MURDER AND MISTLETOE

BARB HAN

DELTA FORCE DEFENDER

CAROL ERICSON

MILLS & BOON

First Published in Great Britain 2018
by Mills & Boon, an imprint of HarperCollins*Publishers*
1 London Bridge Street, London, SE1 9GF

Murder And Mistletoe © 2018 Barb Han
Delta Force Defender © 2018 Carol Ericson

ISBN: 978-0-263-26602-3

1118

MIX
Paper from
responsible sources
FSC® C007454

This book is produced from independently certified FSC™ paper to ensure responsible forest management.

For more information visit: www.harpercollins.co.uk/green

Printed and bound in Spain
by CPI, Barcelona

MURDER AND MISTLETOE

BARB HAN

To my editor, Allison Lyons, for being my dream editor for twenty books now (wow!). Thank you!

To Brandon, Jacob and Tori for being my greatest loves, inspiration and encouragement.

To Babe, my hero, for being the great love of my life.

Chapter One

The normally pitch-black night was lit up with swirling red-and-white bursts. At half past midnight, the normally empty gravel lot teemed with law enforcement and emergency personnel. Dalton Butler's heart fisted as he approached the scene in his sport utility, thinking how much of a contrast the activity was to the normally sleepy town of Cattle Barge. An ominous feeling settled over him. This was the spot where his high school girlfriend's life had ended on a cold winter night fourteen years ago.

As Dalton drove toward the scene, the air thinned and his chest squeezed. A rope hanging from the same tree came into view. Emotions he'd long ago buried stirred, as the unsettled feeling of history repeating itself enveloped him. A shot of anger surfaced and then exploded with rage inside his chest. He white-knuckled the steering wheel as he navigated onto the side of the lot, watching the flurry of activity in disbelief. Why this spot? Why this night?

He parked, lowered his gray Stetson on his forehead and turned up the collar of his denim jacket to brace against the bitter temperatures. A cold front had blown in during the last hour, welcoming the month of December with a blast of frigid temperatures and freezing rain.

Dalton blocked out the image of a young life hanging from that rope as he shouldered his door open against the blazing winds. A gust blew his hat off before he could react. He retrieved it and held it in his hands. The entire scene unfolding before him tipped him off balance as memories crashed down around him like an angry wave tackling a surfer, holding him under and twisting his body around until he didn't know up from down anymore.

A foreboding feeling settled around his shoulders, his arms, tightening its grip until his ribs felt like they might crack. Not even a sharp intake of air eased the pressure. Fourteen years was a long time to hold on to the burden of guilt that he could've saved her if he'd shown up to this spot.

The sheriff stood inside the temporary barricade that had been set up around the perimeter of the tree, a somber expression on his face. Sheriff Sawmill's shoulders were drawn forward as he listened to one of his deputies. Cattle Barge had been overrun with news crews since the end of summer when Dalton's father—the wealthiest man in the county—was murdered on the successful cattle ranch he'd built from scratch. Maverick Mike Butler's rise to riches was legendary. He'd won his first cattle ranch in a gambling match, lost his first wife to alcohol and his bad luck ended there. In death as it was in life, the man always seemed to have another card up his sleeve.

"Sir, you can't be here," Deputy Granger said, extending his arms to block Dalton.

"I need to speak to the sheriff." He had every intention of walking past the man, and there wasn't anything Granger could do to stop him short of arresting him.

Granger seemed to know it, too. He called for Sawmill but kept his arms outstretched.

The sheriff glanced over and did a double take. Stress shrouded him as he made a beeline toward Dalton, stopping behind Granger's arms.

"I appreciate what you're going through and how personal this may seem, but I can't let you walk onto my crime scene and destroy evidence." The middle-aged man looked like he hadn't slept in months. His eyes had the white outline of sunglasses on tanned, wrinkled skin. Hard brackets bordered his mouth and deep grooves lined his forehead. The tight grip he had on his coffee mug outlined the man's stress level. He was on high alert and had been since Maverick Mike's murder, a high-profile case he had yet to solve.

"Tell me what happened." Dalton needed to know everything.

"We haven't established cause of death."

Most of his family might get along with the sheriff now but Dalton would never forget the way he'd been treated after Alexandria Miller's death. He'd barely been seventeen when he'd been picked up in the middle of the night and hauled to the sheriff's office. Sawmill had spent the next twenty-two hours interrogating Dalton, suspecting him of murder and treating him like a criminal.

"Correct me if I'm wrong, but you found her hanging from that tree." Dalton bit back the frustration that was still so ready, so available. He'd go through it all again willingly if Alexandria's murderer would be brought to justice. If her family could have answers. If there could be closure.

Sawmill tilted his head. "Doesn't mean it was the cause of death, and I can't discuss an ongoing investigation with a civilian and you know it."

"Who is she?" Dalton asked anyway.

"I didn't say the victim is a woman." The sheriff was trying to sell the idea that this had no connection to the past. Without proof, Dalton wasn't buying it.

"No. You didn't. She's a girl, not a woman." Déjà vu struck as Dalton glanced at his watch. At around the same time fourteen years ago, Alexandria was being cut down from that exact tree.

"Out of respect for you and your family, for what you're going through, I won't threaten to arrest you, Dalton. But make no mistake that you're interfering with an ongoing investigation and I can't allow that, either," the sheriff warned.

Again, Dalton noticed the sheriff's word choice. He didn't mention murder.

"Another suicide in that tree fourteen years to the day and around the same time?" Dalton folded his arms and planted his boots in the unforgiving earth. "What are the odds?"

"They're high, actually." The sheriff blew out a sharp breath and threw his hands up. "All these reporters drudging up the past, digging into everyone's personal lives. Every story they run increases the odds of a copycat from some crime in the past." There hadn't been many criminal acts in Cattle Barge leading up to this past summer. "There's no respect for the families involved. The people who suffered through losing a loved one and now are being forced to relive the pain as news is being blasted across the internet. They deserve peace, not this."

"There can be no peace without justice. I think we both know that," Dalton shot back. From his peripheral, he saw a woman stalking toward them, so he turned to look. Her face was set with determination, her gaze intent on the sheriff. She had on dark jeans and a blazer. She was tall and beautiful with chestnut wavy hair loosely pulled back in a ponytail that swished back and forth as she walked. An inappropriate stir of attraction struck. Dalton shoved it to the back burner. Charging toward them, she took the kind of breath meant to steel nerves. She clutched something tightly in her left hand as her right fisted and released a couple of times. She was young, early thirties if Dalton had to guess. As she neared, he could see concern lines ridging her forehead.

The sheriff followed Dalton's gaze, which admittedly had been held a few seconds too long toward the object of his attention.

Sheriff Sawmill immediately spun around to address the stalking female, who was only a couple of feet away from them by now. "I'm sorry, ma'am, but this is a restricted area. Only law enforcement personnel are allowed beyond—"

The woman cut him off by holding up the item clenched in her left fist, a badge.

"My name's Detective Leanne West. Tell me exactly what went down here, Sheriff," she demanded, with an intensity that made Dalton believe her interest in this case extended beyond official duty. She wore a white button-down oxford shirt under the blue blazer and low heels, which also told him that she wasn't from around these parts. The butt of a gun peeked out from her shoulder holster. If he had to guess, he'd say it was a SIG Sauer. His first thought would've been FBI if she hadn't already identified herself.

"I'll have my secretary issue a full report to your supervising officer when we've concluded our investigation." Sheriff Sawmill crossed his arms and dug his heels in the hard dirt.

"My SO? Why not tell me? I'm standing here in front of you—he's not." Her determined voice had a musical quality to it that reached inside Dalton. This wasn't the time to get inside his head about why. He wanted information as badly as she did and, at least for now, nothing was more important. If he had a chance to put his demons to rest and give peace to the Miller family, there were no walls too high to climb.

She was getting further with Sawmill than he had been, so, if necessary, he would be her shadow from now on.

With the sheriff's back to Dalton as he was being distracted by the detective, Dalton turned toward the hanging rope and palmed his phone. He angled his cell toward the rope as anger stirred in his gut, remembering the specific knot used in Alexandria's hanging. The trucker's knot. Alexandria would have had no idea what that knot was. She hadn't had a brother or male cousin who she spent time with and she wore more skirts than jeans. Furthermore, every Boy Scout knew that the whole conglomeration could be untied with only four pulls in the right places, meaning she could've freed herself at any time if she'd known. And anyone who knew how to use the knot would know how it worked.

With a quick swipe across the screen, Dalton blew up the focal point, zeroed in on the spot and snapped a pic. The knot could tell him a lot about whether these two crimes were related. All his warning flares were firing, but he couldn't ignore the sheriff's argument. A lot of time had passed. News stories had been drudging up the past. There was a possibility that this incident wasn't related, other than someone being a copycat or inspiring a young person to imitate what she thought was a suicide in the same spot.

"Because I'm not ready to risk details of this case leaving this lot and being broadcast across the state." Sawmill's normally steady-as-steel tone was laced with frustration. "In case you haven't noticed, this town has had its fair share of exploitation for the sake of ratings in the past three months."

"I can assure you that won't happen." The detective's shoulders straightened and her chest puffed out a little at the suggestion she'd bring in the media. The words had the sharp edge of a professional jab.

Sawmill tipped his head to one side. "Forgive my being blunt, but so can I."

LEANNE WOULD'VE HANDCUFFED the good-looking cowboy for taking a picture of the hangman's rope herself if the sheriff was cooperating. Since he wasn't and she figured the two were in the same boat with Sawmill, she'd let it slide and figure out a way to find out what he was so interested in.

The cowboy was hard to miss at six-four and he was using her as a distraction, which had her mind spinning with even more questions. Did the man, who was professional-athlete tall with a muscular build and grace to back it up, know Clara? His hair was a light brown with blond mixed in and his eyes were a serious blue. Under different circumstances, she'd have enjoyed the view. But her niece had been taken down from that tree…

Leanne's heart nearly burst thinking about it. As difficult as it was, she had to keep her emotions in check and focused. Keeping a tight grip on her sentiments was proving more difficult than expected, and she'd put the sheriff on the defensive already because she wasn't restraining those very feelings.

For the sake of finding Clara's killer, she would do almost anything and that included swallowing her pride. The last thing she wanted to do was cut off her best source of information.

She softened her approach. "I apologize for getting off on the wrong foot, Sheriff."

The sheriff nodded. "If you'll excuse me, this case needs my full attention."

Sheriff Clarence Sawmill was much older than Leanne and he had more experience. She was a solid detective, but her emotions were getting in the way and she was blowing it big-time. The sheriff was already on high alert and, from the looks of him, had been since his town had gone crazy following the news of Maverick Mike Butler's death. Leanne had read about the famous murder that was still an open investigation and she worried that her niece's case would get swept under the rug.

"In the spirit of cooperation, I'd like to offer my assistance," Leanne said, hoping the softer tact would sway him. She didn't care how she managed to get the sheriff's agreement. Only that she got it.

"Again, with all due respect, we have this covered." His tone was final as he walked her toward the temporary barricade that had been set up to cordon off the scene. He seemed to realize the cowboy wasn't following when he stopped and turned. "Dalton."

The cowboy seemed to be taking full advantage of the sheriff's split attention. She needed to figure out his interest in the case.

"I'm coming, Sheriff," he said, jogging to catch up.

Since Leanne never seemed to learn her lesson about fighting a losing battle—and face it, this battle was lost—she spun around to try yet another approach. It was the equivalent of trying to grasp a slippery rope while tumbling down a mountain, but she'd do anything to find out what had really happened. "I can call my SO and have more resources here than you'll know what to do with. Surely, you wouldn't want to—"

"I doubt the city of Dallas will throw personnel at a teen suicide investigation in my small town." The sheriff's brow creased.

"Is that how you're classifying it?" Leanne balked. "What makes you so sure it's not murder?"

"For one. There were no other footprints leading up to the ladder against the tree." The sheriff took in a sharp breath as though to stem his words. No doubt, he hadn't meant to share this much. "I'll include all the details in my report."

"How soon will that be available?" she asked, figuring she was already overstepping her bounds. Might as well go all in at this point.

"You'll be one of the first to know." The sheriff signaled for one of his deputies to escort her and the cowboy, Dalton, the last few steps to the barricade.

A cruiser parked and the passenger side door opened. Leanne started to make a beeline toward the vehicle because she had a sinking feeling her sister would be the one stepping out. She wasn't ready to reveal her relationship with the victim but that was about to be done for her.

"Excuse me." The sheriff grabbed her arm to stop her.

Leanne muttered a curse, wishing she could shield Bethany.

"I'm afraid you're done here," the sheriff warned.

"Not anymore."

"This is my county and my business." The sheriff's voice fired a warning shot.

"That may be true, Sheriff. But that's my sister, and I have every intention of staying by her side through this," Leanne ground out. Technically, Bethany was Leanne's half sister. "So I'm not going anywhere until I know she's all right."

Bethany had been fragile before and Leanne was worried the situation was about to get a whole lot worse.

"The victim was your niece?" It was the sheriff's turn to balk.

Leanne nodded.

"Why didn't you say something before?"

"Would you have allowed me to stay? To have access to your investigation?" she shot back.

The sheriff hung his head in response, and she was certain Dalton made a shocked noise. Everyone knew the answer to that question, and she'd been forced to tip her hand before she was ready.

Dalton turned and then made a move toward the barricade. She couldn't let him disappear without finding out what he'd captured on his phone.

She touched his arm and fireworks scorched her fingers.

Ignoring the heat pulsing between them, she said, "Please, stay."

"What happened to my baby?" Bethany's legs folded and a deputy caught her as she slumped against the cruiser. Leanne bolted toward her sister as her stomach braided.

Even with the best of intentions, Bethany would only hurt Clara's case.

Chapter Two

"Please, sit down," Sheriff Sawmill instructed, pointing to one of two small-scale leather chairs opposite his mahogany desk. He glanced toward Dalton, who was helping Bethany walk. "I thought I made my position clear at the scene, Dalton."

"My presence was requested, Sheriff," he responded. When she'd almost fainted a second time, he'd been there to scoop her head up before it pounded gravel.

"I asked him here, sir," the detective interjected. "I'll be sticking around the area for a few days and my sister is in no condition to offer assistance. I needed someone local to the area to give advice on the best place to eat and stay."

"My office would be more than happy to make recommendations." Sawmill stared at Dalton a few seconds too long before blowing out a breath and focusing on the victim's mother.

To Dalton's thinking, Bethany Schmidt didn't look anything like her sister. Her shoulder-length hair was stringy and mousy-brown. Her red-rimmed eyes were a darker shade, a contrast to the honey-colored hue of the detective's. Bethany's sallow cheeks and willowy frame made her look fragile. She carried herself with her shoulders slumped forward and the bags under her eyes outlined the fact that she'd been worried long before today. Grief shrouded her, which he understood given the circumstances, and this much grief could change a person's physical appearance. He'd seen that almost instantly with Alexandria's parents.

His heart went out to her, knowing full well how difficult it was to lose someone and yet how much worse it must be when it was her child. Bethany had seemed too distraught to say a whole lot on the ride over, so he'd offered her a sympathetic shoulder.

The detective from Dallas hadn't said much on the ride over, either, and Dalton figured she didn't want to upset her sister by talking about the case. Besides, he could almost see the pins firing in her brain, as she must've been cycling through every possible scenario. He'd watched from his back seat view.

Alexandria's mother had pushed him away and it felt right to be able to offer comfort to someone who was living out what had to be their worst version of hell.

"First of all, I'm deeply sorry for your loss, ma'am," Sheriff Sawmill began. He sat down and clasped his hands, placing them on top of his massive desk, which was covered in files. An executive chair was tucked into the opposite side. The sheriff's office was large, simple. There were two flags on poles standing sentinel, flanking the governor's picture. In the adjacent space, a sofa and table upon which stood a statue of a bull rider atop a bronze bull that had been commissioned by Dalton's father. Maverick Mike had been a generous man and had given Sawmill the gift after he'd gone above and beyond the call of duty in order to stop a gang of poachers. The heroics had cost Sawmill a bullet in the shoulder.

There was a half-empty packet of Zantac next to a stack of files. Dalton had been inside this room too often for his taste in the past few months. Activity down the hall had slowed since the last time he had been here. The temporary room set up for volunteers to take calls about leads in the Mav's case was still in the conference room at the mouth of the hallway, but there were fewer phone calls now and leads had all but dried up.

Bethany sniffled, clutching a bundle of tissues in a white-knuckle grip.

Dalton kept to the back of the room, near the door.

"I apologize again for asking you to give a statement so soon. Anything you can tell us might help close the investigation." Dalton noticed that Sawmill didn't mention the word *murder*. Was he being careful not to set false expectations that he would treat this as anything other than a suicide?

The detective noticed it, too. She sat up a little straighter and her shoulders tensed. Her gaze was locked on Sawmill like she was a student studying for final exams.

"I'll help in any way I can." Bethany's weak voice barely carried through the room in between sobs. Helping her walk into the coroner's office to verify what they'd already known at the scene had been right up there with attending Alexandria's funeral. Too many memories crashed down on Dalton. Memories he'd suppressed for fourteen years. Memories he had every intention of stuffing down deep before they brought him to his knees. His anger wouldn't help find answers. Finding the truth was all that mattered now.

"Can you confirm the deceased's name is Clara Robinson?" His voice remained steady.

"Yes." It seemed to take great effort to get the word out.

"I identified the body at the scene, Sheriff," Leanne interjected and the tension in Sawmill's face heightened. It was just a flash before he recovered, but Dalton knew it meant he'd never cooperate willingly with the Dallas detective. That also made her of no use to Dalton.

"And your full name is?" Sawmill continued.

"Bethany Ann Schmidt," she supplied before looking up.

"Okay. Mrs. Schmidt, can you describe your relationship with your daughter?" the sheriff continued.

"It was all right. I guess. I mean, she's…*was*…a teenager. We talked as much as any mother and her seventeen-year-old can." Bethany shrugged as if anything other than a complicated relationship would require skills no one could possibly have.

Dalton couldn't speak on authority but he picked up on the tension between the detective and her sister.

"How were the two of you getting along lately?" Sawmill leaned forward.

"Okay, I guess," she responded with another shrug.

"Had you been in any disagreements recently?" he asked. Dalton couldn't help but remember a very different line of questioning when he was in the interview room with the sheriff. Another shot of anger burst through his chest, and he had to take a slow deep breath to try to counter the damage. The sheriff had spent too much time focused on the wrong person back then and because of it, Alexandria's killer still walked the streets. He'd wondered if the man had ended up in jail for another crime or died, considering how quiet life had become until recently in Cattle Barge. If he'd been in jail, the timing of another similar murder could be explained by a release.

"No. Not us. Nothing lately. I mean, we argued over her helping out more around the house yesterday. Her little brother is a handful and she barely lifts a finger," Bethany said on an exacerbated sigh.

Again, Leanne stiffened but this time it happened when her sister mentioned the boy.

"How old is her brother?" Sawmill continued.

"Hampton will be four years old in two weeks," Bethany supplied before taking a few gulps of air and then picking back up on the conversation thread. "And we didn't have a knock-down-drag-out or anything. It was more like me reminding her to help pick up toys and her rolling her eyes for the hundredth time. I swear that girl communicated more with her eyes than her mouth."

The sheriff nodded like he understood and then waited for her to go on, hands clasped on his desk.

"We got along okay other than that," Bethany said through sniffles.

Based on Leanne's reaction so far, she didn't agree. Questions rolled around in Dalton's mind. Was Bethany telling the truth about her relationship with her daughter? Why was Leanne so tense? Was she expecting her sister to drop a bomb at any minute? Or was it fear? Was she afraid that her sister would say something wrong?

Leanne had secrets. Dalton intended to find out what they were, because if he could uncover any connection between this and Alexandria's murder he might be able to bring peace to her family. Only this time, he wouldn't involve the sheriff. Sawmill had let Dalton down all those years ago, still was with his father's murder investigation, and he didn't trust the man to do his job.

"How did the two siblings respond to each other?" Sawmill asked.

"About the same as any, I guess." Bethany shrugged again. There was a note of hopelessness in her voice. "Hampton gets into her stuff and she goes crazy. My Clara is—" she shot a glance toward the sheriff "—*was* particular about all her belongings being right where she left them. She didn't like anyone getting into her stuff and that caused a lot of friction in the house."

"Between you and her?" the sheriff asked.

"No. I expected it to some degree. She was used to being the only child for most of her life and then suddenly she was not. She had all my attention before I met Gary." She flashed her eyes at the sheriff. "My husband. She had a hard time with me being in a relationship and then Hampton came along quicker than we expected." Bethany blew her nose and then took in a deep breath. "So, we decided to get married. Clara and me weren't as close after that. I chalked it up to hormones. She was a normal teenager and she was thirteen when Gary and me tied the knot."

Leanne shifted in her seat as though she couldn't get comfortable. Her movements were subtle. If Dalton hadn't been watching, he might've missed them. What was she holding back? Something was making her uncomfortable and she seemed a skilled-enough investigator to know to cover her physical reaction as best she could.

"How did your husband get along with your daughter?" Sawmill picked up a packet of Zantac.

"Clara didn't like him much." Bethany shrank a little more into her seat, a helpless look wrinkling her forehead. "Like I said, I spoiled her with my attention before we met."

Leanne's fingernails might leave marks in that chair if she gripped it any tighter.

"Those two were fire and gasoline from the get-go," Bethany added.

"Which wasn't Clara's fault," Leanne interjected hotly. "Gary yelled at Clara all the time and for no good reason."

LEANNE FUMED. SHE shouldn't have confirmed that Gary and Clara didn't get along. Watching her half sister, whom she loved but would never understand, defend Gary over her own daughter lit the wick that caused an explosion she couldn't contain.

The sheriff's brow arched. He was looking for evidence that this was a suicide and Leanne might've just handed it to him with her outburst. She bit back a curse, wishing she'd inherited more of her mother's ability to stay calm in a crisis. In times like these, she missed her even more than usual.

Leanne could feel the cowboy's eyes on her, and there came a flitter of attraction that was out of line. Leanne had no plans to let him out of her sight until she knew what he'd captured with his phone, magnetism or not.

"The reason Clara didn't get along with Gary is that he treated her more like a servant than a daughter," Leanne said as calmly as she could. Someone had to stand up for the girl.

"That's not true." Indignant shoulders raised on Bethany like shackles on a scared or angry animal.

"A seventeen-year-old girl shouldn't have more responsibilities around the house than her mother." There. Leanne had said it. The truth was out.

Bethany gasped in what sounded like complete horror and guilt knifed Leanne. She didn't want to upset her half sister, but Clara wasn't around any longer to defend herself. Besides, the sheriff was getting the wrong picture. Clara wasn't a mixed-up hormonal teenager who fought with her stepfather and then killed herself.

"Is that the real reason you came to pick her up?" Bethany blurted out.

More of the truth was about to come out, so Leanne may as well come clean. She turned her attention to the sheriff, ignoring the glare her sister was giving her. Another pang of guilt hit. Leanne didn't want to cause her sister any more pain and losing a daughter was up there with the worst anyone could experience. But. And it was a big *but*. She wouldn't allow her niece's murder to be classified as a suicide when it wasn't.

Or to let a killer walk around scot-free.

Nothing would ever be gained from skirting what had really happened, and a small part of Leanne couldn't help but wonder if Bethany was somehow relieved that Clara was out of the way. Not necessarily that her daughter was gone, but that she wouldn't have to fight with Gary anymore over doing the right thing for Clara.

"I came down here to pick my niece up so she could live with me," Leanne explained.

"What do you mean *live*? I thought she was just going to stay with you a couple of weeks until I could smooth things over with Gary during Christmas break. Give the two of them some breathing room." The hurt in Bethany's tone wounded Leanne.

She turned to her sister. "I'm sorry you have to find out like this. But I know for a fact that Clara wouldn't have done this to herself, and if we aren't honest with the sheriff, none of us will ever know the truth about what happened."

"What good would that do now?" Bethany shot back with the most fire Leanne had ever seen in her sister's eyes. At least there was some spark there when all too often her sister looked dead since marrying Gary. "It won't bring her back." Her voice rose to a near-hysterical pitch. "Who cares why she's gone. She's gone."

Bethany slumped forward in her seat and Leanne reached over to comfort her. Her sister drew away from her as though she was a rattlesnake ready to strike.

The sheriff's gaze narrowed in on her. He didn't seem to like the fact that Leanne had been withholding information. She'd been on the other side of that desk and could appreciate his position. She couldn't, however, allow this farce to go on. Clara had been murdered.

"What really happened, Detective West?" The sheriff's dark tone said he wasn't impressed.

"She and Gary, her stepfather, had had a huge argument and Clara couldn't take living with them anymore." It dawned on Leanne that Bethany might not want that information getting out because it wouldn't cast Gary in the best light. Leanne further knew that he'd just topped the suspect list. So be it. If that man was involved in any way, she'd…

Bethany bristled and Leanne shot her half sister an apologetic look.

"She said you needed help with Mila," Bethany countered, talking about Leanne's six-month-old daughter.

Leanne hated the deception, but her back had been

against the wall and Clara had sounded desperate. Leanne had planned to sit Clara down and explain all the reasons the two of them needed to tell Bethany the truth.

"I know she did." Leanne turned to her half sister and her shoulders softened. "I'm sorry we lied to you, but Clara insisted you'd never let her come otherwise and she was desperate to get out of the house."

"So that made it okay to deceive me?" More hurt spilled out of Bethany.

"I'm sorry for that. But I also know that my niece wouldn't end her own life. She has a boyfriend she cares about and only one year left at home. Something happened, and if we don't impress the sheriff with that knowledge, her killer will go free," Leanne implored.

"What's her boyfriend's name?" Sawmill asked.

"Christian Woods." Leanne turned to her sister.

Deep grooves lined Bethany's forehead and dark circles cradled her eyes. Leanne could see that she was getting through, and she prayed the woman would do the right thing by her daughter in death even if she hadn't in life.

Then it seemed to dawn on her that Gary could be investigated when her pupils dilated and her lips thinned.

"How do you know she didn't feel guilty for lying to her mother? Or maybe she and her boyfriend had a fight? Kids do all kinds of crazy things in the name of love," Bethany countered. She perched on the edge of her chair as she focused on Sawmill. "My daughter was mentally unstable. She said that kids were bullying her at the new school. She didn't fit in. I can't remember how many times she threatened to harm herself. I didn't take any of it seriously at the time, figuring she was just blowing off steam. Now, I'm not so sure."

"Can you provide a list of names?" Sawmill took notes. Leanne saw that as the first positive sign. "How long ago did you move to Cattle Barge?"

"We've been here around seven months. Gary thought it would be best to move the family before the end of the last school year, so Clara could make friends before summer." The fear in Bethany's voice gave Leanne pause.

Was she afraid of Gary being investigated? Afraid of the possibility of bringing up another child alone? Or, looking closer, just plain afraid of Gary?

Leanne scanned her half sister's arms for bruises. She had on sweatpants and a sweater with the sleeves rolled up. Bethany had had problems with substance abuse when she was younger. Leanne learned after locating her half sister that Bethany had been in and out of rehab twice during high school. Then she'd had Clara instead of her senior year and, by all accounts, turned her life around. Without a high school diploma or job skills to fall back on, it had been a tough life. She'd worked hourly wage jobs. Bethany had struggled to make ends meet until she'd met Gary five years ago. An almost immediate pregnancy was quickly followed by marriage performed at city hall. Gary had driven a wedge between Bethany and Leanne.

According to Clara, the man was an iceberg when it came to emotion. Leanne wondered how well her sister really knew her husband.

"I apologize for the questions," Sawmill said. "Can you tell me more about your husband and daughter's recent fight?"

"Yes, it happened the other day, but Gary was only reacting to Clara's moodiness," Bethany admitted. It galled Leanne that her half sister would defend his actions. She neglected to mention the times Gary had forced Clara to get up off the couch for no good reason, saying that she had to ask permission before she sat down. Or when he'd made her kneel for hours on end because she'd worn what he considered too short of a skirt. Gary's father had been an evangelist. Gary used the same punishments he'd received as a child on Clara.

Clara was a normal teenage girl who wanted a little freedom.

"What about alcohol or drugs?" the sheriff asked and it was Leanne's turn to bristle. She already knew the answer to that question.

"I found an empty bottle of beer in her room last weekend," Bethany answered truthfully.

"What did Mr. Schmidt think about that?" Sawmill asked, and Leanne could tell by his line of questioning that he wasn't taking her murder claim seriously.

"He never knew. I hid it because Clara begged me to," Bethany said.

"What would've happened if he'd known?" Sawmill continued.

Bethany blew out a breath. "Another fight."

"He'd been threatening to send Clara to a super strict all-girls school," Leanne interjected. "And that beer belonged to Renee, not Clara."

Renee was the daughter of one of Gary's friends. Clara didn't care for the girl but couldn't turn her back on her because Gary would shame her.

Bethany turned sideways to look at Leanne. The woman shot a look that could've melted ice during an Alaskan winter.

"And you believed her?" Bethany asked.

Chapter Three

"Of course, I did. Clara never lied to me," Leanne responded with a little more heat than she'd intended. So much for keeping things cool in front of the sheriff.

Bethany made a harrumph sound and pushed to her feet. "I'd like to speak with the sheriff alone."

Leanne started to protest but the sheriff cut her off.

"There's coffee at the end of the hall and everything said here will go into my report," he said, motioning toward the door.

It was his witness, his investigation. With no other viable choice, Leanne stood and walked out the door. She'd been too harsh with her fragile half sister and this was going to be the price. Everything had balance, a yin and yang, she thought, except for her personal life, which had been turned upside down since having a baby six months ago. She wouldn't change a thing about her life with her baby girl, except maybe more sleep. Definitely more sleep. And if she could turn back time, she would make sure that Mila's father wouldn't have died on her watch.

Dalton followed her out the door and she could feel his strong presence behind her.

"Coffee's this way," his low rumble of a voice said,

and the sound penetrated a place deep down, stirring emotions she had no desire to acknowledge as existing anymore. Her traitorous body wanted to gravitate toward the feeling and bask in it. A little reality and a strong cup of coffee was all she needed to quash those unproductive thoughts.

She stepped aside, allowing the man with the strong muscled back to lead her down the unfamiliar hallway. He made a left before what she figured was an interview room. She closed up her coat, shivering against the cold temperature in the building.

A dark thought struck that the sheriff might be hauling her sister to the interview room any minute. Bethany had no idea how much her actions were about to impact her life, and a mix of protectiveness and frustration swirled in Leanne's chest. Bethany might be clueless but she'd had a rough start, had cleaned up her act, and Leanne knew deep down that her sister was trying her best. Was it good enough? Before having Mila, Leanne might've judged her sister more harshly. After having a baby, she realized the job wasn't easy and didn't come with instructions.

"The coffee here doesn't taste like much, but it's strong," Dalton said, pouring two cups and handing one to her.

She took the offering, wondering why he knew so much about the quality of the coffee at the sheriff's office. "I'm afraid I'm at a disadvantage here. You already know my name and more about my personal life than I share with even my closest friends, but I don't have the first clue who you are." The part about having close friends was almost laughable. Happy hours after work and shopping with the girls had never been high on her list of priorities. She'd worked hard to make detective by thirty and there hadn't been room for much else in her life.

"Dalton Butler. And I'm pleased to meet you." He switched hands with the mug and offered a handshake.

She took his hand—his was so much larger and rougher than hers—and realized making physical contact had not been a good choice. Electricity exploded through her, bringing to life places she didn't want awakened. She reasoned that it had been a long time since she'd had sex and her body was reacting to the first hot man she touched, but there was so much more to it, to him, than that.

From the callouses on his skin, she deduced that he must work outside, which in these parts most likely meant on a ranch. His outfit of jeans, boots and a denim jacket had already given the same impression.

"Why does that name sound familiar?" She examined him, his clear blue eyes that seemed to hold so many secrets. She was beginning to hate secrets.

"My father owned a famous ranch in the area," he conceded as the contents of his mug suddenly became very interesting.

"Maverick Mike Butler of the Hereford Ranch?" That explained why the man seemed to know the layout of the sheriff's office so well. At first, she'd feared he might have been previously on the wrong side of the interview table, especially with the way he related to the sheriff. Now, she realized he'd been there because of his father's murder. The fact that the case still wasn't solved would explain his chilly response to Sawmill.

But what did he want with *this* investigation?

"What's on your camera?" she asked, figuring she

could ask at another time why the son of a famous rancher—and one of, if not *the,* richest men in Texas—would have so many callouses on his hands. There were other things she didn't want to notice about him, like the half-inch scar above his left brow at the point where it arched. And the crystal clearness of his blue eyes.

He fished his phone out of his pocket and held it out on his palm between them. Leanne stepped closer to get a better look at the screen and that was another mistake because she inhaled his scent, a mix of outdoors and warm spices. A trill of awareness shot through her. She blinked up, trying to reset her body and thought she caught the same reaction from him as his pupils dilated.

Chalking the whole scene up to overwrought emotions, she studied the picture he brought up on his phone.

"Why is this important?" She shot him her best don't-feed-me-a-line look.

"It's the type of knot used." He enlarged the hangman's rope and her heart squeezed, looking at the device that had killed her niece.

"Which is?"

"The trucker's knot," he supplied.

"Why is this significant other than I'm guessing that only a Boy Scout would know how to tie it?" Examining the knot shot pain through her. She had to set aside her personal feelings, block out emotion and focus on finding the jerk who'd done this to Clara. "Justice for Clara" was Leanne's new marching orders.

"Right. A Boy Scout would know this and that has to be taken into consideration in finding the killer, but the person who did this gave them an out." His inflection changed and she could sense his relief at talking about this... But relief from what?

"You said *killer*. How do you know this wasn't a suicide?" She latched on to the first piece of good news in hours. Hours that felt more like days.

"Was your niece ever a Brownie? Girl Scout?" he asked, ignoring her question.

Leanne shook her head and his lack of surprise made something dawn on her.

She blinked up at him, searching his eyes.

"I know it wasn't suicide." His tone was finite and his jaw muscle ticked.

"How can you be so sure?" She wanted to hear those words so badly.

"The knot. One tug in the right place and they could've been free," he supplied.

There was more to the story based on how much he seemed to care. There was something else present behind his eyes, too. Hesitation? Lack of trust? Her investigative experience had taught her when to press and when to back off. This was time for the former.

"Can I ask a question?"

Dalton nodded.

"Why do you care about what happened to my niece?" And then she thought about what else her police training had taught her. Actions were selfish. People were motivated by their own needs and rarely put anyone else's first. She'd seen it time and time again through her work as a detective in a major city. The only reason he'd care about Clara was if her death was connected to something important to him.

He glanced at her and that one look spoke volumes.

And then she realized that he'd said the word *they* and not *her*.

"How many others have there been?"

DALTON STOOD IN front of the beautiful detective trying to decide how much of his hand he should show. It sounded a little far-fetched even to him that the same murderer would strike fourteen years later. But he knew without a doubt this was the work of one person. And the odds increased when he considered the event had happened on the exact same day at the same spot. "As far as I know, one. But there could be others in different locations."

Proving his theory was a whole different story, and he also had to contend with the fact that the detective was about to find out that he'd been the prime suspect in his then-girlfriend's murder.

"How long ago did the first occur?" Her voice was steady, calm. There was so much going on in the detective's mind that he could almost hear the wheels churning behind those intense honey-brown eyes.

He hesitated before answering, wondering if she'd accuse him of being out of touch like the sheriff had. On balance, she needed to know.

"Fourteen years," he said, expecting her to end the conversation and try to get back into the office with her sister.

"Other than the knot, what makes you think these two crimes are connected?" She stared at him, and he got the sense she was evaluating his mental capacity.

"Same day and location, same tree and same method," he stated.

"The knot." She took a sip of coffee as she seemed to be considering what he'd said. "But fourteen years apart."

"There could be others that I'm not aware of." Dalton saw this as the first positive sign that someone other than one of his siblings was listening. Of course, they'd been supportive. The Butler children had always been close. But shortly after the crime, his twin and best friend, Dade, had signed up for the military. His sisters had been busy with college and high school. His father, the Mav, had slapped his son on the back and told him the calves needed to be logged and the pens needed to be cleaned, like his teenaged heart hadn't just been ripped out of his chest. Guilt ate at him, even today.

Dalton mentally shook off the memory and lack of compassion his father had shown.

"Have you considered the possibility of a copycat?" She had that same look the sheriff had worn so many times when he discredited what Dalton had told him.

"Enjoy your coffee." He turned to walk away and was stopped by a soft touch on his arm.

"Hey, slow down. I wasn't saying that I didn't believe you."

"Yeah, you did." Dalton had no plans to go down that road with anyone again.

The detective held up her free hand in surrender. "I'll admit that I was skeptical, but that's what makes me good at my job. I don't take anything at face value. But I'm also good at reading people, and whether there's a true connection to these cases or not, I can tell you're not lying. You believe the two are related and I want to hear you out."

"Tell me everything I should know about your niece," he said, testing the detective to see how far the information sharing would go. If she trusted him, she'd open up at least a little.

The detective bristled. "She's in high school."

Dalton set his mug down, turned and walked out. He had no plans to share his information with someone unwilling to go deep. Telling him a seventeen-year-old was in high school was like saying coffee beans were brown.

The detective was on his heels.

"Hold on a minute. I just said that I know you believe what you're saying is true and I told you something about her," she argued.

"I know," he said out of the side of his mouth. He'd seen the distrust in her eyes. She thought he was as crazy as the sheriff had all those years ago. And since he had no more plays left in present company, he walked outside to where his truck was parked. He'd had one of the ranch hands drop it off since he rode here in the back of a deputy's SUV. Reporters had started gathering in bigger numbers, no doubt looking for something to report since news—and leads—about the Mav's murder had gone cold. He shooed them away as he made large strides toward his truck, ignored the detective and shut the door, closing him in the cab alone.

Dalton pulled out of the lot, squealing his tires, although not meaning to. His adrenaline was jacked through the roof at the thought that a murderer—*her murderer*—was still in Cattle Barge. One of the reasons he'd believed there'd only been one murder in town since was that he thought the killer had moved on. But now?

This guy was shoving the murder in their faces. And he could be anyone. For all Dalton knew, he could be walking right past the bastard every day. Greeting him when the man should be locked behind bars for the safety of other teenage girls.

A question tugged at the corner of his mind. Alexandria's killer had been quiet for fourteen years. Why strike now?

There had to be a trigger. Dalton intended to figure out what the hell it was and finally put to rest the crime that had haunted him for his entire adult life.

The one spark of hope was that with modern-day forensics, the sheriff would be able to find a fingerprint and nail the jerk. Either way, Dalton had plans to see this through. Tonight was the closest he'd been to Alexandria's killer, and he could feel it in his bones that these two crimes were related beyond a copycat. He knew for a fact that the use of the trucker's knot had not been reported in any of the stories. He shouldn't read them, but how could he help it? He owed Alexandria that much.

Hell, he'd been the one to point out to the sheriff that was what they were dealing with when Sawmill had shown him the picture of the hangman's rope fourteen years ago. Pointing out the type of knot used had also most likely helped put him on top of the suspect list. At seventeen, he had been naive. He'd believed that he was helping the investigation.

Dalton was no longer a kid. And he didn't give up so easily.

HOURS PASSED BEFORE Dalton deemed it safe to revisit the crime scene. The sheriff had said that he wanted it cleaned up as fast as possible before copycats got any more ideas and reporters fed them with notions. His remarks were further evidence that Sawmill was considering this a suicide.

The sun was beginning to rise in the eastern sky, allowing enough light to see clearly since the trees were barren of leaves.

It was the dead of winter, close to Christmas but Dalton wasn't in a festive mood. There were two killers on the loose, his father's and a teenage girl's. Plus, no matter how complicated Dalton's relationship might've been with the Mav, he couldn't imagine the holiday without his father's strong physical presence.

A foreboding overcame Dalton every time he came near the spot where Alexandria had died and this morning was no exception.

Between law enforcement and emergency personnel, there were too many footprints leading up to the tree. Dalton took out his phone and started snapping pics of everything. The unforgiving earth leading up to the tree. The oak from every angle. The perimeter of the crime scene.

He didn't know when he'd get the chance to return and evidence was still fresh even if it had been trampled all over. He had no idea what could be significant, so he figured he'd capture everything and study the photos later.

The tree was mature, coming in at a height of forty-plus feet. It was majestic and had been around for as long as Dalton could remember. He'd seen it more times than he could count going back and forth to town from the ranch as a kid.

This location was between Dalton's family ranch and Alexandria's house in town. He could almost still see her silky blond hair flirting with the breeze on a warm summer night. Her nervous smile. The way she tugged at his arm when she wanted him to put it around her.

When Sawmill couldn't prove that Dalton had anything to do with her death, he'd ruled suicide. Did Alexandria have a difficult relationship with her parents? Yes. There was no question about it. That didn't mean she took her own life.

Tires crunching on gravel caused him to spin around. The detective parked her sedan and exited the vehicle. The sun was to her back, rising, creating a halo effect.

"What are you doing here?" he bit out sharply.

"Looking for you." There was so much hurt in her voice, even though her set jaw said she was trying to put up a brave front. He knew exactly how difficult it was for her to be there, in this location, facing down that tree.

"How'd you know where to find me?"

She tucked her hands into the pockets of her blazer and shivered against a burst of cold air. Dalton hadn't really noticed before but his hands were like icy claws. He put them together and blew to warm them.

She shrugged. "This is the first place I would come if I were in your shoes."

"You don't know anything about me," he stated. He had no intention of discussing Alexandria with her. Since there was nothing else to say, he stalked toward her because she was in the way of getting to his sport utility.

"Hold on," she said as he passed her.

He paused as he heard the hum of a car engine on the farm road. The noise was growing louder, which meant the vehicle was moving toward them. It was probably nothing but he didn't like it. He should've heard her approach as well, but he'd been too lost in thought and the winds had blasted, muffling other sounds.

Dalton watched as it turned toward them into the empty lot where all kinds of summer fruit stands had been set up over the years. There was only one time that growers had moved to a different location, because this one had had bouquets of flowers all around the tree's massive trunk and the ground had seemed sacred.

Or maybe they were afraid. Afraid the place was cursed. Afraid a murderer was still out there, watching, searching for his next victim.

This sedan seemed out of place at this time of morning. There were no signs of law enforcement and that got all of Dalton's radars flashing on full tilt.

Had news of Clara's murder leaked? The sheriff had intended to keep details as quiet as possible, but then it seemed like reporters were everywhere since the Mav's murder and especially since the will would be read on Christmas Eve.

Would the media play to Dalton's advantage? Surely, reporters would be just as suspicious as he was about two suicides playing out in the same spot and on the same day fourteen years apart.

On the other hand, media coverage this early could work against them. There'd been a reporting frenzy after his father's murder and the sheer amount of false leads that had been generated as a result had bogged down the sheriff's office.

Dalton didn't want to risk the same thing happening to this case.

The detective muttered the same curse he did, seeming to realize how little the sheriff might appreciate the two of them being photographed at the scene of his investigation.

Dalton needed to create a distraction. But what?

One thing came to mind. Plan A might get him punched in the face, but there was no plan B and he was running out of time.

He hauled the detective against his chest—ignoring the feel of her soft skin and the way her breasts pressed harder into his chest with her sharp intake of air—and then dipped his head to kiss her.

Every muscle in her body chorded as he pulled hers flush with his in an embrace. He half expected the feisty detective to bite him but then she seemed to catch on. This maneuver would keep her face away from whoever was behind the wheel.

Dalton Butler was well-known, but she wasn't. As long as he shielded her, it would be next to impossible to figure out who she was. That would most likely keep her name out of the headlines. It was a risky move, though. There were a dozen ways this could come back to haunt them, but time was the enemy.

Out of Dalton's peripheral, he watched a young man pop out of his small sedan. He stood in between the opened door and his vehicle, causing Dalton to brace for the possibility that the young man had a gun, but stopped short of closing his car door. His body remained wedged in between the car and door with one hand on the wheel and the other on the door casing.

"Excuse me," the young man said.

Dalton's hands tunneled into the detective's hair as her palms pressed firmly against his chest. She repositioned, wrapping her arms around his neck and a sensual current coursed through him when her firm breasts pressed further against him as they deepened the kiss. Heat penetrated layers of clothing and caused his skin to sizzle.

He was going to need a minute when this was over to regain his bearings, because in that moment, this stranger felt a little too right in his arms.

"Sorry to bother you, but I'm lost," the young man said.

Dalton took in a sharp breath before pulling back. As he looked at the man, he saw a camera being aimed at him.

"Don't turn around," he said under his breath to the detective before looking straight at the guy who had to be a reporter. "What the hell do you want?"

"Nothing," the startled voice said in reaction to Dalton's tone. "I already got what I came for."

Chapter Four

"Dammit," Dalton said, cursing again under his breath. "Keep your face covered in case he tries to shoot another picture."

The reporter hopped into his sedan and then tore out of the parking lot, spewing gravel. Before the small gray car could disappear, Dalton palmed his own phone and snapped a pic of the back of the vehicle. He'd open his own investigation on the man and see what he could find.

"This isn't good," the detective said. "I could lose my job if this thing plays out wrong."

"We need to go." Dalton started toward his sport utility, feeling a cold blast of morning air penetrate his thin jacket.

"Where?" Detective West asked.

"You can go wherever you want," he shot back. Other than engaging in a kiss that did a little too much damage to his senses, nothing had changed. She still didn't trust him, a sentiment that went both ways.

"The sheriff said there was only one set of footprints leading up to the base of the tree before she was taken down. Now there are many," she said and her words stopped Dalton in his tracks.

"How much did your niece weigh?" he asked.

Leanne must've known the question was coming because she answered without hesitation. "Around a hundred pounds or so."

"He could've carried her," he countered, keeping his back to her. He stomped on the ground. The earth was cold, hard, unforgiving. "I'm a big guy and I'm barely leaving a footprint."

"I'm trying to talk the sheriff into treating this as a murder investigation," she said. "Maybe if you come with me, I'll have a chance."

"Being with me will only hurt your cause in case you haven't noticed." Dalton needed to get back to the ranch where he could be productive. Besides, he wanted to examine the pictures he'd taken in detail. "Good luck."

There were no sounds of footprints behind him, which meant the detective was standing her ground. "If Sawmill treats this as a suicide, we both lose."

"He won't change his mind and especially not with me around," Dalton said. "It's a matter of pride at this point."

"Then we have to think of a way to change it for him." The despair in her voice nearly cracked the casing that locked down his emotions. He'd buried them so deep in order to survive all these years he was caught off guard that anyone could come close enough to touching that place inside him.

"You've never met the guy. He'll stay the course," he said.

She shot him a curious glance and he decided not to go into detail about how he knew Sawmill so well. "We need him. I can't call in favors in Dallas to investigate leads. Not without putting people's jobs in jeopardy and

I won't do that to my friends. If you and I put our heads together, we might just get somewhere."

"I have to go to work," Dalton said, figuring he'd given enough of his time to this lost cause. If she thought he could make an impact with Sawmill, she'd have a better chance without his involvement. That part was true enough.

"My niece is dead because of me. It's my fault. I should've been here. We were supposed to meet and I was late." Damn, the sound of anguish in her words tugged at him. It was a pull he couldn't afford. He should walk away right now and not look back.

Instead, he turned around, wishing there was something he could say to ease her pain. "Blaming yourself won't bring her back. Believe me."

"Who did that tree take from you?" she asked, and her eyes here wide bright brown orbs.

Dalton started to answer but held back.

"I'll find out either way. I'm sure there's been coverage, and I still have resources at the department who can check into a cold case. Why not just tell me and make this easier on both of us?" she asked.

Trying to force his hand was as productive as trying to drink milk from a snake.

"Because it's none of your damn business." A surprising explosion of anger rattled against his chest. His blood pressure spiked and adrenaline-heated blood coursed through him.

A grunt-like noise issued from the detective. "This whole situation stinks for both of us, but this could go easier if we work together. And you might just get the answers you need as desperately as I do."

"Good luck, Detective." He walked away.

She stalked behind him and poked him on the shoulder. Dalton stopped but didn't turn.

"Name your price. I'll do whatever it takes to get your help."

Damn that he was about to agree to help her.

LEANNE WALKED INTO Sawmill's office ahead of the tall cowboy. She didn't like the way she could feel his masculine presence behind her without needing to see him. She chalked it up to his intensity and did her level best to move on.

"Thank you for agreeing to see us again, Sheriff." Leanne held her hand out.

Sawmill politely shook it and greeted them but stopped short of inviting them to sit this time. He stood near the door, making it all too clear that he had nothing else to add and expected this meeting to last a minute or two at best. From the grooves around his eyes, she sensed that his patience was running thin.

"I appreciate how much you have on your plate right now..." she started but was met with a get-on-with-it response in the form of the sheriff leaning back on his heels.

Okay, she could work with his emotions. See if she could get his agreement to move forward with a murder investigation instead of wrapping this case as a suicide.

"We just came from the scene," Leanne said, figuring the sheriff needed to be aware since the guy who was most likely a reporter had taken a picture of them. "Someone showed up and had his phone out. I'm sure he took a picture but we did what we could to hide my face. The story could leak."

The news didn't seem to sit well with the sheriff. He

folded his arms in a defensive tactic. He was shoring up his reserves when she was trying to lower his guard by sharing and being honest. All she needed was his word that he would open an investigation.

"I'm sorry about that. It's not good if my name is linked to the scene and I know it," she quickly added.

"What were you doing at my scene? What's the real reason you requested this meeting?" Sawmill asked.

When Leanne hesitated, he added, "I don't have the resources to follow every bunny trail, including professional courtesy cases. If I did, I'd be more than happy..."

"This isn't a case of departmental cooperation or respect. I have no intention of wasting your resources or time." Leanne shouldn't allow herself to become so heated, but this was Clara. Her sweet niece was never coming back and she knew in her heart Clara hadn't committed suicide. Leanne suppressed a sob. "I know for a fact that my niece never would've done this to herself."

"I'm listening," the sheriff said. His posture had improved; she had his ear and she wouldn't look a gift horse in the mouth by overanalyzing it.

"Gary didn't like her," she added, fighting the personal disdain she had for her brother-in-law.

"That's nothing new in my business," Sawmill responded flatly. Any hope she had that he could be taking her seriously fizzled.

"Of course it isn't, but how often do you have a detective telling you there are holes in your case?" she said a little indignant. Damn, why'd she say that? Putting Sawmill on the defensive would only move him further away from her goal.

Dalton touched her arm and heat crackled at the point of contact. "We're done here. He won't take you seriously."

"Whatever's between us happened in the past, Mr. Butler. This has nothing to do with it." Sawmill was really on the defensive now. Dalton had struck a chord. She hadn't thought bringing him into the equation would actually hurt her case, even though he'd insisted that it would.

"We don't need him to find out what happened," Dalton said, and his commanding voice sent another jolt rocketing through her, a jolt that couldn't be more inappropriate under the circumstances.

"I do. I have no intention of working outside the law or putting my career on the line no matter how personal this case is," she shot back. That was mostly true. She was willing to stretch boundaries when the time was right, but she wasn't anywhere near there yet.

"There's no incentive for him to open another murder investigation he can't solve." Now the cowboy had stepped on the sheriff's toes.

But then her rational appeals were netting zero.

"All the resources I have are invested in keeping this town safe while I track down a killer," Sawmill defended. "A suicide—" he flashed his eyes at Leanne "—no matter how upsetting or personal the case might be, has no place sitting in a murder jacket."

"Are you calling me a liar?" Leanne was taken aback.

"I'm saying that your judgment is compromised and I don't blame you. There's a reason it's against department policy to work on a conflict-of-interest case in every law enforcement agency in the country," he said, again with that even tone.

It infuriated Leanne, but Dalton touched her arm once more and the spark distracted her for a split second.

"Who knows, you just might solve two cases at once. Forensics has come a long way," Dalton continued and she was pretty sure the sheriff's ruddy complexion became even rosier, another sign this meeting was going south. He was right about one thing. Keeping her emotions in check was going to be more difficult than she'd estimated.

"It has." The sheriff's tone was steadfast.

"Then we're wasting our time here like I said before." There was anger in his voice now as he spoke to the sheriff. "If you won't believe a detective, I have no chance of convincing you. Besides, I tried once and we both know how that turned out."

"These cases aren't related," Sawmill said.

"Really?" Dalton took a step back. "Same method. Same tree. Same knot. Hell, it was the same day at around the same time. Are you planning to look me in the eye and tell me this is a coincidence?"

Sawmill stared at him but said nothing at first.

And Leanne figured she and Dalton were about to be escorted out the way they had come in when the sheriff lifted his gaze to meet the handsome rancher's.

He stared for a long moment without saying a word.

And then he issued a sharp sigh. "I owe it to you to take this seriously, Dalton. One of my deputies will pull her cell phone records. We'll see who she was talking to leading up to last night. There are a few other pieces of evidence I can have processed. If anything comes up to change my initial opinion, you have my word I'll open a criminal investigation. Between now and then, I'd like to keep this as quiet as possible."

This was a huge win and she had no plans to push her luck. "Thank you, sir."

"Let's see if there's anything there to be concerned with." He held up his hands, palms out.

"Anything you can do is appreciated," Dalton said before escorting Leanne out of the building.

Neither spoke until they reached the safety of the sport utility.

"It's obvious that you two have history. Do you plan on telling me what any of that was about?"

The doors were locked and the windows were up.

Dalton turned the key in the ignition. "I'd rather talk about our next step. You shouldn't leave your car at the lot today."

"What are the chances we can go back to get it unnoticed?" She wondered how much damage there'd be if her name was linked to the case.

"Slim. Especially now that the sun has come up."

"Did he get my license plate?" Leaving her car there could pose a problem, too.

"Not that I could tell. I was a little preoccupied." She could've sworn a small smirk dented the corner of his lips.

If it did, he suppressed it just as quickly.

She'd been thinking about that kiss, about the contrast of his hard, muscled chest and the tenderness he'd shown when he pressed his lips to hers. About how good he tasted, like coffee and mint…and she shouldn't be thinking these destructive thoughts right now.

"Where should we go?" She bit back a yawn.

"I'll drop you off anywhere you want," he said.

"Can we talk through what happened while the details are fresh?" she asked.

"The ranch needs me," he said.

What was he up to?

"I can drop you off at your sister's," he said.

"After the way we left things, I doubt it," she responded. "And since I'll be sticking around a few days, I'll need a recommendation for a place to stay while my sister cools off."

There was no way Bethany was going to give Leanne access to Clara's room after everything she'd said to her half sister.

Besides, Gary had most likely torn it apart already.

THE BLACK COFFEE burned Dalton's throat as he took a sip. It felt good. Reminded him that he was alive. He took another, still trying to figure out what he was doing with Leanne West when he should've dropped her off so he could examine the photos on his phone in privacy. But then a part of him realized she had a right to know if he found something there. Besides, with her trained eye, she could be useful in evaluating them.

"Thanks for not dropping me off and leaving," the detective said. "And for everything you've been doing to help so far. I never would've gotten that far with the sheriff on my own."

Dalton nodded.

The detective ran her index finger along the rim of her coffee cup. She took hers with cream and two packets of raw sugar. He didn't want to notice those details about her. She wasn't a date. And even the women he'd spent time with never stayed long enough for him to figure out their coffee habits. He knew very little about the woman sitting across the booth from him in the empty café off the highway.

There were other details he'd cataloged about her. The fact that she didn't wear a wedding ring. He told himself the only reason he noticed was because of the kiss—a kiss so hot he didn't need to think about it, either—and a necessary apology that would have gone to her husband if she'd had one.

Dalton set his cup down. He also noticed that she'd picked at the hem of her navy blazer four times since sitting down and figured she was nervous. Was it because she was with him?

"If we're going to work together, we should probably know some basics about each other, Detective," he started, figuring information might come in handy if they somehow separated.

The detective blew out a burst of air. "Okay. First things first, call me Leanne."

He nodded.

"I'm from Dallas, but you already know that. I have a six-month-old daughter." She paused long enough to pull out her cell phone and show him a pic of a partially toothed little girl. "Mila."

"Cute kid," he said. His newly found half brother, Wyatt, had a six-month-old kid.

"There's no father," she said with an awkward half smile. "I mean, there was a father, but he's not... *around.*"

"He's an idiot," Dalton said before he could stop himself. He probably shouldn't insult a man he didn't know, but anyone who could walk out on a face like the one on the cell phone and not look back had to be a first-order jerk.

Leanne shot a warning look, which surprised him and told him there was more to the story. "My neighbor has been a gift. She loves kids, has more grandkids than I have fingers on one hand and she's keeping Mila for a few days."

"Sounds like a good setup."

She nodded. "Other than that, there's not much to tell. I worked my butt off to make detective before thirty. I've been on the job two years, so still earning my stripes to some." And then turned the tables on him. "What's your story?"

"You already know my name is Dalton Butler. I have a twin, Dade. We're identical, so if you bump into someone who looks a helluva lot like me but says he's not, he's not lying." He chuckled at her wide eyes. "What? You've never met twins before?"

She made a gesture. "I guess I have. Haven't known a lot personally."

"My father was fairly famous in Texas." He paused before adding, "Infamous in some circles."

"I heard a lot of good things about him," she said casually, like it was common knowledge.

She obviously didn't know the real man. But then, who really did?

"I'm one of six kids, unless someone else comes out of the woodwork before the reading of the Mav's will on Christmas Eve." He tried to suppress the anger in his voice and figured he wasn't doing a great job based on the look she shot him. "Four of us grew up under one roof and had the same mother."

"Do you work on the farm?" she asked.

"It's a ranch. And the answer is yes," he said indignantly, picking up a packet of sugar. He should've realized a Dallas detective wouldn't know much about ranching but calling Hereford a farm was a lot like calling a horse a cow. "All of us do in some capacity, including the new ones."

A moment of silence passed between the two of them before Leanne's gaze intensified.

"Why do you care so much about this case?" She pinned him with her stare, and he couldn't tell if she was looking at him or through him. "Who did you lose?"

"It's been fourteen years, so the number fourteen might be important," he said, redirecting the conversation. He tossed the sugar packet on top of the table.

Leanne sat there for a long moment, like she was expecting—hoping?—he'd return to the original conversation thread. She'd have to figure it out as they went along. He had no plans to rush. Drudging up that pain held no interest to Dalton.

On a resigned-sounding sigh, she pulled a small notepad and pen out of her purse.

"Fourteen," she parroted as she jotted the number down. "The date might be significant."

She wrote, *December 7.*

"Also, the digital date of twelve-seven," he added.

"Right. The tree is oak." She twirled the pen around her fingers and shot an anxious look at Dalton. "He put them on display."

He could see that she was trying to hold back a flood of emotions.

"He likes to show his work," Dalton ground out through clenched back teeth.

"Because he wants the bodies to be found." Leanne gripped the pen and removed the cap before replacing it. Nervous tick? Or was this one of her little habits when she concentrated?

Dalton broke eye contact and focused on the black

liquid in his cup. Anger was an out-of-control tide rising inside him. One he needed to get under control.

"He likes young girls," Leanne said. "Was your friend in high school?"

A sharp sigh issued. If the two of them were going to come up with a profile of the killer, he needed to talk about her. Although, nothing inside him wanted to. *Do it for Alexandria*, a little voice in the back of his mind said.

"A junior," he said and those two words were harder to say than he figured they would be.

"So was Clara. She was already making plans for senior year," she said, and her voice was anguished.

There was a pull toward it, maybe because it mimicked his own pain.

"Your niece. Was she blonde, like her mother?" he asked. "And alone on the night of the seventh?"

"Yes and yes, but everything about Clara was full of life. My sister—" she paused long enough to look up at him "—half sister used to look more like her daughter based on the pictures I've seen of her. Now, she's just faded, washed-out. Exhausted."

"The two of you didn't grow up in the same house?" he asked.

"No. We have different mothers. Our father was some piece of work." She rolled her eyes and embarrassment flushed her cheeks.

"How'd the two of you meet?"

"I tracked her down after my mother passed away when I was a rookie. Before then she'd asked me not to try to find my father. Looking for siblings felt like a betrayal and that last year with Mother's cancer was hard." Leanne looked flustered. "My sister was a mess when I found her, but then we got her into rehab and she cleaned up her act."

"Speaking of your family, the sheriff will follow up with your brother-in-law," he said.

"I'd expect him to," she said in that determined voice he was beginning to recognize.

"What are the odds he'll find something there?" Dalton had to ask.

Leanne stared out the window for a long moment.

"They'd better be slim-to-none," she finally said through gritted teeth. "What kind of clothing was your girlfriend wearing?"

"I never said she was my girlfriend," he countered.

"You didn't have to." There was compassion in her voice now. No trace of the rage he'd heard when she spoke of her brother-in-law. "This is deeply personal for you and that's the only reason you care about my niece's case. Don't get me wrong, I'll take all the help I can get, but based on your reaction so far I'd say the two of you used to be close."

Perceptive.

"We dated in high school. I'm the reason she was in that lot in the first place. She was waiting for me but I was out partying, having a good time. We'd had a dustup over my drinking, so I didn't want to show up with alcohol on my breath." Damn, those words were bitter tasting as they passed over his lips. "I left her there alone. By the time I show up, it was too late. Since I was the last person she'd seen and the first to find her—"

"You were the only suspect," she cut him off.

"That's right," he said.

"And that's the undercurrent I feel between you and the sheriff," she added.

"That and the fact that he still hasn't found my father's murderer." Dalton took another sip of coffee.

Her cup suddenly became very interesting to her. "I'm sorry about your friend. And I'm so sorry that you lost someone you cared about, especially while you were so young. This situation would be difficult for anyone, but a teenager…"

Dalton acknowledged her sentiment but nothing could ease the pain.

Leanne didn't speak. She looked up at him and caught his gaze, searching his eyes for something. A sign that it was okay to move on?

He nodded slightly to prod her into speaking again. At least for the moment, he had no more words ready.

"We'll come back to clothing. So, this person likes seventeen-year-old girls. Both events happened on the same day in December but fourteen years apart. The timing has to be significant."

"There was no sign of struggle at either scene," he added in a shaky voice—unsteady from anger. "I've gone off the assumption we're looking for a man all these years. You see anything to give me another direction?"

"No. A male is a safe assumption. I mean, cases like these are almost always male. This person had to be strong enough to hoist her up." Leanne's voice broke and a tear slid down her cheek. She seemed caught off guard. "Sorry."

Dalton reached across the table and thumbed it away. A hum of electricity pulsed through him at the contact and he bit back a curse. He resisted the urge to tuck the few tendrils of loose hair behind her ears.

Solving Alexandria's case was priority number one.

He needed to keep the thought close, because his damn hands wanted to reach for the beautiful determined woman across the table.

It was a case of sympathy, two people in a rare but similar circumstance. Or maybe a primal need for proof of life had him wanting to be her comfort. There was no way real feelings could be developing, considering he'd known the woman less than twenty-four hours.

Or could there?

Chapter Five

Both Leanne and Dalton had ordered, the food had arrived and she was doing more rearranging bites on her plate than actual eating. She'd ordered a full Southern breakfast of eggs and bacon along with biscuits and gravy mostly to appease Dalton, who seemed determined to get a warm calorie-laden meal inside her. The smell of food turned her stomach and she missed her little girl so much she ached. Despite working a full-time job, Leanne had been the one to put Mila to bed every night since her daughter was born six months ago and her heart wanted to be there for her daughter more.

If Leanne hadn't been so preoccupied with her newborn, she might've read the signs of trouble within Clara more accurately. A now-familiar pang of guilt struck deep and hard.

"Mind if we review your pictures?" she asked. The pain was never far from her thoughts and she needed to distract herself by maintaining focus on the case, on finding Clara's killer rather than being caught up in her emotions. The sheriff had made a good point. There was a reason investigators didn't work cases when a conflict of interest was present. The legal implications were only one part of the problem. Emotions were the other bigger issue. Get too caught up in her feelings and she could miss something important, something that could crack the case wide open.

Dalton studied her plate and she got the message. He wanted her to eat. But how could she? Her niece was gone and the person responsible was walking around free.

Pushing a clump of overcooked egg with her fork, she said, "I'm not hungry." Before he could protest, she added, "Mind if I sit on your side?"

Dalton shook his head.

Leanne came around the booth and slid in beside him. Her left arm grazed his right, reminding her how bad of an idea making physical contact with him was. Even through layers of clothes and jackets, there was a spark of attraction along with a free-falling sensation in her stomach.

"I shot everything I could think of, so there's a lot on here and I can't guarantee any of these will be useful," he warned.

"Let's just go through them one by one." She picked up her coffee cup and held it in two hands, appreciating the warmth on her palms.

"I hoped there might be something here to tie the crimes together," Dalton said. "But fourteen years is a long time and I don't have any photos from the original scene."

"The sheriff does. Maybe we can convince him to let us take a look at those. Compare."

"Doubt it. Do they even keep evidence from a suicide?" he asked.

"Good point. Every agency is different. We need to figure out a way to get him to check the database to see if there have been any other similar crimes in the past fourteen years." She was trying to offer hope. Losing her niece as an adult was horrific. She could only imagine the horror of losing a girlfriend at such a tender age. Then to become the prime suspect must've added insult to injury. What she knew from interviewing dozens of teens was that they carried a lot of guilt. They almost always found a way to blame themselves when tragedy struck.

The strong, virile cowboy next to her also seemed to carry the weight of the world on his shoulders even now. Fourteen years later.

Had the sheriff done the right thing accusing Dalton? One of the first rules of a murder investigation was to look at who was closest to the victim. She would need to know more about the case to make a better determination. For the sheriff to rule the death a suicide must've been a double blow, especially to someone Dalton's age at the time. "Maybe he'll get a hit on her cell phone and we'll have something more to go on."

She studied him. He would've been Clara's exact age. Everything had been so intense with her. It was one of the main reasons Leanne hadn't dropped everything to run to Cattle Barge when Clara first sounded the alarm. Leanne remembered the sense of urgency in her niece's voice and another wave of near-crippling guilt washed over her. Knowing she'd heard that same tone when Clara thought she might've done poorly on a test when she'd scored a B had normalized the emotion and made it seem like she was reading a cereal box instead of crying for help.

"In your experience, does this seem like the work of a serial killer to you?" Dalton asked and she didn't realize he'd been studying her for the past few minutes when she'd been inside her thoughts.

"There's a strong possibility but it's too early to tell. Contrary to how they're depicted on television, most serial killers have a cooling-off period in between murders. Fourteen years isn't too long for a second strike," she informed. "Why didn't you hire your own investigators when your friend died?"

"Because being a Butler means I'm supposed to have money coming out of my ears?" His tone was defensive and his muscles chorded with tension.

"Sorry. I didn't mean—"

"The Mav wouldn't allow it. He said I should get back to work and forget it ever happened." Dalton paused for a beat. "I'm pretty sure he was angry that I didn't thank him for sending in his lawyer to get me off the hook. I never really knew if he believed I was innocent."

"The whole situation is a lot for a teenager to take in." She softened her voice even more. Being a detective, she was used to choosing her words carefully and using tone to manipulate the suspects she interviewed into giving more details than they'd planned or getting a confession out of them. Talking to Dalton, she wanted to take her investigator/interviewer hat off and be a woman. He'd been through so much, too much, really. No one should have to endure it, although she'd seen this and worse in her job so many times.

She admired the strength in the man sitting next to her.

Most people, her sister included, reached out to find pain relief in the wrong places and in turn piled more problems on top of a bad situation. Problems like addictions to drinking, narcotics or both. Chemicals were the express train out of pain that most people took.

Not this man.

And she respected him for it.

"There was no sign of a struggle in my niece's case. I'm guessing with your friend, too. That's partly why the sheriff is reluctant to call this a homicide. So, I'm wondering how this guy could manage to pull that off. I know my niece and she would fight if someone came at her," she said.

"Unless she knew him personally or he disarmed her in some way," he said with an apologetic look.

"You're right. Now that I really think about it, she would also help anyone in need. The person could've been familiar to her," she said. "I wonder who would know both victims fourteen years apart?"

"Good question." Dalton used his thumb to flip through pics, giving enough time to study details. Most of them were of the ground or the tree. "Off the top of my head, they went to the same school. Could be a bus driver or male teacher. Even an administrator."

"True. I wish I had access to her laptop. She might've been communicating via email," she said on a sharp sigh.

"Maybe the link between them is location," he offered. "Alexandria and I were supposed to meet at the tree. How about you and Clara?"

"I expected to pick my niece up at her house," she admitted. "Although, she didn't like to be there more than she had to."

"Maybe she needed air." Dalton took a sip of coffee. "Could she have gone for a walk and ended up there? Where does Bethany live?"

"That's possible, but how much do you believe in coincidence? Even if I miraculously put them at the same tree fourteen years apart to the day and then suppose they both knew the person responsible, where's the struggle?"

"The first location might've been by accident but the second could've been chosen," he conjectured, thumbing another picture of the base of the tree.

"There are no marks going up the trunk to the branch." She pointed.

"With Alexandria," he thumbed another pic but didn't turn to look at her, "I assumed she was already knocked out and that's why she didn't put up a fight."

"There are drugs like ketamine that could've come into play," she offered and when he lifted a dark brow she added, "It can be crushed up and put in almost anything. It knocks them out and is easy enough to get."

"The date-rape drug?"

"Yes." She needed to ask this next question delicately. "Do you remember if the sheriff tested your friend to see if she'd been…*abused*…in any way?"

"No. Guess he didn't think he needed to," he said after a thoughtful pause.

"Meaning there were no indications of forced acts," she clarified.

"From the so-called interview, I found out that there were no signs of struggle, nothing under her fingernails, no marks on her arms. It's why the sheriff initially hauled me in. I was the last person who was supposed to have seen her alive and she had no marks or bruises to indicate she'd been in a fight," he said. "When they figured out that I was telling the truth, he shifted gears to suicide."

"Based on what else?"

"Alexandria had problems at home. Her parents weren't getting along. They were having marriage problems, serious financial problems, problems with her older brother. She wouldn't let me tell anyone. We'd been fighting about that and my drinking," he informed.

"The family was on the verge of losing everything. She could've believed it was her fault somehow." She brought her hand up to her face. "Stress could be a factor, but..."

He stared at her and she couldn't tell if he was looking at her or through her, but she already recognized that look he got when he had an idea. "What is it?"

"I was just thinking that suicide by hanging seems like something a guy would do," he said.

"You're right. Statistics put death by hanging as a far more common method of suicide for males than females. The latter usually rely on something less violent like taking too many pills. When they *are* violent, they normally take an object to their wrists. I'm glad you brought that up. That struck me as odd about these cases and I meant to mention it before." Everything had been moving so fast they'd barely had time to think.

"Which makes two in the same location, by two teenage girls, even less likely." He picked up his coffee mug but held it midair.

"Even so, if I look at this purely from an investigator's point of view, I walk up to a body hanging in the air, no sign of struggle. In your friend's case, I talk to a few people and find out that she was supposed to meet you, so you hit the top of my suspect list. Keep in mind the biggest threat to any woman is the person closest to her. Oftentimes that means we look hardest at the person the victim was in a relationship with. I'm guessing threatening you with charges was the sheriff's way of trying to get at the truth. I'm also assuming he believed it had most likely been a suicide from the onset. And if that's the case, he wouldn't truly have treated it as a murder investigation aside from trying to shake you down."

"Meaning?" Dalton asked, and he was following what she was saying with renewed intensity.

"There isn't going to be a whole lot of evidence that has been collected in either case, which will make it even more difficult to tie these two crimes together." She studied the picture of the tree trunk again, wishing it could speak. It held the answers, and there wasn't anything anyone could say or do to dig out the truth.

"Then we solve the current case," he said.

The waitress showed with the brown-rimmed coffee carafe and topped off their twin cups.

"Thank you," Leanne said as the waitress seemed to be waiting around for acknowledgment. The place was empty and she was most likely bored, Leanne thought, until Dalton glanced up and offered a polite smile.

The waitress's face flushed. "You're welcome. Anything else I can get for either of you?"

Leanne read the name tag. "No. We're fine. But thanks, Makayla."

Makayla lingered, like she was expecting Dalton to speak. When he didn't, she said, "Holler if you need anything else."

"We will," Leanne said, hearing the defensiveness in her own voice.

Makayla moved on and quickly disappeared behind

the counter. Leanne shouldn't have cared one way or another if the waitress flirted with Dalton. But she did.

Her phone buzzed. She checked the screen. The call was coming in from her babysitter. Her heart stuttered.

"Excuse me while I take this," she muttered, scooting out of the booth as she answered on the second round of her ringtone.

"Everything okay?" she asked, skipping right over niceties, needing to know the answer. Her hands shook. Her blood pumped. And her internal alarms sounded.

"Fine here. How about on your end?" Mrs. Blankenship must've picked up on the stress in Leanne's voice.

"Sorry. I didn't mean to make you worry," she responded. "My niece's case is a bit more complicated than I'd expected. I'm most likely going to need to stick around for a few days. Is that a problem?"

Mrs. Blankenship lived on the same block as Leanne in Dallas. The grandmother of seven almost always had a grandchild being picked up or dropped off at her house and she always said how much she loved children. But Leanne didn't want to impose on her kind neighbor or overstay her generosity.

"No. Mila is just fine. She's been a little fussy. Might be getting in one of those teeth we've been talking about," Mrs. Blankenship said in her usual pleasant tone. She was the ideal image of a grandmother: white hair, generous stomach and gentle nature. That, and she loved to bake. If Leanne had had a grandmother, she would've wanted her to be like Mrs. Blankenship.

Mila loved her and she'd been a godsend when Leanne had returned to work, unable to drop her six-week-old baby—because that was all the leave she'd accrued—off with strangers at the day care she'd meticulously vetted. All it had taken for Mrs. Blankenship to offer her services was to see Leanne sitting on her porch step, cheeks and eyes soaked with tears while she held on to her baby in that little pink blanket when she was supposed to be back at work.

Mrs. Blankenship had taken the sleeping baby from her arms and told Leanne to go on. After a quick tutorial in her formula and feeding schedule, Leanne had handed over her daughter and a decent portion of her paycheck ever since. Her neighbor was worth every penny and more. Mrs. Blankenship was the rare neighbor who still baked cookies and personally delivered them on most major holidays. She had a knack for remembering birthdays, too. Every May 2, a card with a homemade treat was waiting for Leanne on top of the chair on her porch. The older woman had a quick smile and more energy than Leanne had ever seen. With her grandkids, she'd throw a ball or hop into the pool with them. Mila was lucky to be counted as one of her flock.

"I hate to impose with your grandkids coming over this weekend, but I might not be back until Monday," she said into the receiver, wishing her daughter was in her arms. "Can you hold on until then?"

"Don't worry. I just hope you find the person who did this," Mrs. Blankenship said in a hushed voice. It was the softest Leanne had ever heard the woman speak and there was so much sadness. Her husband of thirty-two years still held down his day job. Although, he had been threatening to retire for the past couple of years, according to his wife. Mrs. Blankenship had chuckled when she told Leanne. He'd taken an early pension from the force and worked as a security guard detail at a high-rise in Turtle Creek. The man had no plans to retire, no matter how many times he'd said this year would be his last.

"Thank you, Mrs. B." It was the nickname the fifty-nine-year-old woman had asked to be called the first time they met. "This means a lot."

"Find the person who did this to her. She was a good kid." Mrs. B's voice started to break, but she seemed to quickly catch herself. She was one of the few people who understood law enforcement types.

"Give the baby a hug and a kiss for me?" Leanne asked, trying not to focus on just how much her heart ached at being away from her daughter this long. Other than an occasional late night on a case, this was the longest Leanne had been away from Mila. She'd underestimated how powerful that pull would be after going a full day without seeing her baby.

A grunt came through the line before Mila's unmistakable cry.

"She's waking up. I bet she's hungry. Be careful out there," Mrs. Blankenship said.

"You know I will."

Leanne ended the call and took a moment to breathe in the cool air outside. She turned and saw the waitress had wasted no time returning to the table. Why did a pang of—jealousy?—strike Leanne? She had no ties to the handsome cowboy and he certainly had none to her. The two of them were trying to solve a murder case, two actually, which reminded her that she needed to ask for his friend's file from fourteen years ago. Surely, there was some obvious link between these cases.

Makayla threw her head back as though cracking up at something the cowboy had said. Leanne's feet jutted forward and before she could say the words, *Back up*, she was standing next to the waitress and politely asking her to move so she could reclaim her seat.

Making a show of being put off by the request, the waitress blew out a breath and walked away from the table.

"Who were you talking to out there?" Dalton asked, picking up his phone and where they'd left off.

"The person who's taking care of my daughter while I'm here," she supplied.

"Everything all right?"

She nodded. "But I've been thinking about what you said."

Leanne pulled out a couple of twenties and tossed them on the table. Dalton sat there, a surprised look on his features.

"Take your money back. I already paid," he said, and she figured he was operating from some cowboy code, which meant arguing would do absolutely no good. He picked up the twenties and handed them to her.

"I'd ask you to at least let me leave the tip, but I'm guessing that's already taken care of, too," she said.

"It is," he confirmed.

"Well, if we want to figure out who murdered Clara we need to start with my sister." She issued a sharp breath. "Ready?"

Chapter Six

Dalton didn't pry in other people's business. He couldn't help but notice the strained relationship between the detective and her sister earlier. This visit should be interesting if she allowed them past the porch, which he doubted based on the way the pair had left things. Deception pushed people away from each other. It didn't matter how good the intentions might have been.

Several taps on the door to the small redbrick bungalow netted zero on the other side. It was well past noon and there was no sign of activity in the house. For all he knew, Bethany had taken her young child and disappeared. There was a chain-link fence around the property. The house sat on about a quarter of an acre of land if he had to guess. And there were no cars under the porte cochere.

Leanne knocked again, harder this time.

Just when he was about to urge Leanne to come back later, the door cracked open.

"Are you trying to wake Hampton?" Bethany spoke in the same quiet, angry tone May, the Butlers' longtime nanny and housekeeper, had used to keep young kids quiet in church. It was the one that said he'd be more than damned if he didn't get his act together. Bethany's eyes were dry. The tip of her nose was red, giving the impression she'd been crying earlier. She wore pajamas.

"Please let me in, Bethany. We need to talk," Leanne insisted.

"Why should I?" The fire in those words didn't reach Bethany's eyes.

"Because I want to find out who killed Clara and bring him to justice." Leanne's voice was composed, but a flood of anger stood like barking dogs behind a fence and threatened to unleash if her half sister didn't comply.

"You can't help with that."

"Don't be—" The door slammed shut in Leanne's face.

"Want me to give it a try?" Dalton figured he couldn't do much more damage than Leanne. Her sister might see him as neutral.

The detective stepped aside. "It can't hurt."

He rapped on the door of the modest house, using his knuckles. He'd need to take a lighter tactic than the bull-in-a-china-shop approach Leanne had used. "Mrs. Schmidt, this is Dalton Butler. I'd appreciate it if you'd open the door and hear me out. Your daughter's case could be tied to one close to me and I'd very much like to find out if there's a connection."

She complied. But, again, she peeked through a small crack.

"Thank you for—"

"You were in the back of the car with us earlier," she cut in. "And at the sheriff's office."

"That's right. I couldn't be sorrier for your loss, ma'am." Every word was true and he could tell by her slightly softened expression that she sensed it. "I lost someone a few years ago in the same spot. Any chance you'll let us in and hear me out on this?"

"I don't know. Gary could be home any minute and he won't like the two of you here," she hedged, and there was a nervous twitch above her left eye.

Leanne took an impatient-sounding breath—the bull returning—so he touched her arm, ignoring the frissons of heat scorching his fingertips.

"We certainly wouldn't want to cause any problems between you and your husband, especially now while you have so much to deal with," Dalton said sympathetically.

His approach was working. He was gaining ground and he could see it. She shifted her weight from her left to right foot and chewed on her chapped bottom lip.

She swept the outside with her gaze, cracked the door open enough for them to slip through and said, "You can only stay for a few minutes. Hampton's sleeping and he doesn't know what's going on yet. If Gary sees your car out front, he'll freak out so make it quick."

All the honor codes that made Dalton the man he was, one who respected women and took it upon himself to protect anyone or anything smaller or weaker than him, flared up.

Was Gary physical with Bethany?

If he was, Dalton had to consider the possibility that he could've been involved in her daughter's murder.

Dalton followed the frail woman into the living room. He couldn't see into the kitchen with the boxy layout but a square dining table with four chairs, one with a booster seat that he presumed was for Hampton, filled the room. Based on the layout, he imagined the kitchen was to the left of the dining room.

A well-used sectional anchored the room with a matching ottoman that held several remote controls along with a few magazines. It was clear by the reading material that Gary owned guns. If Clara had been shot, the case might have been a no-brainer. Dalton filed the information in the back of his mind. It wasn't exactly unusual for a household to have a hunting rifle or shotgun in Texas. Most folks kept them for protection from animals.

But then again, the sickest animal in Cattle Barge seemed to be preying on teenage girls.

This conversation was going to be tricky in his estimation because Leanne, who seemed like a fine detective, was too emotional with her half sister to keep a clear mind. Her presence seemed to upset Bethany and that was another strike. The fact that her husband could come home any minute also seemed to put Bethany further on edge. Sure, he was a jerk but was he a murderer?

Dalton couldn't ignore the possibility that the man might've read about Alexandria in the news—maybe even found a reference Dalton didn't know about—and decided the time was right to get rid of the problem he had at home. Glancing at a picture on the fireplace of Gary with Bethany and Hampton said the guy had enough bulk to pull off carrying the teenager.

"You want coffee?" Bethany asked. "I just put on a fresh pot in case Gary came home."

Dalton picked up on the fact that she'd said *in case*. The woman didn't know when to expect her husband?

"If it's not too much trouble," he said as Leanne issued another sharp breath.

"None at all." Bethany's cheeks flushed. And then she looked at her half sister. "Leanne?"

Luckily, although to be fair Dalton didn't believe in luck, she'd kept quiet so far. She seemed to realize as much as he did that her talking would get them kicked to the curb quicker than she could find a penny at the bottom of her purse.

Seeing the relationship between these two helped him appreciate how close his own family was. The four kids who'd grown up together—Ella, himself, Dade and Cadence—had learned to band together early in life growing up with a father like Maverick Mike.

Their other two siblings who'd been kept secret until recently had been welcomed into the family and shown their rightful place as heirs. Not all of it had been easy, but he could see that it had been worth the extra effort on everyone's part as he watched Leanne and Bethany's relationship unravel under duress.

No matter what else happened, Butlers could be counted on to stick together.

"Yes, please," was all Leanne said. Good. Maybe she realized the importance of keeping her sister on an even keel.

The kitchen was where he thought it was, around the corner from the attached dining room. The walls in this place were most likely thin, so he didn't speak. Instead, he moved to the fireplace mantel to get a better look at Gary. He was decent-sized, five feet eleven or so if Dalton had to guess. The guy had massive arms. He must lift weights and he had a tattoo running up one side that Dalton couldn't make out. He stood in front of something that looked a lot like a fishing cabin and he was holding his kid upside down by the boy's ankles. Gary didn't strike Dalton as someone who was rocking an overload of IQ points but this guy wouldn't care about quantum physics.

He was a trophy hunter based on the other shots on the mantel and the fact that a deer head hung over the brick, no doubt a prize buck from a hunting trip.

Leanne made eyes at him when he glanced at her.

"Wasn't sure how either of you took it," Bethany said, returning to the room holding out two fists of mugs and looking at Dalton.

"Black's fine for me," he said. Hadn't Leanne added sugar and cream to hers in the coffee shop? The fact that her sister didn't know said a lot about their lack of a relationship since reuniting. He didn't know much more about Leanne's past other than that she had a small child and no husband. That last part shouldn't have made his heart skip a beat as fast as it had. She was giving up precious little about herself and anytime he asked a personal question, she dodged giving a straight answer. He didn't think she was out to sabotage their working relationship, but she kept her vest buttoned all the way up. Which also made him not want to notice little things about her, like how she took her coffee.

Instead, he focused on the room, trying to memorize as much as he could about the place in case Gary showed up and cut their visit short. There were toys scattered around that obviously belonged to a little boy. Several pictures of Hampton hung on one wall, the fireplace covered another, and in the corner sat a fairly large flat screen television. There were no pictures of Clara.

"Sorry for the mess," Bethany said, bending down to pick up a couple of small cars before setting them on top of the ottoman. "Hampton just went down for his nap and I haven't had a chance to straighten up."

"That him?" Dalton pointed to the picture on the mantel.

"Yes. This picture was taken over the summer. Gary thought it would be a good idea to take Clara, so she and her brother could spend more time together."

"Don't you mean so she could watch him while Gary drank himself into a stupor?" Leanne said under her breath.

Thankfully, Bethany didn't seem to hear. She straightened up the magazines on the ottoman and lined the remotes next to each other until they looked like piano keys. An opened decorative box revealed a bottle of pills that he hadn't noticed before.

"I never did much decorating. Gary moved here first and sent for us once he was established," Bethany offered, as she held her hands out toward the dead buck mounted above the fireplace.

This must be her way of explaining why her home looked more like a hunting lodge than a place for a family. There were normally more feminine touches around when a woman lived in a house, in Dalton's experience, which also led him to believe that Gary was the one in charge.

"Sit down," Bethany said.

"Thanks for the coffee." Leanne gripped her mug but didn't take a sip.

"My Gary likes to take care of us so I don't have to worry," she said by way of explanation.

"Sounds like a decent man," Dalton said mainly to check her reaction. He took a seat near her and, now that Bethany was close, he could see that she'd taken whatever was in the medicine bottle.

He must've looked at the bottle a second too long because Bethany's eyes flew to it.

"Doctor likes me to keep these on hand to help me deal with…*things*," she said by way of explanation.

That gave him the impression the pills were some kind of antidepressant.

"Where's your husband?" he asked, figuring the question would come off better from him than Leanne. It was obvious to everyone, including Bethany, that her sister didn't care much for her spouse.

"He's probably out at the deer lease," she said with a shrug and awkward glance toward Leanne. "I couldn't reach him, which isn't unusual because cell coverage is spotty on a good day, and with the cold snaps we've had it gets even worse with all the wind."

If Gary was on the deer lease, someone would be able to corroborate his story.

"Who'd he go with?" Leanne's tone was sharp. She'd picked up on the same thing he had.

Bethany gave a noncommittal shrug. "I'm not sure."

"How do you know that's where he is?" Leanne asked outright. If he let her keep going, they'd be kicked out of there in a matter of minutes.

"What smells so good?" Dalton asked, trying to re-direct the conversation.

Bethany's gaze bounced from her sister to him. "Cookies. I decided to make some for Hampton." She looked away when she said, "To soften the blow of what I have to tell him about his sister."

"Half sister," Leanne pointed out and that elicited a glare from Bethany.

He shot Leanne a severe look.

"Are those chocolate-chip?" he asked, trying to pull the attention back to him.

"Snickerdoodle," she responded. And then it seemed like the air staled and she had nothing else to say.

Dalton wasn't sure how far they could push her. She seemed fragile, like she was hanging on by a thread but also a little too quick to sweep the whole incident under the rug. Her reactions sent up warning flares about Gary. Did she believe he was as innocent as she said?

"Did Gary say when he'd be home?" Leanne asked.

"I'm not sure. I left messages. It's not unlike him to show up without calling me back first," she said, but something flashed behind her eyes. Fear? Dalton didn't comment on how strange the relationship seemed to him. If or when he was ready to commit to someone, he'd have the decency to let them know where he was and be sure he could be contacted in case of an emergency. If she knew who her husband was with, although he had to consider the possibility that she was protecting Gary and his friends, she was covering pretty damn well. Out of loyalty or fear? Or both? "Did you say there was another case?"

"Yes, I did," Dalton said. "Can you tell us anything about your daughter that might help us figure out if this case is connected to mine? Who were her friends?"

"She didn't have a lot of them. Gary said he wanted us to move before the end of the school year last year so she could make friends but that didn't happen," Bethany said. "She missed her friends back home and didn't even try to make new ones while she lived here. She kept threatening to leave, saying this friend or that had said their parents didn't mind if she finished school there, but Gary wanted her here with us where she belonged."

"What did you think?" Dalton asked, leaning forward.

Those bony shoulders of hers rose and fell again in another shrug.

"Who was I to stand in the way?" Bethany asked. "He was making an effort with her."

"What about being her mother and doing what was right for her?" Leanne ground out.

Dalton shot her another severe look but she seemed unfazed. She had a right to be angry. Hell, he'd wanted to fight the world after Alexandria's murder. But her attitude was putting Bethany on the defensive. Based on the tight grip Leanne had on the coffee mug, she knew it, too. It seemed to be taking all the strength she had to contain her anger. Even so, it was boiling over like an active volcano spewing hot lava all over their case.

He turned to Leanne and didn't speak until they locked gazes.

"Do you want to wait outside while I speak to your sister?"

"Half sister," Bethany clarified.

LEANNE GOT IT. She was blowing it. Dalton's message rang loud and clear. Get a grip or leave so he could finish what they'd come here to do. She shot her best look of apology and mouthed the words in case he didn't get the message. She really was sorry. Putting Bethany on edge—no matter how much she disliked Gary—would do nothing to help.

She chalked her anger up to Bethany not protecting Clara the way she should have. Bethany might be in a difficult situation with her current husband, but that was no excuse to allow him to make Clara miserable.

"Did she have any local friends that you knew of?" Dalton asked. "I grew up here so I might know the family."

"Other than Renee, I'm not sure. She was the only one who ever came over to the house," Bethany said.

"Why is that?" Leanne asked, using a much softer tone. In an interview, it was sometimes a good idea to throw a witness off by upsetting them. In this case, Leanne could see that her sister would just buckle and most likely kick them out.

"Gary didn't like strangers in the house," she said, looking to Dalton as though another man would obviously see the logic.

Dalton looked unmoved. "Renee Paltry?"

Bethany nodded after shooting a surprised look at him. She must've realized he'd know most of the families.

Leanne glanced at the medicine bottle and wondered if her sister was taking something on a regular basis. Clara had already said that Hampton was a handful when he was awake. A wild four-year-old was the least of her half sister's problems now. Because the sheriff would come after Gary and, at the very least, bring him in for questioning. Her brother-in-law wouldn't take kindly to having anyone poke around in his business.

Leanne wanted to march into Clara's room and gather evidence. Since she'd convinced the sheriff to look into the case, it would only be a matter of time before he sent a deputy to her niece's room. If Leanne's prints were all over the place, she'd be hauled in front of the Internal Affairs Division (IAD) to explain herself. Losing her job wasn't an option with a child to support by herself. So, she'd play it by the book.

"Did Clara have her cell phone on her?" The question was probably useless. Leanne had learned to ask them anyway. She never knew when an unexpected answer would break a case open.

"I believe so," Bethany said.

Leanne made a mental note to ask the sheriff about it. Her personal belongings would be released to the family unless he collected them as evidence. She'd left his office so abruptly earlier that she'd forgotten to ask. "I know this is hard but have you been inside her room?"

Bethany shook her head and tears welled. "The door's closed and I didn't have the heart to open it." She released a dry sob. Bethany had loved her daughter in the best way she knew how.

"What about her laptop? Is it normally in her room?" Leanne asked.

Before Bethany could answer, the back door smacked open, causing everyone to jump to their feet.

"What the hell's going on in my house, Bethany?" Gary's voice boomed from the other room as his boots smacked against the flooring. The floor groaned under his weight.

"You'll wake your son," Bethany said in a hushed tone.

"Whose SUV is parked out front?" Gary stalked around the corner and froze the second his gaze landed on Dalton. He must have known on instinct that he'd be no match for the cowboy whose head almost touched the ceiling.

Dalton's heft blocked Gary's view of Leanne.

"I'm afraid your wife has bad news." Dalton immediately repositioned himself so that he'd be in between Bethany and Gary. Leanne moved to her sister's side.

"I tried to call but couldn't reach you," Bethany said.

Gary looked the same as his photograph on the mantel, reasonably tall with a spare tire around his midsection and a ruddy face with pockmarks from too much acne as a teenager. Everything about him was big, from his big horse teeth to his big attitude. His mouth was big, too. Leanne sensed Dalton wasn't the type to put up with too much lip.

Bethany delivered the news about Clara.

Gary got quiet, listened.

"I'd like to speak to my wife in private," Gary said after a pause.

"Now, don't get upset, Gary. My sister is here to pay her respects and this is her new boyfriend." She glanced at Dalton, who supplied his name. "There's nothing going on and they were on their way out." Bethany stepped aside and pushed Leanne toward Gary. Leanne could feel her sister's hands trembling against her skin, a stark contrast to contact with Dalton. Leanne didn't correct her sister about Dalton being her boyfriend. Her sister had said it to calm Gary about another man being present.

A sinking feeling pounded her chest. Was he abusing Bethany? Clara?

Why would Clara cover that up when she spoke to her aunt?

Her niece had said she wanted—no, *needed*—to talk to Leanne about something. Was this it? Leanne had dismissed it as Clara becoming desperate to get Leanne to pick her up. But physical abuse? Every time she'd asked Clara, her niece had denied it. But now the signs were obvious.

"I'm sorry for your loss, Gary," Leanne said, her tone

laced with spite she hadn't intended. She didn't want her emotions to be transparent.

Her comment seemed to get him going, as his ruddy complexion turned a few shades darker red. For a split second, she wondered if he knew what she was even talking about.

"You have no idea. I loved that girl," he said a little too defensively.

"I'm sure you did." She was goading him but getting a witness upset was an interview technique she'd employed many times in her career to catch someone in a slip. Besides, she could handle Gary.

"If you'd learned your place, maybe none of this would be happening. Did you ever think of that?" He fired the words like buckshot. They penetrated because she had in fact thought that exact thing. Leanne would eat one of her own bullets before she'd let him know just how accurate he'd been.

"I don't know, Gary. Why should I be the one to learn my place when you never did?"

Her brother-in-law's face took on a cartoon-quality expression. So much anger. Was he trying to throw blame on her to release his own guilt? Guilt at what, though?

Bethany jumped in front of Leanne, facing her, breaking her line of sight.

"You've done enough already. Go home, Leanne." Bethany's words were more plea than fight, and it broke Leanne's heart to hear the desperation in her sister's voice.

If Leanne had realized how bad the situation at home had become, not only would she have pulled Clara out sooner she would've gotten help for her sister, too. A little voice in the back of her head reminded her that she couldn't force anyone to do anything they didn't want to. It still stung and frustrated her to no end that she'd missed the signs.

"Get out of my house," Gary demanded, throwing his arms in the air and taking a threatening step toward Leanne and her sister.

Dalton had Gary pinned against the nearest wall before Gary could finish his sentence. His head banged against the drywall so hard a picture of Hampton flew off. The frame broke and the glass shattered as soon as it made contact with the floor.

"I'm going to tell you this once and you better remember it because if I have to come back, you're not going to like what's going to happen to you." Dalton used his forearm to press Gary against the wall. "Man to man, if I hear of you so much as grabbing your wife's arm too hard and leaving a mark, it'll be the last thing you do on this earth. Do you understand me?"

Gary's ruddy cheeks flamed brighter and he seemed to need air.

"I'm going to take a step back and you're going to apologize to the ladies in the room." Dalton leaned forward like he was about to whisper in Gary's ear. Gary winced and Leanne could only guess that Dalton had increased pressure against his windpipe.

"Are you ready to show some respect?" Dalton asked loud enough for the women to hear.

Her brother-in-law's head was still turned to the side but he nodded almost imperceptibly.

"Okay. Nice and easy. And you apologize." Dalton must've eased some of the pressure because Gary gasped.

Leanne should have wiped the smirk off her face,

but Gary had had this coming far too long for her not to enjoy it at least a little bit. And if he'd done anything to hurt her niece, Dalton pinning him to the wall for a few uncomfortable seconds would be the least of the man's problems. She'd have him arrested and throw the book at him herself.

"Sorry," came out on a rasp. Gary's hand came up to his throat where a red mark already streaked his neck. He carried the disposition of a child who'd been reprimanded. Bullies backed down the second they met their match. She'd seen it time and time again when the seemingly toughest men on the outside broke down, cried and begged to be released after a few days in prison.

Dalton pressed his hand to the small of Leanne's back and then guided her out the door. The move felt protective. Even though Leanne could hold her own in a confrontation, she liked the thought of letting someone else be in control for a change. It was nice for someone else to have her back when she'd felt so alone for most of her life.

Leanne barely closed the door of the sport utility when words exploded from her mouth. "He's hiding something and I don't like it. Where the hell's he been all this time?"

Dalton, the ever-cool cowboy, started the ignition and compressed his lips as he backed the vehicle off the parking pad and onto the street. "What was Gary's relationship like with Clara?"

"You've heard some of the stuff he pulled with her," she said, and a feeling deep in the pit of her stomach stirred. Call it intuition, but something was off.

"I don't mean any disrespect to her, but is there any chance there could be more to it than that?" He was talking slowly, choosing his words carefully and that sent up so many warning flares.

"Like what? A relationship beyond…" Leanne couldn't bring herself to say the rest. Acrid bile scorched her windpipe. She was shaking her head, praying there couldn't be any truth to his idea. "Not if she had anything to say about it."

"Hear me out for the sake of argument." His voice was a study in calm.

"Okay." Leanne took in a deep breath, meant to fortify her, but all it did was cause more acid to rise.

"He convinces her, possibly even threatens her, into entering into a relationship with him." He paused as though allowing her to take in what he was saying, like if he went too fast her head might explode. "Maybe she doesn't even like it, but she thinks he'll hurt her or her mother if she doesn't do what he says."

Leanne's chest tightened and it was getting difficult to take in air. Her mind couldn't even go there hypothetically. Her brain screamed *no*.

She listened for something to blow a hole in the story because it sounded like other horrific stories she'd known about.

"Maybe this goes on for a few days, weeks—" he paused another beat "—maybe longer. One day she freaks out. Says she can't keep doing this to her mother behind her back and threatens to come clean. He can't have that, so he kills her."

Chapter Seven

Leanne stared out the windshield. She brought her fingers up to the bridge of her nose as though trying to stem a headache. Dalton didn't like saying the words any more than she liked hearing them. But they had to discuss the situation.

"There are so many possibilities at play here. Aside from the fact that I think Clara would've told me something like that, I don't think it could've gone down that way. Let's just go down that road for a minute." Her mind seemed to be reeling at the thought of it happening right under her nose. "Say the two were in a…relationship. I know it would've been forced, because my niece couldn't stand Gary and I can't blame her. For argument's sake, what if he had threatened her mother and she gave in but she feels guilty about it. Eventually, the guilt eats her inside out and she tells him she can't do it anymore. He tries to convince her to keep quiet but she says she has to tell her mother. In the heat of the moment, he decides to silence her. A passion killing. He's hotheaded, so he'd use the first thing available. We already know he has guns but even if they were locked up, he'd grab the first thing available, a rock, a knife. Those heat-of-the-moment murders tend be ugly crime scenes."

Dalton wouldn't know from personal experience, but her points sounded solid. There were gun magazines and signs of hunting everywhere. In fact, Gary was supposed to have been out at the deer lease when Bethany couldn't reach him.

"Okay. How about this? Could he have seen the news coverage and decided to copycat?" he asked.

"He honestly doesn't strike me as someone who's bright enough to execute a plan as complicated as that," she admitted.

"I guess that theory doesn't quite match up with his quick temper," Dalton said, relief washing over him. He wouldn't rule Gary out, but he didn't want to believe the man in Clara's life who was supposed to protect her would hurt her. He turned the wheel onto the farm road 254. "We won't get anything else out of your sister now that he'll have a chance to work on her."

"You're right about that."

Leanne's cell buzzed. She fished it out of her purse and then checked the screen. "It's her." Her voice broke. "He better not have done anything to her."

Dalton pulled off the road and into the parking lot of a grocery store as Leanne took the call.

"What is it, Bethany? Are you okay?" There was silence but he could hear screaming through the receiver. "Calm down. I can't understand what you're saying." Leanne's forehead wrinkled in concentration, another little thing he didn't want to notice about her. "Start from the beginning and tell me everything that's happening."

Dalton drummed his fingers on the steering wheel.

Whatever was going down was big and curiosity was getting the best of him.

"Okay. Here's what I want you to—" She paused and listened as though she'd been cut off midsentence. "No. There's no need for—" Another stop. "I'm going to break it down for—"

Leanne moved the phone a few inches from her ear. The sounds of her sister working herself into hysterics filled the cab. A kid screamed and wailed in the background.

"Don't do anything or go anywhere. We're on our way." Leanne ended the call and then looked at Dalton.

"We need to go back. I could barely understand what she was saying." The resignation in her voice had Dalton pulling away from the curb and making a U-turn.

"You didn't tell your sister to get a lawyer." He spoke his observation aloud.

"If Gary has nothing to do with this, he won't need one." Dalton could've guessed her answer. He'd thought the same, and it was the exact reason he wasn't offering up his family's attorney, Ed Staples. The man was the best in the state, probably the country, but he worked exclusively for the Butler family.

"The media is going to be all over this story once it breaks," he said. "Ever handle a high-profile case before?"

"Nothing that will get the kind of coverage this could draw," she admitted. She didn't have to say it but he knew—his name wasn't going to help keep this quiet.

The rest of the ride was spent churning over events. There was no preparing either one of them for the barrage of media already outside her sister's house, even though Dalton probably should have been used to it by now.

Dalton circled the block.

"This isn't good."

"These guys need something to put on the air. Your sister seems…" He didn't want to insult Bethany.

"Fragile," Leanne said for him.

"She has a little boy depending on her, and I don't like what this could be doing to her mental state," he stated.

"Agreed. Hampton might be a pistol but he's just a kid. Clara's voice always softened when she talked about her little brother. I think she secretly wanted a big family. Lots of kids running around and to be the big sister to them all," Leanne sighed, and it seemed to catch her off guard that she'd done it.

Was that what she wanted?

Dalton was in no way ready for a wife and kids. Hell, he couldn't begin to sort out his tangled emotions when it came to his relationship with his father, let alone try to make a family of his own work. The Mav and his mother—who'd abandoned the family when his youngest sister was still in diapers—weren't exactly the best role models for making a marriage work. All the kids were dealing with the fallout.

"Any chance Bethany might agree to let my family's housekeeper take care of him until this whole situation settles? She could stay on at the ranch, too. It would give her a chance to grieve her daughter and not have to worry about cooking or taking care of a little one," he said. "I don't have a lot of experience with kids but based on what I've seen when I'm out in public, those little guys can be a handful."

"You'd do that?" she asked, sounding a little caught off guard. "You'd offer up your own home to strangers?"

"If you think it'll help," he said. "And we're not exactly strangers anymore."

Most folks were surprised by the generosity of the Butler family, even though his sister Ella practically dedicated her life to serving the community through volunteer work. Ella fought to expand shelter space for stray animals. She worked tirelessly for the rights of the elders in their town. And yet, their reputation would always be that of their charismatic and unconventional father.

"I do. I just hope Bethany will be smart enough to take the help. When my sister breaks down, she tends to go inside herself and then use pharmaceuticals to equalize her moods. I can be hard on her sometimes, but she had it rough. We couldn't be more different, and I think that's part of the reason we ended up on opposite paths."

"How long do you think Gary will be held?" He circled the block once more before settling down the street where they could keep watch on the activity without being seen by reporters or deputies.

"Not long, if I had to guess. Sawmill must've found something on Clara's cell phone records that gave him enough to search the house. Gary was most likely brought in for routine questioning. The most they can hold him is seventy-two hours before they'll have to cut him loose," she said. "I'd call on favors to get more information from the sheriff but with the way this case is going, anyone at my department who's connected to me could end up hauled into IAD." She seemed to catch herself that he wouldn't know what those initials meant. "Internal Affairs Division," she explained.

Dalton admired the fact that she refused to put her colleagues—friends?—in the line of fire to get at the end she so badly wanted. He admired her sense of loyalty and respected the internal compass she possessed to keep her on the straight and narrow.

Her good qualities were racking up and he didn't want to notice or like any of them, dammit. And especially since the kiss they'd shared wound through his thoughts more times than he needed to allow. Tight-gripped control on his emotions had gotten him through some dark days during his childhood and in high school. And throughout his adult life.

"She's a mess. We need to go in before she comes out and does or says something she'll regret," Leanne said before taking in the kind of breath meant to fortify. She palmed her cell. "I'll let her know we're coming in the back way."

REPORTERS TEEMED ON the sidewalk outside. Entering through the back door, Leanne looked at her half sister. Bethany seemed so lost and alone, so small, as she paced from room to room.

Anger and frustration flared inside Leanne. She'd put away dozens of killers and predators in her time on the job, vowing to bring justice for those who couldn't speak for themselves. Why couldn't she make things right for her own family?

Locking away that unproductive thought, she squared off with Bethany, who was wearing a path in the linoleum floor, covering the kitchen with her pacing. Hampton was on her hip and already more than half the size of his tiny mother. Bethany's hair was disheveled and her cheeks streaked with tears. She was still in her pajamas and there was an opened beer on the counter.

The woman looked to be on the edge of a meltdown and none of this was good for the child on her hip, who was sniffling and rubbing his eyes.

"Can I hold him?" Leanne asked. She wasn't sure if her nephew would even come to her. She'd been so tied up with Mila and her job that she hadn't been out to see him in the past year. At his age, he'd most likely forgotten her.

Bethany looked to be holding on to the toddler for dear life as she shot a panicked look at Leanne. At least she wasn't yelling like she had been over the phone.

If Leanne had to guess, all the commotion coupled with his mother's over-the-top emotions had thrown him into quite a crying fit. Clara had said her little brother could throw a temper tantrum like a pro.

"I could take him to play in the living room. He won't be out of your sight," Leanne added. She'd read something about kids being able to pick up on their caretaker's energy and how, as such, their emotions could be impacted later in life if they experienced too much trauma. She could only pray that her daughter didn't feel the absence of her father. Dating her partner had been stupid, but she and Keith had been together almost all the time. If the department had found out, they would've been out of jobs. The one time she went against her better judgment and gave into emotion she let herself fall down that rabbit hole. Both had seemed to gain their senses quickly, breaking off the affair. Being partners became awkward after.

A few weeks later, the sickness came and she started throwing up every morning. Part of her must've known what was going on, even though she wouldn't—couldn't!—allow herself to consider pregnancy as a possibility. Their working relationship would be ruined. One of them would need to transfer, and she could've handled all that if Keith hadn't moved on and started dating a desk jockey. Then he was shot. Killed. And time had run out to tell him he was going to be a father.

Chin up, she was forced to pretend she had been in a relationship that had gone sour before it had gotten off its feet in order to save face for both of them.

Leanne refocused on her sister. Bethany's body was strung as tight as her emotions. Talking to her sister would require a balancing act and as long as Leanne could keep her own emotions out of it, she should be fine. She'd done this countless of times in interviews. Now shouldn't be an issue, she reminded herself. She rolled her head side to side, trying to diffuse some of the tension in her neck.

"You want to go with your auntie?" Bethany finally asked.

Hampton shook his head in a definite no.

The confident cowboy seemed to know the perfect time to step in. The big guy moved with athletic grace as he swooped down to pick up the nearest toy, some kind of cartoon character airplane, and then swirled it through the air. Seeing him be so charming with the tyke put a chink in the armor around her heart. She reasoned the reaction came from wishing Mila's father was around, not for Leanne's sake, but for her daughter's. Leanne hated that history was repeating itself given that her own father had never been around growing up. As much as she believed, preached, that people made their own destiny, she sure as heck hadn't seen that one coming when she'd started dating Keith. Granted, it wasn't his fault that her heart had broken after losing him, but the result was the same. All Mila had was her mother.

Hampton laughed despite huge tears welling in his eyes when Dalton dropped the plane low until it almost crashed against the floor. He made up a commentary about how the pilot saved the day and then popped back up, making the plane nearly collide with the ceiling in the small ranch-style house.

The little guy ate it up like spaghetti on his plate. He belly-laughed and Leanne marveled at kids' ability to be so in the moment they forgot everything—from tragedy to anger—in a manner of minutes.

She wished there was a toy shiny enough or that possessed enough magic to make her do that, too. She'd love to be able to shift gears and leave the past in the dust. Adults were so much more complicated.

And seeing Dalton Butler entertain her nephew was one of the most attractive sights she'd seen, even though she didn't want to see the handsome cowboy in that light. *Or any light*, her mind argued.

"Mr. Butler offered his family's ranch as a safe house for you and Hampton until all this attention dies down." Keeping her out of sight was one reason he'd made the offer. She kept to herself the part about wanting to separate her sister from Gary so he wouldn't influence her decision. And about needing Bethany to get off whatever pills she was taking to ease the pain of Clara's death.

Based on how hard Bethany was shaking her head this was going to be an uphill battle. "Gary won't like it when he comes home if we're not here."

This wasn't the time to try to talk some sense into

her sister about the man she'd married. Leanne thought about Clara and about how much her niece had loved Hampton. For his sake, she needed to convince Bethany and not lose her cool.

"I understand," she started saying but Bethany cut her off.

"Do you?" Bethany drew her thin shaky hand to her forehead. "Because when all this blows over and it's just me and him, do you know what that'll be like for me? For us?"

"There are organizations that can help if you want to leave," Leanne said in as calm a voice as she could muster.

"Is that what you think I'm saying? I happen to love him and I don't want to go anywhere. Life has been good. Was good," her sister said, eyes brimming with tears.

"Really? Was it? Who was it good for? You? Clara?" Leanne couldn't help herself.

"That's not fair." Bethany released a sob and her eyes were wild, but Leanne could also see the fog starting to lift and a good dose of anger stir. Good. Because that was so much better than her sister being too numb to feel anything.

"I'm sorry about what happened." Leanne put so much emotion into those words. She was sorry. So sorry. Sorry that she'd let everyone down. "If I'd come sooner, maybe none of this would've happened." She meant it. She meant every word. Guilt was a relentless pit bull nipping at her heels.

Bethany dropped to her knees and put her head in her hands.

Leanne scooted beside her half sister and wrapped

an arm around her. "I know how much you loved your daughter." Every word was absolutely true. Bethany had loved Clara as much as she was capable. It was part of the reason Clara had waited so long to ask her aunt for help according to her message. She didn't want to leave her mother and Hampton alone with Gary.

Gary was a bad husband, stepfather. But was he a murderer?

"Sheriff and his deputies took her laptop and her diaries," Bethany said. "What are they going to read about us?"

"Clara knew you loved her. I'm sure that comes across in all her communication," Leanne clarified.

"Will they take Hampton away?" she asked and her voice was weak again.

"For what, Bethany?" Didn't that get all of Leanne's warning flares going? "What are you keeping from me?"

Bethany didn't offer a response. She rubbed her still-red nose with a fistful of tissue she fished from her pocket. "I've already lost my little girl. I can't lose anyone else."

"Come with us to the ranch. Bring Hampton. You don't want to stay here alone until Gary is released. Not after everything that's happened." Leanne stood and opened the curtain to the front window. "Take a good look, because those people aren't going anywhere. Every time you leave the house, they're going to follow you and that could create a dangerous situation for Hampton."

Again, she was digging up everything in her arsenal to convince Bethany.

"What's Gary looking at? Honestly?" Bethany stared blankly at the wall.

"Depends on how questioning goes. I'm guessing he'll be detained for seventy-two hours. If they get anything out of him that they don't like, he's looking at a longer stay and a possible arrest." Leanne wanted to lie to her sister and make her think he would be in longer. But she couldn't. Not while looking at the fragile creature she'd become.

"That's three days."

"At a *minimum*," Leanne emphasized. There was a possibility that Sawmill might release him sooner if his alibi for the other night checked out. Being at the deer lease didn't exactly qualify unless one of his buddies could corroborate his story.

"Where's the deer lease?" she asked.

"Bonham." Bethany rubbed her raw nose again.

"That's what…about two or three hours from here." Leanne performed a mental calculation. "Maybe three and a half if traffic is bad on the highway."

Bethany just shrugged.

"How long was he there?" Leanne asked. She'd rather be asking these questions somewhere else. Anywhere else than here, because there was a possibility that Gary could walk in that door at any moment. It was slim, almost nonexistent. But possible.

Bethany's cell phone rang. She darted to it like it was lifesaving water to douse a raging fire. "I don't recognize the number."

"If it's Gary, he's calling from a line at the station. He wouldn't be allowed to use his cell phone," Leanne advised.

A mix of hope and fear flashed in Bethany's eyes as she took the call. "Hello."

It must've been Gary because her shoulders fell slack for a split second.

"Okay." She ran to the kitchen and rummaged through a couple of drawers before locating a scrap of paper and a pen. "Okay. Got it." Bethany jotted down a note. "Why do you need someone like him?" She fell silent for a few beats. "I'll call right now."

Bethany ended the call.

"Who does he want you to call?" Leanne asked, splitting her attention between her sister and the handsome cowboy keeping her nephew entertained.

"A lawyer."

Leanne knew exactly what that meant.

Gary was under arrest.

Chapter Eight

Bethany's phone rang in her hand, startling her. She fumbled it before recovering and checking the screen. "Another unknown number."

"It's not him," Leanne said, and Dalton knew she was referring to Gary. "Let it roll into voice mail. Whoever it is can leave a message."

Her sister was close to agreeing to come with them, and Dalton figured that Leanne didn't want to lose momentum. He'd watched Leanne work on her, and it really was the best thing for Hampton and Bethany to get away for a few days. Leaving town immediately following his father's murder had done wonders for his state of mind. His eldest sister, Ella, had stayed on to manage ranch business until Dalton and Dade realized she was being targeted for murder. They'd flown home immediately and stayed at the ranch ever since.

The white-knuckle grip the woman had on the cell outlined her stress along with the deep grooves carved into her forehead and the brackets around her mouth. She seemed worn out and greatly aged, even though she wasn't more than a few years older than Leanne.

"Whoever it is, they're done." She held out the phone,

showing that the voice-mail message icon had the number one written in the top left corner.

"Do you want me to check it for you?" Leanne offered.

"I'll put it on speaker." Bethany glanced toward her son. She turned the volume down so as not to draw Hampton's attention away from the airplane.

This is Carson Trigg with NewsWhenYouNeedIt! *I'd love to hear your side of the story.* He left a contact number before reminding her that she had an opportunity to speak on behalf of her daughter and help other families dealing with similar tragedies.

Dalton fisted his hands. Jerks like Carson who dug into other people's business in order to display their pain in public for ratings were some of the lowest bottom-feeders.

"It won't be long before all those people out there get your number and your phone won't stop ringing," Dalton warned.

As if on cue, her cell buzzed again. She looked at it with a mix of fear and shock. "Unknown number."

"That's probably another one of those creeps who prey on other people's tragedies," he said with disdain.

"How do you know?" she asked.

"My father was Maverick Mike Butler."

"Oh." The word was so faint that he almost missed it.

And then the impact of his admission must've hit her full force because recognition dawned. Whether it was positive or negative remained to be seen, but he capitalized on the moment anyway.

"Hereford has the best security. You and Hampton would be safe on the ranch. Reporters wouldn't be able to get to you and there's plenty of help available so you can rest when you need to."

Leanne chimed in. "Hampton's a great boy but kids his age can be a handful. And you need time to catch your breath, process everything going on."

Bethany seemed to be considering it as her phone vibrated in her hand again.

"It might not hurt to have a little help. For Hampton's sake," Bethany said, and she seemed to be making up her mind. She shot a look at her sister. "I lost my temper with him for no reason a little while ago. He spilled juice on the kitchen floor and I snapped at him. Then I felt so bad we both sat on the floor and cried."

"You're under too much stress," Leanne said, and there was no denying the genuineness in her tone. She cared for her sister even if from an outsider's view their relationship was complicated. Hell, complicated relationships were a little too familiar to Dalton. He had no use to add to the list. But he would offer a hand-up to any decent person in need.

"How long do you think they'll keep him?" She was referring to Gary.

"I can't be certain until I speak to the sheriff. It's a long shot that I'll get much information given my connection to the case, but I might be able to get a few details out of him," Leanne admitted.

"The ranch is probably a good idea." Bethany exhaled and she looked exhausted.

"You need help packing a few things?" Leanne asked.

Her half sister shook her head as she pushed up to standing.

"Once we get her settled we can figure out our next

move," Leanne said to Dalton. For reasons he didn't want to overanalyze, he wanted to make sure Leanne ate and had a chance to rest, too. Her sister wasn't the only one running on empty, and they still had a lot of road to cover if they were going to find out who killed Clara.

He told himself it would be good for the case if Leanne refueled, but there was something far more primal at work. He cared.

Dalton excused himself to make a couple of phone calls. He only needed two. One to his twin brother, Dade, who put the other siblings on conference as Dalton explained the situation. The other to the family's longtime housekeeper, May, to let her know what was going on and see if she could handle a few more mouths to feed. When she heard another child was coming to the ranch, she practically squealed. As he ended the second call, he realized he'd been white-knuckling his cell.

Frustration nipped at him.

The truth about what had happened to Alexandria felt like it was slipping away again with each passing minute. Answers that had felt so close hours ago were just out of reach.

What were they missing? They didn't have long to find out. He didn't have to be a detective to know the more time passed, the colder the evidence would get.

"YOU WANT TO take a walk?" Dalton asked Leanne once her sister was settled in one of the guest suites in the main house. May was already doting on Hampton and the little boy was eating up the attention. Of course, it probably didn't hurt that she was the kind of person everyone wished they had for a grandmother. Case in point, she'd thrown a batch of her made-from-scratch chocolate-chip cookies into the oven the minute she found out a little guy was coming. She knew how to make the shorter set feel at home.

By the time they'd arrived, she had had the guest room ready to go, cookies coming out of the oven and had dug out some of Dalton's and his brother's old toys from storage. The woman was a force of nature and had been a surrogate mother to the four siblings who'd grown up under the same roof. The two siblings they'd gained since summer were getting their bearings and figuring out how they fit into the family. Accepting them had been easy. They were decent people despite having Maverick Mike Butler for a father. His absence from their lives growing up had most likely helped more than hurt them.

The one thing all six kids had in common was that no one had really known their father. Ella, Dade, Cadence and Dalton might've grown up with the man, but he'd stayed outside working the land and played his cards too close to his vest when he was alive. Ella had probably been the closest to their father. Several of the other children had made their peace with the Mav. Dalton wasn't sure how he fit into that puzzle. It was hard to resent a man who was dead. And yet, Dalton couldn't help but feel like their relationship was left unfinished.

The fact that the Mav's relationships were so complicated probably made it difficult for the sheriff to find his murderer.

"What could the sheriff have on Gary?" Dalton asked once he and Leanne were out of earshot of Bethany.

"If I had to venture a guess, I'm betting his alibi didn't pan out. Which means he wasn't where he said he was," Leanne said matter-of-factly. "It seems too soon for the sheriff to have any real evidence, but that would be enough to keep Gary in a holding cell for a while and let him sweat. He doesn't have a history of violent crime, but that doesn't mean he couldn't have escalated."

"We both know he's a jerk, but is he a murderer?" Dalton had his suspicions after talking it through with Leanne earlier. What if Clara had told her stepfather that she was moving to get away from him? Leanne had made a valid point about a heat-of-the-moment killing. But what if that wasn't the case? Could Gary be smarter than they'd given him credit for?

"That's the question," Leanne said, interrupting his heavy thoughts. "My professional instinct doesn't think so. I don't trust him, though."

"That last part's a safe bet." A selfish part of Dalton didn't want Gary to be the guilty party. There was no way the man had a connection to Alexandria fourteen years ago. He wasn't from the area and, as far as Dalton knew, never had been. Gary's age didn't match the age of the suspect to Dalton's thinking. Although, he couldn't rule out that a young person could be responsible for Alexandria's death, but it seemed more likely that it would be someone older. And that someone would be in his late thirties by now, early forties at most.

"If I had to guess I'd say Gary is seeing someone on the side and didn't want to give her name up," Leanne said. "My sister will be devastated, but I'm going to look into some programs for her. Get some referrals. From what Clara told me he isn't faithful. If Bethany can see it, she'll do what she should've done before— walk out on him."

"There should be a special place for men like Gary."

Dalton flexed and released his fingers again. He wouldn't mind five minutes alone with the guy so he could see what it was like to fight his equal. But then, fighting Dalton wouldn't be a level playing field for the jerk. At six feet four inches, Dalton had a solid five inches on the guy and Gary's marshmallow for a spare-tire stomach had nothing on Dalton's athletic build. He came by it honestly, working the ranch.

With the physical labor he performed every day, there was no need for a gym membership and he'd been doing morning push-ups since he was old enough to have a patch of hair on his chest. The push-ups were as much of a habit as brushing his teeth. He could ac-knowledge that some of his rituals had come from need-ing to blow off steam. There was no better release than a quick morning workout followed by a long day on the land working the ranch.

Although, glancing at the curve of Leanne's hips, another thought came to mind as a way to work off stress. The thought was inappropriate. He chalked it up to too many nights without female companionship. Since everything he did made news, he'd been shy-ing away from spending time with anyone out in pub-lic. Plus, he needed a little more than hot sex if he was going to spend time with someone. One-night stands hadn't interested him since he became old enough to buy a lottery ticket.

A relationship in the midst of all the chaos he'd been through was about as likely as a dust storm in Dallas. It could happen, but it would make news.

Don't get him wrong, he wasn't ready to trade his sport utility for a minivan and had never seen himself as the kind of man who would ever be behind that wheel.

But the maturity that came with being old enough to grow hair on his chest also kept him from slipping under the covers with a woman without knowing more than her first name. All hot quickie sex did was ease a few tension knots. Real release accompanied interesting sex, and he had to be beyond courtesies with someone from the opposite sex for that to happen.

Leanne was studying him when he snapped out of his unproductive revelry. There was something about being back on his family's land, his home, that made him take stock in his life.

"What were you thinking about just then?" Leanne asked.

He wasn't ready to come clean and he'd never been much of a liar. "Things I shouldn't."

She looked him in the eyes and her honey-brown irises intensified as it seemed to dawn on her that his thoughts might've included her.

There was also something else he didn't want to see in those eyes—a familiar spark of excitement.

And then it dimmed like she'd turned a switch.

They stood there, neither of them moving as though at a stalemate.

It took a minute for her to speak but when she did, she'd recovered a cooler stare. "Maybe we should agree to keep a professional distance. It's best for the case if we don't get too...*personal* with each other."

"Done." It was true. Anything more than a working relationship was tempting fire based on his body's reaction to her so far.

She stood there, staring at him. Hesitation was written all over her features. And he almost made a stupid mistake when she dropped her gaze to his lips. She slicked her tongue across hers, and it took all his will-power not to reach for her and find out for himself just what she tasted like at this moment.

Drawing on all his considerable self-control, he turned away from her and looked out onto the land that had brought him so much peace. No matter what his relationship with the Mav had been, Dalton always felt settled on the land. *Until now.*

He chalked it up to old feelings being dredged up about Alexandria's case.

"What if I missed something?" Leanne asked, taking a step beside him. He could feel her feminine presence standing next to him and he could admit that it was nice. Maybe more than nice.

"Would Clara have come clean with you if you'd grilled her about her intentions?" he asked, needing a distraction.

"My experience interviewing people of all ages and from all walks of life has taught me that economic status, grades, none of that matters. When it came to teenagers, they were remarkably similar. All of them had secrets," she admitted.

"Makes sense," he said when he thought about it. "It's part of separating from parents, evolution. Plus, most of the people you interviewed had committed, were suspected off or had ties to criminal activity."

"When you put it like that, it's true. Most of the people I deal with have secrets."

"Which is a good point. What if Clara and Alexandria uncovered someone else's secret?" A picture was starting to emerge. One he didn't like but couldn't rule out. By the way Leanne's gaze narrowed, she couldn't, either. She compressed her lips, and that usually meant she was onto something. Now that he'd spent time with her, he was starting to pick up on her habits. Habits he probably shouldn't have allowed himself to notice.

"A secret worth killing for," she said. "Leads me to believe there would be a trail. You know. I mean we have no real information from the past. It doesn't sound like the sheriff did much investigating with your friend's case and obviously, the trail froze up years ago. It'll be harder to make a correlation between the two."

"Maybe not. Doesn't it depend on what they had in common? I mean, when we find out what it is."

"How are we going to do that?" There was frustration mixed with exacerbation in her tone.

"Sawmill thought he had the right person. I was supposed to be the last person to have seen Alexandria alive. I was going through a rough patch personally and she'd threatened to break up with me if I didn't stop partying. Then, when I found out what happened I was in too much shock to say what I needed to. That I was innocent. I felt like it was my fault because of the problems we'd had," he admitted.

"And you still do," she said so quietly he almost didn't hear her over the wind. She shivered and rubbed her arms as though to warm them.

"What makes you say that?" he asked. She couldn't possibly know him well enough to read him, and he was certain he'd done a damn good job of stuffing his emotions down so deep that even he didn't think about them anymore.

"Because this situation with my niece is going to haunt me for the rest of my life if I don't find out who killed her and bring him to justice. And even if I do, who knows if this weight will lift," she said in that same small voice.

"This is the first hope I've had in fourteen years that there could be a breakthrough in Alexandria's case. I haven't given life much thought past finding her killer." Was she telling him there was no escaping the demons? There had to be a way to put them to rest, because all his hopes were riding on finding out who killed Alexandria. If that didn't bring him peace, there was no hope. "Is it time to bring in a professional?"

"A professional investigator?" she asked.

"Why not?"

"I've thought about bringing in someone who could be more objective than me. We'll alienate the sheriff even more. Believe it or not, he's our best chance right now at getting at the truth. He has resources even a pro wouldn't have. Then there's my job. I have to consider the consequences if I get caught interfering with a murder investigation. I'll do whatever we can to find out on our own without stepping on the sheriff's toes. We don't want to end up hurting things when we're trying to help," she said after a thoughtful pause.

"We're facing the same problem with your case as I did with mine. The sheriff already ruled this a suicide in his mind. Even though he said he'd look into as a murder investigation his heart isn't in it," he said.

"On the surface, it's an easy assumption." Leanne compressed her lips. "But Sawmill arrested Gary and got a search warrant for my sister's house. He has something and he has a solid reputation. I asked around."

Dalton issued a disgusted grunt.

"He's learned from the mistakes he made early in his career," she admitted.

"I hope so. For all of our sakes."

Leanne opened her mouth to speak but his cell's ring-tone rang out and she clamped her mouth shut instead.

"What's going on, Dade?" he asked his twin brother.

"I'm guessing you haven't seen the news coverage," Dade said and the ominous quality to his voice sent up a warning shot.

"What is it?" Dalton asked.

"Check your phone and then call me back. Let me know what help you need," Dade said before exchanging goodbyes.

Dalton pulled up the internet on his smartphone and thumbed through headlines reporting local news. Dread wrapped around him as he read.

"Dammit."

Chapter Nine

"The reporter?" Leanne asked, grabbing his wrist to reposition the phone so she could get a better view.

The picture was damning because the reporter was able to get enough of Leanne's face in it to identify her. The pair were caught in an embrace while standing underneath the tree where her niece had been murdered less than twelve hours prior to the picture being taken. Okay, this looked bad. From this photo, no one would buy the fact that this had been staged. The headline read, *Dallas Detective Brings Death to Cattle Barge*.

"First of all, I didn't *bring* anything and especially not *that*." She pointed at the word *Death* with a shaky finger.

Leanne would have a lot of explaining to do. First, to her sister who could interpret the entire situation wrong while under duress. Complicating their relationship further wasn't exactly on Leanne's agenda, and her heart rate climbed thinking about the fallout. Dealing with the sheriff was going to be a whole other issue that raised her blood pressure up a few notches. There was no telling how he would look at this, and he could misconstrue her and Dalton's relationship and, worse yet, cut her completely out of the process.

And then there was her boss. She'd told him that she needed time off to be with family after losing her niece. How was this going to go over?

So, not only had this reporter violated her privacy but he'd done it in a way that could have her ending up in the unemployment line with no way to care for her daughter. Being fired from one law enforcement agency would make it impossible to get a job in another one due to civil service laws.

Even if that didn't happen, say that was the worst case, at the very least her credibility had just taken a huge hit. Her reputation was on the line.

Leanne felt sick.

"This jerk is going to sabotage the investigation and my career," she said, adding, "I need a minute to catch my breath." She took a few steps away from the handsome cowboy. She didn't need her superiors knowing that she was in Cattle Barge investigating in the first place, but how else could she explain herself? She'd worked long and hard to make detective before age thirty and she needed a steady career even more now that she had Mila. Being a single parent was difficult enough without being jobless to make matters worse.

Being with Dalton could hurt her own investigation, and his friend's case had gone so cold her fingers would become frostbitten if she touched the file—which, by the way, no one was going to let her do and especially not now.

She needed to perform damage control with her boss and with Sawmill. Where would she even start?

"I know what you're thinking." The low rumble of a voice came up from behind her, sending all kinds of inappropriate sensations skittering across her skin. He was close enough that she could hear him breathing and for a split second she wanted to lean back against his chest and absorb some of his raw masculine strength.

Instead, she turned around. Her body moved slower than she expected, as though turning too fast would overload her senses and she somehow sensed it on instinct. Breathing too much, too fast would only usher in more of his scent—raw, masculine. And all Dalton.

Leanne bit back a yawn, fighting against the tide of sleep that wanted to suck her out to sea and spin her around again and again until she gave in.

"You're not going to want to hear this but nothing else can be done tonight. You need a warm meal and a decent bed. We have both of those here at the ranch and I think it'd be best if you stayed over rather than risk reporters stalking you at a roadside motel." He was right. She needed all those things plus a shower and a toothbrush.

But how would she get her mind to stop spinning long enough for any of those normal things again? She'd let Clara down in the worst possible way. Doing something as menial and ordinary as eating seemed...selfish.

He was also right about sticking around the ranch. She wanted to make sure her sister was going to be all right and that someone was available to help with Hampton.

"Does that offer include a hot shower?" she asked, hoping she could clear the dense fog smothering her brain.

"It does." His blue eyes twinkled in the moonlight.

"Thank you for helping my sister. Part of me acknowledges that you aren't doing it for my benefit. You want answers and helping us figure out who killed Clara is a means to that end. We find Clara's killer and you might just be able to put your friend's case to rest. But something else makes me think your cowboy code would have you offering to help anyway. I appreciate everything you're doing for us and for my niece," she said. And she meant every word. No matter how confusing or upside down her life became, she was grateful to the handsome cowboy for everything he'd done and was doing. She knew that would also stop her from cutting him out of the investigation. He deserved to know the truth about Alexandria. It was the only way he'd be able to put his ghosts to rest and begin to think about letting go of the guilt that had obviously eaten at him for almost a decade and a half.

He nodded by way of acknowledgment. Something also told her he wouldn't let himself accept anyone's appreciation until he found the killer.

"Let's get a few hours of sleep and we can start fresh. We'll put our heads together and figure out a plan for damage control with the media. I'd like to include the family lawyer in that discussion. He's the best and knows how to spin a story in a better direction," he said. "Think Sawmill's finished with Gary yet?"

"Probably not. If he thinks my brother-in-law's involved in some way he'll keep him in the interview room all night if he has to," she clarified.

"Then you might wake up to find this nightmare is all over," he said, extending a hand to lead her toward the main house. "And you'll be able to pick up your life where you left off."

Was that something she even wanted anymore? Her life seemed somehow empty now. But that was silly, at best, to think being with Dalton for such a short time could alter her perspective.

Even at night she could tell the land was beautiful, and she could only imagine how much more enchanting it would be in spring when the bluebonnets were in bloom. But even in this setting she didn't believe in fairy-tale endings. Her niece was gone and her life would never be the same again.

Leanne had noticed the grandeur of the Butler home when she was getting her sister settled earlier. The house was a sight unto itself. It looked like something out of a resort brochure with its rustic charm and wood-beamed arched ceilings in the main room.

"I'll heat something in the kitchen," he said, hooking a left.

"Mind if I take a shower first?" she asked.

He gave her a once-over, which made her feel a little self-conscious before he said, "Hold that thought."

A few moments later, he returned with a woman trailing behind.

"Hi. I'm Ella. Dalton's—"

"Sister." Leanne nodded, smiled and shook the extended hand. Ella had a firm shake and an honest face.

She also had a bundle under her left arm, which she pulled out and held between them. "I wasn't sure about your size but I think we're close. These will be better than sleeping in your work clothes." Ella was a similar height and build to Leanne and that's where the similarities stopped. Ella had cornflower-blue eyes and bright red hair. Her complexion gave the impression she had some Irish in her.

Leanne had read about the elder Butler's involvement in charity work, and the woman was striking and seemed to be the genuine article, too. She took the offering. "Thank you."

"I don't want to keep you. I've been somewhat in your shoes and I know what it's like to finally get a hot shower," Ella said. "I'll just help Dalton in the kitchen. Make yourself at home."

"I can handle the kitchen," Dalton defended.

Ella rolled her eyes and laughed. "I was just trying to be helpful. Don't go all caveman on me."

Leanne laughed and it felt good. She'd become so used to seeing the dark side of life, it was refreshing to see something so basic as siblings teasing each other good-naturedly. Her relationship with her own sister was complicated. She held up the bundle, wishing her relationships were as easy as what she was seeing between the Butlers.

"And if you're so capable of domestic duties, why haven't you brought the tree home yet?" Ella teased.

Dalton shrugged, but Leanne saw something dark cross his features. Regret?

"Thanks, again," she said to Ella.

"Your room's this way," Dalton said with a half smile back at his sister. "I thought you'd want to be close to Bethany and Hampton."

"Your nephew is adorable." Ella's eyes looked like they'd been sprinkled with fairy dust. Leanne recognized that look. It seemed the older Butler sister wanted a baby.

"He's a handful but he's sweet." Leanne was embarrassed to admit how long it had been since she'd seen him. She'd been relying on Clara for updates. Bethany had made excuse after excuse as to why she couldn't come visit Leanne and the baby.

Leanne wondered how much the excuses had to do with Gary forcing his wife to stay home. Was he sealing her off from family in order to isolate her?

In order to hide what was going on at home?

THE SHADES WERE closed in the comfortably furnished guest room, blocking out the sun. Leanne stretched. Coffee. She needed caffeine.

It was 6:20 a.m.

There were no sounds coming from the room next door. Was it possible she'd woken before Hampton? Leanne never slept more than five consecutive hours since the baby came. Mila would sleep longer, but Leanne would wake to check on her daughter and make sure she was okay. Having a little girl had changed her in many wonderful ways. It had softened her and made her more sympathetic. It had also put her on guard 24/7.

And, it had also hardened her toward Bethany for her relationship with Clara. Babies were so small and vulnerable that Leanne couldn't imagine not moving mountains to protect them as they grew and especially after waking every few hours just to make sure her own daughter was comfortable and still breathing.

It was too early to call Mrs. B and check on Mila. She considered firing off a text to let her babysitter know that everything was fine and to respond when she had a few minutes to talk.

Leanne would wait until after she had a cup of coffee in her before trying to communicate with anyone. Her autocorrect had sent a few interesting messages before she was fully awake. Glancing at the clock again told her that Mila would be awake in another hour at the latest, but she'd need to be changed and fed right away.

Leanne sat at on the edge of the bed for a long moment, gathering her thoughts. Life moved fast, especially in her line of work. It was important to take a few minutes every day to slow down and breathe. A solution to a problem often came when she took the time to quiet her mind. She squeezed her eyes shut, wishing something would pop into her thoughts about Clara.

It had been thirty-six hours since her niece's body had been found. With every second that ticked by, the killer took another step away from the light.

Forcing a breakthrough wasn't working, so she pushed off the bed and headed into the adjacent bathroom. Her and Bethany's rooms were connected via a Jack-and-Jill bathroom so she tiptoed around, not wanting to disturb her sister. Leanne brushed her teeth, washed her face and then wandered down the hall toward the kitchen. The ranch-style layout had been easy enough to memorize. A fact she appreciated this morning with the fog engulfing her brain.

As she neared the great room, she heard voices. One of them belonged to Hampton.

"Good morning," she said to May.

"You're up early," May said, scooting her chair back from the table where she was playing cars with Hampton. "Did you get any sleep?"

"A surprising amount, actually. Thank you for having us," Leanne responded.

"You're no trouble at all. It's nice to have babies in the house again," she said, rising and moving toward the coffee machine. "I asked Dalton and he said you drink coffee."

"Yes, but please let me get it myself. You're already doing too much for us." Embarrassment heated

Leanne's cheeks. She wasn't used to letting others do things for her.

"It's nothing." May waved her off.

"Really, I insist. It's the least I can do after you've shown so much hospitality." Leanne was by the woman's side, urging her to reclaim her seat at the table.

"Aunt Lee-Lee, look," Hampton said with a big smile. He pointed to a yellow car on the blue track. Even he was in a better mood today, and she wondered how much his mother's moods were affecting him. Kids were so good at picking up on emotions. And then there was this magnificent ranch. It would be hard to be in a bad mood waking up to this every morning.

"That's awesome, buddy," Leanne said, walking over to get a better look. He'd started calling her Lee-Lee when he was too young to say her whole name and it had stuck because Clara had encouraged it, thinking it was adorable. Leanne had to admit her niece had had a point. It was pretty stinkin' cute. She tousled his blond curls, thinking how much his eyes looked like his sister's, and said, "Good job."

May reclaimed her seat and Leanne poured a cup of fresh hot coffee.

"Dalton wanted me to tell you he's on the back porch," May said.

"I can take Hampton with me," Leanne said. Although, she half feared he'd cry the minute she tried to pull him away from his toys. And May. She had a calming presence that Leanne appreciated.

"Don't worry about us, right, Hampton?" The older woman handed him a red car.

"No way." He took the toy, rewarding May with another toothy ear-to-ear smile.

Leanne let a small sigh escape. This ranch had a magic she'd never known. A family magic that she'd never experienced with a mother who worked two jobs just to keep food on the table. Leanne and her mother had been close and she loved her mother. They had been more like sisters than parent and child. Her mother had done what was necessary to make ends meet.

The outside of the ranch was decorated to the nines for Christmas and the smell of fresh-baked bread filled the kitchen. The best thing about Christmas to Leanne's mother had been the extra seasonal jobs she could pick up so they could stay ahead of the bills. Leanne had worked from her earliest memories and the two had gotten by all right, combining funds to keep the lights on.

Her mother had kept a solid roof over their heads, clothes on their backs and food on the table. She was a practical woman who'd had no patience for emotions. Abigail West lived hard and took care of business. She never trusted men after Leanne's father had walked out despite bringing home several "uncles."

Her death had left a hole in Leanne's life, in her heart.

Life was hard. Kids were simple.

When she really thought about life, adults made it complicated. In her own case, she could acknowledge that her mother had never forgiven Leanne's father for walking out on her during her pregnancy. And, in little ways, she'd most likely blamed her daughter for their struggles, for how hard she'd had to work.

Her mother never would've said anything outright, save for the occasional outburst of angry words in the heat of the moment, which she later apologized for. She'd try to make it up to Leanne by making her favorite dessert. But Leanne had always known that she was the reason her mother had had a difficult life.

"Shout if you need help with him." Leanne wrapped lean fingers around the mug to warm them as she walked to the back door leading to an enclosed porch. Dalton was there. His long legs were stretched out in front of him. He stood the minute he heard the door creak.

"Morning," he said. "Come on out."

"Sorry. I didn't want to disturb you," she said. The screened-in porch was grand in scale, like everything at the ranch. There had to be half a dozen pairs of white rocking chairs. A small table with a checkerboard on top and two chairs nestled underneath sat on one side of the room.

The sun was rising in the east, not yet visible over the tree line, but casting a warm glow in that part of the sky. Dalton motioned for her to take the seat next to his. A small table was nestled in between.

"I was thinking about what we know so far," he said.

Taking her seat, she said, "I woke up thinking about it, too."

He shot her a glance that said he understood. It was a small gesture, really, but even so, it sent warmth circulating through her.

"Going over the sheriff's initial assessment, I can't make sense of his line of thinking. Christmas break is almost here. Clara would have gotten time off from school. Why would she commit suicide now?" he asked.

"Exactly."

"She and her stepdad didn't get along." Dalton restated what they already knew.

"Not a bit." She took a sip of the steaming brew. "I

can admit that she wasn't in a good place about a lot of things. She missed her friends in San Antonio. She didn't feel like she fit in here in such a small town with nothing to do besides help her mother and work at the whim of her stepfather."

"We know she wasn't making new friends here in Cattle Barge. What about a boyfriend?" he asked.

"His name is Christian," she said. "And he lives in San Antonio."

"Have you spoken to him?"

"Not since this all started. No." She took a sip of fresh brew.

"How long have they been together?" His forehead creased and she realized why he'd be concerned about the boyfriend.

"A year, I think. At least, she told me about him last Christmas and I got the impression it was a new thing," she detailed. "He works three mornings a week plus weekends in a bagel shop in order to save money for college, going in at four o'clock in the morning before school. From everything Clara said about him, he's a good guy."

"He shouldn't find out something like this about his girlfriend on the news." His deep voice was low and his jaw clenched. There was so much pain. "If they're like every other young couple, he's already worried that she isn't answering her texts."

Having gone through something similar, Dalton would know what to say. Leanne drew a blank, which wasn't normally an issue for her but this wasn't an ordinary situation. She was too personally involved and shutting out her feelings—again, something she'd learned to do in order to survive—wasn't an option.

She felt for Christian. "We'll make the call in a few hours when he wakes up."

"I can talk to him."

"That would be nice," she offered.

"What else do you know about her home life?" he asked, refocusing toward the landscape beyond the screen.

"Gary's punishments were becoming worse. That's why she wanted to stay with me. She needed to escape and figured he would cool down if she was gone for a while," she admitted with that now-familiar guilt.

"It's not uncommon for teenagers to rebel," he offered.

"I'm not saying my niece was perfect by any means. I've heard her snap at her mom. But she wanted her mom to be happy and for Hampton to have both of his parents in the home. She tried to get along with Gary and not create any friction, and I think she felt like it was her fault they didn't click."

"Kids have a way of blaming themselves for everything." He paused for a couple of beats. "Which is another reason it's important for us to speak to Christian. He'll walk around the rest of his life with the guilt that he didn't realize what was going on and help her."

Based on what she knew about Dalton so far, he most likely fell into that same category. Would he ever be able to let go of the guilt that caused dark circles to cradle his too-serious-for-his-age blue eyes?

It struck her that while most people their ages were settled down and well into establishing their own families, she and Dalton were single and grieving. She had Mila and that was the beginning of more of a home life. Before the baby, all Leanne did was work and eat out. She didn't cook, not that that was a requirement, especially since she worked. But wasn't it a little odd that she couldn't melt butter on a stove if she had to?

Did it even matter? Would Mila notice? Or would her daughter have a similar childhood as her mother? The thought hit deep. By twelve, it wasn't uncommon for Leanne to stay in the apartment alone overnight while her mother spent time with an "uncle" when most kids her age were having sleepovers.

Last night, when she'd pulled the covers over her, she went to sleep thinking about Dalton's easy relationship with his sister and what growing up in a supportive family might feel like.

There was something intimate about sitting on the porch with Dalton, being able to read some of his thoughts.

The kiss they'd shared, their embrace, trickled into her thoughts, too. She'd felt something stir when she'd been in his arms, and it was something that had been absent in physical contact with all her past relationships combined...*chemistry*?

With Keith, sex had been more about being together so much they'd felt like a couple. They'd had a similar sense of humor and work schedule.

Speaking of which, she wondered how she'd ever put the pieces of her life back together. The past couple of days had felt like an out-of-control Ferris wheel, spinning and churning. And nothing would ever be the same without her niece.

There was no room in her life for a man, no matter how much her body wanted to feel Dalton's on top of her, blanketing her with his athletic frame.

Talk about lost causes. This man was haunted by a

ghost from his past. Even if they decided to date—and that was a ridiculous notion for more than just logistical reasons—how could she ever compete with the memory of the girl from his past?

She didn't even want to try. The two of them had been together when they were barely more than kids; life was about what to wear to prom. It was all promise and young love. Pure. Nothing was complicated.

Dalton had hinted at a difficult relationship with his father but Leanne couldn't imagine that it could've been too difficult, considering he grew up in a warm place like this with siblings around. She could already see that his and Ella's relationship was special.

Leanne knew nothing about siblings. She hadn't even known about her sister until she'd turned sixteen and her mother sat her down and told her. It had taken another half a dozen years to decide to track Bethany down.

Leanne's cell buzzed, breaking through her revelry.

She fished it out of her pocket, looked at the screen and gasped.

"It's Gary."

Chapter Ten

"Hello?" A beat passed and Leanne's body tensed. Her face muscles pulled taut, tension written in the lines of her forehead. "I'm not telling you where she is, Gary."

He'd made his one mandatory phone call last night. Unless Dalton was missing something, the man must've been released.

"She doesn't have her phone right now." Leanne's voice was a study in simmering anger.

Dalton sipped his coffee, listening to one side of the conversation.

"No, I won't go get her. I didn't say we were in the same place," she said tersely. And then seemed to realize she might be making things worse for her sister when she added, "She just lost her daughter. She needs a little time. Surely, you can underst—"

He must've cut her off and said something to offend her because her shoulders flew back and her posture became rigid.

"I'm sorry if you can't understand what's happening. All I can tell you is that she's safe and—"

Leanne blew out a frustrated-sounding breath. "No, the best place for her isn't home." She paused. "The reporters are one thing—" Another beat passed. "Maybe if you'd listen instead of flying off—"

She set her phone down in her lap. Dalton could hear the yelling even though the words were difficult to make out.

After taking a sip of her coffee, she picked up the phone. "You do realize that you just threatened a law enforcement officer. That's a felony offense in case you were unclear, and I won't care who you're married to when I file a complaint against you."

Now the line was quiet.

"Not exactly your brightest move, considering you're still under suspicion for my niece's murder. And I will testify against you to get the truth, Gary. Harass my sister and I'll haul you in myself," she bit out. "If you ever hurt her again, you won't make it that far."

Gary seemed to be taking in that last comment based on the silence that followed. That was the funny thing about bullies. They usually knew when they'd met their match and it didn't take long to buckle. Dalton felt nothing but pride for Leanne standing up for her sister, for herself. His chest swelled with it.

Leanne ended the call and looked at Dalton with defeat. "She might not be answering now because she's asleep, but the minute she realizes he's out, she'll go home."

"Maybe not."

"Past behavior is always the best predictor. She always jumps as soon as he snaps his fingers. That's what Clara told me," she said.

"I wish they'd held him longer, given us more time." He couldn't argue her point, so he didn't. But he hoped recent events had caused Bethany to rethink her home situation. And maybe make a better choice moving forward.

"Seventy-two hours was the maximum. I'm not surprised he's out. We should speak to the sheriff and do some damage control," she said and he agreed.

She pulled up his direct line on her smartphone, tapped the name and then put the call on speaker.

"I have Dalton Butler here and he's on the call with us," she informed the sheriff after the perfunctory greetings.

"Dalton," the sheriff said by way of acknowledgment. It was short and his voice was tight, signaling he wasn't thrilled with the photo of the two of them from the parking lot the other morning.

"Morning, Sheriff."

"Sir, you released Gary Schmidt this morning," she began.

"My office has a strict policy of not commenting publicly on an ongoing investigation," Sawmill said in that matter-of-fact voice Dalton had heard used before with the media.

"I understand your position but I'm not a run-of-the-mill citizen or media outlet," she defended.

"That may be. However, I'd advise you to call your supervisor if you want more details. I agreed to release information to him in my report as a professional courtesy, which I'll have to him later this morning." Dalton had also heard that tone before. This issue was done. Over. Applying more pressure wouldn't help.

"Will you at least tell me how you're classifying this case?" Tension lines creased her forehead as she brought her hand up to cup it.

"I'm not at liberty to discuss the details with you."

She seemed to realize at the same time he did that Bethany was most likely the only one who could get more information. Even that was questionable, considering her husband had been interviewed as a possible suspect.

Talking to Sawmill was as productive as trying to climb a wall wearing mittens.

"Can you tell me if my niece was violated?"

He stalled for a long moment and Dalton figured he was debating with himself about telling her. On the one hand, Leanne had a right to know if her niece had been assaulted.

The sheriff finally said, "She was not."

"Thank you for your time, sir," Leanne said before ending the call and turning to Dalton. He could see the relief moving behind her honey-brown eyes.

"That boyfriend of Clara's. Any chance he's up and working a shift at the bagel shop today?"

"It's possible." She glanced at the clock on her phone.

"San Antonio isn't that far of a drive." He leaned forward, resting his elbows on his knees. "I'd like to be there in person. See his reaction to the news about Clara."

"You don't think he's involved, do you?"

"No."

"I'll get dressed." She stood and then hesitated before entering the house. "I leave Bethany here and she'll be out the door the second her eyes open."

"That's highly possible." He rose to his feet. "But we have other problems to deal with right now."

LEANNE FEARED THE minute she walked out the front door her sister would wake up, see the messages from Gary and run right back to him. That line of thinking almost had her canceling the visit to see Christian.

There were no guarantees that Bethany would stick around, even if Leanne stayed inside the house and waited for her to rouse. She could wake her sister up. But, again, that wouldn't do any good once Bethany heard one of Gary's messages. She must've turned off her phone or she would've already been gone. But then, she'd assumed that Gary was going to be in jail for a few days.

There was no telling how Bethany would react to finding out he'd been released. But Leanne was pretty sure this was the last time she would see her sister. Gary would never allow the two to communicate again after the way she'd threatened him and with Clara out of the picture, there was less of a reason to. Gary would never allow Leanne to be as close to Hampton.

With a deep sigh, she brushed her hair and pulled it off her face into a ponytail before dressing in jeans that were a size too big. She belted them and put on the shirt, grateful her undergarments had been washed and folded and were waiting on the bed. Then, she put on her shoulder holster and covered it with her blazer.

Before leaving, she cracked the door to her sister's room and peeked inside. Bethany's slow, even breathing said she was still asleep. A peaceful sleep? Not with the way her covers were bunched around her, making it look like a tornado had blown over the bed and somehow missed everything else in the room.

She prayed recent events wouldn't overwhelm her sister, causing her to slide into old patterns. Hampton needed his mother. And, dammit, Leanne needed a sister. Losing her mother and being faced with having no family ties left had been the reason Leanne had tracked her half sister down in the first place.

Bethany had been teetering on the edge when Leanne located her. Leanne found a rehab facility that she could afford and threw her energy into finding parenting classes for her sister. She'd gone to a few with her just to ensure Bethany showed up. Despite growing up in difficult circumstances, Clara had been such a bright light. Her life had been filled with so much promise.

It wasn't an easy road but Clara had been thriving in San Antonio. She and her mother had been on a good path when Bethany met Gary. The unexpected pregnancy threw in a few wrinkles but Gary came off like he was happy about it. He seemed to make an attempt to have a relationship with Clara by driving her to school every morning on his way to work. Everything had seemed fine on the surface.

Until he'd lost his job and started drinking.

Clara had protected the situation when Leanne first noticed the changes and asked about them. Her niece had defended his actions, saying she thought it was better if she caught a ride to school with a friend instead of getting a ride with him, so he would have more time to look for a job. She'd had a solid group of friends in San Antonio where she'd grown up. It was one of the reasons Clara had wanted to stay home—and, in hindsight, why Clara had covered her stepfather's actions—when Leanne asked about their home life.

Leanne could be honest enough to admit that Clara was known to keep a secret if she thought sharing would hurt the other person or upset the applecart too much. *I should've listened. I should've taken you more seriously, Clara.*

Kicking herself again wouldn't do any good. She knew that on some level. And yet, she'd never forgive herself. What if she'd gone to pick up her niece a week earlier? If Dalton was right, the date was important.

Bethany took in a deep breath, popped her head up off the pillow and then resettled almost immediately. Leanne froze.

When she was certain her half sister was asleep again, she slowly shut the door and tiptoed down the hallway until she was far enough away to exhale.

Would San Antonio give her the answers she craved? Or, like everything else, would it cost more valuable time?

"I KEEP RUNNING around in circles in my mind trying to figure out if he's involved," Leanne said, after spending a half hour in companionable silence.

"I've been thinking that we should let the sheriff take care of the obvious," Dalton said, adding, "Maybe we should focus on the ways the girls might've been linked."

"That's a good strategy. I'm getting nowhere without being able to access the evidence and the sheriff isn't going to cooperate, so it's all speculation on my part." He was right. She needed to move on to what she could control instead of stressing about what she couldn't. The sheriff would be covering traditional bases. She had to assume he'd found something or he wouldn't have been able to detain Gary. Releasing him this quickly could mean his alibi had held up, at least for now. Concentrating their efforts on the road less traveled was a good strategy. It could also keep them from bumping heads with Sawmill. They'd already brainstormed a few possible connections, so she took out a notepad and scribbled them down.

"We could start at Cattle Barge High School. See if they had any of the same teachers," he offered. "Think your sister would give you her schedule?"

"It would be easier than trying to go behind her back and get it from the school," she said. "We might even get her full cooperation if we tell her that we're trying to find someone besides Gary to name as a suspect."

"Worth a shot," he agreed, pulling off the highway. "There's another angle we owe it to ourselves to consider."

"And that is?"

"It's possible that someone could be using this situation to get at me." His words were heavy, and she could tell he'd been carrying around the guilt associated with the possibility. "I've read everything I could get my hands on that's been reported about Alexandria. The sheriff is right. Reporters drudged up details of the past after my father was killed. I'd been avoiding the reports but stayed up last night reading everything I could find."

That explained the dark circles cradling his eyes today and the reason he'd rubbed them several times on the ride over.

"If we're going to consider this," she began carefully. It was obvious the possibility was agonizing for him, even though he'd never admit how deeply it seemed to cut. "We could also say that someone could be trying to rattle you. To get at you or throw you off balance. With your father's recent murder, someone could be trying to get revenge on the family."

Was Clara an innocent victim in a plot aimed to make the Butler family suffer?

"My father lived an exaggerated life. He did things none of us are proud of. I'm sure he had a long list of enemies," he admitted.

"But why would someone specifically target you?" she asked. "With all due respect, he's already gone."

A revenge-against-his-father plot didn't work for that exact reason. Why target someone's child when the person was gone and therefore wouldn't be around to see it?

"True. I still think we need to put it on the table for consideration." She could tell that he was committed to finding the truth, even if it cost him something precious—the answer to what really happened to Alexandria. Because if this was some sort of revenge killing, that meant Alexandria's murderer might never be brought to justice. And he'd been waiting fourteen years so far to figure it out.

"Okay, then we have to consider motive. It's murder investigation 101. Who stands to gain from tipping you off balance? Why wouldn't they just go after you?" she asked.

"Maybe they want me to be distracted so they can go after something on the ranch," he threw out there.

It didn't stick.

"You have how many siblings and staff working there every day, day in and day out?" she asked.

He started rattling off names. She waited a few seconds before politely interrupting him.

"That's a whole lot of people. If you're distracted, the ranch still runs just fine. Am I right?"

He nodded.

"So we can probably rule that out as a motive." She

thought for a long moment about non-Gary possibilities. "Have you kept in touch with Alexandria's family?"

"I'm pretty much the last person they want to see," he admitted tersely.

"Did she have any siblings?" she prodded. Based on the increased tension in his posture he was still uncomfortable discussing details of her life.

"She was the youngest of three kids. Her brothers were a few years older than us and a year apart from each other." He followed GPS onto a side road as buildings came closer together. Traffic had noticeably thickened as he made a right onto a road that promised to take them into the suburbs.

"Did her parents ever divorce?" she asked.

"Took another six months, but they did. Mrs. Miller stayed in Cattle Barge but her husband moved years ago. I think to Houston."

"I could reach out to them. See what they're up to now." She wasn't sure if it would net anything, but it wouldn't hurt to make a couple of calls.

The voice on his GPS interrupted her, telling him they'd arrived at their destination. There was a strip shopping center on the left, so he pulled into it.

Leanne scanned the storefronts for the eatery. "There."

"Got it," Dalton said, cutting the wheel right. He seemed to zero in on the place because he was parked a few seconds later. He took a deep breath before exiting the vehicle to meet her in front of his sport utility. "Will he recognize you?"

"I'm sure Clara sent a picture of us. You know how kids are with their cell phones these days," she said.

"Good. We won't have to waste time explaining who you are or gaining his trust," he said.

"I'll handle his supervisor," she said as they walked toward the door. She dreaded this part. Having to tell someone a person they cared about was gone. It hit twice as hard since it was Clara.

First, she'd have to speak to his supervisor. Leanne reached inside her purse and dug around for her badge. The conversation would flow better if Christian's boss saw her credentials first.

A short woman in her early forties with dark hair greeted them from behind the cash register. "How can I help you?"

"I'm Detective West," Leanne flashed the badge in her palm, "and this is my associate, Dalton Butler." Leanne worried his last name would garner a reaction but the woman seemed to fixate on the badge instead. It was a common reaction when a detective showed up out of the blue in someone's life. Their next move was to check for a gun. Hers was tucked in her shoulder holster underneath her navy blazer that she'd thrown on over the borrowed shirt from Ella.

Her gaze searched for the weapon. Found it.

"I'm looking for the manager," Leanne said.

"She's right here." The woman gestured toward herself by sweeping her hand in front of her body. She had the build of a seasoned baker, full and round. Everything was short about the woman, her haircut, her height and her fingers. Dark circles cradled her eyes.

Leanne glanced around. "Can I speak to you for a moment privately?"

"Am I in some kind of trouble?" The woman's light brown eyes widened.

"No. Nothing like that. I have a sensitive matter to discuss with one of your employees," she reassured.

"Christian?"

"How'd you know?" Leanne asked.

"He's the only one here right now," the woman said as he emerged from the kitchen, holding a fresh tray of bagels for the counter display case.

He glanced from Leanne to his boss and then to Dalton, seeming to take the whole scene in. "What's going on?"

At seventeen, he was tall for his age, a little more than six feet, and hadn't filled out in the chest yet. He was a good-looking, hardworking kid and Leanne hated the news she was about to deliver.

"Let's talk a walk," Leanne said, motioning toward the door.

Christian's gaze followed her hand and then snapped to his boss for approval. He had a suspicious, lost look in his brown eyes.

"Go on," the woman urged. She seemed to catch on that he was about to get terrible news or maybe she was trying to score some brownie points with a detective when she added, "Take all the time you need. I'll leave you clocked in."

Either way, Leanne appreciated the goodwill.

The three of them walked out front as a blast of wind knocked the door out of Dalton's hand. He righted it and then secured it closed.

"You're Clara's aunt." It was a statement. "What are you doing here?"

"We came to talk to you about Clara," Dalton said. His low rumble of a voice held so much compassion. He put his hand on the guy's shoulder, and the move seemed to calm Christian's nerves. His breathing was shallow and his complexion was already starting to pale. He knew this was going to be bad. But she could tell that he had no idea just how bad it was about to be.

"I've been trying to get a hold of Clara like crazy after a sheriff called and asked where I was the other night. She hasn't been returning my calls or texts," he said, his voice rising at the end like he knew something was wrong. "I figured her stepdad—" he glanced at Leanne and then Dalton "—she called him Gare-the-grumpy-bear. Well, anyway, I thought maybe he took away her phone once he found out."

Found out about what?

Chapter Eleven

"Where is she? What happened? She's okay, right?" Christian started firing off words, sounding more desperate with each question. His gaze darted from Leanne to Dalton.

Leanne would circle back around to his comment once Dalton filled the kid in.

Dalton looked the young man directly in the eyes. "She got involved with someone who took her life."

Dalton paused as Christian sucked in a burst of air. Tears welled as his gaze bounced from Dalton to Leanne and back in sheer disbelief.

His legs seemed to give but Dalton held him upright with a strong hand on his arm. "This is my fault. I should've told—"

"I'm going to stop you right there, son. There was nothing you could've done to save her," he reassured, walking him over to one of the chairs on the small patio area.

Christian sat down, his expression stunned. "Are you sure it was her?"

A quick nod confirmed the worst.

"This can't be happening." His face paled as shock kicked in. "I just saw her last week."

"Did she talk about meeting someone new or making a new friend?" Leanne asked, taking the seat opposite Christian.

"No. She couldn't stand anyone where she moved." He looked up with wet brown eyes. "That's why she wanted to kick it at your place for a while."

"Had she and Gary been in a fight?" she asked, needing to know if she could rule him out.

"Which time?" He sucked in another burst of air. "You don't think it was him, do you? He started getting rough with her mother after the move."

Based on his shocked expression, Christian was having a difficult time processing this news, as expected. It was clear that he cared a great deal for Clara.

"Hitting her?" Leanne braced for the answer.

"Grabbing her by the arms and leaving bruises." Fire glinted behind his eyes. "Clara wouldn't let me confront him about it. She said it would only make things worse for her mother."

"You said something about him taking her phone away. Why would he do that?" she asked.

"Yeah, I thought maybe he found out what she was doing and took it away as some kind of punishment," he admitted, and he seemed to think everyone knew what he was talking about.

"What was she doing that would upset him?" Leanne asked.

Christian looked from Leanne to Dalton like one of them had to know what he was about to say. "You didn't know?"

"I'm afraid not," Leanne said. Clara had another secret.

"She was searching for her father," he said, putting

one hand on the table and grabbing his forehead with the other.

"Did she have any success?" This was the first Leanne had heard about her niece's search, and she wondered if her sister had uncovered it or was trying to cover it up. Sawmill would figure it out soon if he hadn't already based on her browsing history or cell phone records. Well, he'd deduce that she was looking for someone, even if he didn't know whom.

"Yeah." He ran his hand through his brown hair. "He lives in Dallas."

Dallas? A whole string of warning bombs detonated. Was that the real reason Clara had wanted to come live with her aunt? Why had her niece kept this from her?

There were so many secrets. First, Clara hid just how bad things had gotten between her and her stepfather. She'd downplayed the fights between her mother and stepfather. And she'd hidden the fact that she was searching for her father.

Of course, trying to relate any of this emerging picture to the hanging and especially Dalton's friend nearly made her head explode with questions. Because the story developing was that Clara had located and contacted her father in Dallas, and either the man had decided for one reason or another to meet with her and get rid of her, or Gary had resented it and gotten rid of her. Tying the murder to a past crime in Cattle Barge could've been to confuse law enforcement.

Bethany didn't talk much about that part of her past. She hadn't said much more than she'd been in a dark place during dark times when she'd met Clara's father. She'd explained it like a bad storm and that, rather than focusing on the devastation, she wanted to rebuild her life. Just how bad had it been? How many more secrets were there under the layers?

Leanne shivered against the cold chill gripping her spine. Bethany didn't exactly have the best taste in men, but wouldn't she have known to stay away from someone so evil he could murder his own child when she reached out to him?

More questions swirled around in Leanne's head but she had trouble grabbing and holding on to just one. Had her sister been in a relationship with a murderer? Leanne had checked into Gary's background when the two had started dating and he'd been clean. She hadn't been around to do the same thing during Bethany's relationship to Clara's father.

"Did she tell you anything about her father?" Leanne hated to dredge this sore subject up with Bethany. Her sister had never wanted to discuss Clara's father and Leanne respected her privacy. Now, she wished she'd done more digging, demanded answers.

And yet, everything she knew about investigating murder said that the closest ring of people around the victim would most likely be as far as they had to look for the killer. Sadly, a woman's number one danger came from the person she lived with day to day, her spouse. Or in Clara's case, potentially her stepfather. Her own father killing her made no sense unless he had something to lose if news of her being his child came to light.

But what would it to do him?

And why would a stranger want to hurt his own daughter? All he would've had to do was blow her off and tell her to go away. She would've listened.

Unless there was more to the story and in Leanne's line of work, there almost always was.

What else were you hiding, Clara?

"CLARA'S FATHER WAS in a band, living in a loft with some friends and doing odd jobs. That's as far as we got during her search." The look in Christian's eyes was a sucker punch to Dalton's gut. Kids were honest about pain, unlike adults, who had years of practice burying theirs. Dalton should know. Seeing the kid in such a devastated state brought back a flood of memories for him, none of which he welcomed.

"Do you know his name?" Leanne asked.

"Adam Robinson, but he goes by Havoc because of his antics on stage," he supplied and it looked to be taking him a great effort not to break down. "His last name starts with an *h*. That's all I know."

Leanne had kicked into detective mode and Dalton wanted to protect Christian while still giving her the room she needed to dig for answers. The more questions she asked, the further the two cases moved away from each other. He could see that she was honing in on those closest to her niece for suspects and he couldn't argue the logic, no matter what that beating organ in the center of his chest wanted to say. Deep down, he wanted—needed!—these cases to be locked together in order to find answers for Alexandria's family and maybe put to rest some of his own torment.

This twist took him down a road he didn't want to go but couldn't ignore now that it was out there.

"Will you excuse us?" Dalton looked to Leanne for approval, still a little unsure why it suddenly seemed so important to get her stamp. This was shaky ground for him, because Dalton rarely cared what anyone other than his family thought about his actions.

Christian followed, swiping at a loose tear.

When they rounded the corner toward the side of the strip center, Dalton said, "I know what you're going through is hell, because I've been in your shoes."

The young man's eyes widened but he maintained focus on the patch of concrete in front of them. It was easy enough to see that the guy was doing everything he could not to break down. He needed to know it was okay to go with what he felt.

"I lost someone important to me when I was your age in a similar way," he said, leaving out the main difference of him being a prime suspect at the time. "Someone will be down to speak to you. Most likely a deputy. I want you to call me if he starts asking questions that make you scratch your head in any way."

Christian glanced up with a look of confusion.

"Trust me when I say these investigations can turn in all kinds of unexpected directions," he offered by way of explanation. "I want you to be prepared, so take this."

He pulled a card with his personal number and pressed it to the kid's palm. "Call me if any of the questioning seems out of line, like the deputy is grilling you or not taking you seriously. Definitely call me if he takes you in for questioning. Understand?"

"Sort of. I guess," Christian admitted.

"If you have a question about any of the news coverage coming out about her death, call me. I'll filter through it for you," he added. "Until then, it's best to stay away from news sites on the internet. There'll most likely be social media posts, too. You might want to avoid that if possible."

He knew all about how to avoid the media, including social sites. Then again, he'd never been on those to begin with. He'd left the state after his father was killed in order to get away from reporters for a little while. He came back the minute he heard Ella had been targeted, and thankfully, the man responsible was serving time.

"So, they don't know who did this to her?" he asked after a long pause and several tears.

"Not that I know of," he responded. "They called it a suicide at first, but we argued against it."

Dalton didn't need to finish that sentence because the kid was already shaking his head.

"She would never do that. We were happy. Everything was solid between us and we had a future." More tears streamed as the kid spoke.

"I know. They might not believe you. Stick to your story, which is the truth," Dalton said. "And here's the hard part. Find a way not to blame yourself."

"How am I supposed to do that? I never should've told her she should find her father. She was so unhappy and she said the situation with her aunt would be temporary, so when she said she wanted to look for her father I thought it was a good idea. I was trying to help. She was miserable with Gary and he was getting worse every—" He stopped midsentence. "Was he involved in this somehow?"

"We're not sure. On the surface, it looks like he could be," Dalton admitted. "But there was a similar case fourteen years ago that makes me think not."

And then it seemed to dawn on the kid.

"This happened to *your* girlfriend and you think it's the same guy," Christian said.

"The sheriff is going to come after you to ask questions, like where you were two days ago around midnight. Whether or not you and Clara were fighting. He might even throw in details in order to throw you off track," he said.

"That's easy—I was home watching my brother while my parents went out to dinner." He said it like it was a no-brainer, but a skilled investigator could pick it apart.

"How old is your brother?"

"He's twelve, but he doesn't like to stay home at night alone." Christian's eyebrow arched. "Why?"

"They'll ask, and you need to be prepared to answer just that honestly every time in case they try to play a head game with you," he said. Dalton needed to think of the right way to ask his next question. "Was Clara in any kind of trouble?"

"No. She was a good person."

"How about emotionally? She had a rough situation at home—"

"Oh, no. I can assure you she wouldn't try to hurt herself if that's where you're going with this," he said, and his tone was so matter-of-fact that Dalton wanted to believe him. One thing was certain, the kid believed it wholeheartedly.

"It was set up to look that way," Dalton admitted.

"She wouldn't hurt herself. We had a future. We were planning on going to college and then getting married our senior year before we start working." His words started breaking up as his emotions intensified with the memories of their plans. His face twisted in pure agony and Dalton's heart wrenched.

"I'm sorry, man. I know how much this hurts." Dalton put his hand on Christian's shoulder and was surprised when the kid barreled into him with a hug. Christian held on and seemed to let go of the pent-up emotions he'd been barely keeping at bay since hearing the news. Having a future ripped out from underneath like a rug unleashed more shock than Dalton had ever known at that age. He remembered feeling the exact same way Christian had at first. That initial shock followed by disbelief.

"She didn't deserve to have this happen," Christian said, sucking in another burst of air.

"No. She didn't. Neither did you," Dalton reassured. "I want you to use that number I gave you anytime you need to talk to me. Day or night. I'm here for you, buddy. I mean it. Any time."

"I will," Christian promised, and there was honesty in his brown eyes. He wiped at his cheeks, swiping away tears while his head was down before asking, "We should probably go back to Clara's aunt."

"Not until I know you're all right," Dalton said.

Christian rocked his head, but there wasn't much conviction in his eyes. Dalton had just turned the kid's world on its axis and tossed it around as if in a hot dryer with no off button. Nothing would be the same after this day. Christian would look at the world differently from now on.

Dalton sure as hell did.

"How about you and your parents?" he asked.

"We're good. I mean, they care. They're not perfect, but they try," he admitted.

That was good to hear. Because he was going to need them and a whole lot more to get through the next couple of days, weeks. And especially when that angry beast called guilt that Dalton had contained for nearly a decade and a half started eating away at its chains.

Dalton led Christian around the corner and back to Leanne.

The sound of her ringtone broke the conversation. She quickly glanced at the screen and Dalton knew she was hoping for a call from the sheriff. He also doubted she'd get one.

"It's my babysitter," she announced along with an apology for needing to take the call.

"What happened?" Everything about her voice said she'd shifted into panic mode. Her back stiffened and she leaned into the earpiece, listening with the intensity of someone receiving the code to unlock a nuclear weapon.

"Where are you right now?" She listened for a response. "I'm on my way."

Leanne locked on to Dalton's gaze.

"A man wearing a ski mask just approached my daughter and her babysitter at the park." She flashed her eyes at him. "We have to go."

Chapter Twelve

"Your daughter will be picked up and brought to the ranch. I don't want you on the road. If someone's targeting her because of this investigation, they could be watching for you." Dalton made a few calls to set everything up.

Leanne seemed to be thinking up an argument. She'd told him the basic facts. Someone had approached the babysitter at the park and then made a play for Mila. Mrs. B, as Leanne called her, had pulled out her stun gun and blasted the guy with fifty thousand volts.

While he was flat on his back, squirming in pain, she got the baby safely inside her vehicle and called the police. Having a husband who'd spent most of his life in law enforcement and stressed the importance of being prepared helped her stay calm during the incident. Before Dallas Police could arrive, the man hopped to his feet and took off in the opposite direction. He'd managed to evade capture. Mrs. B had given as much of a description of the assailant as she could, considering the attacker was wearing a ski mask and it had all happened so fast.

He was roughly six feet tall, maybe a little shorter, and large.

Mrs. B and the baby were at the north central division. She was waiting for her husband and planned to stay with Mila until the flight crew and friend of the Butler family arrived. The crew was already in transit to pick up Mila and bring her safely to the ranch.

"It's the fastest way to get the two of you in the same location and keep both of you safe along the way," he continued. "I sent the best and she'll be in good hands."

After exhaling slowly, Leanne agreed.

He could only imagine what she must be feeling but based on her expression, it was as bad as he thought it might be.

"Christian, I'm sorry to leave you like this but we have to go," she said, her angst written across her expression.

"Don't worry about me," he said. Based on the change in his demeanor, he was more concerned for the little girl who might be in danger than his own emotions. Dalton had picked up right away that Christian was a good kid. His family didn't have enough money for college. Dalton had personal plans to see to it that a scholarship was set up to take care of tuition and anything else the kid needed. He deserved a future, and what had happened with his girlfriend would alter his thinking for the rest of his life. Dalton would talk to Ed Staples, the family lawyer, about the scholarship and maybe setting Christian up with a counselor and money in a trust to take care of college-related expenses. Dalton had no idea how to make any of this right, but based on his own personal experience of going inside himself, he knew *not* talking about it with someone was a worse idea. And yet, that's exactly what he'd done. "A friend of mine is going to call you in a day or two. His name is Ed Staples and he's a lawyer."

Christian's eyes grew wide again.

"Not because I think you're going to need him to get yourself out of trouble, but because he's going to check on a few things for me and then contact you. Okay?" Dalton asked.

"Thank you," Christian said before the two embraced in a man-hug. "Talking to you about it is helping a lot."

This kid had no idea just how long the road ahead of him was going to be, but Dalton had a good feeling about Christian and he'd do whatever it took to help shorten the journey to healing.

"Anyone at home right now?" Dalton asked.

"My mom is," he responded and it was obvious from his expression that he was still in shock.

"A car will be here in a few minutes to pick you up." Dalton pushed a few buttons on his phone to order a service. "The driver will take you home to be with her."

"I have work to—"

"I'll make sure you have a job when you return," Leanne said.

"I need this in order to go to college—"

"Consider me a family friend who wants to help and can," Dalton said. "Don't worry about money."

He could see the hesitation in Christian's eyes. The kid, his family, had learned to get by using hard work and not handouts.

"This isn't charity. I'm investing in you because I believe in you. And we'll figure out a way for you to pay it back some day. Deal?" Dalton extended his hand.

Christian seemed tentative at first, but then he gripped Dalton's hand and gave it a good shake.

"I don't know how to thank you," he said, and there was so much gratitude in his eyes.

"You will," was all Dalton said before entering the kid's number into his phone. The two finished saying their goodbyes while Leanne disappeared to speak to his supervisor. With the right support, Dalton felt that Christian would be okay. And he intended to check up on the kid. "Call your mother and let her know that you're on your way home."

Helping made Dalton feel another peak of light in his soul. Something he'd stuffed away long ago surfaced and a little of his darkness released.

Leanne returned and he ushered her into the SUV. They were pulling out of the parking lot as the driver was pulling in.

"He's a good kid," Dalton said as he navigated onto the highway. It felt good to be able to help someone else. Dalton had never been comfortable with the money he'd been born into. He'd never needed much to be comfortable. But being able to help someone else who needed it felt right in a way he'd never experienced. He'd put it to Ella's influence. His older sister was always out doing good somewhere in the community. But this desire to release some of the grip on his old ghosts and be a better man came from somewhere else.

And it probably had a lot to do with the person sitting next to him. He wanted to be her comfort. "You can take my phone if it'll make you feel better. I asked for updates about your daughter's location every fifteen minutes."

"I'd like that very much," Leanne said without hesitation. She picked up the phone sitting in between them and studied the screen.

"If you pull up the map feature you'll be able to track your daughter in real time."

"Seriously?" The sense of hope and relief spoken in that one word was all the thanks he needed. "This is beyond." She looked up from the screen for a second. "Thank you. It's hard to focus on anything else for long after what happened."

"It's understandable." And probably what made her a good mother. Though, he'd keep that last part to himself.

The crew was half an hour from the ranch as Dalton pulled past the security gate at Hereford and then parked the SUV in his usual spot.

"Does anyone know where Gary is?" Dalton asked as he pulled the key from the ignition.

"No. But I'm half-surprised he isn't here throwing a fit on your front lawn," Leanne said with an eye roll.

"He'd never get past security," Dalton quipped. The past few days had been heavy—for good reason—and he wanted to put a smile on her face, even if it didn't last.

Glancing over at her, Dalton couldn't help but notice the exhaustion lines on her face.

"You think it was him?" She checked her watch. Depending on when he'd been released, he might've had time to make the drive. Although, when he really thought about it the timing was off.

"It's possible. Then there's Havoc to consider."

"We need a description of him," Leanne said. "But we don't have a last name."

"How many men named Havoc can there be in Dallas who are also in a band?" he asked.

"Of course. I'm not thinking straight or…"

"Your thoughts are right where they're supposed to be. On making sure your daughter is safe," he said.

She pulled out her phone and after a couple of minutes said, "According to Blue Potato Bar in Deep Ellum, his band is scheduled to play next month." She paused long enough to pull up a picture of the band. "These guys are skinny. It's hard to believe any one of them would have the strength to carry her. Also, according to his website he played a gig on December 7 in Oklahoma. There'd be witnesses."

"Then we just ruled someone out."

Silence stretched on for a few minutes after Leanne put her phone away.

"You did a good thing for Christian," she said. "Thank you."

Those two words cracked a little more of the casing inside his chest. Allowing a little more light to bleed through. "He's a decent kid. Sure as hell didn't deserve any of this."

"Neither did you," she said quietly.

"I wasn't as good as him," Dalton said in response.

"You couldn't be this good of a man if you weren't a decent kid. I have enough experience dealing with people from all walks of life to be certain of that," she said. "Kids make mistakes, Dalton. It's part of growing up."

He let the words sit between them.

"I didn't ask on the way over because part of me didn't want to know. But before I go in there, is my sister here?"

"She stayed," he said and hope lit in Leanne's chest like a fledgling campfire in a severe storm watch.

So many emotions bubbled to the surface that Leanne was at a loss to contain them. Rather than deal with any of those, she distracted herself by leaning over and kissing him.

The second her lips pressed to his she realized her mistake. It was most likely the primal need for proof of life that had her melting into the kiss, hungry and wanting more.

He brought his hand up to the back of her neck and cradled it as he drove his tongue inside her mouth. There was no hesitation in his skilled movements and his actions robbed her of her breath.

An explosion of need rocketed through her. Need to be with this strong man. Need to feel his arms around her. Need to…*escape*. Hold on a minute.

The last thought caused her to put on the brakes. She cursed her overactive mind as she pulled away. The best kiss she'd had in…her… What?… Entire life? And she couldn't shut down random thoughts that had run wild. The realization about the kiss was sad but accurate. It was the best she'd ever had. Not even with Mila's father had Leanne felt that kind of sizzle.

"I'm sorry," she said, turning and reaching for the door.

He stopped her with a hand on her shoulder and the shock of electricity stemming from contact reminded her why the two of them together was a bad idea. There was too much stray voltage that could damage everything around them.

Besides, all she could think about was seeing her daughter again, holding her and making sure the little girl was safe.

"Don't be." And then he removed his hand—leaving an immediate feeling of cold in its place—before getting out of the SUV.

"How do most murder investigations work?" Dalton asked.

"What do you mean?"

"Who do you usually start investigating first?" He stopped next to his vehicle.

"Those closest to the victim. Family. Friends." She arched a brow. "Why?"

"Because we've done that. We talked to your sister, Clara's boyfriend and her stepdad. What happens if all the family members check out?" He leaned an elbow against his SUV.

"We funnel out from there." Leanne took in a deep breath. "We'd look at friends, known associations, places the victim frequented."

"I keep going back to the tracks leading up to the tree. There was only one set, which means there was no resistance. If they were drugged, who has access?" His eyes sparked with possibilities.

"A pharmacist comes to mind first. Dentist or doctor." She studied his face.

"The town pharmacist has a son who could be the right age. What about a bus driver? Someone they knew or had met."

She rocked her head in agreement. "Not to put a damper on your ideas but both girls were upset and maybe a little naive. They were at a vulnerable age. A stranger could disarm them and lower their guard if he knew what he was doing."

"Let's think about on it some more," he said.

She followed suit and with every step toward the main house, her tension increased. By the time she walked across the threshold and marched into the kitchen, her pulse blazed. Her sister sat at the table where Leanne had last seen Hampton. She was smiling and playing with her son.

When Bethany looked up, there was an empty expression in her eyes. Was it possible she didn't know Gary had been released? Anger shot through Leanne at thinking he might be involved in her daughter's attempted abduction. Why would he do that?

The answer came almost immediately. To punish her.

"How's everything going in here?" Leanne asked, suddenly afraid to bring up the subject. Maybe she could work on her sister a little bit and convince her to stick around and get healthy.

"Good," Bethany said.

Hampton looked up with a huge smile plastered on his face. "Lee-Lee."

"Hello, buddy." It was good to see him genuinely happy. Her heart squeezed, thinking how much she missed Mila. Her little girl was safe. She was on her way.

Leanne refocused on Hampton. She'd worried that taking him out of his environment would be stressful. Turns out, he was acting like he was on the best vacation ever. She could admit the ranch held a certain unexplainable magic that had her tension ratcheting down a few notches.

"He's out," Bethany said with those same dead eyes.

"I know." Leanne was surprised by her sister's reaction.

Tears welled and Bethany turned her head as though she didn't want her son to see her cry.

"Can I play?" Dalton seemed to pick up on the tension. He pulled out a chair on the other side of Hampton. "I used to hide this truck so my brother wouldn't get to play with it."

"You did?" Hampton giggled like the two were conspiring.

Leanne moved to Bethany's other side and took a seat. "I'm sorry I didn't call. I wanted to tell you in person."

"How do you know?" There was such hollowness to her voice that it made Leanne's heart ache. She wished she could take her sister's pain away.

Leanne held up her cell.

"He said if I didn't come home now that I shouldn't bother. There wouldn't be one to come back to," Bethany said quietly. She glanced toward Hampton who was invested in playing with Dalton.

"It's an idle threat. You know that, right?" By no means did Leanne want her sister to go back to that creep, and she had yet to determine if he was also a criminal. Bethany needed to make a decision. Trying to force her would only push her toward him instead of away. Leanne also knew the pitfall of tying up her self-worth with a man who didn't deserve it.

The first real relationship Leanne had been in after graduating high school had been with an older man who'd manipulated her into thinking she was special to him. He'd said all the right things—things she'd wanted to hear but didn't have the experience to know whether or not they were sincere—and she'd taken the bait. Then the little insults had started.

He'd commented about her hairstyle not fitting her face and that he thought she'd enjoy it more if she cut it short. When she accepted that criticism, because she'd always been good at seeing her flaws, he added a few more. Her clothes were too tight. Her lipstick too bright. Later, she'd realized that he'd believed in breaking her down and by making her believe she was less than him so she would stay. It didn't take long to see through him, but she'd allowed herself to fall for the guy—or at least that's what she'd believed at eighteen—and he'd been a first-rate jerk. She'd picked up what was left of her self-esteem and moved on.

The only good thing about youthful relationships was that while emotions might run high, they didn't run as deep.

Walking away from him had proven the easy part. Trying to regain confidence in herself and her judgment about people had been the tricky stuff. Leanne had always been too hard on herself.

Bethany seemed to be teetering on an emotional ledge. Leanne needed to know which way she was going to fall, because one of those choices would kill her ability to help her sister. In these situations, a straightforward approach was always best.

"Are you going back to him?" Leanne asked outright.

Bethany drew a sharp breath and the attention of Hampton, who locked on to her.

"Mommy?"

"It's okay, sweetie. Mommy's fine," she reassured.

When Hampton went back to playing with the toys, she leaned toward Leanne and said, "How am I supposed to tell my little boy his sister is gone?"

"It'll be hard but he needs to know." Leanne realized that her sister had changed the subject.

"He wasn't at the hunting lodge the other night. I

called my friend and she said they didn't go. He went drinking instead," Bethany admitted.

Which was suspect but didn't necessarily mean that Gary was a murderer or kidnapper.

"He and Clara didn't get along too good and especially lately. Those two were oil and water," she said.

Leanne further wanted to point out that they were like gasoline and fire, but she let her sister continue.

"What if he was invo—" Bethany released a sob and surprised Leanne by wrapping her arms around her. Bethany's body trembled.

"Then we'll nail the bastard," Leanne said low and into her sister's ear. "But right now you need to let Hampton know what's going on."

A look of resignation passed behind Bethany's eyes. She walked over to her son and dropped down to his level. She said a few quiet words to him as she patted him on the back and both cried.

"GARY'S ALIBI IS blown and it's only a matter of time before the sheriff finds out," Leanne said to Dalton.

The two had walked outside for fresh air after Bethany had calmed down and decided to take a nap with Hampton.

"She told you that?" he asked, wide-eyed, and she fully understood his surprise at the admission. Bethany had been so adamant about protecting him. The woman was on an emotional roller coaster as her world crumbled around her. Without Mila there, Leanne could relate to the out-of-control feeling.

"Yes."

"Did you advise her to tell Sawmill?" His dark brow

arched in clear surprise that she might not have after looking at her.

"Of course." But something had been nagging her from the start. They'd been focused on Gary. Too focused. While he might explain Clara's murder, it didn't make sense that he would've known Alexandria. She needed to look at this from another perspective. "Can I see those pictures again?"

He pulled out his cell and thumbed the photo application open. "Which ones?"

"The tree." She moved next to him and her arm grazed his, causing a little too much electricity to jolt through her.

He handed the phone to her to let her scroll through the photos until she stopped on one of the tree and examined it closer.

"How high is this branch?" she asked, knowing she was heading into dark territory with him because it was the one the girls had been hung from. It hit her, too, in a spot dark and deep. Maybe shared pain was the reason she felt so connected to a man she barely knew. Although, after spending two intense days with him, she felt like she'd known him her entire life.

Looking at the photo again made every beat of her heart hurt. Her brain scrambled from the onslaught of emotion bearing down. But she was on a mission, so she shoved those thoughts, those emotions to the side. She'd deal with them later, and she'd pay the price for bottling them up.

"About seven feet tall," he said, looking closer.

"The rope probably hung a foot and a half from the branch to the victim's neck." She wouldn't use the victims' names anymore. She couldn't. It would be too personal, and she had to keep a laser focus. "How tall was your friend?"

"She was around five feet five inches," he supplied. "Why?"

"You said something about the knot that has been sticking with me," she admitted. "He's proving a point. With one pull in the right direction, the girls could've freed themselves."

"Thinking about it takes me down a different path than Gary. I'm guessing it does the same for you." He rubbed the two-day scruff on his chin, as he seemed to be catching on. Dark circles cradled his intense blue eyes.

"If my calculations are right, the victims' feet would've been inches from the ground," she added. "Meaning he might've been proving a point."

"Or shoving it in our faces," he added bitterly.

"And what is he ultimately saying?"

"That he's smarter than everyone else," he deduced.

"This guy thinks he's better than us. Superior," she said, and her shoulders deflated. "Gary doesn't fit that profile, and I know for a fact he was never a Boy Scout."

"I know."

"This person knows the area well, which leads me to believe he's local and not someone passing through," she added. "I don't think Gary's ever been to Cattle Barge before."

"Except that he was the one who chose this place to live, right?"

"True. I thought about that, too. He came here for work but then lost another job," she said.

"Wouldn't that shoot him up the suspect list? He's

frustrated. Wants to show the world his real power. That he's better than everyone else," he theorized.

"The arguments with my sister intensified as a result of him losing his job. And I think that might've been his outlet." She paced in front of the house. "I keep going back to the fact that he's a hothead. The timing of the killings might've been opportunistic but I believe the acts were premeditated."

Dalton muttered a curse and something about the man responsible being right under his nose this whole time. "Why would he wait fourteen years to strike again?"

"My best guess is that he's a serial killer. It's not uncommon for them to have long cooling-off periods in between killings," she confided. "Was anything missing from the victim in your case? Jewelry? Article of clothing?"

"I remember the sheriff asking where her other earring was. It struck me as odd at the time." Dalton raked his hand through his hair as though trying to tame the out-of-control curls. The fact that his thoughts were heavy was written all over the tension in his face and body.

"He most likely kept it as a souvenir," she said with disdain, and wondered what he'd kept of Clara's and if the sheriff would even tell her if anything was missing. That familiar anger raged inside her and she knew it would cloud her judgment if she didn't keep it in check. She couldn't afford anything less than crystal clear focus.

What if she gave Bethany a list of questions to ask? Surely, the sheriff wouldn't deny information from a mother who was curious about the investigation into her daughter's death. Sawmill had seen her and Bethany react to each other. He wouldn't assume the two were talking. This could work.

"I'm guessing by the spark in your eye that you're thinking the same thing I am," Dalton said. "Do you think Bethany's up to asking the sheriff a few questions?"

Chapter Thirteen

"My sister wants to find out what happened to Clara. I can't deny that it might be so she can find out if Gary's in the clear or cheating on her. If he's not involved, she might actually take him back," Leanne said with disgust.

"Hampton's a good kid," Dalton said. "He deserves a better life than watching his father berate his mother."

"My sister needs to tell him about Clara." A tear rolled down her cheek. "My family must seem crazy to someone like you," she said.

"Families are complicated and none of them are perfect," he responded quickly and it made her wonder about his. She already knew he was close to his siblings, but he hadn't said much about his parents. "Were your mother and father close?"

"I'm not sure. My mom took off when we were little. My father was Maverick Mike Butler. He didn't exactly light a campfire every Friday night, rally the children and talk about his feelings." There was no emotion in his voice.

"So you don't know much about their story?" She wanted to know more about the handsome cowboy.

More than she could read in a headline. And a part of her couldn't deny that she wanted him to confide in her.

"Everything my father did made news. And yet, he managed to keep many of his personal exploits out of the public eye. Can't say there was much between us other than him giving me and Dade orders," he said.

"So the two of you weren't close?" she asked.

"My brother and me, hell, yes. But Maverick Mike was a different story," he admitted.

"Do you miss him?" She glanced around at all the holiday decorations. Christmas was the loneliest time of year for her since her mother died. She'd been looking forward to this year's, as it would be Mila's first. Clara would have been with them and the three of them together would have been the most family she'd had under one roof in as long as she could remember.

But then the desperate call from Clara had come.

"His presence? Yeah. The man? Not as much as I probably should." His admission caught her off guard. He was opening up and telling her something very real about himself.

"I'm sorry," she said softly for lack of anything better. She said it all the time in her work and meant it, but it had never felt so hollow until now. Was it because she suddenly realized how inadequate those words were after losing Clara? Her niece didn't even have a name anymore. She would forever be referred to as a victim.

A tear surprised her, springing from her eye and spilling onto her cheek. She mumbled another apology, but Dalton responded by lifting her chin until her eyes came up to meet his. His complicated family relationship made him more relatable to her and the pull toward him even more intense.

"Don't apologize for showing emotion." He thumbed the tear from her cheek and there was so much tenderness in that one move.

"If it makes you feel any better, this is Mila's first Christmas and I don't even have one decoration up. No tree. Nothing. Looks like I won't be up for mother of the year."

"That doesn't make you a bad mother."

She flashed her eyes at him.

Leanne couldn't think of one word to say against the tug she felt. She wanted to argue that her timing was awful—and it was—but she couldn't deny the urge to kiss Dalton again.

So, she popped onto her tiptoes and did just that.

He groaned as she pressed her lips to his and then his tongue slicked across hers. This time, he wrapped his arms around her waist and pulled her flush against his hard, muscled wall of a chest.

She brought her hands up to brace herself, but instead found herself gripping his shoulders and digging her nails into him, pulling him closer. Desire rocketed through her and sensual shivers skittered across her exposed skin.

His mouth covered hers and both of their breathing intensified. Electricity hummed though her nerve endings, awakening every cell and she surrendered to the feelings engulfing her like wildfire in a dry forest.

The bucket of cold water came in the form of tires on gravel out front. *Mila?*

DALTON PULLED BACK, muttered a curse along with his frustration about timing before threading his fingers with Leanne's. He led her toward a shortcut to get to the small parking lot.

Dalton had seen the serious side of Leanne. He'd seen the devastated side. But nothing prepared him for seeing her tender side. The look on her face when she saw her daughter had the effect of showering light into a black hole. Everything about Leanne relaxed when she looked at her little girl.

The way her daughter's face lit up when she saw her mother was enough to melt a diamond in the icebox. The little girl was all round angelic face and big brown eyes, the color of honey just like her mother's. She had a sprinkling of hair, her fist in her mouth and a bright smile.

His heart stirred and cracks in the veneer exploded at seeing the interaction between mother and daughter.

He needed to get his thoughts together, because he was thinking about the three of them as a family.

Dalton excused himself and walked away.

After refilling his coffee cup, he stepped onto the back porch in order to breathe in the fresh air and think about what they'd discussed.

Taking a seat and leaning forward, he thought about the kind of person who would have access to the girls. Someone they'd be comfortable with. Years ago, he'd read in a crime journal that predators usually knew their targets and gained their trust beforehand. That could explain why neither girl showed signs of a struggle. Was there some type of drug involved? Leanne had made a good point about the girls being vulnerable. He couldn't speak for Clara but Alexandria had been angry. She might've acted out of character or put herself in a bad situation.

The local pharmacist, Larry Wentworth, had been living in the community for three generations. Dalton went to school with his son, Bartholomew. It would take someone strong to lift the girls and Mr. Wentworth had to be in his early sixties. Everything about him was short. Short height. Short legs. Short hands. Due to the fact that he was both short and thin, Dalton doubted he was strong enough to lift the girls, let alone pull off the murders.

Bartholomew was Dalton's age and he could be strong enough. Had he married? Dalton thought about the fact that many of his classmates had settled down by now. Even Dade had found love in a stable relationship.

He and Cadence, the baby of the family, were the only two who were still single.

Personally, Dalton was nowhere near ready for that kind of commitment. Not until he brought justice to Alexandria's murderer. Not until he got past the anger he felt toward the Mav. And not until he could feel something in his chest besides anger and betrayal. His mother had disappeared when he was too young to remember her. Alexandria had been taken from him. And the only woman he'd been serious enough about to consider moving in with had walked out days before signing the lease, saying that he was still in love with a ghost.

Was that true?

Dalton refocused on the coffee mug, rolling it around in his hands. Alexandria deserved justice.

What was he missing?

There was no way Christian had done anything to hurt Clara. It was obvious the kid was head-over-heels in love with her. He was a decent kid, hardworking, with good grades and a solid future. He seemed to have the support of his family. He didn't fit the stereotype of a murderer, not to mention the fact that the two were on solid ground, according to Christian. He had no reason to hurt her and he would've been three years old at the time of Alexandria's murder.

Dalton knew that losing her in this way would affect every relationship Christian had with the opposite sex for the rest of his life. It had for him.

"Can I join you?" Bethany asked from the door, surprising him.

"Be my guest." Dalton gestured toward the chair opposite him, the one Leanne had sat in earlier that morning.

"Thank you."

The screen door opened behind him.

"Got anything to drink out here?" Bethany took the seat and pulled her legs up, wrapping her arms around them.

"Afraid not." And she didn't need anything, especially with the emotional state she'd been in.

"I can't imagine what you must think of our family," she said sheepishly. "We must seem crazy to someone who grew up in such a nice place."

"All families have their moments," he said. "Believe me, ours is just like everyone else's."

"I doubt it," she said, waving a hand around.

"Right. The money. Don't get me wrong, we're grateful to have food on the table and a roof over our heads. Kids need more than that," he defended.

There was an awkward silence.

"I keep running through everything in my head, and I just can't imagine Gary doing something like this. He and Clara had their differences, but…" She twisted her fingers together.

Dalton didn't speak. This wasn't the time to play his hand, and she might confess something that could lead them to the killer.

Bethany rubbed her eyes.

She released a sob. "It's possible. I can't deny it. He wasn't where he said he'd be the other night."

"I know I said it before but I couldn't be sorrier for your loss," he said.

"She was a good girl," she admitted. "Never got into trouble at school. Well, except when other kids bullied her, and then she'd get called out for talking when she told them to leave her alone. Seems like the teachers here have their favorites, and those kids get away with…" She stopped herself from finishing the sentence as she rubbed her eyes again.

"This town can be pretty tight. Folks have grown up together and it can be hard to break in," he said.

"My Clara was smart and a few kids didn't seem to like the fact that she made better grades," she continued.

"What about that bullying you mentioned? Did any of them make any real threats to her safety?" he asked.

Bethany shrugged tired shoulders. "She may have mentioned a couple of names of kids who elbowed her into her locker. You know, typical acting up."

"Did she tell the principal or talk to a teacher?" From the sounds of it, she was enduring more than standard jokes. It seemed like there were even more ways to make kids miserable these days. Forget the grapevine that ended with a handful of smart-mouthed kids. Now, rumors could be spread via the internet on social media.

"Said it would only make things worse," she said.

"Than what?" he scoffed. And then he really thought about it. High school for someone who didn't feel like they fit in could be hard. Scratch that. It could be hell. Especially if that person was being bullied. Being in a new environment was never easy.

He didn't want to believe it was possible that local kids could've been hazing her and not just because that would mean his theory that the cases were linked would go up in smoke. Part of him, and it was a very big part, wanted to believe that kids in Cattle Barge were decent human beings. But he didn't want to be selfish when a young woman had lost her life. He had to consider the possibility that Clara's situation had nothing to do with Alexandria's murder and that even in a small community kids could go unchecked.

Kids were smart and they could dig up facts on the internet no one else seemed able to. He wouldn't take anything for granted. As much as he wanted— no, needed—to put Alexandria's case to rest, he had to make sure the right person was caught and prosecuted.

Was it possible that a few kids could've found out the details of Alexandria's case? Could Clara's "suicide" have been staged to look like she'd done it to herself? He'd read some horrific stories about the cruelty of college kids' hazing pledges to fraternities. Dalton had never been the "join-in" type, and he couldn't see why anyone would want to be part of a club so badly that they'd be willing to chuck their dignity.

Guess his independent streak would've never allowed him to be that desperate to conform. From what he'd been told about Clara so far, neither was she and he respected her for it. Such a shame that a life could be cut down so young.

Thinking about his conversation with Bethany caused something to click. He and Leanne might not be able to get to her laptop, but they could check out her profile and recent posts. Maybe there'd be a clue in there, because he was getting frustrated by the lack of anything else to go on.

And he wondered how reliable any information from Bethany would be.

"How often have you been taking the medication lately?" Dalton asked.

"Not much. I just take it when I need it," she said a little too defensively. Dalton knew on instinct that she was downplaying her usage.

And that could mean she'd missed a lot of signs.

At this point, they'd covered Gary well enough. The sheriff was investigating him and Dalton had to believe if there was anything there, Sawmill would see it.

"What about her father? Have you heard from him?" he asked.

Bethany seemed taken aback by the questions.

"He hasn't been around since Clara was a baby," she scoffed.

Opening up to her about his personal life might build a sense of comradery, which in turn could help her relax and open up a bit more. She'd been on the defensive with her sister in every conversation he'd observed so far.

"Same with my mother," he admitted.

Bethany's eyes widened with shock. "I'm sorry for saying this, but I figured someone who grew up in a place like this would have a perfect life."

"Most people think the same thing."

"I guess that saying about money not being able to

buy happiness is true," she said before adding, "It's sure hard to be happy without it, though."

"Money isn't the source of happiness or the root of evil," he said. "A man only needs enough to put a decent roof over his family and good food on the table. Whatever else he does with it is up to him."

Using it to help a decent family in need of a break sure as hell made him feel proud, though. Maybe that was the trick to having money and feeling good about it, sharing it with people who deserved better than what they'd been handed.

"You don't think her father knows anything about what happened, do you?" he asked, trying to gauge if she knew about her daughter reaching out. Based on what he knew about their relationship, he didn't think Clara would have mentioned it to her mother, but there were a lot of spying devices that could be used to monitor texts, social media pages and emails. Most devices or applications were easy enough to find on the internet following a quick search. Privacy wasn't guaranteed when it came to using technology, no matter how much people felt secure with it.

"No. He had no interest in her," she supplied.

"Even so, he deserves to know what happened to his daughter." It wasn't Dalton's place to tell Bethany that Clara had reached out to her biological father. He and Leanne needed to make an appointment with the sheriff to discuss it, along with a couple of other theories, in order to cover all bases.

If Sawmill locked on to an idea, he might have a tough time seeing alternatives. If they could shed light on an area that he hadn't considered and help with the investigation of Clara's murder, he might just find out what had happened to Alexandria, too.

And then something must've dawned on Bethany, because she squinted her eyes and her lips compressed.

"I didn't think much about it at the time, but she mentioned some guy hanging around and giving her the creeps," she said.

"Recently?" he asked.

"She brought it up not long after school started again. I guess that's why I didn't think about it the other day," she supplied. "I should've listened to her more."

"But she didn't say anything lately?"

"No. But that could be my fault." The familiar pains of guilt darkened her features. "When school started, she got real homesick. Seems like San Antonio was all she could talk about. When she wasn't singing its praises, she was complaining about everything in Cattle Barge. I didn't think she was giving it a chance here, so I got on her case pretty hard. I guess I reached a boiling point, you know?" She looked to him for what he interpreted as approval, or maybe just a sign he wasn't judging her too harshly. Based on her expression and the pain wilting her body, he figured she was doing enough of that on her own.

"Teenagers can make everything overblown and seem worse than it is," he said. "You wanted her to give it a chance here."

She nodded and seemed grateful for the understanding.

He remembered enough of his and Dade's teenage years to know his statement was true, even before Alexandria's murder.

A thought struck. Was he remembering all the harsh

words and actions of his father while excluding anything good the man had done? It was so easy, especially for a young person, to file someone in the "good" or "bad" category, leaving them there whether they still deserved it or not.

Dalton could admit that his father had turned a new leaf in recent years. In holding on to his hurt from the past, he'd robbed himself of getting to know the man his father had become.

"She describe the guy to you?" he asked.

"No. But I'm not at all surprised with the way I shut her down. She didn't mention him again or the bullying, but I could see how unhappy she was." A sob escaped. "I should've let her live with one of her friends in San Antonio and then my baby would still be alive."

"Hindsight might give us perfect vision, but I can see how much you love Clara," he defended, knowing she would carry that guilt for the rest of her life. "You didn't know this would happen, and you can't blame yourself."

Didn't saying that make him feel like the world's biggest hypocrite? Hadn't he been carrying around guilt over Alexandria's death for the past fourteen years? It had become part of him, squeezing the light out of everything inside him.

Leanne was breaking down his walls, though. He had no idea what that meant for the future but he wanted to be around her, in her life somehow.

But could he?

Was there even room?

Chapter Fourteen

Bethany and Hampton were resting. Mila was down for her afternoon nap. Hampton had insisted the baby be allowed to stay in his room and Leanne figured he was most likely missing Clara, so she agreed.

Walking helped Leanne think when she was stuck and this case had her head spinning.

Stepping out the back door, she saw Dalton walk into the barn carrying a bag of something. Feed? She followed him, wanting to pick his brain again. He'd been quiet after leaving her alone with Mila.

"Hello?" she said as she stepped inside the partially opened door.

"In here," he responded, and she could tell that he was in one of the horse stalls.

"I figured a barn on a ranch like this would be booming," she said.

"Not at this time of day. Everyone's out taking care of the cattle, checking fences and making necessary repairs."

"This one's beautiful." She walked over to the mare.

"This old gray mare?" he asked with a smile, and she could see how much pride he had in the horse. "Name's Lizzie. She's mine. Rescued her from Lone Star Park after a trainer took pity on her when she lost a race and then found out she had health problems."

"What did her owner say?" she balked.

"He wanted her euthanized. Billy 'Big Heart' Willy slipped her out the back door, looking for someone, anyone, who promised not to race her again. He'd lose his job if his boss saw her on the track again." He patted her on her long neck. "She's been with me six years with no signs of slowing down."

Lizzie looked like she was actually smiling.

"I feel like I should know more about horses growing up in Texas. There aren't a lot of barns where I grew up in east Dallas," she confessed. "I know you were born into ranching, but is it what you wanted to do?"

"Yes. There's something about being on the land, working with my hands that makes me feel alive. I've always known my place was at Hereford," he admitted. "What about you? Did you always want to be a cop?"

"Me? No. Not until I was a teenager and lost my mother. I started getting serious about my future then. We shared a small apartment and whenever we were home at the same time, which was rare, we were climbing on top of each other." She smiled at the fond memory. "I decided that I wanted a career with a solid future."

"I guess we both lost people we loved early in life."

Was that part of the pull she felt toward the handsome cowboy?

"The two of you were close," he acknowledged.

"We were more like sisters, because she was a young mother and we were figuring it all out together," she said. "Times were hard but we made it through."

In losing her mother, she realized that she'd lost her

belief in people being good. Letting anyone truly get close to her afterward had been off the table.

She stood there, looking into his eyes and she could feel the change in temperature. Her thighs heated as they locked gazes. Her pulse pounded. And rational thought blew out the window.

He stood there like he was debating his next move.

Which lasted for all of about a minute until he stalked toward her, brought his hands to cradle her neck and then kissed her.

She could taste coffee on his lips as he deepened the kiss.

This time, any resistance faded, her mind quieted and her body ached with need as he pulled her flush against his solid wall of a chest. Her breasts swelled and her nipples beaded as his hands slid underneath her blouse and cupped her lacy bra.

Heat engulfed them as urgency roared, building with a tempo she'd never experienced before.

She pulled back enough to say, "Don't stop this time, Dalton."

It was all the encouragement he seemed to need, as she pressed her fingertips into his shoulders. Tilting her head toward his gave him better access to her mouth and his tongue lunged inside.

He made a guttural groaning noise from low in his throat, and it was the sexiest sound she'd ever heard.

She dropped her hands and started unbuttoning her blouse. Her body had so much pent-up need that her fingers trembled. Dalton joined her and helped her out of her shoulder holster and shirt before walking her to an office across the hall.

The room was the size of two horse pens. Concrete

flooring was covered with a soft rug. Furnishings were simple. Across from a handmade desk and chair stood a comfortable-looking leather love seat.

Leanne placed her shoulder holster with her weapon on top of the desk along with her shirt. She kicked her mules off before unsnapping her bra and shrugging out of it. Next, she shimmed out of the borrowed jeans, taking her lacy underwear off in the same motion.

When she looked up at Dalton again, he was completely naked and her pulse skyrocketed at the sight of him. Anticipation mounted as he stood there, looking at her, appreciating her. It had been a very long time since she'd felt adored by a man, maybe never. Certainly not with this level of intensity.

"You're beautiful," he said. Her stomach free-fell in the best possible way.

She was normally embarrassed by her body and especially now that she'd had a baby. Her hips were fuller than before and there were marks that had never disappeared.

The hot cowboy didn't seem to notice any of her flaws.

"So are you," she said with a flirty smile. Her gaze slid over his chest and down to that dark patch of hair. A little farther south and she could see how much he liked seeing her naked based on his straining erection.

It turned her on.

"I want to feel your hands on me, Dalton," she said.

It took only three strides for him to stand in front of her. He pulled a condom from the wallet on the desk and she helped him put it on, stretching it over his tip and down his stiff length.

And then he tilted her head back and captured her

mouth. Her bones went liquid when he kissed her so thoroughly, her body hummed with anticipation as she stood there.

Every cell inside her cried out to touch him, so she did. She smoothed her flat palm across his muscled chest, letting her fingers glide over the strong lines. The thought of making love to someone had never seemed this good of an idea or *this* right.

It should scare her.

But it didn't.

DALTON'S HEART THUNDERED as he explored Leanne's taste. He feathered kisses along her jawline, her neck before cupping her full breast with one hand and slicking his tongue across the other. Her back arched and her nipples beaded, flooding him with heat.

He picked her up and repositioned her on the edge of his desk before sliding his tongue south. He gripped her sweet round bottom as he slicked his tongue inside her sweet heat. She moaned and wiggled her hips as he moved his mouth along the inside of her thigh until she begged for release.

He stood and she wrapped her legs around his midsection before grinding against his erection.

When she scooted closer until his tip entered her mound, he had to strain to maintain control—which threw him for a loop. He'd never been early to the races, but she was so damn sexy with her curves and silky skin that he nearly detonated before it got interesting.

Her bare breasts pressed against his chest as she pulled closer, digging her fingers into his shoulders as he entered her.

"Dalton." She said his name so low, but it was the sweetest sound. He wanted to hear it again and again until she screamed it in release, so he dipped inside a little deeper, waiting to make sure she was okay.

Her wet heat surrounding his erection was the second time he almost lost it. *Damn, Butler. Way to slow down.*

She was that sexy. Her body was one thing and, yes, it was his idea of perfection. But the sexy sparkle in her honey-browns when she looked at him threw him into a whole new stratosphere of attraction. She was sharp and warm, a rare combination of spunk and tenderness.

And when she bucked him in deeper, he gripped her sweet bottom and drove them both home.

The next few minutes were a frenzy of tongues melding, hands exploring and friction building.

Deeper, she welcomed him, answering his strides with a fever pitch until her muscles strung tight and he could sense she was on the edge.

Thrusting. Faster. Harder.

She cried out his name in sweet ecstasy as her muscles contracted around his hard length.

His pace was steady as he guided her toward that sweet release she craved until she shattered around him.

And then he detonated, too. Driving steady and deep until everything drained from him.

Panting, he held on to her. Both seemed to need this moment in the present. Because experience had taught them tomorrow wasn't guaranteed. Both seemed to realize their paths could break in opposite directions at any time now.

"This changes things for me," Dalton said quietly.

He had no idea if she'd heard him, was speechless or just plain old didn't feel the same way.

THE SHERIFF'S REFUSAL to meet with Leanne gave her no choice but to show up at his office. Thankfully, the baby was safe at the ranch. Mila's presence seemed to distract Hampton and Bethany, too. Her sister had lit up when she saw Mila, constantly expressing how much she'd wanted to visit after the birth.

It seemed that Bethany was channeling some of her extra energy into Mila. Her sister was brighter today and Leanne hoped it was because she wasn't taking the medication that blanked her face and the fact that she'd made a decision not to go back to Gary.

"I need to speak to the sheriff. It's urgent," Leanne said as Janis, the sheriff's receptionist, came around her desk with her hands out in front of her.

"Hold on there. Slow down a minute." The older woman had a kind but firm way about her. She was tall, close to six feet if Leanne had to guess. And she was using every inch of her height to block the hallway leading to Sawmill's office.

"Let him know I'm here, and I'm sure he'll agree to see me," she defended.

Dalton was behind her, but he didn't seem to have a play.

Since making love, his normally tense expression had relaxed and he was even more attractive. She'd let his last words sit between them, unsure of what they meant or what either of them could do about them, anyway. Her life was in Dallas and his in Cattle Barge.

Leanne had a daughter who would always be her priority. Trying to add someone else to the equation of her already-complicated life seemed like looking for disaster. She couldn't make the math work, no matter how much her heart wanted to argue.

Cattle Barge was hours away from Dallas. Dalton loved the land he lived on. Their lifestyles were on the opposite end of the spectrum. She had a job that required long hours and a child who deserved her attention when she wasn't working. As much as Leanne loved her mother, there were many times she felt left out when her mother was seeing someone new. Eating dinners alone before the age of twelve was about the saddest thing she remembered.

Leanne needed Mila to know she came first.

A little voice in her head said circumstances were completely different. Mila was a baby. But then that made things even worse. What was she supposed to say to Dalton? "Hold on while I burp my baby"? "Sorry, she just threw up on your good pants"? None of it worked.

And yet, when his hand came up to her shoulder, everything scrambled in her logical mind and she wished they could give a relationship a shot.

Didn't he say that working a ranch was a seven-day-week job?

"Please let me in there," she begged.

Janis studied her for a long moment. "I can't do that or I might lose my job."

Leanne started to argue, but Janis's hand came up again. "You seem like the kind of person who won't take *no* for an answer." She craned her neck like she was using her head to point to the back parking lot. "And he's due any minute. He'll most likely come through that back door." More of the head movements. "And there's not much I can do if someone wants to wait out there on public property in order to speak to him."

It dawned on Leanne that Janis was actually helping her out.

"My job wouldn't be hurt at all. Nothing in my file—"

She didn't need to finish her sentence, because she was already shushing them out the front door. Leanne understood.

"Thank you," she mouthed, careful not to say it too loud.

"No one's ever thanked me for kicking them out before," she said a little too loudly, and Leanne knew it was for the benefit of anyone who was trying to listen to their conversation.

Bolting around the station, Leanne caught the sheriff as he opened the back door.

Chapter Fifteen

"Sheriff Sawmill," she shouted to get his attention as she rounded the corner, desperate to get to him before he pretended not to see her and slipped inside the door.

"I'm on a case right now, Detective West." His tone was irritated, but he rested his hand on the half-opened door.

"We'd like to speak to you about the victims—"

"We've already been over this," he insisted. "I sent a report to your supervisor this afternoon."

"I haven't spoken to my SO today," she admitted. "Dal—Mr. Butler and I have been thinking and we'd like you to hear us out."

Sawmill glanced around as a reporter dashed around the corner. Normally, she didn't appreciate media interfering but in this case, it might actually help her out.

"Come inside," he said after a second.

"Thank you, sir." Leanne knew she was putting her job on the line.

Sawmill led them inside his office and closed the door behind them. "I'm willing to hear you out this time but make no mistake about it, this is a favor."

"Understood," Leanne said, grateful to have the sheriff's ear.

He didn't sit down, so neither did they. She pulled out a notepad from her purse.

"Dalton and I have been looking at the cases from a different angle, trying to infuse another approach," she started.

"I've already—"

"Come on, sheriff," Dalton interrupted. "You can't tell me these cases don't look enough alike to at least make you question it."

Sawmill nodded in response. "I'm already thinking the same thing."

"Hear what she has to say. If you don't agree, the only thing you've lost is a couple minutes of your time," Dalton continued.

"Okay. I'm listening."

"The bodies showed no signs of putting up a fight. So, it's possible they were drugged and that's why there are no signs of struggle. The victims are both a little more than five-feet-tall blondes, both seventeen years old. They were hung from the same tree on the same night fourteen years apart," she said.

"Tell me something I don't know," Sawmill responded with an even tone.

"I made a few phone calls last night and found out that one of the bus drivers at the high school has a biology degree," Dalton said. "He quit his job and moved home after his mother died."

"Ted Brown has a biology degree?" Sawmill asked.

"He's strong enough to carry the victims," Dalton said. "He was twenty-six when the first victim was hanged. Forty years old now and strong as an ox."

"One of my deputies collected coke caps from the

underbrush at the scene. Maybe we'll get a DNA hit," the sheriff said.

"Ted doesn't have a record that I know of," Dalton said. "I didn't know him personally, but people said he came back from school after an accident. Said he hasn't quite been right ever since."

"I checked the database and didn't get any hits for other victims on December 7," Sawmill admitted.

"It's not uncommon for a serial killer to have a cooling-off period," Leanne chimed in. "He would need to have other victims, of course, to fit this classification."

"Seems like someone with a mental impairment or brain injury would have a difficult time pulling off two murders without leaving a trail," Sawmill said. It was true that most killers had low IQs and were caught early as a result. It was also true that the really smart ones literally got away with murder.

"I believe he's showing off. He thinks he's superior, so he's rubbing our noses in it," Leanne stated. "The trucker's knot. The public display. He wanted the victims to be found, because he's thumbing his nose at us."

"You don't believe your brother-in-law is involved?" Sawmill asked.

"If he is, throw the damn book at him. I just can't reconcile it. He's a hothead, my brother-in-law. I found out he's been physically rough with my sister a few times." She flashed her eyes at the sheriff. "Believe me, I had no idea any of this was going on. They kept me in the dark. I'm guessing they knew what my reaction would be."

"Which would be understandable, but that doesn't solve my case."

"Yes. But right now I'm thinking my brother-in-law

is your best suspect and you can see the holes in that theory better than I can. You have another higher-profile murder investigation sitting on your back and while you figure out who did that, you need this win as badly as we do." Leanne didn't hold back, and she hoped it wouldn't get them kicked out.

The sheriff took a step closer and looked at the notepad she was holding.

"You believe the suspect is male. Strong. Brown is at the top of your list," he said. "But Bartholomew, the druggist's son, is on there, too. The man has a family. Goes to church on Sunday."

"So did the BTK Killer. Having a family and going to church didn't stop him from stalking and killing women," Leanne interjected.

"But you want access to Brown."

"Yes. But I can't touch him without putting the case in jeopardy, and I won't do anything that might damage your investigation." She studied Sawmill. Tired? Check. Listening? Check.

This was the most progress she'd made with him since they met a few days ago. Had it really only been a handful of days? Barely sleeping for most of it stretched the days into what felt like weeks. It was impossible that she and Dalton had only known each other for a short time. Her feelings for him ran deeper than anything she'd known before. A little voice reminded her that they were in an intense situation and that could bring out all kinds of extra hormones.

Was it hormones? Really?

A blind attraction that would fade?

She hoped not, because she'd felt struck by a stray lightning bolt from the minute she met the handsome cowboy. Getting to know him only made her respect him even more. He was the kind of guy she could see herself with long term under different circumstances. If the relationship had time to take hold before she returned to the city.

Long distance rarely worked without all the complications they had. Leanne didn't have it in her heart to try again with anyone.

Did she?

"THIS IS GOOD investigative work," Sawmill finally said after they gave him a few more choices for suspects. He folded his arms.

Dalton knew that he was also signaling that it was time to end the meeting.

"We appreciate your time, Sheriff," he said, offering a handshake.

This meeting was going a long way toward rebuilding trust and the sheriff seemed to realize it when he took the outstretched hand in a firm grasp.

"Can I take a picture of that page?" Sawmill asked.

"Absolutely," Leanne said with pride.

Dalton liked it when she smiled. He wanted to talk to her about the possibility of spending time together once she returned to Dallas. He'd shelve the thought for now, but his chest was lighter than it had been in longer than he could remember. The chinks in his armor, allowing some of the pain to seep out, had the benefit of him carrying a lighter load.

"I'll follow up on these leads and see where these people were on the seventh," Sawmill promised.

The pair stood after thanking the sheriff.

Dalton walked Leanne to the SUV, stopping to give her a kiss before opening her door.

"You think she's still asleep?" Leanne asked, referring to her daughter. "I want to call and check on her, but I don't want to wake anyone."

"Let's give it a minute," he said. "Besides, I have an idea."

The smile on Leanne's face broke down more of the casing around his heart. He was falling. Hard. He just hoped there'd be a life raft when she walked away.

He didn't tell her where they were going, but it wasn't far out of town. The two chatted easily on the way. Leanne seemed pleased the sheriff was taking them seriously and he couldn't deny that he was, too.

It was Christmastime and his turn to bring home the tree. The Butlers had a tradition that no other decorations could go up inside without first having a tree.

Dalton realized something about the sheriff through this process. Sawmill had a tough job. He had a lot of pride in his work and even if he made a mistake, it wasn't because he didn't care. There was an odd comfort in the sentiment.

"Okay," he finally said. "We're almost there."

"Great, because all I see is farm road," she quipped. There was a lightness to her voice that he liked. Was it because they were making progress in the case? He figured that was part of it. Seeing her daughter had improved her mood considerably. And then they'd made love.

Dalton couldn't remember when it had been so right. He wanted to make Leanne happy.

"You were talking about feeling like a failure earlier for not being more prepared for your daughter's first Christmas," he began as he winded down the path.

"Yes. So, why are we out in the sticks? I thought the ranch was remote until you brought me out here. Is there even cell reception?" She checked her phone for bars.

"Maybe. Maybe not," he teased.

"Tell me again why we're all the way out here," she pleaded.

"Hold on," he said. And then he rounded the bend, revealing the best Christmas tree farm in Texas. "Here."

"This…is…beautiful." She wiped a tear.

"There's no need to get emotional," he said, but his chest swelled with pride.

"I've never been to a real Christmas tree farm before. When Mila is older, I want to bring her back here."

There were more pines than he could count. He parked the SUV and hopped out so he could open her door for her.

"This is…" She seemed to be searching for the right word. She also seemed at a loss, so he kissed her.

She responded in a way that got him aroused. Bad idea out here. And when he looked up afterward, he smiled when he saw mistletoe hanging over the trellis leading to trail to the small forest.

"You ready to pick out your first Christmas tree for your daughter?" he asked. Leanne deserved this. So did Mila. The kid was as cute as a button. He briefly envisioned bringing them here for hayrides and hot chocolate as Mila grew older.

"Can we get any one of these?" Leanne took off running toward the plantings. This close to Christmas the lot had a fair amount of vehicles, mostly trucks.

Dalton hoped he had a way to tie off whatever tree she picked as he chased her through the forest of evergreens.

"What do we do?" she finally asked, out of breath, as she stopped in front of one.

"Get an ax," he said.

"No." She spun around, grabbed him and pulled him closer until he could breathe the same air as her. "They're too perfect. I don't want to spoil them by taking an ax to one."

"I can understand your point," he said, tugging her toward him. "I can."

He could feel her heartbeat against his chest. Hers pounded from the run, and it reminded him of another time her pulse raced alongside his.

"But this family grows these trees as a source of income. This land is dedicated to growing trees to be chopped down, so it's not hurting the environment. In fact, it's helping out a very good family," he explained before kissing her again. The taste of convenience-store coffee was still on her breath from when they'd stopped earlier to pick up a couple of cups.

"Need any help?" A bear of a man walked toward them. He couldn't be much more than forty years old.

"Dalton Butler." He stuck out his hand.

"Hardy." The man gripped his hand and Dalton was immediately aware of the strength in his handshake.

"Do you work for the Santanas?" Dalton asked. He didn't remember seeing Hardy around before.

"Pamela's my aunt," he said by way of explanation. He wore lumberjack-type clothing and wielded a hefty-sized ax. He wore a serious expression and something darkened his eyes as his gaze landed on the area of Leanne's shoulder holster. "You like this one here?"

"Yes." Dalton pulled Leanne closer to him. It was probably just because the guy almost matched him in height and build, and was wielding an ax that caused him to want to keep her within arm's reach. Primal instinct. Nothing more. "You live here, too?"

"Nah. Just come when I can get away from home. My uncle's getting up there in years and Pamela can use a hand." Hardy shrugged, pulled the ax sideways and then got off his first shot at the trunk. He had the form of a professional golfer with similar precision. Wood chips flew from the contact as he made a large dent in the side of the tree. He turned to Dalton and Leanne. "You might want to step back."

He tagged the tree before pulling a slip of paper out of his pocket and handing it to Leanne. Something else flashed behind his eyes, but it happened so fast Dalton couldn't be sure.

Dalton put his body in between Hardy and Leanne, linking their fingers as they took a few steps back.

A few hacks at the trunk later and Hardy hauled the tree up onto his shoulder. "What are you driving?"

"Sport utility. Black." Dalton supplied the license plate number.

"Take that slip I gave you to my aunt to pay. I'll have this strapped to your vehicle by the time she runs the charge," Hardy said.

"Will do," Dalton replied.

"I've never had a real Christmas tree before," Leanne admitted when they were out of earshot.

"There's nothing like waking up to the smell of pine to tell you the holiday is here." Dalton had mixed feelings about this year and that was most likely the reason he'd been stalling on finding a tree. Then again, it was his turn this year and he'd been dreading it. Being with Leanne, seeing her eyes light up when she saw "the one" gave him a warm feeling in his chest. Was that cold heart of his finally thawing out? It had been frozen for a very long time. *Too long,* a little voice in his head said. The voice sounded a whole helluva lot like Alexandria's.

Deep down, he knew she'd want him to be happy. In the past, attempts to reclaim his life had felt hollow. Not this time. Not with Leanne.

She squeezed his hand with the excitement of a little kid. But the kiss she planted on his lips next was all woman. It also got something stirring they couldn't deal with out here in the cold.

He smiled at her and she seemed to catch on.

The sparkle in her eyes told him all he needed to know about what she was thinking, too.

"Thank you," she said, looking right through him to his core. "I haven't felt this happy, this alive in longer than I can remember."

"Me, either." Happiness had always been fleeting in Dalton's life. And he feared this time would be no different. Yes, his feelings ran deep for the woman at his side, as they linked their fingers again and strolled through the pine forest. But they'd be out of the woods and back to reality soon.

The small wood hut at the entrance to the gravel parking lot had a window for transactions.

"Pamela," Dalton said as he walked up. She was short. He couldn't see much more than her platinum blond hair, which was piled on top of her head when he first approached.

"In the flesh," she chirped.

She wore too much blue eye shadow over brown eyes and had a nice but worn dimpled smile.

"Hardy said I should give you this." He handed over the slip of paper.

"Excellent choice," she said, looking over the small sheet. "A nine-foot Leyland cypress. That's my favorite kind." She looked harder at him. "I'm sorry I can't keep you and your brother straight. Are you Dalton?"

"Guilty," he admitted, pulling out his money clip and peeling off a few twenties after hearing the price.

"It's a pleasure to see you again. I'm real sorry about your papa," she said, taking the bills being offered. Her eyes widened. "This is too much."

"Give whatever's left over to Hardy."

"He'll appreciate it," she said on a sigh. "As a boy, he went through more than anyone should have to endure in one lifetime. For a while, I thought he wouldn't come out the other side after witnessing his mother bring man after man parading through the home, each one with his own set of problems. There were severe punishments that…let's just say that each new male figure seemed to have a new way to torture Hardy. Later on, he got into trouble but he learned his lesson while he served his time," she glanced up and seemed to have revealed more than she'd wanted to, "and here he is."

"I'm sorry to hear about his past. Nice of him to help out," Dalton said, noticing she'd called Hardy a boy instead of a man.

"It gives him running money." Pamela flashed eyes at him. "Sorry, I shouldn't talk about other people's problems."

"I thought I knew everyone in Cattle Barge," Dalton added. "Did he grow up around here?"

"No. He's not from around these parts. Me and my husband bought this farm fourteen years ago to make a fresh start after he lost his job." Pamela had a wistful look on her face, but she reined it in real quick and then handed him a receipt. "You folks have a nice holiday. Come back and see us next year."

"We will. And you, too." Dalton took the paper and stuffed it inside his front pocket.

He and Leanne walked to his sport utility as another car pulled into the parking lot. Hardy was already tying another tree on top of a sedan. The place seemed to do a steady business.

On the road again, something was bugging Dalton.

Chapter Sixteen

"I have a weird feeling." Leanne hadn't been able to shake it since she and Dalton left the tree farm.

"Same here."

They'd winded down the lane and onto the road leading toward the highway.

"Can't put my finger on it," she admitted. "Did Hardy rub you the wrong way?"

"He did."

A few seconds later, Dalton mashed the brake and pulled onto the shoulder of the two-lane road. He bolted out of the SUV and released a string of swear words.

"What is it?" she asked.

"Check the sign," he said.

She glanced around the road and locked on to a sign. They were on Farm Road 1207. Immediately, 12-07 shot to mind. The date.

Leanne flew out of the vehicle, because she knew exactly what he was doing. Checking the knot.

"Is it the same one?" she asked.

"Yes," Dalton said after muttering a few more curse words. The same ones she was thinking. He pulled a slip out of his pocket and then muttered more. "His aunt mentioned that he'd served time. Could explain why there haven't been any murders in between Alex-andria and Clara."

"She also mentioned something about a traumatic childhood and not being from around here," she said.

"And that he had a whole mess to deal with back at home."

"There's always a trigger with serial killers," Leanne added as anger filled her.

"Get in." Dalton was already reclaiming his seat.

"No, Dalton. Stop. Whatever you're thinking is the wrong move." She knew based on his actions that he wanted to go back and spend a few minutes alone with Hardy. "We don't have proof and as much as I want to hurt him, if he's the one responsible, we'll only do more damage if we go vigilante."

Dalton was the kind of man who was used to taking care of business himself. It was one of the attributes she admired most about him.

"I'm going back to ask a few more questions." His white-knuckle grip on the steering wheel intensified.

"Let's think this through first." Sure, his anger was running high now. And she wanted revenge as much as he must. "We want the same things."

"Then get in and put on your seat belt." His voice was a low rumble.

"If he's guilty, I want him to pay for the rest of his life, Dalton. I want him thrown behind bars so he can remember every day what he's done. We go back there, find out it's him and take his life, then what? He's gone. It's over for him. I want him to suffer for the rest of his life."

Dalton stared out the windshield, but she could see that her words were making an impact.

"Let's do this instead. Let's call the sheriff and tell him what's going on," she said.

"What if it's him? What if he runs and they don't catch him? He'll continue to walk free. He'll hurt more girls and a helluva lot sooner this time." The anger was still very much present in his words, but she was chipping away at his emotions by using logic. Dalton was a logical man. If she could continue to appeal to that side of him, she had a chance at doing this the right way.

"They'll go after him. They'll find him. And if they don't, we will."

"But I'm right here. I can take care of this right now. I can make sure that bastard never sees another sunset. As long as he's breathing and free, he'll find another target." The intensity of his voice softened ever so slightly, but she could tell she was making headway.

"Let's make the call. Do this the right way. He isn't going anywhere. He doesn't suspect a thing, Dalton. We have the element of surprise on our side, and Christmas isn't for a few weeks. He'll be right here. And now that the sheriff will know what he's looking for, he'll build a solid case that will make sure he doesn't see daylight for the rest of his life."

Dalton sat there, grinding his back teeth. She knew that the man in him wanted to take Hardy in his bare hands and squeeze the life out of him for what he'd done. It was primal, but Dalton was a good man. She had to believe that he'd act on reason. Or maybe if she was honest with him, she could give him a better emotional reason.

"I have a selfish reason for not wanting you to circle back, Dalton. I'm falling for you, hard. I've never felt this way about another man, and I want to figure out a way to see each other when this is all over. I can admit that I don't know how it'll work with our lives, but I want to try. See where this thing goes. I want us to have a chance. And we can't do that if you're behind bars."

His gaze intensified on the road ahead. Finally, he ground out, "Make the call. Ask Sawmill if anyone saw pine needles around the parking lot or the tree."

Leanne wouldn't look a gift horse in the mouth, and her heart leapt at the thought that he might want the same things.

He'd already pulled his cell out and he was checking the photos from the scene.

She wasted no time retrieving her cell from her purse and making the call to Sawmill. She intentionally left her door open so that Dalton couldn't change his mind without talking to her first.

"They're right there." He cursed and showed her a picture of the base of the tree with pine needles nearby.

After relaying this new information to the sheriff, she ended the call and looked at Dalton. "He's putting every available resource toward tracking down what happened to Hardy and his family. And Sawmill is on his way."

"I need to go back and look him in the eyes right now," Dalton said, his intensity returned. "I can't walk away when I'm this close, Leanne."

DALTON STALKED TOWARD the trees. If he cut a path straight through them, he could get to Hardy within minutes. Anger fueled his steps; fourteen years it had built up inside him like a simmering volcano, and he'd finally found the release valve.

Hardy needed to pay for what he'd done.

"Dalton, stop," Leanne called after him, and he could tell she wasn't far behind. Her voice broke through the ringing noise in his ears.

So much anger. So much pain. And the reason stood a football field away.

"We don't have all the facts yet." Leanne's voice sounded desperate. And that dented some of his armor.

"I know all I need to." He stomped through the underbrush of the nongroomed area of the tree farm.

"Please, stop," she continued. "If we do this the wrong way, he could go scot-free. I know you don't want that any more than I do. If you assault Hardy, you'll be the one in trouble. The sheriff will be here any minute. Alexandria wouldn't want you to go to jail, Dalton."

Those words slowed his pace.

"From what I can gather, the two of you cared a great deal about each other. Ask yourself if this is what she would wish for you." Damn those words were having an effect on him.

Maybe it would be better to think this through instead of acting on his rage. Thinking back, no good had ever come out of his making a decision or reacting from anger.

At this point, he didn't care what happened to him— although that wasn't completely true now that he'd found Leanne—but she made good points about Alexandria. One of the things he'd loved so much about her was her compassion.

The feeling of an explosion rocketed his chest.

Leanne was right. Alexandria wouldn't want this.

Hardy deserved to spend the rest of his life in jail. He deserved to face punishment for what he'd done. He deserved to suffer for the innocent lives he'd cut short. He deserved to wake up every day knowing the pain he'd caused.

Taking in a sharp breath, he spun around. His action wasn't fast enough to react to the large sharp rock being hurled at his head.

And then he blacked out.

DALTON BLINKED HIS eyes open. He lay sprawled out on the ground. His head hurt and his eyes burned. He brought his hand up to his forehead and immediately drew it back. Pain shot through him as everything came back to him in a jolt. *Leanne.*

Footsteps sounded nearby. More than one pair? Running away or coming toward him?

He'd been too caught up in his own anger before to realize they were being hunted. He forced himself upright and scanned the area. *She* was being hunted. Clearly, Leanne was the one Hardy wanted, considering she was nowhere in sight.

The sounds of footsteps drew closer. Was Hardy coming back for round two in order to finish him off?

Dizziness made it difficult to get to his feet. A burst of adrenaline helped but nausea quickly followed. He stabilized himself by grabbing hold of a tree trunk.

A man in a brown uniform moved through the trees. Dalton recognized the sheriff immediately.

"Over here," he said loud enough to get the sheriff's attention and hopefully no one else's. It occurred to Dalton a few moments too late that Hardy would know this land better than anyone else.

Sawmill shifted his direction toward the sound of Dalton's voice. His eyes widened when he got close enough to look at him.

"I'll call for an ambulance," he said.

Dalton had ignored the liquid he felt running down the side of his face. He touched it and drew back his hand, his fingers now covered in blood.

"I'm fine," he said. "He got Leanne."

Deputy Granger came up behind the sheriff. He'd stood back and had been surveying the area.

"It's clear," he said.

"The address to the tree farm is 14 Pine Lane. The farm road is 1207. He hung both girls in a tree. And now the bastard has Leanne," Dalton said.

"Let's secure the area and interview the aunt and uncle," Sawmill said.

"She said something traumatic happened in his past and that he's served time." Hardy could've taken Leanne anywhere on the property. He could've killed her already and buried her.

"Moved from where?" Sawmill asked.

"She didn't say."

"I want that interview now," Sawmill barked.

Pamela was still in the shack with a small line of customers when they arrived a few minutes later.

"What happened?" she immediately asked, her gaze flying to Dalton's forehead and the fresh blood. She burst out the side door. "Follow me. I have a first aid kit in the house."

She must've thought Dalton had brought the sheriff back to have her arrested based on how scared she looked.

"We're looking for your nephew, Hardy," Sawmill said.

She stopped in her tracks.

"What did he do?" Her question was peculiar. There

didn't seem to be any doubt in her mind that he deserved to be arrested. More warning flares lit in Dalton's mind.

"You said he served time. What was his crime?" Dalton asked.

"Drugs." Her gaze bounced from the sheriff to Dalton.

She stared toward the sky. "I thought he cleaned up his act. He found religion and—"

"When was he released?" A picture was emerging that clenched Dalton's stomach.

"Six months ago."

"Is he here?" Sawmill was surveying the area.

"I haven't seen him, and that's why I have a line of customers waiting to be helped." She motioned toward the shack. "I need to fetch my husband."

"Ma'am, we need your cooperation. We believe that your nephew has taken a female law enforcement officer hostage." Sawmill's voice had a sense of urgency.

"Norman," she called out.

"Ma'am, do you know where he is?" Sawmill continued, trying to direct her back onto the right path.

"No, I don't. I wish I did. This is bad." She shook her head and tears welled. "We knew something was wrong, but we thought he was holding it together. You say he took a woman?"

"Yes."

"He hates law enforcement after what happened," she confessed. "He's always talking about making them pay. About them being too stupid." She flashed her eyes at Sawmill and Deputy Granger. "I'm sorry. They were his words, not mine."

"What happened?"

"His younger sister was abducted when she was seventeen by their mother's boyfriend. She was found before he killed her…" Pamela made apologetic eyes at them for needing a minute. "But she couldn't adapt after the ordeal and a few weeks later, on December 7, she hung herself. Hardy found her," she said. "He blamed the way law enforcement handled her case for her suicide. He never did get over it. He got so sad. I guess he used drugs to numb his pain. We had no idea he'd do anything like this or we never would've brought him here."

Sawmill steadied himself, because it looked like his legs were about to give. "He killed two girls, both seventeen years old, and fourteen years apart."

Sawmill cursed, and it was the first time Dalton saw the man almost lose his composure. He regained his footing and jumped into action.

Within the hour, law enforcement had descended on the surrounding area, searching for Leanne by air, four-wheelers and on foot. Calling her phone was the first thing they'd tried. She couldn't be tracked using GPS, either. Hardy must've disarmed her. If she had control of her weapon or her cell phone Dalton would've heard from her by now.

There was no sign of her or Hardy.

"I put out a 'be on the lookout,' a BOLO. I'll put in a call to Texas State Troopers in order to warn them personally in case he's on the highway somewhere."

"I need to talk to her sister and tell her what's going on." Dalton knew Bethany would be worried. She knew Leanne wouldn't disappear without checking in with her since Mila was there. "Call me if you get a hit?"

It would be breaking protocol, but it was worth a shot to ask the sheriff.

"I'll let you know the second we get anything," Sawmill promised.

Dalton hitched a ride back to his SUV, which was parked on the side of the road. He thanked the deputy before taking off.

The road in front of him seemed to stretch on for mile after empty mile. Darkness covered the land. At this time of evening, there weren't many vehicles on the highway.

And then a thought struck.

This was personal. While all available resources were at the tree farm, Hardy had the perfect opportunity to deliver a devastating blow to Sawmill.

Dalton bit down a curse and jammed his foot onto the gas pedal.

Chapter Seventeen

Dalton had a hunch that Hardy would take Leanne to the tree. He just didn't know if she'd be dead or alive.

Instead of banking a left on the farm road that would take him to Hereford, he turned the wheel right. He made good time back to Cattle Barge.

Driving up to the spot when it was still dark outside would make his headlights give him away. It seemed like the surest way to get Leanne killed.

His stomach lining braided thinking about what could have happened to her already. He knew he shouldn't go there.

Whatever was going on, he'd face it.

For three hours he camped out near the tree.

Dalton found a place to watch. Seeing the tree was difficult but he'd see anyone walking up to it. The sheriff and his deputies were canvassing neighboring ranches around the tree farm and checking out the list of possible hiding places that Pamela had supplied.

A burst of adrenaline shot through Dalton as he inched closer and saw Leanne's limp body hanging from the oak tree. Dalton palmed his weapon. Hardy was there. From this distance, he could see that Hardy was supporting her weight, using his shoulder as he tied the knot around her neck.

Dread was a hard knock as Dalton faced the very real fear that she might already be dead.

But then he remembered what she'd said about ketamine and a burst of hope filled his chest that she was out and not gone.

Hardy most likely had her gun but his hands were currently full, which played to Dalton's advantage.

Biting back a curse, Dalton bolted out of the woods. He covered the distance between them in a few quick strides before diving toward Hardy's knees.

Making contact, Dalton drove Hardy a step back and heard a loud crack. A bone?

Fighting back, Dalton connected a fist with Hardy's jaw. Another crack.

And that's where Dalton's advantage ended.

With an animal-like grunt, Hardy pounded his fists against Dalton's body, connecting with his ribs, arms and face.

Leanne hung in the tree a few feet away behind him, and Dalton feared no matter how quickly he subdued Hardy, it would be too late for her.

Fourteen years of rage exploded inside him and, just like a bomb detonating, he exploded against his enemy. On the man who had taken so much from him.

Dalton pounded his fists against Hardy, delivering punch after punch in rapid succession. He worked on Hardy's gut and face until the man threw his arms up to block. Putting Hardy on the defensive, gaining ground, Dalton pummeled harder.

Thoughts of Alexandria—her pure smile, her sweet personality—tore through him like an out-of-control storm. And then, there were his feelings for Leanne—feelings that ran steady and deep.

Hardy wrestled Dalton for control, managed to get it. Anger surged and Dalton flipped the big guy on his back again. The guy was pinned, momentarily secure, but Dalton was paralyzed. One wrong move and Hardy would gain the upper hand. And if he didn't get to Leanne soon, it would be too late.

The image of her limp body dangling from that tree momentarily distracted him. Hardy landed a punch that most likely broke Dalton's nose and threw him off balance enough to tip the scale in Hardy's favor.

Hardy bucked, knocking Dalton off him.

And then Hardy launched into a terror of flying fists, grabbing and punching anywhere and everywhere on Dalton's bruised body.

Dalton captured Hardy's right hand and rolled several times, separating himself for a brief moment.

Hardy flew toward Dalton and as he was about to land on top of him, Dalton threw a punch, his fist connected with the man's face, jutting it awkwardly to the left.

When Hardy landed, he lay in a lump on the ground. Dalton's gaze flew toward the tree as he forced himself upright. His twin brother, Dade, was running toward Leanne.

"She's alive," Dade said. "She freed herself before I got here."

Leanne had propped herself up, and she was leaning against the trunk.

Dalton looked at the tree that had taken so much from him.

But not this time.

"An ambulance is on the way," Dade said as he made it to Dalton's side and offered a hand up. "Let's get you over to her."

"She's alive," Dalton repeated softly as a surprising tear leaked from his eye.

"You did it," Dade reassured as he helped Dalton to Leanne. "I stopped by to bring food before starting my workday and saw it unfold. You did it, Dalton."

Dalton was too exhausted to say much. He took Leanne's hand as Dade said he'd keep watch over Hardy's body until authorities arrived.

Leanne's face was pale and her breathing shallow.

"Please don't leave me, Leanne," he whispered, adding, "I know how crazy this might sound but I love you."

LEANNE WOKE IN unfamiliar surroundings. She blinked her eyes open with a gasp as memories of being abducted by Hardy came back in a flash. She pushed up to a sitting position and looked around the room, steadying her rapid heartbeat.

The sun was blazing in the sky. She threw her feet over the side of the bed, checked to make sure she had clothes on. Exhaled a slow breath when she saw that she did.

She had to remind herself that she wasn't in the freezing cave that Hardy had dragged her into and kept her in a drug-induced haze for days. She'd spent several more in the hospital before being released.

And then remembered where she was. The Hereford Ranch. But this wasn't the bedroom she'd slept in.

She managed to get to her feet on shaky legs. A bathrobe was on a chair next to the bed. She slipped the white cotton robe on and tied the belt. A toothbrush waited for her in an adjacent bathroom and she was so grateful. It tasted like she'd slept with cotton balls in her mouth. She was so thirsty she bent down to take a drink from the faucet and then splashed some cold water on her face.

Commotion in the bedroom caused her to turn a little too fast. She gripped the doorjamb to steady herself and was glad she did when she saw Dalton holding Mila. Her daughter was cooing at him and she'd never seen him look so happy.

The expression morphed when he saw her standing there. "You should be in bed."

"How long was I asleep?" she asked.

"Not long enough. The doctor said it'll take a few more days before you start feeling like yourself again," he informed.

Her concern melted a little when she looked at her happy baby. Mila was all smiles.

"We did it, Dalton," Leanne said, remembering that Hardy would go to jail for the rest of his life with the evidence against him.

"We sure did."

She leaned into him and cried.

When there were no tears left, he helped her onto the edge of the bed.

"I can't bring her back," she said on a sob.

"I know."

Mila made a cooing noise at her mother and Leanne smiled through her tears.

"You want a cup of coffee?" Dalton had several days' worth of scruff on his chin, but his face was more relaxed than she'd ever seen.

"Sounds like heaven, actually," she said, wanting to

hold her baby but afraid she wasn't strong enough yet. "Have you slept much?"

"Me?" he scoffed, and it made her laugh. "I don't sleep. I've been setting up a scholarship for Christian. I hope you don't mind, but I set it up in honor of Clara and it bears her name."

"She would've loved that," Leanne admitted. She looked at her baby. "I wish I could hold her."

"You could sit on the floor," he said.

Leanne leaned on his free arm for support, anchoring herself against his strong biceps and the bed as she sat down. She stretched out sore legs.

He set Mila next to her with a pillow behind the little girl's back for support.

"I'll be right back." He feathered a kiss on Leanne's forehead before jetting out of the room.

Dalton returned, as promised, a few minutes later with two mugs of coffee and joined them on the floor.

Leanne immediately took a sip. It tasted perfect. Being here with Dalton and Mila was perfect. But perfect had a shelf life.

"This might sound crazy, but hear me out." Dalton flashed his eyes at her. "In the past few days, I've fallen for you, Leanne. I'm all in. Your daughter is the most beautiful baby, but don't tell my brother that." He smiled and it warmed her heart. Was he saying what she was hoping? That they'd somehow figure out a way to see each other after going back to their lives. A life that felt hollow somehow without Dalton in it.

"We might've just met, but I feel like I've known you my entire life. I see how hard you fight for what you believe in, for the people you love. And that's all it takes to make a relationship work. I want you to know that if you have the same feelings for me, if you love me, I have every intention of asking you to marry me."

Warmth cascaded over Leanne at the sound of those words.

"I do love you, Dalton. I can't imagine living one more day without you in my life," she said. "So, what are you waiting for?"

A slow smile spread across his lips.

"I promise to love this little girl and protect her as the child of my heart that she is. And I vow to live each day to bring a smile to your lips and make sure you know how much I cherish you. Leanne West, will you do me the honor of being my wife and making the three of us a family?"

"Yes." Tears of happiness and joy spilled down her face. "I will marry you, Dalton."

Dalton leaned over and kissed her. Mila giggled at the wonder of her own hand and the two of them laughed with her.

After playing on the floor without having to watch the clock, hunger finally made its presence known. "I could eat for two days straight right now."

"Wanting food is a good sign," he said with a smile.

"How's my sister?" she asked, needing to know what she'd be facing when she walked down that hallway.

"She's good. She's been hanging around with May and spending time with Hampton. He's loving it here, and there's talk in the family of finding a permanent job for Bethany and setting her up with a place to stay."

"Has she mentioned Gary?" She hiked a brow.

"Yes," he admitted. "You should know that Gary admitted to hiring a guy to go to the park in Dallas, but he swears he never had any intention of actually taking the baby. He was trying to scare you and get you to go home so he could work on Bethany. He knows it was stupid. He turned himself in to the sheriff."

Leanne took a minute to let that sink in. Gary wasn't the brightest and she could see him following down that path of logic, crazy as it was. "Is he being held?"

"Our family lawyer put a call in to the judge who said they wanted to sweat him out. Give him a couple of days to really think about what he's done," Dalton said.

"Serves him right. But it would be best for my sister and Hampton if Gary got his act together," Leanne admitted after careful thought. "I'm not saying I think she should go back to him after he got physical with her. But he needs to learn to be a better man."

"Ella is certain she can reform anyone if she has the right resources and they're willing. He says he is, but Bethany said he's going to have to change big-time and prove he's worth another shot before he's allowed to be in the same room with her or their son again. It'll take time for her to trust him. Losing his family and Clara seems to have finally sunk in."

"Whether he's in the picture at some point or not, at least my sister's on the right track," she said.

"We all know what it's like to grow up without a father. No one's giving up on helping Gary become the man he needs to be. Whether they all live in the same house or not will be up to them when the time is right. For now, he's willing to work on himself and earn the right to be a father and husband again."

Warmth spread through her at hearing those words.

People deserved second chances.

Dalton made a move to get up, but she touched his

arm. "Did you get the answers you were looking for about your relationship with your father?"

"Don't need 'em." There was so much sincerity in his eyes when he looked at her. "I already have the two of you."

With that, she tilted her head toward the sky and kissed her future husband, the man she loved with her whole heart, the man who was her home.

* * * * *

DELTA FORCE DEFENDER

CAROL ERICSON

Prologue

A bug scuttled across his face, but Major Rex Denver didn't move one coiled, aching muscle. Twenty feet below him at the bottom of the hill, an army ranger team thrashed through the bushes, their voices loud and penetrating in the dead of the Afghan night.

Rex clenched his jaw as if willing the rangers to do the same. Didn't they realize this mountainous area was crawling with the enemy?

His eye twitched. To those rangers, Major Rex Denver *was* the enemy.

He didn't blame those boys for being out here searching for him. Hell, he'd be out here hunting down a traitor to his country, too.

He resettled his rifle and rested his finger on the trigger, not that he'd ever use it against any branch of the US Military. If the rangers found him, he'd go peacefully—but they'd never find him.

He'd started as a ranger himself, and after twenty years in Delta Force, leading his own team, he'd honed his skills at subterfuge and escape to perfection. They wouldn't catch him, but he'd die before he allowed the enemy that roamed these hills to catch those rangers.

One of the rangers yelled out. "Come out, come out, wherever you are."

Rex rolled his eyes. If that soldier was on his team, the wrath of hell would come down on him for that behavior. Rex had to bring the hammer down on Cam Sutton, one of the younger Delta team members, more than a few times for reckless behavior.

Someone issued a whispered reprimand from out of the darkness.

The young soldier answered back. "I don't care, sir, this is wrong. Major Denver's no traitor."

Rex believed he had the loyalty of most of the soldiers who knew his reputation, but the evidence against him was overwhelming. Why him? He and his Delta Force team must've stumbled on something big for someone to take them out of the picture. And he hoped to have a long time to figure it out.

A twig cracked to his right, and Rex's gaze darted toward the sound. Something glinted in the thick foliage. He flipped his night-vision goggles over his eyes and picked out the man crouched in the shadows, his focus on the team of rangers below.

Adrenaline flooded his body, and his heart hammered in his chest. Were there more? He scanned the area beyond the stealthy intruder. If this interloper wasn't solo, his companions weren't within striking distance of the rangers…at least not yet and not before the rangers could respond with their own firepower.

If Rex took out the enemy, he couldn't do it quietly. And once he made his position known, the rangers would swarm the mountainside and capture him.

He cranked his head around slowly, eyeing the steep drop-off behind him. He'd seen worse.

Rex popped up from his hiding place, and in the same motion he took the shot. It took just one. The enemy combatant pitched forward, his gun shooting impotently into the sky above him.

The rangers came to life as they fanned out and charged the hill.

Rex clutched his weapon to his chest, and rolled off the edge of the cliff into the dark unknown.

Chapter One

Martha's head pounded, and her hand trembled as she clicked open her email. Holding her breath, she scrolled past all the new emails that had come in since she'd taken lunch.

When she came to the end of the batch, she let out that breath and slumped in her chair.

The most sinister email that had come through was a reminder to submit her time sheet. She picked up her coffee cup and had to set it down as the steaming liquid sloshed over the rim onto her unsteady hand.

"Hey, Martha. Did you have a good lunch?"

Martha twisted her head around and smiled at her coworker Farah. "Errands, you?"

"Hot lunch date with the mystery man."

"I hope he's not married like the previous one."

"The previous one is still in the picture. A girl has to keep her options open." Farah winked and pushed away from Martha's cubicle almost bumping into Sebastian.

He held up his hand in an awkward wave. "Everything working okay with your computer after I dialed back that program to the previous version?"

"It's back up to speed. Thanks, Sebastian." Martha made a half turn in her chair back to her desktop, hoping he'd take the hint. They'd dated once or twice, but she wanted a relationship with some flying sparks for a change.

Sebastian took a step back, tapping the side of her cube. "Okay, then. Let me know if you need anything else."

Yeah, sparks.

Martha swung around to fully face her computer and jumped when another email came through. When would this fear go away? Those emails had started trickling into her inbox four months ago. She'd turned them over to the appropriate authorities and washed her hands of them—or tried to.

She chewed on her bottom lip. She hadn't forgotten about those emails. How could she, when they'd resulted in a huge investigation of some hotshot Delta Force commander, who'd then gone AWOL? How could she, when ever since she'd clicked on those emails, someone had been spying on her, following her?

She glanced over her shoulder at her coworkers in the CIA's translation department. Why had she been chosen for the honor of receiving those anonymous emails accusing Major Rex Denver of treason and colluding with the enemy?

What would've happened if she'd deleted those emails and never told a soul? Would she be the nervous wreck she was today?

She tapped her fingernail against her coffee cup. She couldn't have ignored those emails any more than she could jump up on her desk right now and scream in the middle of a CIA office that she had a bomb under her desk.

Maybe if she'd gotten rid of the emails like she was

supposed to do, the people who'd sent them would leave her alone. But why would that matter? The senders had gotten their desired response. She reported the emails, which prompted the investigation of Denver, which then led to the discovery of his traitorous activities. The man had gone rogue. How much more guilty could you get?

But some gut instinct had compelled her to hang on to the emails. When she first received them, she'd copied them to a flash drive, which she wasn't even supposed to insert in her computer, and taken them home. She'd told everyone, including her slimy boss, Gage, that she'd deleted them. Then the IT department had come in and wiped her deleted items off the face of the earth.

She had her own suspicions about how those messages had gotten through to her email address at the Agency. It had the fingerprints of Dreadworm, a hacking group, all over it, but not even Dreadworm had claimed responsibility for forwarding those emails.

Martha had wanted to take a more careful look at the messages because of the phrasing. She spoke several languages, and she'd told Gage that the emails sounded like a foreigner had composed them.

He'd brushed her off like he always did, but she'd gotten her revenge by keeping those emails for herself.

Now she had someone stalking her.

Sighing, Martha straightened in her chair and shoved in her earbuds. She double-clicked on the file she'd been working on before lunch and began typing in the English words for the Russian ones that poured into her ears from one of the radio broadcasts the CIA monitored and recorded. After about an hour of translating,

Martha plucked out the earbuds and stretched her arms over her head.

She swirled the coffee in the bottom of her cup and made a face. Then she slid open a desk drawer and grabbed a plastic bag with a toothbrush and toothpaste.

When she returned to her desk ten minutes later with a minty taste in her mouth and a bottle of water, she plopped in her chair and tucked her hair behind her ears, ready to tackle the remainder of the afternoon.

She glanced at the bottom of her computer screen, noticing a little yellow envelope on her email icon, indicating a new message. She double-clicked on it and froze. Her blood pounded in her ears as she stared at the skull and crossbones grinning at her from the computer screen, its teeth chattering.

Hunching forward, she resized the window and scrolled from the top to the bottom of it. No text accompanied the image. She scrutinized the unfamiliar email from a fake email account at the top of the window.

She glanced over her shoulder, and in a split second she forwarded the email to her home address. She deleted it and then wiped it clean from her deleted items. She knew it still existed somewhere in cyberspace, but not unless someone was looking for it. And why would anybody be checking her emails? She'd been the good little soldier she always was and turned over the others. The people up the chain of command had no reason to suspect her, and Gage thought she was a lifeless drone, so she didn't need to worry about him.

If Gage cornered her right now and asked her why she didn't tell anyone about the skull and crossbones, she wouldn't have an answer for him. Maybe because she'd been dismissed so thoroughly after turning over the first batch. Not that this message had anything to do with the others—did it?

Of course it did. The same people had just sent her a warning, but she didn't know why. She didn't know anything about those emails or what they meant—but she was determined to find out.

The rest of the afternoon passed by from one jumpy incident to the next. Her scattered focus had been worthless in her attempts to translate the recorded broadcast.

Fifteen minutes away from quitting time, Farah hung on the corner of Martha's cubicle, her dark eyes shining. "I'm meeting my guy for a drink after work tonight. Do you want to come along?"

Martha crossed her arms. "And be a third wheel? No, thanks."

"He might have a friend." Farah made her voice go all singsongy on the last word as if to heighten the temptation.

"That's even worse than being a tagalong. A blind date?"

"Oh my God, Martha. Get used to it. It's the way of the world now."

"Seems to me all online dating has gotten you is a couple of sneaky married men."

Farah pouted. "It's fun. Not every date has to be a lifetime commitment."

"Go then and have fun for me." Martha waved her hand.

Not that she'd have accepted Farah's invitation under any circumstances, but after the day Martha had just had, she'd rather be home with a good book—and those emails.

She wrapped up her work and logged out of the computer, removing her access card and slipping it into her badge holder.

Waving to the security guard at the front desk, Martha pushed out the front doors and snuggled into her jacket. Winter in DC could be mild, but this November weather was already putting a chill in her bones.

She caught the next plain-wrap CIA van that shuttled employees from Langley to Rosslyn. When the van finally lurched to a stop, Martha stashed her book in her bag, rubbed her eyes and readjusted her glasses. She stepped out of the van and into the cold night, making her way to the Metro stop on the corner.

Descending into the bowels of the city with the rest of the worker bees, she welcomed the warmth from the pressing crowd as she turned the corner for her train. She jostled for position among the crush of people, gritting her teeth against the screech of the train's wheels slowing its progress.

As the lights approached from the tunnel, a man crowded her from behind. Martha tried to take a step back, but found herself pitching forward instead as someone's elbow drove into her back.

The train screeched once more, and Martha felt herself teetering on the edge of the platform. She thrust her arms in front of her as if to break a fall…but the only thing breaking this fall was that train barreling toward her.

Chapter Two

Cam curled his arm around the waist of the woman floundering on the precipice of the platform and pulled her back against his chest. He jerked his head to the side, but the man who had been crowding Martha Drake from behind had wormed his way through the crowd, the black beanie on his head lost in a sea of commuters.

Martha's back stiffened and she tried to turn in his arms, but he tightened his hold on her until the train came to a stop in front of them.

The doors whisked open, and Cam nudged her forward, whispering in her ear. "Go on."

She squeezed into the train with a mass of other people, grabbed a pole and spun around, her eyebrows snapping over her nose. "Take your hand off me."

Cam's jaw dropped open and a rush of heat claimed his chest. He'd just saved the woman's life, and this was the thanks he got?

He wrapped his fingers around the pole above her hand and twisted his lips. "You're welcome."

"I—I..." She shoved some wispy brown bangs out of her eyes, which blinked at him from behind a pair of glasses. "Yes, you're the one who pulled me back. Thank you. But..."

Lifting his eyebrows, he asked, "Yes?"

"How do I know you're not the one who was crowding me from behind in the first place?"

"I wasn't. That guy took off."

Martha's eyes, a lighter brown than her hair, widened and her Adam's apple bobbed in her delicate throat.

His statement had scared but not surprised her, and he dipped his head to study her face for his next question. "Any reason for somebody to push you into the path of an oncoming train?"

"No." She pressed her lips together. "It was crowded. Everyone was moving forward. I don't think that was an intentional push."

"It's always crowded. Commuters don't generally fall onto the tracks."

She shifted away from him, and the odor from the sweaty guy behind him immediately replaced the fresh scent that had clung to Martha, which had been the only thing making this tight squeeze bearable.

"Well, thank you." She tilted her chin up, along with her nose, and dismissed him.

Looked like she'd perfected the art of dismissing obnoxious men, but Cam had a date with Miss Prissypants here, even if she didn't know it.

He left her in peace for the remainder of the ride, although her sidelong glances at him didn't go unnoticed, and the knuckles of her hand gripping the pole had turned a decided shade of white. He'd planted a seed of suspicion in fertile ground.

When the train jerked to a stop, forward and then backward, Martha peeled her hand from the pole, hitched her bag higher on her shoulder and scooted out of the car, with a brief nod in Cam's direction.

He exited the train and followed Martha up the stairs and out into the night air, its frigidity no match for Ms. Drake's.

Three blocks down from the station, she stopped in front of a crowded Georgetown bar, clutching her bag to her chest, and turned to face him.

He sauntered toward her, then wedged his shoulder against the corner of the building, crossing his arms.

"Why are you following me? I'm going to call the police." She waved her cell phone at him.

"We need to talk, Martha Drake."

She choked and pressed the phone to her heart. "Who are you? Are you the one who sent the skull and cross-bones?"

Skull and crossbones? That was a new one. He filed it away for future reference.

He shrugged off the wall and straightened his spine. "I'm Sergeant Cam Sutton, US Army Delta Force, and you discovered some bogus emails that compromised my team leader, Major Rex Denver."

Martha's expressive face went through several gyra-tions, and then she settled on suspicion, which seemed to be one of her favorites. "How do I know you're tell-ing the truth?"

He pulled his wallet from his pocket and slipped out his military ID. He held it out to her between two fingers.

She wasted no time snatching it from him and hold-ing it close to her face, peering at it through her glasses. After perusing it for at least a minute, she handed it back to him. "Bogus emails?"

"Major Denver never did any of those things in those emails—" he jabbed the corner of his ID card in the general direction of her nose "—and if you hadn't turned them over to the Agency, Denver wouldn't be in the trouble he is now."

"If I hadn't…" She stamped one booted foot. "What did you expect me to do with them?"

"We can't keep talking out here. Let's go inside." He jerked his thumb toward the bar.

Her gaze bounced to the large picture window of the bar over his shoulder and back to his face. The crowd inside must've reassured her because she dipped her head once.

Cam circled around Martha and opened the door, holding it wide for her to pass through. As she did, he got another whiff of her fresh scent, which seemed to cling to her.

DC office workers, unwinding at the end of the workweek, packed every inch of the horseshoe bar. They seemed more interested in socializing and watching the football game on the TVs over the bar than quiet conversation, leaving a few open tables toward the back of the room, near the restrooms.

Cam placed his hand on the small of Martha's back and steered her toward one of those tables. She'd twitched under his touch but didn't shrug him off. He'd take that as a good sign.

When he pulled out her chair, her eyes beneath her arched eyebrows jumped to his face, and she mumbled, "Thank you."

After he took his own seat across from her, he folded his arms and hunched over the table. "Why weren't you surprised that somebody tried to push you onto the subway tracks?"

Her nostrils flared, and then she pursed her lips. "I told you. I thought it was an accident. I still think so."

"Really?" He reached across the table so quickly she didn't have time to pull back, and smoothed his thumb over the single line between her eyebrows. "Then why are you jumpier than a long-tailed cat in a roomful of rocking chairs."

Martha's mouth hung open, and Cam didn't know if it was because he'd presumed to touch her petal-soft skin, or because he'd laid on a thick Southern accent. That slack jaw made most people look stupid, but Martha couldn't look stupid if she tried. It made her look—adorable.

"Cat?" Her soft voice trailed off.

"You know—long tails, rocking chairs going back and forth." He hit the table with his flat hand, and she jumped. "Nervous, jittery. Don't deny it."

A cocktail waitress dipped next to their table and tossed a couple of napkins in front of them. "What can I get you?"

Cam plucked a plastic drink menu from a holder at the side of the table and tapped a picture of one of the featured bottles of beer. "I'll have a bottle of this."

"I can't just point at a picture." Martha snatched the menu from his hand and flipped it over, studied it for what seemed like ten minutes and then asked about twenty questions about the chardonnays. When she finally tucked the menu back in its holder, she said, "I'll have a glass of the house chardonnay."

When the waitress dived back into the crowd, Cam drummed his fingers on the table. He needed to start at the beginning with Martha. She clearly liked to take things in order.

He took a deep breath and started again. "Can you tell me about those emails? Where they came from? What they said, exactly, or close to it?"

"I should report you." She flicked her fingers at him. "What are you doing in DC? Why aren't you on duty?"

Cam narrowed his eyes. She didn't want to report him. Her voice had quavered, and she'd broken eye contact with him. If she'd turned those emails over so quickly, there shouldn't be anything stopping her from turning him over—but she didn't want to go there.

"I'm on leave. I'm not here on any official business, just my own." He crumpled the cocktail napkin in his fist. "Look, I know Major Rex Denver, and I know he's innocent of these charges."

"He went AWOL." She sniffed. "Running indicates guilt."

"Not always." He smoothed out the napkin and traced the creases with the tip of his finger. "Not if you think there's a conspiracy against you and you're going to be railroaded."

"A conspiracy?" Her eyes widened and seemed to sparkle in the low light from the candle on the table.

"Here you go." The waitress set down their drinks and spun away before Cam could tell her to close out the tab and that he didn't need a mug.

He watched Martha over the bottle, as he tipped the beer down his throat. Maybe this night would be longer than he expected.

"We think someone is framing Denver, and it started with those emails."

"We?"

"The Delta Force team that Major Denver commanded. We were all—" he put down the bottle harder than he'd planned "—dragged in for interrogation. Do you know what that's like? You're doing your job, doing the right thing, and *bam*. They're lookin' at you like you're vermin."

She nodded and took a big gulp from her wineglass. "I do know what that's like. I turned over those emails and all of a sudden, I'm suspect. They're checking out *my* communications, *my* files."

Cam's pulse ticked faster. That's why Martha was none too anxious to report him. They'd grilled her, too.

"Exactly." He touched the neck of his bottle to her glass and the pale liquid within shimmered and reflected in Martha's eyes. *Whiskey.* Her eyes were the color of whiskey. And right now he was a little drunk just looking into them.

Cam cleared his throat and rubbed his chin. "I don't trust them, any of them. All I know is Denver is not guilty of those crimes, and I'm gonna prove it."

Martha took another sip of wine from her half-empty glass, her cheeks flushed like a rose stain on porcelain. "I'll start at the beginning with the emails."

"Did the CIA determine where they came from?" He scooted forward in his seat.

"I didn't get all the details because why would they tell *me* anything? I'm just the one who discovered them and turned them over." She cupped her glass in her two hands and rolled it between her palms. "They were looking at Dreadworm though, you know that hacking group?"

He nodded, not wanting to interrupt her flow. This stuff had been bothering her for a while, and he just became her receptacle—a very willing one.

"But I don't know if they ever determined how my

email inbox became the target, or at least they never told me. Dreadworm was just the messenger, anyway. The conduit for the message, if you will—and that message was that Major Rex Denver had been working with a terrorist group plotting against the United States."

Cam slammed his fist on the table, the tips of his ears burning.

Martha held up her index finger. "But I noticed something strange about those emails."

"Yeah, they were filled with lies."

"Well, I don't know about that, but it didn't seem as if the person who composed the emails was a native English speaker."

Cam blinked his eyes and took another swig of beer. "Go on."

"If it were a foreign entity who sent those messages, why? Why would they care to warn US Intelligence about an American serviceman?"

"Our allies would care."

"Why wouldn't our allies just use regular channels to communicate with our military or even the CIA? But an unfriendly entity might have every reason to plant those stories about Denver."

"You've been thinking about this."

"It's more than just the emails." Martha waved her hand at the passing waitress. "Another round, please."

Cam cocked his head and took in Martha's empty wineglass and flushed cheeks. She'd downed that pretty fast. Although even in low heels she stood taller than most men, she was as slim as a reed, and the booze seemed to have loosened her tongue and her attitude toward him. He'd take it.

"More than emails?" He wrapped both hands around his bottle.

She looked both ways in the crowded bar and hunched forward, wedging her chin in the palm of her hand. "I'm being followed."

"The guy on the subway platform."

"I don't know." She drew back from him…and her earlier pronouncement, and tucked a lock of silky hair behind her ear. "Nobody has ever made physical contact with me before. That push could've killed me."

The fear in her whiskey eyes plunged a knife in his gut. "Maybe it was just a warning, maybe a coincidence after all."

"You don't believe that."

"How do you know you're being followed?"

"I can feel it, sense it."

He rolled his shoulders and thanked the waitress as she brought them their drinks. Maybe Martha was just paranoid. She'd been dwelling on those emails, and he didn't blame her. They'd started a firestorm.

"And then there's the skull and crossbones."

He coughed and his beer fizzed in his nose. "You mentioned that before. Someone put a skull and crossbones on the emails?"

"Not the original messages. Someone sent me an email, just this afternoon, with one of those animated gifs of a skull and crossbones—blinking eyes and chattering teeth." She took a gulp from her new wineglass, and Cam placed his hand over her icy cold one.

"Why is someone sending you threats? You obviously took the intended and hoped-for action. You turned over the emails and got Denver in a heap of trouble. Why the harassment?"

"I—I do have an idea."

"I'm all ears." He curled his fingers around her hand in encouragement. Why would anyone threaten Martha Drake, a by-the-book CIA translator worker bee who'd reacted exactly as the sender thought she would?

"It might be because I copied all of the emails from my work computer to a flash drive, and now I have them at home."

Chapter Three

Cam Sutton's warm hand tightened around her fingers for a second. "Whoa. I bet the emailer wasn't expecting you to do that. Why *did* you do that?"

How could she explain it? She'd never done anything against the rules in her life. "I don't know exactly. There was something about those emails that didn't sit right with me."

"You said before that they might've been written by a foreigner." Cam tapped his temple. "You're a smart woman."

"I think it was the sentence structure and the word choice. Too formal or… I don't know what." She squared her shoulders and slipped her hand from Cam's. "When I first reported the emails, I tried to tell my supervisor about my suspicions, but he brushed me off."

"I take it nobody at the CIA knows what you did with those emails?"

"N-no." She pulled her bottom teeth between her lips and traced the stem of her wineglass. Farah didn't count, did she?

"You seem unsure. Did you tell anyone you forwarded the messages to yourself at home?"

"I didn't tell anyone anything."

"If someone's been following you and sending you poison-pen emails, somebody knows. Otherwise, they would've left you alone after verifying you'd turned over the messages."

"I don't see how someone could know I have the emails."

He hunched forward, and his energy came off him in waves and engulfed her, sweeping her up in his world. "You seemed hesitant before. Do you think your supervisor might suspect you?"

She snorted and took another swig of wine. "No way. If he did, he would've just reported me to security and gotten me fired…or worse. He wouldn't be hiring people to shove me onto the train tracks."

"You've got a point." He rubbed his hands together. "It has to be the party who sent the emails, the people who wanted to bring down Denver."

Her gaze dropped to his fingers drumming on the tabletop. "You're *glad* someone's after me."

"Wait. What?" He smacked his chest with the palm of his hand. "That's dumb. I don't want to see anyone hurt over this."

"No, but you tracked me down because I'm the one who initiated the fall of Major Denver, and you probably expected some CIA drone that you could bully and instead you've discovered a chink in the story, a new twist you weren't expecting."

He cocked his head, and a lock of hair curled over his temple. He shoved it out of the way like a man accustomed to a military cut and whistled. "Are you sure you're just a translator and not an analyst?"

"*Just* a translator? I know four languages in addition

to English." She ticked off her fingers. "Russian, German, French and Spanish."

"Okay, okay." He held up his hands. "You also have a big chip on your shoulder."

"I do not." She crossed her arms, covering her shoulders with her hands. "I'm just sick of being underestimated."

"Clearly." He leveled a finger at her. "And that's why you stole those emails."

"Are you sure you're *just* a Delta Force grunt and not military intelligence?" She held her breath.

He opened his mouth, snapped it shut and hit the table with his fist. Then he laughed, and what a laugh he had. A few heads turned at the loud guffaw.

"Shush." She kicked his foot under the table.

"Did those spies pick the wrong CIA drone to mess with or what?" He shook his head. "Why *do* you think they targeted you?"

"Honestly? I think they picked me because I have a reputation for following the rules. Everyone at work knows that."

"That's kinda scary."

"What? Following rules? You're in the military. You must do a lot of that."

"Not the rule-following, but the fact that the people who sent the emails knew that about you." He rubbed his knuckles across the sandy-blond stubble on his chin. "Inside job? Some kind of bug?"

"A few minutes ago you called them spies. Do you think this is some foreign entity or worse, a foreign country?"

"I don't know." He tapped her wineglass. "Are you done? I want to see those emails."

"You mean, at my place?" Her heart fluttered. It was one thing talking to this hunky military guy in public, but bring him back to her town house?

"You still don't trust me?" He slumped in his seat and finished off his beer. "What can I do to remedy that?"

"It's not that I don't trust you…exactly. I'm just not comfortable bringing strangers to my place."

He rattled off her address and winked. "I already know where you live, Martha."

"This is all really creepy. How long have you been following me around DC? Maybe my feeling of being tailed was coming from you."

"I swear, I just started following you from the Langley bus stop today."

"How do you even know about the Langley bus stop?"

"I have friends in high places."

She rolled her eyes. "Obviously not if you're dogging a lowly translator."

"I mean it." He grabbed her hands. "I want to see those emails. I know Denver. I'd be able to detect any falsehoods in those messages. I mean it's all false, but I might be able to see something in the emails, some clue."

An edge of desperation had entered his voice, and the easygoing frat boy had morphed into this earnest man with the serious blue eyes, desperate to clear his commanding officer's name.

Despite herself, she felt a twinge of pity and then steeled herself against the emotion. Her father had always employed the same tone when trying to wheedle compassion from her.

She blinked as Cam tugged on a lock of her hair.

"C'mon, Martha. I saved you from an oncoming train. If you don't want me in your personal space, you can bring your computer out to someplace neutral, if you have a laptop."

She inhaled the fresh, outdoorsy scent coming off him and counted the freckles on his nose. Cam already *was* in her personal space, and she didn't mind one bit.

"All right. I'll take you back to my town house."

Cam waved at the waitress for the bill, and as soon as she plucked it from her apron, he snatched it from her fingers. "I'll get this."

Martha didn't even hesitate as she pulled a five and a ten from her wallet and flicked them onto the table. "That's too much like paying for information. I'll get my own wine."

Out of the corner of her eye, she could see Cam raising his eyebrows at her, but she ignored him and stashed her wallet back in her purse. "Is it all there?"

"Yes, ma'am." He tucked his bills and hers beneath the candle on the table, along with the check. "Walking distance?"

"You know my address." She folded her arms, regretting her decision already.

"I know your address, not the area, but I figured you were close if you got off at the Metro stop." He pushed back from his chair and stepped to the side to let her go first.

As she shuffled past him, she noted his height again. At five foot ten, she hit eye level with most men, but her nose practically brushed the chin of this one.

When they reached the sidewalk, Cam hunched into his jacket and flipped up the collar against the wind. "It's not gonna snow, is it?"

"I hope not." She peered at the light gray sky and pulled on her gloves. "That would be pretty unusual for November."

They walked along the busy Georgetown sidewalk, occasionally bumping shoulders, which oddly reassured her, although she couldn't figure out why. Cam had the type of solid build that screamed strength and fitness. Physically, he could have his way with anyone, even a tall woman like her.

She hunched her shoulders and stuffed an errant strand of hair back under her hat. *Dream on, Martha.* Cam was the type of guy who'd wheedled homework assignments out of her. Just like in college, she had something he wanted—just not her body.

She stopped in front of the town house she owned but shared with a roommate, and grabbed the iron handrail. "I'm right here."

"Door right onto the street."

"Yeah? So what?" She fished her key from the side pocket of her purse, and for the first time in a while hoped her roommate, Casey, was on the other side of that door.

"Not that safe."

"If you haven't noticed, this is a nice area."

He looked up and down the street. "Lots of foot traffic though."

She looked up from turning the key in the lock. "I'm a very careful person."

"And yet, here I am."

She opened the door and blocked it with her body. "Are you telling me not to trust you? Because I can change my mind right here and now."

Casey yelled from the inside. "Close the door. You're letting in the cold air."

"My roommate. Protection." Martha jerked her thumb over her shoulder.

"Good thinking." He rubbed his gloved hands together. "Now can we go in? It *is* cold out here."

Martha pushed into the room, and Cam followed on her heels.

"I was just on my way…" Casey tripped to a stop in her high heels when she swung around and almost collided with Cam. "Well, hello there."

"Hey, what's up?"

"Casey, Cam. Cam, Casey, my roommate."

Casey stuck out her hand and wiggled her fingers, her long painted nails catching the light and glinting like she was casting a spell. "Nice to meet you. You're the first guy Martha's ever brought home."

The heat washed up Martha's face, and she ground her teeth together. "It's not like that. He's not a guy."

Casey fluttered her long—fake—eyelashes as she gave Cam the once-over. "You could've fooled me."

"I think what Martha means—" he hooked his arm around Martha's neck in a total buddy move and pulled her close "—is we're just friends."

"Of course you are." Casey turned toward the kitchen, giving Cam a view of her derriere in her tight dress. "Do you want a beer?"

"I thought you were going out?" Martha ducked out of Cam's hold and shed her coat.

"Just showing a little hospitality."

"Don't worry about it. He's *my* guest. I can get him a beer if he wants one."

"I'm good." Cam held out one hand as if refereeing

an MMA fight. "We don't want to hold you up, Casey. Nice meeting you."

Her roommate's pretty face fell, and Martha couldn't help the little spark of satisfaction that flared in her belly. "Have fun, Casey."

"Nice meeting you, Cam." She swept up her coat from the back of a chair. "Hope to see you again sometime."

The door slammed behind Casey in a gust of perfume and hairspray.

Cam cocked an eyebrow at her. "Not a good friend, I take it?"

"Not a friend at all, and she's a horrible roommate—messy, noisy, brings guys back here all the time."

"And you mean *guys*."

"Yeah. She's a real pain."

"Move."

"It's my place."

Cam's gaze flicked around the town house, still sporting the expensive furnishings Mom had favored and she couldn't afford to replace. "Government's paying some solid wages."

"Anyway, I can't just move." She had no intention of getting into her personal finances—or her notorious background—with Cam.

"Kick her out."

"She signed a lease."

"How long?"

"Four more months. I think she's gearing up to move out anyway."

"I'm sure you're counting the days." He clapped his hands once and she jumped. "The emails?"

"Do you want a beer? Or something else?"

"Just some water." He tipped his head at the door. "She doesn't know about the messages, does she?"

"Casey?" Martha snorted. "No. She wouldn't care, anyway. She's in DC to sleep around and maybe snag a book deal, and she has a good start on both."

"Who knew the capital was such a cesspool."

"I hope you're kidding." She strode into the kitchen and reached for a glass. As ice dispensed from the fridge, Cam joined her in the kitchen, making the space feel claustrophobic.

"I am kidding, and I'm convinced someone, some-where in this cesspool has it out for Major Denver." He took the glass from her hand, his fingers brushing hers and giving her a jolt.

Leaning her hip against the kitchen counter, she tucked the hand behind her back. "Why would they have it out for him? Why frame him? By all accounts, he's a good soldier."

"The best and maybe that's why." He gulped down the water. "Maybe he stumbled onto something he shouldn't have."

"Again, that could point to a foreign entity."

"I agree, especially after what you told me about the emails, which are…"

"On my laptop." She brushed past him. "In my bed-room"

Leaving him in the kitchen, she jogged upstairs and pulled the door closed on Casey's messy room. She ducked into her own room, swept her laptop from the desk and tucked it under her arm. By the time she got downstairs, Cam had settled on the sofa in the living room, his long legs stretched out in front of him.

She sat next to him and opened her computer. "I put them in a folder on my hard drive."

"Where's the flash drive? You copied them to a flash drive when you stole them, right?"

She tapped the keyboard harder than she intended. "I didn't steal them. They were addressed to me."

"Addressed to your CIA address, but I'm not judging. Hey, I'm glad you did steal…take them, but where's the original flash drive?"

"It's in a safe in the office."

Raising his eyes to the ceiling, Cam asked, "This place has an office, too?"

"Yes." She zipped her lip and double-clicked on the folder holding the emails. "Is that secure enough for you?"

"I don't know if it's such a good idea to have the messages in two places. You're doubling the opportunity for someone to take them."

"Why would anyone else want them? The CIA already has them." She pointed to her screen. "This is the first of the three emails I received."

Cam moved in closer and his warm breath bathed her cheek as he read the email aloud, slowly. "'Look at Major Rex Denver, Army Delta Force, and track his actions and communications. You will understand his behavior as treason. He has many contacts in region.'"

"Sounds stilted, doesn't it?"

"Wow." Cam slumped back and kicked one foot on top of her coffee table. "That's enough to raise suspicion and get you investigated? Good thing nobody ever sent the CIA information about my activities."

"There are two more emails with more details." Her hand hovered over the keyboard. "*Your* activities?"

"Not treasonous. I'm just saying stuff happens in the field, and it's better for everyone if it stays in the field." His hand dropped to her head, and he messed up her hair with his fingers. "Don't worry. I'm not doing anything to compromise national security—and neither was Major Denver."

She jerked away from him with a scowl, smoothing her wavy hair back into place. "Do you mind?"

"Sorry. I have a younger sister, and I'm accustomed to teasing her." He tapped the keyboard. "Next email."

She huffed out a breath as she opened the second email. Great. The hottest guy she'd run into in months thought of her as a little sister. Typical.

Tipping the display toward him, she drew back and watched his profile as he digested the next message, his lips moving silently as he read it, his finger following the words. He must've read it a few times, as it took him a while to peel his eyes from the display. When he did, his jaw hardened and his eye twitched.

For all his carefree, easygoing ways, Cam really did care about Denver, and a strong desire to help him clear his commanding officer washed over her. She hated seeing anyone unfairly accused, and she'd had a feeling about these bogus emails ever since they landed in her inbox.

"Worse, huh?" She reached across him and opened the final email.

Cam took his time reading this one, as well, and when he finished, he punched the pillow next to him. "This is such garbage. All the CIA had to do was ask anyone who's ever served with the major. Even now nobody in the field believes Denver was conspiring with terrorists."

"Why'd he take off? Why didn't he just face the music and prove his innocence?"

"It's not supposed to work that way, is it? As a suspect, you don't have to prove anything. It's up to the prosecution to come up with the evidence to convict you. I'm guessing Denver recognized a setup when he saw one and figured the fix was in. There's no fighting against that when evidence is fabricated."

"He should've trusted the system." She jutted her chin.

"Really?" He bumped her knee with his own. "Like you did? C'mon, even someone like you knows there are times when the system breaks down and you have to take matters into your own hands."

"Even someone like me." She drummed her fingers on the edge of the laptop.

He cleared his throat. "You know, someone who likes to follow the rules…which is usually a good idea. I'm not knocking it."

"No offense taken. I have my reasons." She shoved the computer from her lap to the coffee table. "I'm just wondering how someone knew to target me."

"The CIA must've investigated the source of the emails. Let me guess. Fake IP address?"

"Yes, which they wrote off as coming from Dreadworm."

"So the sender got a bunch of CIA email addresses from Dreadworm, picked one at random and sent out these lies about Denver? I don't believe that for a minute, do you?"

"No, I think I was specifically targeted, but I don't know why I'm being harassed now. I did what the sender expected and wanted me to do." She shoved at her laptop with the toe of her boot.

"Because somehow they know you still have the emails, and they don't like that." He sat forward and dragged the computer to the edge of the coffee table. "You're not quite the good little soldier they anticipated."

"Serves them right." She grabbed Cam's water glass. "Do you want more water or something else?"

He held up one finger. "Does this LED light on your laptop monitor blink like this all the time?"

She squinted at the blue light at the tip of his finger. "I don't know. I guess so. Doesn't that just mean it's on?"

"Maybe, maybe not." He pulled the computer onto his legs and started clicking around.

"What are you doing?" She wrapped her hands around the glass. "Are you some kind of computer whiz, too?"

"No, but..." He dragged an icon from a system folder onto her desktop and turned toward her, his face tight. "This is a Trojan, and someone's watching you...us, right now through your computer's camera."

Chapter Four

Martha swallowed. Her gaze darted from Cam's blue eyes to the blue eye on her laptop. She snapped shut the computer. "How do you know that?"

"Shutting it solves the problem right this second, but that Trojan's gonna have to be removed from your computer as soon as possible. It's not just computer keystrokes and actions. The person on the other side can see you as long as your laptop is open and powered on."

"Oh my God." She covered her mouth. "I wonder how long this has been going on."

"A tech can probably tell you that by looking at the program. It'll have a date on it."

"But how did you know? How did you know where to look?" The veil of her preconceived notions about Cam Sutton lifted—and she liked what she saw even more. Brawn *and* brains.

"About a year ago, my sister was being stalked." A muscle ticked in his jaw. "It became apparent that her stalker was watching her in her private moments. One of her friends, a real computer geek, came over to inspect her computer. First she watched for the blinking LED, and then she did a search for a common Trojan used to infect the computer and allowing an outside source to gain control of it. I looked for and found that same virus on your laptop."

Martha's mind raced and reeled over the times she'd had her laptop open in her bedroom, not bothering to shut it down. She hugged herself, digging her fingers into her upper arms. "Get it off. Can you get it off?"

"I can delete it. Hell, *you* can delete it, but I don't know if that removes it from everywhere. It's probably best if you take the laptop in or call someone to do it." Cam tapped his chin with his index finger. "I wonder if they could hear us, too."

"At least we were spared that. The microphone on my laptop doesn't work. No sound in. No sound out."

"That's an unexpected bonus." He hunched forward, digging his elbows into his knees. "Whoever was watching you saw me, but at least that person won't know who I am and how I'm connected to Denver."

She handed him the glass and pushed at his solid shoulder. "Put that in the sink or get yourself more. I'm going to open this up and delete that program. Then I'll take my computer in and get the virus removed from everywhere else."

Glass in hand, Cam pushed up from the sofa while Martha flipped open the laptop, keeping her thumb over the camera lens. She gasped and nearly drove her finger through her computer as a parade of skulls and crossbones marched across her display, the word *busted* floating between the grinning teeth.

Cam clinked the glass on the countertop. "What's wrong?"

"Come and look at this. He knows I…you discovered the commandeered camera. He's admitting he's busted."

"Son of a gun." Cam hovered over her shoulder. "Cheeky bastard."

"I wish I could just communicate with him and ask him what he wants. Oh." Martha put her fingers to her lips as her email icon blinked, indicating a new message. "Maybe I can."

"If you open that email, don't click on any links. That's how your computer gets infected. He might be trying to load something even more insidious on your laptop."

"More insidious than a program to take over my camera to spy on me? That would be hard."

"Hold on." He backtracked to the kitchen. "Do you have any masking tape in here?"

"Post-its in the drawer to the right of the dishwasher."

He returned with two pink Post-it notes stuck to his fingertips. He slid a finger beneath the pad of her thumb, covering the eye of the camera with one Post-it and stuck the other on the edge of the first one to hold it in place.

"Go for it."

She opened the email and licked her dry lips.

"'Do you want to…play?'" Cam read the message out loud, which took off its sinister edge and made it sound almost sexy.

Of course, Cam could make anything sound, or look, sexy.

Dragging in a breath, she put her fingers on the keys.

"Wait." He cinched her wrist with his fingers. "What are you going to write back?"

"I'm going to write 'Hell, yes.' What do you think?"

"Shouldn't you ask him what he means? Ask him what he wants? That's what he'd expect out of you. If you agree too quickly, he's going to wonder if he picked the right person for the job."

His thumb pressed against her pulse. Could he feel it throbbing with excitement? She couldn't tell if the buzz claiming her body was coming from the email or Cam's warm touch. Did it matter? The two had mingled in her scattered brain.

Rotating her wrist out of his grasp, she said, "You're right. I'll take it slowly."

She voiced the words as she replied to the email. "'Play what? What do you want? Who are you?'"

She clicked Send and held her breath.

Her heart stuttered when the quick reply came through. She clicked on the email and read it aloud to Cam. "'I'm a patriot.'"

Cam snorted and she continued. "'I'm a patriot. That's all you need to know. You did the right thing. Leave it alone, or you might not like the game.'"

She whipped her head around to face Cam. "He's threatening me."

This time her hands trembled as she held them poised over the keyboard.

Lacing his fingers through hers, Cam pulled her hand away from the computer. "Ask this patriot why he's so nervous if the information he revealed in the emails about Major Denver is true."

"Shouldn't I ask him about his threats? If he's the one who pushed me at the Metro?" She untwined her fingers from his.

"He's not going to give you a direct answer or admit that he tried to harm you, but I'm interested to see his lies about why he wants you to stop digging."

"I haven't even started digging." She puffed at a

strand of hair that had floated across her face, and Cam caught it and tucked it behind her ear.

"He knows you saved the emails and shared them with me." He flicked his finger at the Post-its. "And he knows you're on to him."

"If you say so." As long as he kept finding excuses to touch her, she'd do just about anything he asked. She cleared her throat and her mind, and then typed in Cam's question.

They both jumped when a message showed up in her inbox, but it was an ad for ink cartridges.

"Come on, patriot." She flexed her fingers over the keys. "I think we scared him off."

"Or he's thinking up a good story." Cam stretched his arms over his head before standing up. "I'm going to get more water. Do you want something from the kitchen?"

"No, thanks." She wedged the toes of her boots against the coffee table. "We lost him."

"Do you think my question was too direct?" He called back at her over the running water from the kitchen faucet. "We must've hit a nerve. He wants you to stop because he doesn't want the truth revealed—that the claims in those emails were all bogus."

Instead of an answer, grinning skulls danced across her screen, giving her the chills. "Ugh. He really is just playing games."

Cam returned to the living room and hung over the back of the sofa. "Idiot. I don't think he plans to tell you anything. He does want you to stop snooping though, and he's trying to scare you off."

"All the more reason to continue." She rolled her shoulders in an effort to release the tension bunching her muscles. "Maybe I should turn all this stuff over to the CIA."

"Martha, you committed a crime by making a copy of those emails. Even if you're not prosecuted, you'll lose your job." He reached past her and closed the lid of her laptop on the skulls. "It's not worth it. Do you want to wind up in federal prison?"

"No!" She dumped her computer from her lap to the sofa cushion. "You're right. I'm not telling the CIA a thing."

He drew back at the violence of her exclamation, but she didn't have to explain herself as the key turned in the door.

"Casey's home early." Her eyes wide, Martha watched the door handle turn and released a sigh when Casey crept into the room on tiptoes.

"Oh, you're still up…and *you're* still here."

The reason for Casey's dismay followed her into the room wearing an expensive suit and a sheepish grin. "Sorry to intrude."

"Join the party." Cam spread out his arms and then dropped them to his sides as his invitation was met with silence. "Just kidding. We were just wrapping up."

"Take your time." Casey circled one finger in the air. "Bob and I will be upstairs. Bob, this is my roommate Martha and her friend Cam."

They all managed awkward hellos and goodbyes as Casey led Bob up the stairs of the town house.

When she heard the door click above, Martha made a face. "She usually doesn't bring them home this early. I never have to meet them."

Cam whistled. "I can see why she doesn't."

"Why?"

Jerking his thumb at the ceiling, Cam whispered. "Old Bob up there is Congressman Robert Wentworth from some district down in Florida."

"What? Are you serious? How do you know that?"

"He's on the House Intelligence Committee—and he's married, as far as I remember."

"That makes it doubly worse that they're up there…" She waved a hand toward the staircase and heated up to the roots of her hair. "Why do women go for these married men?"

Martha flicked a glance at Cam's bare left ring finger and let out a little breath. Of course, lots of men didn't wear wedding rings.

"Imprudent of him at the very least." Cam leaned forward and lifted the laptop lid. "Still no communication from the patriot, so I'm going to head back to my hotel. Are you going to be okay?"

"I will be once I power down my computer and stick it in the office tonight."

"How many rooms does this place have?" He raised his eyes to the ceiling.

"Just three bedrooms. I could sublet the other room, but I'd probably go crazy with another roommate." She tucked the laptop under her arm. "Should I…should I call you tomorrow or something?"

"I'll go with you to cleanse your computer. Is that okay?"

More than okay. "Sure."

Cam strode to the kitchen and ripped a Post-it from the pad. He scribbled something on the pink square and then stuck it to the edge of the counter. "My number. Call me when you're ready to roll."

He grabbed his jacket from the back of the chair

and hunched into it. "I'm sure I don't have to tell you to lock your door."

"Nope. I've got that one down. Besides, I have a US congressman upstairs for protection."

"All right, then." Cam stood in the entryway and thrust his hand forward for a shake. "Take care and thanks for trusting me."

She tucked her laptop against her side and took his hand in a firm grip—no nonsense. "Thanks for...rescuing me on the platform and discovering I'd been hacked."

They both released at the same time, and Cam saluted. "All right, then. See ya later."

Martha shut the door behind him and then rested her back against it, hugging her computer to her chest. Had Cam been nervous? Maybe he thought she'd expected a hug or a kiss or something. Did she appear that desperate?

She spun around and threw the locks into place and then launched herself up the stairs. Cam probably hadn't given her much thought at all.

Martha crept past Casey's bedroom door and the low voices murmuring within, and slipped into her own room. At least her master bedroom had a bathroom attached.

Tripping to a stop, she glanced at the laptop in her hands. She didn't want to go into the hallway again, so she made an abrupt turn and stuffed the computer on the floor of her closet under some folded clothes.

She got ready for bed. Several minutes later as she slipped between the covers, her mind was still racing with the day's events.

Casey squealed from somewhere beyond the walls, and Martha burrowed beneath the covers. Her roommate and her lovers always made a lot of noise.

Martha reached into the top drawer of her nightstand for her earplugs and cupped them in her hand as the congressman let out a growl.

Shutting her eyes, Martha closed her fingers around the earplugs. What would Cam sound like in the throes of passion?

Casey yelped, and Martha stuffed the earplugs into her ears as she buried her face in the pillow. One thing she *did* know is that she wouldn't be squeaking and squealing like Casey if she ever did get a chance with Cam.

And with that delicious thought making her shiver, Martha closed her eyes.

What seemed like moments later, Casey's scream punctured Martha's dream state…and her earplugs. She groaned and rolled onto her side.

Didn't the woman have any shame—or self-control?

Casey screamed again, and Martha pulled the pillow over her head, gritting her teeth.

"Martha! Martha!"

The bedroom door burst open, and Martha sat up, the pillow falling from her face. She blinked her eyes at Casey standing in the doorway, a filmy nightgown clutched to her chest. Was she dreaming?

"Martha, wake up. We're in terrible trouble."

"What?" Martha flicked on the light above her bed, and Casey's face looked whiter than it had in the darkness. "What's wrong? What's going on?"

"Oh, Martha." Casey stumbled across the room and

tottered before she dropped to the edge of Martha's bed. "Bob, Congressman Wentworth, is dead in my bed… in your town house."

Chapter Five

Cam glanced at his phone for about the hundredth time that morning. Maybe Martha had decided to get her computer wiped on her own. It's not like she needed him to do it. He didn't know that much about technical stuff, and she probably figured that out about him in a hot minute. She seemed like the self-sufficient type, anyway.

In fact, Martha Drake had a surprising rebellious streak. He never would've guessed she'd be the type to sneak out those emails. The woman had gone rogue—and he was glad she'd decided to do so.

And maybe she was going rogue again by handling the patriot herself. Cam wouldn't put it past her, but he didn't think it was a good idea. What if she'd fallen in front of that train last night? She needed a right-hand man, even if she didn't realize it yet.

He tossed his phone onto the cushion next to him and snatched up the remote. Propping one bare foot on the table in front of him, he clicked over to one of the cable news shows.

He studied the reporters and news vans with a crease forming between his eyebrows. Someone had died, and the street where the buzzing media had gathered looked familiar with all those rows of town houses with shutters and arched windows.

When the words scrolled across the bottom of the screen, Cam choked and his foot slipped from the table. His thumb drilled into the remote to increase the sound.

The reporter breathlessly gushed into the mic. "All we know so far, Carrie, is that Congressman Robert Wentworth, from the Second Congressional District in Florida, died in this town house behind me sometime last night or this morning. There was a 911 call and the DC Metro Police responded. The body has not yet been removed."

Carrie put on a concerned face, but Cam could see the speculative light in her eyes. "Have the police said whether they're looking at foul play here, Stacie?"

"They haven't released any statement yet or talked to reporters."

Cam curled his fingers around the remote and hardly noticed the edges digging into his flesh. The reporter hadn't mentioned anything about anyone else being hurt…or arrested. What the hell had gone down in that town house after he'd left last night?

Cam muted the TV and reached for his phone. Damn that Casey for dragging Martha into her messy life. He stopped, his thumb hovering over the screen. Or was it the other way around?

Could this really be just a coincidence after what Martha had gone through yesterday? What possible connection could Wentworth have to Martha and the emails?

Cam dropped his phone when it hit him that he didn't even have Martha's number. He'd given her his number with the understanding that she'd call him to go with her to fix the laptop. Some understanding. Seemed like he didn't know Martha at all.

He paced the room, juggling his phone from hand to hand, occasionally turning up the TV for more news on the congressman's death. The stiff muscles across his shoulders began to unwind when he didn't see anything about any other injuries or anyone getting taken in for questioning, and then seized up again as Martha had been identified as the owner of the town house.

More than an agonizing hour later, Cam's phone buzzed with a DC number. "Hello?"

"Cam, it's Martha… Martha Drake."

"Yeah, I know. You're kind of famous right now, or at least your town house is. What the hell happened over there?"

"My name's out there, isn't it?"

"Are you worried about your job?"

"I'm worried about a lot of things right now." She sighed. "It looks like the congressman had a heart attack. Casey didn't even realize it until this morning. His body was slumped halfway out of the bed when she woke up."

"A heart attack? Of course, they're gonna do an autopsy before they rule on the cause of death." He wiped a hand across his mouth. "How are you holding up? How's Casey?"

"Casey is hysterical. I'm…nervous."

"Why, Martha?"

"Why do you think?"

"Are you linking this to the emails?"

"Aren't you?" Her voice rose, and for a second she sounded close to hysteria herself.

"Crossed my mind, but I can't see how this can be

related to the emails or how it affects you." He wedged
a shoulder against the window and watched one bare
branch from a tree scrape against the edge of the balcony. "Heart attack, right?"

"Right." She cleared her throat. "We need to talk."

"And clean that computer."

"Don't come anywhere near here. It's a madhouse.
I'll slip out the back and head over to your hotel. The
police are still questioning Casey, poor girl."

He gave her the name of the hotel and the address
before turning up the volume on the TV again. Several reporters were still camped out in front of Martha's town house, and the speculation had begun. Since
Martha owned the town house, the reporters had her
name on their lips.

It wouldn't be long before they dug up the fact that
Martha worked for the CIA, and he hoped it wouldn't
be long before they discovered she hadn't been the one
who'd invited Congressman Wentworth to an after-
hours meeting.

His blood percolated as he listened to the innuendo
linking Martha to Wentworth, but he still couldn't figure out how this had anything to do with the threats
from the patriot.

With the TV still droning in the background, Cam
straightened his hotel room, stuffing clothes back into
his suitcase and shoving toiletries into the plastic bag
hanging from a hook on the bathroom door. He hadn't
needed to see Martha's place last night to figure she'd
be a neat freak, and for some reason he wanted to assure her he wasn't a slob.

He went a few steps further and got a couple cans
of soda from the vending machine down the hall and

stuck them in the mini-fridge. The woman must've had a rough morning.

By the time Martha tapped on his door, Cam had rendered the room acceptable to the neatest of neat freaks.

He opened the door and she barreled past him without even a hello, striding to the sliding door to the balcony.

She turned to face him, twisting her fingers in front of her. "This is bad."

"Tell me what happened." He gestured toward the sofa facing the TV. "Not many details on the news, except that you own the town house where Wentworth croaked."

She perched on the edge of the sofa. "Casey's name will come out. The police are still talking to her."

"At least you won't be portrayed as the other woman for much longer." He yanked the chair back from the desk and straddled it, resting his arms across the back. "Give me all the details."

"After you left, I went to bed and I could hear those two...whooping it up." Two bright spots of red formed on her cheeks. "I have earplugs for just those occasions, and I was able to fall asleep."

"Damn, you need earplugs?" Noticing Martha's pursed lips, he wiped the grin off his face. "Go on. You fell asleep during noisy sex."

"I..." She ran her fingers through her messy hair, dragging it back from her face. "Yes, I fell asleep, and the next thing I knew Casey was in my room hysterical and crying, saying Bob had died sometime during the night."

"What time did she discover him?"

"About six. I ran into her room and felt his neck for

a pulse. He seemed dead to me, but I have no experience in medicine. I called 911 right away."

"The news said possible heart attack, so I'm assuming no blood or visible injuries."

"No." Martha crossed her arms, cupping her elbows. "He was half out of the bed, as if he'd tried to get up but didn't make it."

"Did Casey have anything to say?"

"Not much to me, but the cops were grilling her. They'd met for a drink at a quiet place. Bob wasn't feeling great, and they decided to head back here."

"You'd never met him before? It didn't seem like you had last night."

"No. I'm not saying she's never brought him back to our place, but I usually make myself scarce when she brings guys home, so I'd never met him before."

Cam tugged on his earlobe. "I don't understand why you think some congressman's heart attack is related to you and the emails."

"Who says it's a heart attack?" She jumped up from the sofa and twitched back the drapes at the sliding door, peeked out the window and yanked the drapes back together.

"It could be something else. Poison. He didn't feel well. Or there are drugs out there that mimic heart attacks. Nobody would know the difference and *poof*—" she tried snapping her fingers, failed miserably and flicked them in the air instead "—you're gone."

Cam flattened the smile from his lips and drew his brows together to look concerned instead. He couldn't help it. Even when he listened to Martha talking about murder, he found her irresistibly cute.

"Wait, wait." He held up his hands. "How does that

impact you, unless the patriot plans to frame you for Wentworth's so-called murder...and that's a long shot. How exactly does Casey's illicit affair with a politician affect you and your investigation of the emails?"

"It brings everything back up. It tarnishes me and anything I might have to say about these emails. It's a warning that he can get to me if he wants to." She pulled her bottom lip between her teeth.

"Yeah, okay. It shows he's powerful, although this is a risky way to do that. But—" he frowned for real this time "—what do you mean by bringing everything back up? Finding the emails?"

Her gaze darted to the TV, still humming in the background, and she took two steps toward the coffee table, picked up the remote and aimed it at the TV.

The reporter mentioned Martha's name, and Cam jerked his head toward the TV. A picture of a young Martha with thick glasses and braces stared back at him next to a picture of a gray-haired man, who looked vaguely familiar. He tuned into the reporter's words.

"In a bizarre twist to this story, the owner of the town house is none other than the daughter of convicted stock trader Steven 'Skip' Brockridge, who's currently serving twenty-five years in federal prison for his role in a Ponzi scheme that bilked investors out of millions."

He twisted his head back toward Martha, her arms crossed and shoulders hunched. She raised one hand. "That's me, Martha Brockridge, daughter of a convicted felon."

Cam swallowed. "That's your father, not you. Obviously the CIA already knows about your background. A name change isn't going to throw off the Agency."

"I never tried to throw them off. I was up front about

my father. They knew. I think they even believed that my father's criminal behavior had influenced me to follow the straight and narrow path, and they were right... until now."

Her voice broke at the end, and he jumped up from the chair and took her by the shoulders. He dug his fingers into her tight muscles. "This situation is completely different."

"Maybe, but do you think anyone's going to believe me about the emails now? A convicted felon's daughter?" She shook her head, and the ends of her hair tickled the backs of his hands.

"I doubt the patriot went through all this trouble to discredit or warn you, and the CIA already knows about your father. It didn't stop them from believing you the first time you turned over those emails."

"I don't know what to think. It's hard for me to believe there's no connection between my online conversation with the patriot and the death of Congressman Wentworth."

He blew out a breath. "I don't believe that, either. I don't believe in coincidences, but I can't wrap my mind around his motives."

"You think there might be another reason?"

He smoothed his hands down her arms and released her, stepping back. "How long has Casey been living with you?"

Martha blinked her long lashes. "About eight months."

"You received the emails four months ago, right?"

"You're not implying Casey is involved? That ditz?"

"It could've all been an act. The people who sent you the emails needed someone on the inside, and it would've been too hard to get one of your coworkers to cooperate. How'd that virus get on your laptop? I'm sure the CIA must drill computer security measures into your head and you didn't just click on some random link in an email. Who does that anymore?"

Martha chewed on the edge of her thumb. "I thought maybe he'd used Dreadworm again to get to me."

"How'd you meet Casey?"

"Through one of those roommate finders. She had the money up front—first, last and insisted on a larger security deposit than I'd asked for." She smacked her knee. "I should've trusted my instincts. I thought she was a little too eager."

"Something else about her choice in boyfriends." He straddled the desk chair again just to keep from touching Martha. It felt…manipulative to use her distress to get close to her. She didn't need any more distractions in her life right now, and neither did he.

"Congressman Wentworth?"

"Remember I told you last night I knew him from the House Intelligence Committee? He must have a lot of information on Denver."

She lowered herself to the bed as if in slow motion. "So, this is a twofer for Casey. She moves in to keep an eye on me, and she dates Wentworth to keep an eye on him and Major Denver."

"It makes sense that a lot of that stuff about Denver came from an inside source." Cam's anger at the injustice of Denver's situation burned in his gut. He crouched to grab the sodas from the fridge, cracked one open and took a long swig from the can. He held the other out to Martha, and she shook her head.

Tucking one leg beneath her on the bed, she said,

"We're just guessing. How are we going to prove any of this?"

"Let's start with Casey. Where was she when you left?"

"She was still with the police."

"She'd admitted to the affair?"

"Of course. What other explanation could she give?"

"It's odd." Cam smoothed a hand across his freshly shaved jaw. "Why risk such public exposure? If Wentworth had served his purpose and they wanted to get rid of him, and maybe scare you in the process, why do it so publicly? They could've killed him without dragging Casey into the picture."

"You're asking me?" She jabbed a finger at her chest. "I still don't even know what the patriot wants of me, and I hate calling him that since he's clearly not one."

"I think he wants you to stop thinking about those emails for one thing and delete them. He wants you to drop your investigation."

"It's hardly an investigation, but I'm not dropping anything. People can't just get away with things." She pointed to her laptop case propped up against the wall by the door. "I called a computer repair place, and the guy told me to bring the laptop in today."

"You know this tech guy?" Cam stood up and stretched.

He didn't know how much longer he could be cooped up with Martha in this small room, anyway. He always had these instant attractions to women, and those never ended well, although Martha wasn't his usual type so maybe he'd learned a few lessons.

Her gaze flicked over his body as he reached for the ceiling, and then she took off her glasses and wiped the lenses with a corner of the bedspread. "He's worked on my computer before. He's good."

When she'd been checking him out, he'd had the crazy idea to flex and show off for her, but a woman like Martha would probably laugh at that. All the smart girls in school had him pegged as a meathead jock who couldn't even read. So he'd gravitated toward the pretty cheerleaders who only cared if he could read their flirtatious signals. He'd gotten good at that.

Coughing, he loped toward her laptop and hooked the case over his shoulder. "Have you checked your messages this morning for anything from the patriot?"

"It's one of the first things I did this morning after checking on Wentworth and calling 911—nothing."

He hunched the shoulder with the strap over it. "I'd find it hard to believe, but maybe this really is all a co-incidence."

"You're right. Too hard to believe." She bounded off the bed. "My car's valet parked. We'll take that."

MARTHA DROVE HER hybrid like she did everything else—carefully and precisely. Cam felt like he'd wandered into the middle of a drivers' training video.

When she'd lined up the car perfectly between the white lines of a parking space in a mini-mall, she cut the engine and glanced at his profile. "What?"

"What, what?"

"Why are you grinning like that?"

"Nice parking job."

She huffed through her nose and swung open her car door.

The computer tech in the store didn't blink an eye when Martha walked up to the counter. He either hadn't seen the news yet about Congressman Wentworth croaking in Martha's town house, or he was trying to be polite.

Martha plunked her laptop on the counter and spun it around to face the techie. "Hi, Marcel. I've been hacked, invaded, compromised, whatever you want to call it."

"Ooh, a Trojan?" Marcel flipped up the lid and widened his eyes when he saw the Post-its blocking the camera. "Dude got to your camera?"

"Yes, he's been watching me." Martha wrinkled her nose. "So creepy."

"And pretty sophisticated." Marcel stuck some tape over the camera lens and plucked off the Post-its. "Any idea who your stalker is?"

"No. Just get rid of it." Martha gripped the edge of the counter. "You can, can't you?"

"Oh, yeah." He nodded toward a computer in the corner humming through some diagnostics. "I'm working on that one, but I can get yours started. You can wait. There's a pretty good Thai place two doors down."

"That sounds good. I'm starving." Martha's gaze darted to Cam's face. "I mean, if you want to get something to eat while we wait."

"Absolutely." Cam peeked out the window through the blinds. "It's already getting dark. I had breakfast at the hotel but completely skipped lunch."

"I guess that's settled." She turned to Marcel, waving a slip of paper. "Do you need my password?"

"Honestly, I can get past it, but I'll do it on the up-and-up." He took the paper from her between his two fingers and lifted the laptop from the counter to take it to a station in the back of the shop.

Cam beat Martha to the door and opened it for her.

"The restaurant is to the right. I noticed it when we drove into the parking lot. I already knew I was hungry."

She stuffed her hands into her pockets as she headed into the blustery wind, listing to the side.

"Are you going to get swept off your feet?" Cam placed a hand on her arm.

"No." She dropped her eyes to his hand, and he released her.

"For a minute there I thought you were going to take off with the wind." He felt like he needed some kind of excuse for touching her again.

When they entered the empty restaurant, the waitress on the phone behind the counter waved them into one of a dozen tables scattered around the room.

"I guess we're too late for lunch and too early for dinner." Martha shed her coat and folded it onto a chair at a table by the window.

Ten minutes later, they waited for their food while Martha blew on her hot tea and Cam tipped his beer into a glass. "That must've been rough on you when your father was arrested. You were a teenager?"

"Yes. It couldn't have happened at a worse time."

"Yeah, those awkward teen years, and then you have to deal with notoriety on top of it all."

Her eyes met his briefly and then seemed to search his face before moving in a slow inventory down his neck, chest, across his shoulders and down his arms.

Her study of him felt like a caress, exploratory and featherlight.

Then her brows snapped over her nose. "*You* had awkward teen years? Not likely."

He smiled and his jaw ached with the effort. "We

all have our issues. What was your father's crime? Securities fraud?"

"Something like that." She waved her hand. "It's confusing, but it boiled down to cheating and scamming. He was always good at that."

"How long is he in for?"

"He's been in for ten, and he's eligible for parole in about five more."

"Do you see him?"

"Occasionally."

"He must've made good money—legitimately—at one time."

"He did quite well for a number of years. I did the whole private school thing, and when I started showing an aptitude for languages, he arranged for language schools and tutoring."

"He must've been proud of you."

"The feeling was not mutual." She rubbed the back of her hand across her nose. "What about you? Where are you from? How long have you been in the military?"

"I enlisted when I was nineteen, after one year in college playing football." He tapped his glass and watched the bubbles rise and try to break through the thick head of foam blocking their escape.

One disastrous year when he couldn't keep up academically, no matter how many tutors the coaches sent his way, and flunked out, losing his football scholarship. "Yeah, the military was a good fit, and it didn't take long before Delta Force started looking my way."

"You must be something special. That's an elite unit."

"It suits me."

The waitress interrupted them with several plates

of steaming food, and as Martha removed her glasses, Cam raised his eyebrows.

"The food is fogging up my lenses."

Martha looked cute in glasses, but without them her eyes mesmerized him as they seemed to shift in color and glow like a cat's in the low light.

The soft pink that crept into her cheeks gave him a jolt. He was staring at her like an idiot. She probably dated educated guys with multiple degrees and witty conversation.

"Do you want some rice?" He held up the round container of sticky white rice. *Real witty, Cam.*

For the rest of the meal, they danced around each other, sharing little bits of information about themselves. Cam took his cues from Martha, skimming across the surface of his life and allowing her to fill in the blanks.

He tried to fill in her blanks, too, but she'd perfected the art of the dodge. Maybe she'd learned that from her old man, even though she seemed to reject everything he stood for.

Her cell phone buzzed on the table beside her plate, and she flicked a grain of rice from its display before she tapped it. Her lips pursed as she read the text. "You're not going to believe this."

Cam's pulse jumped. "What? It's not the patriot, is it?"

"No, it's Casey. She wants to meet me—away from the town house. She has a lot of nerve."

"You're not meeting her alone." Cam pushed his empty plate to the middle of the table. "She might be involved in Wentworth's death up to her eyeballs."

"She says she wants to apologize and discuss moving out. She doesn't want to go back to the town house now that she's been outed as Wentworth's mistress."

"Where is she?"

"At a hotel not far from yours." Martha tapped her phone to reply to Casey's text.

"She wants to see you now?"

"As soon as I can get over there."

Cam checked the time on his own phone. "Let's pick up your computer before the shop closes, and then we'll head over there—together."

"I told her to give me an hour." She grabbed her glasses and put them on, peering at him through the lenses. "You're serious? You're coming with me?"

"Like I said—" he reached for his wallet "—I don't trust that woman. And don't tell her I'm coming along. We'll surprise her."

"I didn't mention you, but I still think you're wrong. Casey is too flakey to be some international spy." She plunged her hand into her purse and withdrew her wallet.

Cam's gaze dipped to Martha's hand, pulling out some cash, and he swallowed. No woman he ever dated expected to pay, not that he'd allow it, but this really wasn't a date, and a woman like Martha might be offended if he insisted on paying.

He waved the check. "Uh, fifteen bucks each, but I'll throw in twenty since I had the beer and you had tea."

"Whatever." She tossed a ten and a five onto the table. "I'll pitch in for your beer in exchange for your protection…from Casey. She might poke me with her stiletto or shoot me in the face with hairspray."

"Go ahead and scoff. Congressman Wentworth trusted her and look where that got *him*."

They walked back to the computer store and picked up Martha's newly cleansed laptop. She did a quick check of her emails before putting it away.

As Cam stashed the computer case in the trunk of her car, Martha said, "Now if the patriot wants to contact me about Wentworth's death, he'll have to find another method."

"If he really wants to contact you again, he will. He already has your email address. He doesn't need to watch you."

Martha drove back into DC toward a hotel a few blocks away from his own. She paid for guest parking in the structure beneath the hotel, and they rode up in the elevator to the fifth floor.

As the doors opened and they stepped onto the thick carpet, Martha whispered, "Maybe she wants to tell me what really happened to Wentworth."

"If she didn't tell you in the time you two were waiting for the ambulance, why would she be coming clean now?"

She shrugged, and they turned the corner in the direction of Casey's room. Cam trailed behind Martha just in case his appearance in the peephole scared off the woman.

But he didn't have to worry about a peephole. Casey had propped open the hotel door with the latch, wedging it between the door and the jamb.

Martha raised her brows at him as she knocked on the door and called out. "Casey?"

No response.

"Maybe she stepped out and wanted to leave the door open for me." Martha placed her hand flat against the door. "Casey? It's Martha."

A tingle raced across the back of Cam's neck, and he pulled his gun from his pocket.

Martha jerked back when she saw it. "What are you doing? Where'd that come from?"

"My pocket." He put a finger to his lips. "Shh."

As Martha pushed open the hotel door, Cam followed closely on her heels. Nothing about this felt right. He flicked the lever back and pulled the door closed.

A lamp in the corner illuminated the empty space, a suitcase open on the bed, a curtain billowing into the room from the open door to the balcony.

"Casey?" Martha crept to the closed bathroom door and pushed down on the handle, swinging it open.

Cam hovered behind her.

Martha gasped and choked. She stumbled against him.

He caught her around the waist and peered over her shoulder.

His gut churned as he took in the sight of Casey in a tub of red-tinted water, one hand hanging over the side, pointing at the pool of blood on the tile floor.

Chapter Six

All at once, the smell flooded Martha's nostrils, the metallic taste filling her mouth. She gagged.

Cam dragged her backward out of the bathroom and propped her against the wall while he dashed toward the sliding glass door, his weapon raised.

She blinked and slid down the wall, her legs crumpling beneath her. Where was he going? Was he cold? She was cold. A ferocious shiver had gripped her body, making her teeth chatter and her hands shake.

The cold had crept into her limbs and she couldn't move them, couldn't get up. Cam had left her, had disappeared out the sliding glass door, had left her alone with… Casey.

Oh, God. Maybe Casey wasn't dead.

It took all Martha's concentration to hunch forward onto her hands and knees and turn toward the open bathroom door, but she remained rooted to the carpet, rocking back and forth like a baby learning to crawl.

"Martha!" Cam scooped her up as easily as if she were a baby and wrapped his arms around her, holding her back against his front.

"You don't need to go back in there. Casey's dead."

"H-how can you know?"

"The blood, the…" He walked backward, towing her along with him, and settled her on the edge of the bed. "Stay here. I'll check."

As Cam left her again, her knees began bouncing up and down. She clasped her hands over them and pressed down, digging her heels into the carpet.

Cam returned and crouched in front of her, taking her stiff hands in his. "She's gone."

"Did she drown? I don't understand. Did she slip and fall? Where did all that blood come from?" Her voice began to rise, and she clamped a hand over her mouth to stop the panic burgeoning in her chest.

Cam brought her hands to his lips and kissed her knuckles. "She slit her wrists, Martha."

"No. Oh, no." She shook her head back and forth so hard, her glasses slipped down her nose.

"We have to call 911 and the hotel." Cam pocketed his gun, pulled his sleeve over his hand and picked up the room's telephone.

He murmured into the receiver, hung up and placed another call. Then he walked to the door of the room and wedged it open the same way Casey had left it for her.

Martha watched all his actions, the fog starting to lift from her brain. Casey was dead in the bathtub—a suicide.

Minutes later, a hotel security guard and a hotel manager burst through the door.

Cam pointed to the bathroom. "She's in there. I already called 911."

The two hotel employees crowded at the bathroom door, and the manager screamed, "Oh my God!"

Cam pulled Martha up from the bed and wrapped

her in a hug. He whispered in her ear, "Are you okay? Still in shock?"

Her lips moved against the rough material of his shirt, but she didn't make a sound. She cleared her throat and tried again. "Why would she do that?"

He squeezed her tighter and she closed her eyes, breathing in the scent of him. She never wanted to leave this safe place.

All too soon, the police and EMTs surged into the room and the questions started.

Of course the police had heard of Casey Jessup, the DC intern who'd been too hot for the congressman to handle.

They questioned Martha about her presence here at the hotel, Casey's demeanor, her motives. They hauled some booze and pills out of the bathroom, items Martha hadn't even noticed.

Cam handled everything calmly and confidently, subtly protecting her by moving closer whenever the cop's questioning veered toward the intrusive.

After what seemed like hours, the nightmare finally wound down. Casey's body was still in the bathroom, but the police were letting them leave. The officer had her number and would call if they had any more questions or needed to visit the town house and search Casey's things.

She and Cam said nothing as they walked out of the room, but he entwined his fingers with hers on the way to the elevator. When the doors of the car closed behind them, he let out a long breath.

"I'm sorry you had to go through all that, sorry you had to stay in that room. I would've hustled you out of there and made an anonymous 911 call, but I'm sure the hotel has cameras that would've caught our arrival and departure, and the cops may even be checking Casey's cell and would've identified that text going to your phone number."

He'd released her hand, and she threw it out now to brace against the mirrored back of the elevator car. "We couldn't have left. We found her. Th-that's like leaving the scene of a crime."

"A crime?" He stabbed at the elevator button again.

"Technically, suicide is a crime, isn't it?" She sagged against the elevator wall and twitched when it landed in the parking garage.

As they exited onto their level, Cam held out his hand, palm up. "I'll drive. You're still shaken up."

Biting her bottom lip, Martha rummaged through her purse and pulled out her key chain. She dropped the keys into his hand, and he opened the passenger door for her.

She plopped onto the seat and snapped her seat belt, keeping a tight hold on the shoulder strap. When Cam slid behind the wheel and started the engine, she turned to him. "Why did you go outside to the balcony? What were you doing out there?"

"Why'd she leave that door open?"

"Maybe she was enjoying a last breath of fresh air."

"The police think she may have taken an overdose of pills with some alcohol for good measure. Did she think slicing her wrists in the bathtub wasn't going to do the trick?"

"What did you see on the balcony?" Martha trapped her hands between her knees and trapped the air in her lungs as she held her breath.

"A way out."

"Do you think someone else was in that room?"

"Why did Casey text you? We were there an hour later. You're telling me she drank that vodka, took those pills, climbed into the bath and slit her wrists all before we got there?"

Martha spoke up over the roar building in her head. "She drank the booze and popped the pills before she contacted me. She thought maybe I'd get here before she was dead, so she decided to speed up the process."

"Why would she do that, notify you, I mean? The two of you weren't even close." He hunched over the steering wheel, crossing his arms on top of it. "I could see that original text. She didn't want to go back to the town house and wanted to give you some kind of notice that she was moving out. Maybe she even wanted you to help her out by packing up her stuff and shipping it to her. But why would she want you here at her death?"

Martha lifted her shoulders to her ears and held them there. "She didn't want a loved one or a close friend to find her, but she wanted *someone* to find her."

"Do you really believe Casey was so distraught over Wentworth's death that she offed herself in commiseration? If anything, a girl like that would've relished the attention, gotten a book deal, landed on reality TV. You told me that's what she was all about."

Martha rested her head against the cool glass of the window. "You think she had help. You think she was murdered."

"C'mon, Martha. Use that logical mind of yours— emails, threats, a dead congressman in your place and now Casey's so-called suicide. All coincidence?"

"It all seems so random."

"It does, but I guarantee you, it's not. This is all connected somehow."

"Do you think the police will figure it out? What about those hotel cameras? If they would've caught us, they would've caught Casey's…killer."

"Unless he snuck over that balcony or disabled the cameras."

"I'm scared, Cam."

He reached over and squeezed her knee. "Get rid of those emails. Forget this whole thing."

"What about Major Denver?"

"We'll figure out a way to help him. Hell, he's probably helping himself."

"Oh, no." Martha pressed her nose to the window and took in the reporters still hovering on the sidewalk outside her place. Her breath fogged the glass. "I can't go through that. Wait until they find out this latest news."

Cam ducked his head and swore. "Vultures. Don't they have more important stories to report on? Is there a back way into your place?"

"They discovered it already." She tucked her hands beneath her thighs. She didn't want to be alone in that town house. Didn't want to leave Cam.

"You should stay in a hotel tonight." Cam flexed his fingers on the steering wheel. "If you want, you can stay in my room."

"That would be great…if you really don't mind." Had she just guilted him into that invitation? Did he see her as the poor, little friendless nerd? "I mean, I can call a friend if it's too much trouble."

The car lurched forward, and he squealed away from the curb. "I think it's better if you stay with someone who knows what's going on right now—someone with a gun."

She twisted her head to the side. "You really think I'm in danger."

"Martha, I don't want to freak you out right now, but I have my doubts that Casey killed herself. I have my doubts she even texted you."

"That balcony. You think someone was waiting for me out there?"

"I think he heard us talking at the door. He wasn't expecting you to have company, so he took off." Cam flicked on the wipers and rubbed the inside of the windshield with his fist.

"He could've shot me…us as soon as we walked into the room." She watched a drip of water on the outside of the window join up with another one and then another to form a little stream.

"Who said he had a gun? Who said he wanted to kill you? We don't know what the patriot wants."

"According to you, he killed Casey. Why would he do that?"

"She knew too much."

"I know more than she does."

"She knew the right things." He swung into the driveway in front of his hotel and left the keys with the valet.

As they entered the lobby, Cam pointed to the gift shop next to the elevators. "Do you want to pick up a toothbrush and whatever else you might need?"

After her shopping spree, Martha dangled the plastic bag from her fingers as she and Cam made their way to his room. She'd rushed here this afternoon convinced Wentworth's death had something to do with the emails about Denver. Now another death had been added to the mix, and she wasn't sure about anything anymore—except Cam.

He had her back—whether from pity or his strong desire to use those emails to clear Major Denver, she didn't know and she didn't care. She'd bask in the safety of the protective aura that wafted around him.

He opened the hotel door for her and gestured her through. "Sorry it's not a suite, just the one room. You can take the bed and I'll camp out on the sofa."

Her gaze swept the length of the truncated sofa—almost a love seat—and then scanned Cam head to toe. "You're not going to fit on that thing. I'll sleep there."

"I've slept on worse than that." He held up one finger. "Don't argue with me."

She raised her eyebrows. "I hadn't planned on it. I'll take the bed, and you don't have to twist my arm. And I'll even lay claim to the bathroom first."

"Be my guest." He dragged a pillow from the bed. "I will take one of these."

"Be *my* guest." She twirled the plastic bag of toiletries around her finger and tripped to a stop at the bathroom door. "Do you have a T-shirt or something I can wear to bed?"

"The ones in the closet are all clean. Help yourself."

Martha reached into the closet and yanked a gray T-shirt from a hanger. She made for the bathroom and closed and locked the door behind her—not that she expected Cam to make a raid on the bathroom while she was in here undressing.

Bracing her hands on the vanity, she hunched toward the mirror. Her flushed cheeks and bright eyes were signals of the adrenaline that had been pumping through her system nonstop all day as she bounced from one crazy event to the next.

At the end of it all she'd wound up in the hotel room of this hot Delta Force D-Boy, who had zero expectations of her. And why would he? She'd helped guys like this with their homework and papers many times in college, and they'd never demanded anything from her except the guarantee that she'd help them again.

She let out a long breath and brushed her teeth. She took off all her clothes except for her bra and underwear, and pulled the T-shirt over her head.

Cam's extra-large T-shirt billowed around her tall, thin frame, hitting her midthigh. It would sweep a tinier woman's knees, but she'd never been a tiny person. Tall, gawky and awkward had marked her teen years.

She folded her clothes into a neat pile. Clutching the bundle to her chest, she crept back into the room.

Cam jerked his head up and jabbed at the TV remote, but not before she heard Congressman Wentworth's and Casey's names.

She placed her clothes on a vacant chair. "They're on that like a pack of dogs on a rabbit's scent."

"Until the next scandal breaks." He tossed the remote onto the bed. "Did you have everything you needed in there?"

"I did. Your turn."

As Cam disappeared into the bathroom, Martha turned on the TV but skipped all the news channels. She *was* the news for the second time in her life. She didn't have to watch it. Settling on a nature show, she bunched the pillows behind her and settled back.

Ten minutes into the program, Cam eased open the

bathroom door and poked his head around the corner. "Are you still awake?"

"After the day I just had, I'm wired. I'm going to need a few more hours of watching plants grow in fast-motion before I can even think about sleeping."

He stopped in front of the TV and shook his head. "That would put anyone to sleep."

He turned off the lone light in the room, the tall lamp next to the sofa, and grabbed the hem of the white T-shirt he'd been wearing beneath his denim shirt, pull-ing it up.

Martha got a quick glimpse of his six-pack, illumi-nated by the blue light from the flickering images on TV, before he pulled the T-shirt over his head and she averted her eyes.

As he unbuckled his belt, she shoved her glasses up the bridge of her nose and studied the insects hatching on the screen. And she hated insects.

Yanking down his jeans, Cam turned his back to her and she turned her gaze onto him. His pants dropped down his powerful thighs, and Martha swallowed at the sight of his muscled buttocks in the black briefs.

He kicked his jeans into a corner and then shot her a look over his shoulder.

She cleared her throat and pulled a pillow into her lap. Had he caught her watching him undress?

"Guess I should try to keep the room neater with two people in here."

She waved her hand. "Do whatever you'd normally do."

He walked to the discarded jeans and picked them up. As he draped them over the back of a chair, he said, "I don't think you mean that."

"Sure I do. I don't want to upset your routine."

He cocked his head. "Really? 'Cause I usually bunk in the buff."

A flood of warmth washed into her cheeks. "I—I mean, if that's what you…"

He held up his hands and flashed that boyish grin that pretty much did her in. "Don't worry. I'm not a perv."

What if she admitted she wouldn't mind one bit if he stripped down completely?

"And I'm not a complete prude, you know."

"Prude? I never thought you were." He crawled into the bed he'd made from the sofa, propping his head on the arm of it. "What did I miss?"

"We don't have to watch this if you don't want." She held out the remote into the space between bed and sofa. "Just no news."

"As long as we're both awake, how about you mute this fascinating look at mating insects and we talk instead?"

She squinted at the image on the TV. "Is that what they're doing? I think they're just eating."

"Whatever. Can we talk about what happened today? I know you think Casey was too stupid to be involved, but I think you're wrong."

"Stupid? I didn't mean to imply that Casey was stupid. She's flakey. *Was* flakey." Martha pulled her knees to her chest with one arm.

"Maybe flakey Casey was putting on an act, or maybe they used her, used her flakiness."

"You mean perhaps she was a legit roommate and they got to her *because* she was my roommate, instead setting her up to be my roommate?" Martha rolled her head to the side to face Cam, resting her cheek on her knee.

"That's exactly what I mean." He curled one arm behind his head, bunching up his biceps. "She moved in with you, and they approached her with an offer."

"And Congressman Wentworth? How does he fit into the picture?"

"Maybe once they had her hooked, they told her to target him. She was a beautiful woman. Wentworth already had a rep for inappropriate sexting. It wouldn't have taken much for a girl like Casey to get her claws into him."

Of course, he'd noticed Casey's attractiveness. Had he compared her to her sexy roommate and found her wanting? Her sexy, *dead* roommate.

Martha drew her bottom lip between her teeth. "Do you think they killed her to tie up loose ends? To keep her from talking?"

"Those would be a couple of reasons."

"Why would they, or *he* if we're just talking about the patriot, want to lure me to Casey's hotel room to discover her body?" Martha stretched out her legs, pulling the pillow up to her chin. "Another warning? They got what they wanted from me originally. I turned over those emails to the proper authorities. Now they want me to leave well enough alone. That's the only motive I can figure out."

"It's a strong motive." Cam yawned and slid farther beneath his blanket. "So, why don't you?"

"Leave it alone?" She clicked off the TV and rolled to her side. "Maybe I will."

Of course, if she deleted the emails and let the patriot

know what she'd done and put all her efforts back into her job at the Agency, she'd never see Cam Sutton again.

And she didn't know if she could give him up just yet, danger or not.

THE FOLLOWING MORNING, Martha sat up and squinted against the weak wintry light slipping through the drapes.

Cam yanked them closed. "Sorry."

"That's okay. What time is it?"

"Almost seven. You can go back to sleep if you want. You had a long day yesterday that turned into a longer night."

"I'm awake." She eyed his fully dressed form by the window and rubbed her eyes. And her dream had ended. "It might actually be a good time to drop by my town house and collect a few things. The press might still be sleeping, or maybe some celebrity couple got a divorce overnight and Wentworth and Casey are no longer the hot news."

"Collect your things?"

Cam's gaze darted wildly around the room as if assessing how all her stuff was going to fit in here.

"Don't worry." She whipped back the bedcovers and swung her legs over the side of the bed, tugging on the T-shirt with one hand. "I'm not moving in here. I can relocate to my mom's place."

"Where's that?"

"Maryland."

"She lives here, and you haven't called her yet with all this going on?"

"Her house is here. She's in Florida with her new husband."

"Has she called you? She must've heard about Wentworth dying in your town house—even in Florida."

"She texted me, asked if I was okay and went on with her life."

"She's all right with you relocating to her house?"

"She suggested it." Martha jerked her thumb over her shoulder. "I'm going to shower here."

"Do you want breakfast before we leave?"

"No." Her head jerked up. "We?"

"I'm not letting you back into that lion's den by your-self. You can collect your stuff, drop me off here and hole up in your mother's house." He whipped open the drapes. "And think about letting this go."

She nodded before ensconcing herself in the bath-room. She showered and dressed in record time. The sooner she got away from Cam, the easier it would be to forget about him whether she wanted to or not. And she didn't want to.

She snorted softly as she turned her back to the warm spray from the showerhead. There was going to be noth-ing easy about getting Cam out of her mind.

An hour later, she drove up to her place, Cam in the passenger seat beside her. One news truck had taken up residence across the street, but the hordes of report-ers and cameras had taken a break.

"We're in luck." She parallel parked half a block down from her place. She kept her head down as Cam took her hand and pulled her along quickly to her front door.

As she used her key to open the door, she sucked in a breath. "I need to get Casey's extra key from its hid-ing place before I leave."

Cam followed her closely into the town house. "That's risky, keeping a key like that. I hope it's not under the welcome mat."

"No. It's a good hiding place." She dropped her key chain into her purse and hung it on a peg by the front door. "Casey was always forgetting her keys or losing them, so I stashed an extra for her just in case."

Cam surveyed the room. "At least the police didn't designate this as a crime scene."

"They did search Casey's bedroom and bathroom, but there were no injuries on Wentworth's body, no evidence of foul play. Looked like a heart attack, but we both know there are ways to mimic that with a drug."

"We'll let the police figure that out. Pack up and let's get out of here before the hyenas gather."

"I thought they were vultures…" She put her foot on the bottom step of the staircase and turned. "You can help yourself to whatever if you're hungry."

"I plan to buy you breakfast." He nodded toward the TV. "I am going to take a look at the news though."

"Knock yourself out. I won't be long."

Once in her room, Martha rolled a suitcase from the closet and started packing for her workweek. What would Gage have to say to her about this weekend?

She hadn't done anything to jeopardize her security clearance—at least nothing Gage knew about.

She finished up with her toiletries from the bathroom and even threw in a couple pairs of disposable contacts. She wore them occasionally, even though they dried out her eyes by the end of the day. Wanting to wear contacts had nothing to do with Cam.

She'd dragged her suitcase into the hall and rolled it to the top of the staircase when Cam came bounding up the stairs.

"I'll help you with that." He picked it up by the

handle and carried it down as if it were empty. "Is that everything?"

"What I don't have, I can come back for or buy. Mom has more than enough at her place."

She plucked her purse from the peg and balanced it on top of her suitcase. "I'm just going to get that key, and I'll be ready. Have the vultures started circling yet?"

Standing to the side of the bay window in the front, Cam peeked through a gap in the drapes. "Nope. I'll come with you to get the key."

"It's out back in the garden." She crossed through the kitchen and turned the dead bolt on the back door.

She stepped onto the pavers, kept dry from the recent rains by an awning over the patio. Then she crouched next to a patio chair with a plastic cover and pulled back the zipper on the cover about an inch. She shoved two fingers inside, probing.

When she found the key, it had some paper wrapped around it. "This is weird. Maybe it's the tag from the chair cover."

Cam kneeled beside her. "Did you find the key?"

"I did, but there's some paper wrapped around it." She pinched the key and the paper between two fingers and pulled it out.

She tipped the key into her palm and unwrapped the scrap of paper. Her heart flipped in her chest and she gasped. "She knew. She left me a note. Casey left me a note."

"What does it say?"

Martha read the words from the slip of paper that shook in her hand. "'If anything happens to me, talk to Tony.'"

Chapter Seven

Cam caught Martha's shoulder as she started to tip over. She'd almost been clear of this mess.

"Who the hell is Tony?"

Martha pressed her fingertips to her temples. "I'm not sure. There have so many men since Casey moved in. Tony. Tony."

The rain started up again, pinging the fiberglass awning above them. He took Martha's arm. "Put that away and let's get out of here."

Martha shoved the note and key in her pocket and turned toward the town house.

While she locked up, Cam flicked the edge of the drapes aside and peered out. "They're back. Get ready to do the duck and dodge."

She grabbed her purse from the top of her suitcase and slung it over her shoulder. "Maybe I can use my suitcase as a battering ram through the crowd."

"Don't worry about your bag. I'll handle that. Just put your head down and make a beeline to the car."

They faced the front door, and as he grabbed the handle Martha put a hand on his wrist. "Thanks for helping me out, Cam."

"Since I kinda got you into this mess, it's the least I can do."

"Even if you hadn't shown up when you did, this patriot person would've still taken these actions. Maybe I would've been dead beneath the wheels of that oncoming train two nights ago."

"I'm glad you're not." He pressed a kiss on her forehead and opened the front door.

The media sensed movement, smelled blood and swarmed around the front porch. They shouted Martha's name, Casey's name, Wentworth's name. Cam couldn't make out any of the questions—not that Martha would be answering them anyway.

He put his arm around her shoulders and charged down the sidewalk to her car, dragging the suitcase behind him. He breathed into her ear, "Get in the driver's seat and start the engine. As soon as I get in the car, take off."

Martha hurried to the car, ten feet away, and unlocked the doors. She scurried around to the driver's side, and Cam lifted the lid of the trunk and swung the suitcase inside. As he slammed it shut, she started the car.

He strode to the front passenger door, and someone touched his back. "Who are you? Martha's boyfriend?"

Cam growled, "I wish," and slammed the door in the reporter's face.

"Hit it."

She peeled away from the curb, her eyes on the rearview mirror. "Don't they ever get tired? What do they hope to gain from sitting in front of a building?"

"They just got it—a shot of you hauling your suitcase out of there." He clicked his seat belt in place.

"What about Casey's family. Do you know if they've been notified?"

"The police contacted her mother and sister last night. I've never met them. Casey never talked about her family, but I told the police to give them my contact information when they get to town and I'll let them into the house." She hunched her shoulders. "What awful news."

"And now we know it's murder."

"We should tell the police, give them the note."

"Do you think Tony's going to be willing to talk to the police? Do you think he wants to expose Casey if she'd been doing something illegal?" He rubbed his eyes. "That's if we can even figure out who he is."

"I know who Tony is."

"You do?"

"I remembered when we were running down the sidewalk. He's a bartender. Through all the guys, he's pretty much been a constant fixture."

"Last name?"

"I don't know, but he works at a bar in Georgetown. I'd just need to call to see if he's working tonight."

Her phone buzzed in the cupholder where she'd stashed it, and Cam glanced at the display. "It's the DC Metro Police. Do you want to answer it?"

"Yeah. Speaker."

He tapped the phone for her and put it on Speaker. "Hello?"

"Ms. Drake, this is Detective Merchant with DC Metro. I have a couple of questions for you about Ms. Jessup."

"Go ahead. I'll try to help." She raised her brows at Cam.

"Have you been back to the town house you shared with Ms. Jessup?"

"I have."

"Did she leave a suicide note there or any indication what she was planning? We didn't find any notes at the hotel."

"No notes."

Her jaw tightened, and Cam knew what it cost her to lie to the police.

"Also, do you know what keys she had on her key chain?"

"No. Why do you ask?"

"We didn't find a key chain or any keys at all in her personal belongings or in her purse—just her wallet, some makeup, her cell phone. Did she have a car?"

"No car, but that seems weird she didn't have her house key, at least." Martha turned her head to meet Cam's gaze.

The officer cleared his throat. "Not so strange if she wasn't planning to return to the town house."

"Y-you're right. Do you know if her family is coming to DC to collect her personal items?"

"They'll be in touch and so will we. That's all for now, Ms. Drake."

"Okay, thanks."

Cam ended the call for her. "That's not good, Martha."

"The keys?"

"Exactly. Who has them? Maybe those attack reporters staking out your place saved you from an unwanted visitor last night. If the person who killed Casey took her key, he now has easy access to your place... and you."

"I'll get the locks changed."

"Good idea." He patted his growling stomach. "How about that breakfast I promised you?"

"I don't feel like going out. We can eat at my mom's place if we stop for some groceries on the way. Is that okay with you?"

He tipped his head. "Are you worried about being followed by the patriot, or you're afraid people will recognize you from TV?"

"Do you think he's following me?" She grabbed the rearview mirror and adjusted it.

"I've been watching." He rapped his knuckle on the window toward his own mirror. "Nobody has been following us, not even the press."

Slumping back in her seat, she said, "I just don't want people staring at me. I had enough of that when my dad was arrested."

"I'm more than happy to eat a home-cooked breakfast at your mom's, but I don't think you have to worry about people recognizing you. That picture the reporters keep flashing of you on TV must've been from a while ago." His gaze lingered on her face and hair. "You look different."

"That picture was from my late teenage years, years I just wanted to disappear."

"I can see that from the picture. You wore bigger glasses, baggy clothes and your hair practically covered your face." He reached out and tucked a loose strand of hair behind her ear, his fingers hovering at her earlobe. "I like it this way better—where I can see your face…your eyes."

She coughed and pinned her shoulders against the

seat. "Maybe my appearance won't inspire a paparazzi frenzy, but I'd still rather eat in."

"You got it." He dropped his hand. "I'll even cook, if you like something simple like bacon and eggs."

"Simple? Bagels and toast are about the most complex I get in the morning. You know how to cook?"

"I know the basics."

"I'm impressed."

Cam lifted his chin and smiled. He couldn't help it if Martha's praise stoked his ego. Somehow meeting this woman's approval had become a priority for him.

After a stop at a grocery store, Martha headed east until she hit the coast and then turned north, where Cam caught glimpses of the bay between big houses and rolling lawns. Guess the government hadn't forced Skip Brockridge to give back all the money he swindled.

Martha wheeled her car into the circular driveway and pulled up in front of the double doors.

Cam whistled. "Nice digs. Does she have a bay in her backyard?"

"A bay and a boat dock." She threw the gear into Park. "But no boat."

"Cutting costs?"

"The boats were always my dad's thing—his and mine." She rubbed the end of her nose and exited the car.

He followed her to the trunk and hoisted her suitcase out. He balanced one of the grocery bags on top while Martha snagged the other two. "Did you grow up in this house?"

"This dump?" She swept her arm across the expansive, light blue clapboard front with the wraparound porch. "Mom did have to readjust when Dad was sent to prison, downsize. I don't even know why she bought on the bay. It was never her thing."

"Is there someone here? It doesn't look abandoned."

Martha plucked a key from her key chain and swung it back and forth. "Not right now, but Mom's house-keeper comes in once a week to dust mostly, and the gardeners keep up their weekly schedule."

"You said your mother was in Florida?"

"For the winter—like a bird." She unlocked the dead bolt and shoved the key into the handle to finish the job.

Cam followed her inside, dragging her suitcase be-hind him, his head swiveling from side to side. "Do you share a decorator with your mother? Looks simi-lar to your place."

"The town house was my mother's, from my grand-mother. I can afford to live there—with a roommate—but I can't afford to redecorate."

"Do you want this upstairs?" Cam rolled the suitcase to the foot of a curved staircase.

"You can leave it for now." She held out the two gro-cery bags. "Let's put you to work in the kitchen."

Cam widened his eyes as he stepped into the kitchen, the copper pots hanging above a center island catching the light and reflecting off the shiny granite counters, lined with enough appliances and gadgets to stock a cooking show. "This is way beyond my capabilities."

"If it's beyond yours, you can imagine how I feel walking in here and pouring my cereal in a bowl." She placed the groceries on the island and then rolled up the sleeves of her sweater. "Tell me what to do."

He held up a finger. "You always wash your hands first. That's what my mama taught me."

"Did your mother teach you how to cook, or did she

and your sister baby you and you had to learn on your own later?"

"My mom baby me?" He snorted. "She was a single parent, worked nights a lot so I had to fend for myself."

"Oh." She paused, hugging the carton of eggs to her chest. "What happened to your father?"

He bumped her hip so he could wash his hands at the sink. "My dad took off when my sister Lexie was a baby and I wasn't much older. We never saw him again."

"I'm sorry."

"I'm not. From all accounts he was a bastard, and we were better off without him."

"Funny, I thought…" She shook her head. "Bowls are in that cupboard. I'll leave the egg mixing to you, and I'll start cutting some veggies and grating the cheese."

He lodged his tongue in the corner of his mouth as he cracked several eggs into a bowl. What had she thought about him? At least she'd given him some thought.

"Milk?"

She opened the fridge and pulled out the carton she'd just put away. Looking over his shoulder, she asked, "Do you want me to pour it in? Just tell me when to stop."

He continued whisking. "Okay, pour, little more, little more. Stop."

She put away the milk and tipped her head back to survey the pots swinging above them. "I don't even know which one would work for an omelet."

He reached over her head to grab a pan. "This one will do."

"Is this enough for the filling?" She held up the cutting board for his inspection.

"I've never heard omelet ingredients called filling before, but that'll work."

"I told you I didn't know my way around a kitchen."

"Let me guess. You had a cook."

"We did." Her mouth tightened. "All bought and paid for with ill-gotten gains, but my mother liked to cook. She must've been thrilled when she had a daughter because Mom enjoyed all those typically feminine pursuits, but I was interested in…other things."

"Boating?" The butter sizzled in the pan as Cam swirled it around and up the sides. "I figured you must've spent most of your time holed up with books and studying."

"Oh, the boating." She shrugged. "I did that because *he* liked it."

"Your father."

"Uh-huh." She sniffled. "Too much onion, I think."

"It's fine." Her sniffling had nothing to do with onions. She'd acted like she hated her father before, but that couldn't be further from the truth.

He finished off the first omelet and tipped it onto a plate. Then he constructed the second, messing up the corner when he flipped up the one side.

"I'll take the defective one."

She twisted off the cap of the orange juice bottle and poured two glasses. "They both look perfect to me."

"We didn't get coffee." He slid the damaged omelet onto the second plate with a flourish.

"I'm okay without it."

She carried the glasses to the center island and placed them at the corner of the place mats. He followed her with the plates and centered them on the mats, trying to match her perfection.

"I don't need coffee. I think I'm too wired as it is." She pointed to her laptop case on the coffee table. "I haven't even checked my messages today. What if my friend has some news for me?"

"Unless he can tell you he's going to leave you alone or tell you what he wants from you, his news is worthless." He shook out the cloth napkin next to his plate and draped it over one knee. Martha had brought them back to reality, so he might as well jump in with both feet. "Are you going to call Tony's workplace later to see if he's on tonight?"

"Yes, but I wonder what he knows. Why wouldn't he tell the police or why wouldn't Casey have warned *him* to call the cops if anything happened to her?"

"Maybe she didn't want to involve him." He cut off a corner of his omelet and waved it at Martha. "She warned you instead because you're already involved."

"Great." She poked at her eggs. "This looks really good. I'm sorry I brought up the other stuff. I don't want to ruin your appetite."

"Mine?" He stabbed a mushroom. "Not possible."

They continued chatting, avoiding the issues front and center, and Martha told him about growing up in the Chesapeake Bay area. Her upbringing couldn't have been more different from his on the hardscrabble streets of Atlanta, but the most glaring difference involved father issues. He had no desire to even find out where his was, and Martha had clearly idolized hers—until he'd disappointed her.

No wonder she didn't have a boyfriend on the scene. She must've set her standards high after the fiasco with her father.

They finished breakfast, and Martha insisted on cleaning up since he'd done the cooking.

"You can do the dishes, but I have to help. My mom

ingrained that into me, and she'd smack me upside the head if she found out I let someone else do all the cleaning."

"Your mother still lives in Georgia?"

"Yeah, and I can't get her to leave the old neighborhood." He shook his head. "I keep trying to get her to find another job and move, but she claims she doesn't do the physical work like she used to."

"What does she do?"

"For years she worked as a maid at a hotel. She's still at the same damned place, but now she's the housekeeping supervisor." He shrugged. "She won't give up that job."

Martha dried the plate in her hands and then folded her arms around it, clutching it to her chest. "She worked hard to support you and your sister."

"That she did."

"She must be proud of you now."

"She says she is."

As she stacked the plate in the cupboard, Martha twisted around to stare at him. "She *says* she is. You don't believe her?"

A knot twisted in Cam's gut. "She didn't go to college, so she really wanted me to go. I had a football scholarship to pay for it and everything, but I just couldn't hack it. Couldn't get through those classes."

She turned away from the cupboard and leaned her back against the counter. "Ah, the good-looking jock couldn't find someone to do his homework for him?"

His gaze darted to her face and she flinched, blinking her eyes behind her glasses. Was that what she thought of him? Easy for her to make judgments with all this privilege and the brains to go with it.

"I wouldn't know." He slammed the dishwasher door. "I never tried to get someone to do my work for me. Just tried to do it myself—and failed miserably."

Curling her fingers around the edge of the counter behind her, she said, "I-I'm sorry. I didn't mean..."

"Sure you did." He ground out a laugh. "Girls like you, so superior."

She shoved off the counter and grabbed his hand with both of hers. "It's not even about you, Cam. It's all about me and my shortcomings."

"*Your* shortcomings." He rolled his eyes, but her hands, warm and soft from washing the dishes, squeezed his, and his tight jaw started to relax.

"It's just that you reminded me of all the hot guys in high school and college who used me to do their homework and write their papers, and then completely ignored me in every social setting. Guys I'd studied with all semester would look right through me at the next frat party, and I kept telling myself I wouldn't help them anymore, but I always did. It was one small way to fit in, and I desperately wanted to fit in."

He licked his lips and searched her face for any sign of deception. Her incredible eyes shimmered with tears, and he saw a woman who trusted him enough to be honest and open.

"Those guys were idiots, but even if I'd had a girl like you helping me every night, I still would've flunked out of school."

"I don't know about that. I was a pretty mean tutor back in the day."

"I'm sure you were, but I wouldn't have been able to concentrate with you sitting across from me."

Her eyebrows shot up, and now it seemed to be her turn to study his face. "You're serious."

"Damn straight."

Red flags flew in her cheeks, and she wrinkled her nose. "I'm still sure I could've gotten you through."

"Naw, and it's no reflection on your talents." He twisted his hands out of her grasp and placed them on her shoulders. "I couldn't handle school because I'm dyslexic. I thought you'd noticed before. I can barely read."

Chapter Eight

Martha put a hand to her heart, which Cam's words had just pierced. "I'm the idiot."

He rubbed his thumbs against her collarbone. "You didn't know."

"Yes, but the assumptions I made about you." Her hand crept to her throat. "I feel like such a fool, and I'm so sorry for stereotyping you as the dumb jock. Like I said, I'd been humiliated by plenty of them. And honestly? It probably wasn't even their fault. They didn't twist my arm to help them. I gladly did it to bask in their…hotness."

Cam tipped back his head and laughed at the ceiling, breaking the tension between them although she wasn't sure she wanted it broken. That tension had been building for a while, and she'd assumed it was all one-sided… hers, but he'd called her a distraction. She'd never been someone's distraction before.

"Take it from the dumb jock. You intimidated those dudes. They're used to admiration not admonitions."

"When you say things like that, you don't sound dumb at all. You need to stop calling yourself that." She pressed both hands against his chest. "You have to know that you wouldn't be a member of one of the most elite special ops teams in the military if you were all brawn and no brain."

"I'll make you a deal."

Her fingers curled against his shirt. If she could keep standing this close to him forever, she'd be willing to make a deal with the devil himself. "What kind of deal?"

"I'll stop referring to myself as a dumb jock if you stop referring to yourself as a geek, especially with that tone of voice you use when you do it."

"Do I?" She dropped her eyelashes. "Have a tone of voice when I call myself a geek?"

"You do." He brushed his knuckles across her cheek. "And I don't like it."

"Should we shake on it?" She made no move to remove her hands from his chest, and he hadn't released her shoulder yet.

His gaze dropped to her mouth, and a pulse throbbed in her lower lip. So much better to seal it with a kiss.

Her phone went off, and she almost sobbed with frustration when Cam jerked his head to the side.

"You'd better see who that is. Whoever used Casey's phone to text you yesterday now has your number, and I'm sure he's going to take advantage of that."

She broke away from the already broken spell and lunged for her phone, ready to scream at the person on the other end. She drew her brows over her nose when she recognized Gage's number from the office. "My boss is calling me on a Sunday?"

"Do you mind if I listen in? It might have something to do with the emails."

She tapped the phone to engage the speaker. "Hello? Gage?"

"Martha, I'm here with the section chief, Rand Proffit."

She swallowed the lump in her throat. "Hello, Mr. Proffit."

"How are you, Martha? Pretty rough weekend."

"Yes, it's been crazy. I had no idea my roommate was…dating Congressman Wentworth. If I had, I would've reported it."

She drove a fist into her belly. Would she have reported it? Was that any of the Agency's business? Did she owe them anything?

Proffit's voice reassured her over the phone, like some creepy, condescending uncle. "I'm sure you would have, Martha. I know we can count on you to always do the right thing, but this whole situation has put us in an interesting and unfortunate position. One of our employees, someone with a questionable past of her own caught up in a sex scandal involving a ranking member of the House Intelligence Committee. Doesn't look good."

"Sex scandal?" She ground her back teeth. "I'm not involved in any sex scandal."

Cam had been moving closer to her and now he hunched over the counter, a scowl marring his handsome features.

"Of course you're not, but all that was taking place in your town house…under your nose."

"Hardly under my nose. They were in another room with the door closed." Heat flared in her cheeks as she recalled eavesdropping on the sounds of their lovemaking through the walls and across the hall.

Proffit clicked his tongue, or was that her moronic boss?

"We're not blaming you in any way, Martha, nor are we holding you accountable." He cleared his throat and she held her breath. "However, we're putting you on a leave of absence for the time being—just until the whole situation dies down—and it will be paid leave. So, think of it as a vacation."

"I have work to do."

"Farah can take over." Gage couldn't hide the glee in his voice.

"Farah doesn't speak Russian."

Gage had a ready answer. "We'll get someone in the department to handle your work, Martha. Don't worry about that."

She gripped the phone so hard she thought the screen would crack. "When this…situation dies down, my job had better be waiting for me when I come back, or you'll answer to my attorney."

"Are you going to use your father's attorney?" Gage snorted.

"Damn straight." She ended the call and tossed the phone across the counter.

Cam whistled. "That's the way to handle 'em. They're so sure of you, aren't they? I'd like to see the looks on their faces if they ever discovered you took charge of those emails."

Her anger backtracked to fear, prompting her to worry her bottom lip with her teeth. "They can't ever find out. I'd lose my job and probably wind up in a cell next to my father's."

"They're not gonna find out from me." Cam walked around to her side of the counter and patted the stool between them. "Sit down. You look ready to collapse."

She perched on the stool and folded her hands in front of her. "Gage would like nothing better than to get rid of me."

"I noticed. What's that guy's problem?"

"He's afraid I'm going to take the job he wants." She twisted her fingers. "He probably doesn't have to worry about that anymore."

"If we can get enough proof that those emails were lies, you'll be right in line for that promotion." He patted her back and then strode toward her laptop abandoned on the coffee table. "Are you ready to take a look at your cleaned-up computer?"

"At least my cleaned-up computer won't be looking at me anymore, although now that the patriot and I are like this—" she crossed her fingers "—he'll probably feel free to email me. I'm sure he got my home email address, thanks to Casey the unlikely spy."

"Maybe he'll be kind enough to tell you what the hell he wants." Cam slipped her laptop out of its case, brushed a few crumbs from the place mat and set it down in front of her.

She wiggled her fingers before powering up the computer and entering her password. "If he admits to killing Casey or Wentworth, I'm turning him in. I don't care what the ramifications are for me."

"Even if he admits it, we don't know who he is. Is he one person? A group? Is he the same person who pushed you at the Metro station?"

Her shoulders stiff, she launched her email and watched the messages populate on the screen. She eked out a breath with each email she scanned and discarded. "Nothing from him."

"Maybe he's done with you. Showed you the reach of his power, got rid of a few loose ends and figures you've been adequately warned to let the emails implicating Major Denver drop."

She shoved the laptop away from her. "We're still going to see Tony tonight if he's working, aren't we?"

"Of course."

"Then he figured wrong."

As LUCK WOULD have it, Tony Battaglia still worked at the Insider in Georgetown, and he had a shift that night.

Cam insisted on babysitting her at her mom's house the rest of the day, and she didn't put up much of a fight. She made sandwiches for lunch, her one culinary accomplishment, and they both worked on their laptops until she took him out back for a walk along the shore of the bay.

She'd had an online conversational Russian class that afternoon, but she couldn't tell what Cam's work involved, and she didn't want to ask. He'd requested a quiet place to listen on some headphones and speak into a mic, so she invited him into her mother's library, which was really her father's library since all the books had belonged to him.

She'd shown Cam where to plug in and then had gotten out of there as fast as she could. The sight and the musty smell of her dad's books served as a reminder of all she'd lost when he decided to play fast and loose with the rules.

Like she was doing now.

When they'd come in from their walk, the cold had reddened Cam's cheeks and the breeze had ruffled his light brown hair, giving him the appearance of a model for a men's magazine on the great outdoors. She had a hard time reconciling his Adonis good looks with the insecurities he'd shared about his dyslexia.

Her heart ached for that part of him, while her body

ached for the other part. She couldn't have ordered a more perfect hero than if he'd come special delivery from central casting.

As he removed his coat, he said, "No more of this eating in. We'll go to out to dinner on our way to the Insider—and I'm paying. You've had to put up with me hanging around all day."

The only negative to having him hang around all day was that he was in a different room from her.

She shrugged out of her coat and dropped it on the sofa. "That works for me. I'm going to shower and change. Do we need to stop by your hotel on the way so that you can do the same?"

He brushed his hands over his faded jeans and stomped his work-style boots. "Yeah, I definitely need to clean up."

"Help yourself to anything in the kitchen." She waved her hand in the general direction. "And you can carry on with…whatever you were working on before."

"Reading."

"What?"

"I was working with a reading program. I try to keep at it whenever I'm on leave. If I'd had this program when I was younger, it would've helped a lot."

"That's admirable."

He ducked his head and his cheeks got redder. "I wasn't fishing for praise."

"I know that." She spun around not wanting to embarrass him anymore. "Well, get to work then, and I'll get ready for dinner."

Several minutes later as Martha stepped into the shower, a smile played about her lips. She hadn't felt this connected to a man ever.

She stepped beneath the warm spray and by the time she emerged, she'd lost the smile. What she and Cam had didn't come close to real life. She felt close to him because he'd become her protector, her lifeline in a crazy sequence of events that had just spun out of control. He felt close to her because he liked playing the protector.

If he hadn't come on the scene and all this stuff had gone down, she'd probably be sitting in a police station right now confessing everything. He'd naturally assumed she wouldn't go to the police, and she'd gone along with him on this roller-coaster ride—just like she'd gone along with her father even though she'd discovered his crimes long before the FBI had come knocking on their door.

She ended her shower far from the dreamy state she'd been in at the time she cranked on the water. She yanked her towel from the rack and gave her skin a harsh rubbing. She'd fallen into her old patterns. Some hot guy with a boyish grin crooked his finger at her, and she'd been ready to do his bidding.

But it wasn't exactly his bidding. Cam had saved her, had been there for her, protected her. That all made this a different experience completely.

Buoyed by her renewed justification of events, Martha leaned close to the mirror and popped in her contact lenses, blinking rapidly after she inserted each lens. Nothing out of the ordinary about wearing contacts. She usually chucked the glasses when she went on dates.

She finished getting ready, and then slipped out of the bathroom into the connecting bedroom. She'd already laid out a pair of black skinny jeans and some tall black boots. Pulling a teal sweater over her head, she tugged it into place and resisted the urge to pull at the shoulders to bring up the V-neck. She patted the neckline, which was a long way from plunging.

She put on the finishing touches with a blow-out of her hair and a heavier than usual application of makeup. She wanted to present a different appearance from the one plastered all over the news—at least that was her story and she was sticking to it.

She rested her hand on the bannister as she took one step at a time in her high-heeled boots. By the time she reached the bottom, Cam was there to meet her, his eyes as wide as his grin.

"You look…great." He held out his hand to help her off the last step.

"Thanks." She fluffed the ends of her wavy hair. "I figured I should disguise myself a little just to keep a low profile."

"Uh-huh." He lifted one eyebrow. "Good idea, but I'd hardly call that look low profile. You're gonna have all eyes on you in that getup."

"Too much?" She placed a hand flat against her tummy.

"For a night out in Georgetown? Nope. For me? Not at all."

She moistened her lip-sticked mouth. She hadn't fooled Cam at all with this supposed disguise. She'd dressed for him and had gotten exactly the reaction she'd craved—and she didn't feel silly or nervous or uncertain at all.

She felt beautiful because he made her feel that way.

"Are you ready?" She held up a small black bag. "I'm just going to switch purses."

"I'm ready. My laptop is all packed up." He pointed

to the front door. "I took the liberty of making sure everything was locked up down here. How come that security system wasn't engaged when we got here?"

"Mom's housekeeper leaves it off because she keeps forgetting the code."

"Do you know it?"

"Yes."

"Engage it tonight and leave it activated for as long as you're staying here. You can always call the housekeeper and give her the code."

She looked up from shuffling things from one purse to another. "Is that why you stayed all day? You're afraid I'm vulnerable here?"

"The guy, or guys, killed a congressman and his mistress. I'm not taking that lightly even though we still don't know what he wants from you."

"I agree. Give me two minutes."

While Cam waited by the door, Martha set the alarm system for the house. When she joined him, she said, "All done."

"Better safe than, well…you know."

When they got to his hotel, she insisted on waiting at the bar while he went up and changed to spare them both the awkwardness of having her watch over him while he showered and changed.

"I need a glass of wine anyway."

"Okay, I won't be long." He wagged a finger at her. "Don't talk to strangers."

His warning gave her a little chill, but she laughed it off. "I'll be here when you come back down."

She slid onto a stool at the bar and barely glanced at the scattered couples at the tables. She ordered a glass of red wine from the bartender and took a deep sip, closing her eyes as the warmth spread to her muscles.

"Long day?"

Her eyelids flew open, and she turned her head in the direction of the male voice beside her. "You could say that."

"Same for me." He raised his glass of whiskey. "Travel day. Those are the worst."

"Let's see." She held up her hand and ticked off her fingers. "Lobbyist, congressman back from a home district visit, attorney. Shall I keep guessing?"

"You do know this town." He swirled the amber liquid in his glass. "Lobbyist."

She laughed and fluttered her eyelashes, which seemed to act as some kind of invitation to the stranger. They spent the next half hour exchanging witty repartee. She didn't even know where half the stuff out of her mouth was coming from.

"You know, Martha, you've already made my travel day one hundred percent better. Can I buy you dinner?"

"Oh, I'm sorry." And just like that she'd led someone on even though she hadn't meant to. "I'm meeting a...friend for dinner. In fact, here he is. Nice talking to you, Alan. Have a good week."

Alan cranked his head over his shoulder in time to see Cam making his way through the bar and muttered, "Lucky bastard. Have a nice dinner, Martha."

She met Cam halfway through the bar and nodded. "You clean up nicely."

Cam jutted his chin and glared over her head. "Was that guy trying to pick you up?"

"Just passing time." She took his hand. "Until the main event."

"I don't blame him." Cam interlaced his fingers with hers and did a U-turn to exit the bar. "I figured you wouldn't be flying under the radar looking like a million bucks."

Martha lengthened her stride to keep up with him, noticing a few other admiring glances thrown her way. She flipped back her hair and straightened her spine. Cam could go on about her looks all night, but she understood the difference.

Cam's attentions had given her confidence, and even the plainest girl in the room could command the spotlight exuding confidence.

Even with her newfound assurance, Martha rejected a trendy Georgetown restaurant for a quieter place serving Italian food in a homey atmosphere.

Once they each had a glass of red wine and a basket of bread between them, Cam hunched forward, crossing his arms on the table. "What's our strategy with Tony? Have you ever met him?"

"He's probably the one guy Casey *didn't* bring home, not that I saw much of the others. I swear, running into Congressman Wentworth that night was a rare occurrence." She tapped a fingernail against her glass. "But if Tony's some kind of confidante of Casey's, I'm sure he knows about me or at least knows my name. Why would she blab secrets to a bartender?"

"Are you kidding? Most bartenders probably hear more of people's problems than therapists do." He tore off a piece of garlic bread and pointed it at her. "You're just going to march in and introduce yourself?"

"I'll start slowly and then hit him with the note I found. Who knows? Maybe he's expecting it because

Casey told him she'd be calling him out as some kind of witness if anything happened to her."

"I hope he doesn't plead the Fifth. If it's not crowded in the bar, maybe we'll have a chance to talk to him while he's on the job, or at least make arrangements to talk to him later."

When the waitress arrived with their food, Cam pointed to Martha's glass. "Do you want another?"

"No. I want to have my wits about me tonight, and I already had half a glass at the hotel. That first night after the incident on the Metro platform? Those two glasses of wine were my limit. You wouldn't want to see me after a third."

"Wanna bet? Don't get me wrong. I admire your... restraint, but I can't help wondering what an out-of-control Martha would look like."

"I don't—" she cut off a corner of her spinach lasagna "—let myself go."

"You should try it sometime. It's good for the soul." He broke off another piece of garlic bread. "You should also try some of this bread before I eat it all."

She watched his fingers as he brushed them together, dislodging crumbs into the napkin on his lap and wondered what it would be like to let go with Cam. She was no virgin, but all of her sexual encounters had been very measured and controlled. Probably her fault.

For the rest of the meal they didn't talk any more about losing control or Tony or Casey or the congressman. It was as if this dinner represented a deep breath, a chance to step away from the crazy before plunging back into it headfirst.

They finished their food and, true to his word, Cam

picked up the check. As he placed some bills on the tray, he said, "Are you okay to drive?"

"I think so, although I usually don't drive at all after I've imbibed."

"When it comes to drinking and driving, you can never be too careful." He held out his hand. "I'll take the wheel."

"You've had a glass of wine, too."

"I'm twice your size and drank half as much."

"You have a point." She fished her keys from her purse and dropped them into his cupped palm. "You know where you're going?"

"It's not far from here, right? You can be my navigator."

When they reached the bar, Cam pulled up to the valet parking attendant and left him the keys. As they walked in, Cam ducked to whisper in her ear, "Do you have any idea what Tony looks like?"

She nodded to the bar where a man and a woman were mixing and pouring drinks. "Easy. He's the man."

"At least it's not crowded." He tipped his head toward one of the TVs over the bar displaying photos of Wentworth and Casey. "I wonder how Tony feels about that playing 24-7 in here."

"I guess we're going to find out soon enough."

They claimed two empty seats at the bar, the nearest customer three stools down.

The female bartender got to them first. "What would you like?"

"I'll have one of these." Cam held up a cardboard coaster printed with the name of a bottled beer.

"Club soda with lime for me, please."

Martha tilted her head back and followed the muted

images parading across the TV screen. Even without the sound she could piece together the story—or maybe that was just because it was *her* story.

When the bartender set their drinks in front of them, Cam handed her a folded ten and asked, "Is that Tony Battaglia?"

The bartender's gaze flicked from Cam to Martha, two small lines forming between her eyebrows. "Yes. Do you have business with him?"

"Business?" Cam's hand jerked and a dab of foam leaped over the edge of his mug and rolled down the side. "We have mutual friends."

The woman's scowl deepened.

Martha added, "Just when he has a minute."

"I'll let him know." She snatched up Cam's bill and spun away.

Cam lifted one shoulder. "Weird."

"Okay, so that wasn't just me?"

"Definitely an odd reaction. Maybe the media made the connection between Casey and Tony and have already swooped in for a comment or reaction."

"That's probably it." Martha swirled the straw in her glass, clinking the ice against the sides.

From the corner of her eye, she saw the bartender say something to Tony. He glanced their way, but his face didn't change expression. They waited another ten minutes and three customers before Tony meandered over to them.

He whipped a towel from his waistband and wiped the clean counter next to them. "We have a mutual friend?"

"Casey Jessup. She was my roommate."

Tony choked and bunched up the towel in his fist.

Whatever he'd been expecting from them—that was not it.

"You're Martha?"

Martha's heart fluttered in her chest. "Yes. Casey mentioned me?"

"Uh-huh." He swept his head from side to side, and then he focused on Cam. "Who's he? The po-po?"

"I'm not the police. I'm Martha's friend." Cam narrowed his eyes. "Why are you worried about the police?"

"They don't know about me, do they?"

Martha shrugged. "Not that I know of. I didn't tell them anything about you. Why do you care? Shouldn't one of Casey's friends want to talk to the police about her suicide?"

"Friend? Yeah, I guess we were friends. I told her." He stopped and shook his head.

"Told her what? If you two weren't friends, how did you know her?"

"You really don't know, do you?"

"If I knew, I wouldn't be asking you."

"Casey was a paid girlfriend. You know, an escort."

Chapter Nine

She gaped at him like an idiot and then snapped her jaw closed.

Folding his hands around his glass, Cam leaned in. "She wasn't an intern for some congresswoman?"

"Oh, yeah. She was all that, but she made the big money working as an escort—a professional girlfriend." Tony cranked his head to the side to take in two men in suits talking at the end of the bar. "And I was her facilitator."

"Her pimp, you mean." Cam's voice had roughened around the edges.

"That's a harsh word for what I did. This is an upscale place, and when I ran into someone who was looking for that special girl, I referred that person to Casey. Sure, I got a cut of the action, but Casey was her own boss. She'd tried working for an agency, didn't like it and struck out on her own. She just felt safe having me on her side, and man—" Tony wiped the corner of his eye with his towel "—I loved that girl."

"Tony!" The other bartender called out to her coworker and then held up one hand. "Never mind. You can take a break. It's slowing down."

"Do you want to join us at a table?" Cam jerked his

thumb over his shoulder. "We have a few more questions for you, if you don't mind."

"I don't mind. Better you than the police. God, I hope they don't get suspicious about the suicide story and start digging into Casey's finances."

"Suicide *story*?" Cam lifted one eyebrow.

"C'mon. We all know it was murder. That's why you're here, isn't it?"

Martha's eyes met Cam's as Tony tossed his towel on the edge of the sink. He met them on the other side of the bar, and they crowded around a small cocktail table.

"Before we get started, I want you to know why we're here." Martha dragged the slip of paper with Casey's handwriting from her purse and flattened it in front of Tony. "Casey left this for me where we kept our extra key."

Tony smoothed his thumb over the words. "Inside the chair cover."

"She told you about that?"

"Casey told me everything." He picked up the note and pressed his lips against the paper. "That's why she left this for you."

Having left his beer on the bar, Cam took a sip of Martha's club soda. "Start from the beginning. Are you the one who set her up with Congressman Wentworth?"

"I am, but the setup was a setup." Tony's gaze darted around the room, and he rubbed his upper lip. "Some guy who already knew about Casey's line of work approached me. Wentworth had been in here a few times—they all make it to this bar eventually."

"This guy wanted you to make sure Casey and Wentworth hooked up?" Martha crossed one leg over the other and kicked her foot back and forth.

"Exactly."

"He targeted Casey, didn't he? This man wanted Casey and only Casey for Wentworth. He already knew about her, knew she was an escort…knew she lived with Martha."

Cam's intensity had Tony shrinking back. "Y-yeah. It was all about reaching out to Casey and getting her to spy on her roommate, but Wentworth was definitely part of the equation, too. It had to be Wentworth for some reason."

Martha rubbed the goose bumps forming on her forearms. "It was a plan to get to me."

"I'm sorry. It was." Tony scratched the scruff on his lean jaw. "But I don't know the details about that, and neither did Casey. He instructed her to steal your computer password, stuff like that."

"That's how he hacked into my laptop, how he took over my camera." She smacked her hand on the table, and her ice tinkled in protest.

"Look, Casey never got the impression this guy wanted to hurt you…or her. She wouldn't have done it, otherwise."

"Did she have a choice?" Cam's jaw formed a hard line. "Did he threaten to expose her? Expose her lifestyle? Yours?"

"Maybe there was a little of that, but no way would Casey, or me, be down with violence."

Martha folded the four corners of her cocktail napkin. "What about Wentworth? What was the plan with him?"

"Information. He wanted information from Wentworth." Tony chewed on the edge of his thumb. "The night Wentworth died at your place? Casey had been ordered to bring him back there that night once he started feeling sick. Usually they went to the apartment he kept in town. Casey had access to all his stuff there."

Cam tapped her thigh. "The emails, intel about Denver."

Tony looked from Cam to Martha, a deep crease between his eyebrows.

"Once he started feeling sick?" Martha ran her tongue around her dry mouth. "Did Casey do something to make Wentworth sick?"

"She didn't. No! She wouldn't do that." Tony dug his fingers into his spiky black hair, making it stand on end even more. "But she thinks someone slipped him something because her contact knew Wentworth would become ill that night and she had those orders to bring him back to her place when he did."

"So he'd die in my town house."

"Casey never thought that would be the endgame. She thought it was just a little information, some spy game that wouldn't affect anyone."

"Spy games always affect someone…including the spy." A dangerous light sparked in Cam's eyes. "Now you're going to tell us about this guy. What does he look like? What does he call himself? How does he contact you? Has he been in touch since Casey's murder?"

Tony spread his hands out on the table, his thumbs touching. "He introduced himself as Ben, but I'm sure we can all agree that's bogus. He's average, average everything except his beard. He wears a bushy beard and glasses. Without that stuff, I probably wouldn't recognize him on the street."

Martha glanced at Cam. "Disguise."

"Yeah, probably." Tony rubbed his brow. "Always

wore a hat, too. He comes in here when he wants to make contact."

Martha asked, "Does Ben show up at the bar when he wants to communicate with Casey or just you?"

"Both. He told her to get a temporary phone. They exchange messages that way."

Cam's eyebrows collided over his nose. "Did the cops mention anything to you about Casey having two phones, Martha?"

"No, and I had no idea she had two phones."

"If Ben was in that hotel room with Casey, I'm sure he took the burner phone with him when he left." Tony pinched the bridge of his nose, squeezing his eyes closed. "I can't believe she's gone."

"Why would Ben do it? Why kill Wentworth and Casey unless he got all he wanted from them and decided to tie up loose ends?" Cam drummed his fingers on the table.

"He had gotten what he wanted from them, and everything would've been status quo until he found out I kept those emails." Martha's bottom lip quivered. "I'm the one who caused all of this."

"Emails?" Tony's eyes flew open.

Cam drew his finger across his throat. "Need to know basis. Martha, none of this is your fault. If Casey hadn't been so greedy, she wouldn't have set you up and involved you in all this. If Wentworth had been able to keep it in his pants, he never would've been targeted."

Tony twirled the earring in his lobe. "And let's not leave out Ben himself. What information *did* he have Casey get from Wentworth, and how did it relate to you? Casey told me you were CIA."

"Like I said—need to know, and you don't," Cam growled. "What kind of man is a pimp anyway?"

"Hey, man. It wasn't like that. I protected Casey. I loved her."

"Dude, that's not love."

"A-are you going to tell the cops any of this? I'll deny everything."

"We're not ready to do that yet. We have no proof, but I'm not ruling it out when we do. Don't you want to see Casey's killer brought to justice?"

"I do, but it'll sacrifice her reputation."

"And yours." Cam rolled his eyes at Martha.

"If you're not a cop—" Tony waved at his coworker behind the bar "—why do you care about Ben? Whatever damage he caused has been done."

"I wanna know who he is and who he works for. The damage he did had a huge impact on a friend of mine, someone I admire and look up to. I'm not gonna let that slide. I'm not gonna let him get away with it."

Martha tapped on the table. "I have an idea. Doesn't this bar have security cameras? Would it be possible for us to see Ben?"

"I suppose I can offer to close up on my own, and you can meet me back here at closing. I'd have to disable the cameras or erase the footage so nobody sees you coming back here."

"I can take care of the camera. What time?"

"We close up at two."

Cam tapped his phone. "Almost three hours."

"We can go back to my place for a few hours."

Tony glanced over his shoulder and held up one finger at the other bartender. "I'll let you in the back door. Now I gotta go back to work."

As Tony walked away, Cam slumped back in his chair. "What do you think?"

"I can't believe I was so naive I didn't figure out Casey's real profession." Martha scooped her hair back from her face. "Is everyone in this town scamming?"

"It seems like it."

"Maybe it *is* time to call in the police."

He snorted. "Right. If we do that, you'll have to admit you stole those emails, and then it won't be just the police, it'll be the FBI. Your family doesn't have a great track record with the Fibbies."

"If everyone didn't have something to hide, including me, maybe we could actually get to the bottom of this." She sighed and stirred the melting ice in her glass.

"Maybe it is over for you, Martha." He took her hand and traced over her knuckles with his fingertip. "Ben or the patriot or whatever else he calls himself knows you have the emails, but you already sent them up the chain of command. His work is done. He showed his power and reach by killing Wentworth and Casey, and figures you're not going to do any more investigating. You can leave it now."

"But you're not going to."

He grabbed his coat from the back of the chair. "Let's go to your place."

"I'm going to use this time to pack up Casey's things for her family. Maybe we'll find this phone...or something else."

With one last look at Tony behind the bar and a nod, they slipped outside. Cam took the wheel of her car again and drove back to her place.

As they pulled up to the front, Cam said, "Let's not

forget. Ben could've been in possession of Casey's house key since last night."

Martha glanced up at the glow from the front window. She'd left a lamp on in the living room, so the light didn't surprise her or make her nervous—but Cam's words did.

She peeled her tongue from the roof of her dry mouth. "What if someone's in there?"

"I have my gun." He patted the pocket of his jacket. "Let me go in first."

He parked the car and then led the way up the steps to her town house. After she unlocked the door, he eased it open with his foot. He swung his weapon in front of him and stepped inside.

"Stay back, Martha."

She ducked behind his solid frame, but peeked around his body and surveyed the empty room. She let out a slow breath as Cam crept forward.

He waved his hand behind him, so she hovered in the entryway while he continued farther into the room. He poked his head around the corner to check out the kitchen. "Nobody in here."

He threw open the door to the half bathroom and then checked the lock on the back door. Pointing the barrel of his gun at the ceiling, he said, "I'll take a look upstairs."

"I'm coming with you." She turned and locked the front door although if Ben had Casey's key, that wouldn't do much good.

"Just stay behind me."

Martha followed Cam up the stairs and stayed back as he checked the second bathroom. When he pushed open her bedroom door, she held her breath and then released it when nothing but the silence of the room greeted them.

Cam turned, putting his finger to his lips, and yanked open the door of the master bathroom connected to the room. He shook his head. *"Nada."*

She crossed the hall to Casey's room, but Cam beat her there and pulled her back.

"One more."

He turned the handle and bumped the door with his shoulder. The door swung open and Cam crouched, clutching his weapon in front of him.

Martha gasped and pulled back, flattening herself against the opposite wall. Her fingers clawed against the smooth surface and she squeezed her eyes closed, waiting for…whatever.

Cam swore. "He was here. The bastard was here."

Martha peeled herself from the wall and stumbled forward. Hanging on to the doorjamb, she leaned into Casey's bedroom and a chill zigzagged up her spine.

Someone had torn apart Casey's room looking for something, and Martha hoped to God he'd found it because if he hadn't, she had a feeling he'd come after her next.

CAM SHOVED HIS gun into the waistband of his pants. Whoever was responsible for tossing Casey's room had come and gone. He turned in a slow circle, surveying the damage. "What the hell is he looking for?"

"I don't know." Martha gulped in a breath and hiccupped. "But I hope he found it."

"You do?" Came drew his brows together. "I don't."

"Easy for you to say. It's not your place he's searching."

Cam smacked his fist into his palm. "You should've

had your locks changed as soon as the police told you Casey's keys were missing. It's too late now."

Chewing on her bottom lip, Martha picked up one of Casey's T-shirts with two fingers and dropped it on the bed. "That's an understatement."

"I mean time-wise it's too late. You'll never get a locksmith out here at midnight."

"Luckily, I'm not staying here tonight. I'll get someone out first thing tomorrow morning." She ran her hands over a bunched-up pillow. "I'm sure as heck not going to work."

"What could Casey have that this guy wants?"

"And why didn't he ask her for it before he killed her?"

"Maybe he did and that's why he killed her. She wouldn't give it up."

Tilting her head to one side, Martha put a fist on her hip. "You met Casey. Tony told you what she did. Do you really think she's the kind of person who would die for her country? I'm pretty sure Casey would've given Ben whatever he wanted, especially if she thought it would save her life."

"You knew her better than I did." Cam rubbed his chin. "If Ben didn't ask her nicely for what he wanted or even threaten her if she didn't give it up, why? What is he looking for now? He has the emails."

"That's what I don't get." Martha collapsed on the foot of Casey's disheveled bed. "Ben sent me those emails, knowing I'd send them up the chain of command, and I did. Those messages launched the investigation into Major Denver, which then caused him to go AWOL. Mission accomplished."

"Not quite." Cam leveled a finger at Martha. "Nobody was expecting you to hold on to the emails yourself."

"It shouldn't matter to him. The emails reached their intended target and did the intended damage. So what if I have the emails on an external storage device? The only thing that does is open me up to charges within the Agency."

"It also proves you're suspicious about the emails. You said your superiors didn't take your concerns seriously or at least felt they'd done their due diligence in investigating them. For old Ben, case closed—until you messed things up. He tried warning you. He tried tying up his loose ends by killing both Wentworth and Casey."

"As far as he knows, those actions worked. I'm so terrified, I left my home. Why would he think I'd pursue it further?"

"Maybe he believes case is closed on you, too, but now he has another problem. Casey."

"And whatever evidence she left behind, perhaps linking Ben to the emails."

"He should be worried." Cam joined Martha on the bed. "Because if we find that evidence before he does, we might have some proof that the emails were all a scam."

"Maybe we don't need the evidence if we can ID the guy tonight on the bar's security video."

Cam pushed off the bed and spread his arms wide. "You wanted to start packing up Casey's things for her family. Now you have the incentive. I'll help you clean up this mess."

"Thanks. I'll get some garbage bags in case there isn't enough room in her suitcase for her clothes." Martha headed for the door and stopped. "Ben would've expected Casey to have the burner phone on her, wouldn't he?"

"Probably, if that's the way he contacted her."

"I mean, Tony told us she had a burner phone, but the cop didn't say anything to me about two phones. He mentioned her purse, her wallet and her cell phone. Wouldn't he have said two phones or maybe even asked me about two phones?"

Cam dragged a suitcase from the closet, which had also been thoroughly ransacked. "So, Ben took it, or that's what he's looking for."

"Maybe he found it in here, and now he'll leave me alone."

"If he did, that's one less thread of proof for us to tie him to Casey and the planting of the emails."

"C-can you blame me for wanting to back out of this mess? I know. I started out so full of myself, and now I'm just a coward."

"I wouldn't blame you at all, and you're far from a coward." He flipped open the suitcase. "Let's see what we can find out tonight, and if the video doesn't show us anything, you can call it a night…and forget the whole thing."

She dipped her chin to her chest and pivoted out of the room.

Cam started shoveling the clothes strewn about the room into the open suitcase. At least he had the emails. Martha would turn them over to him, and he could get someone else to look at them. Maybe he could convince someone in intelligence to look at the emails—if there were a way to leave Martha's name out of it.

Then his leave would be over, and he'd get sent on his next Delta deployment, and Martha could get back to doing what she did best—translating and following CIA rules. And their paths would never cross again.

His heart did a strange twist, and he thumped his fist against his chest.

"Playing Tarzan?" Martha leaned against the door-jamb, a garbage bag clutched in each hand.

"Just trying to clear my lungs. Dust." He gestured to the suitcase, half-full with jumbled clothes. "Should I be folding up this stuff neatly?"

"I'll tell you what. You take a bag and fill it with the stuff from this desk." She thrust a plastic bag at him. "I'll pack her clothes."

They worked side by side, the silence broken by the occasional theory or rhetorical question.

Cam thumbed through Casey's papers before tossing them in the bag, but didn't find anything suspicious or out of the ordinary. He looked up when he'd cleared out the desk. "So, I guess professional girlfriends don't keep receipts or records. I've never even heard that term before. Where I come from, we have another name for it."

"I can't believe how naive I am." She dropped the lid on the suitcase and flattened one hand on the top while she zipped it. "I honestly just thought Casey had a lot of boyfriends and dates."

"How were you supposed to know? She hardly fits the profile of a hooker."

Martha raised one finger. "Professional girlfriend, and I guess she *is* the profile."

Cam slid his phone from his pocket and glanced at the time. "It's almost two. We should be heading back to the bar. I hope Tony has something to show us."

Martha followed Cam out of Casey's room and stopped at the door, turning around to look at their handiwork. "Her family hasn't even contacted me to pick up Casey's things. Maybe that's why she did it, the girlfriend thing."

"Why?"

"She just wanted some love, even if it was pretend."

BY THE TIME they got back to the Insider, the traffic on the street had thinned out but not disappeared. Martha parked on a side street, and they slipped into the alley behind the bar.

They reached the door, and Cam pointed to a wedge jammed beneath the bottom of the door to prop it open.

Martha tipped her head back and tugged on Cam's sleeve. "Looks like he already disabled the camera."

Cam looked up and his brow creased. "He sprayed the lens. I guess that way it doesn't look like the camera has been tampered with, as long as it cleans off."

"We'll have to remind him to wipe it off."

Cam used his foot to push open the door, and Martha stepped inside the back hallway of the bar.

She whispered Tony's name.

"He's probably in the office." Cam nudged her back, and she veered toward a closed door past the restrooms.

"Tony?" She knocked, pressing her ear against the door.

Cam stepped around her and opened the door, pushing it wide.

The computer on the desk glowed, and Cam hunched over it. "Looks like he's already been checking the security camera footage."

Martha backed up a step, one arm wrapped around her midsection. "Where is he? He should've heard us come in by now."

Cam reached into his pocket and Martha's heart skipped a beat, knowing that's where he'd stashed his gun.

Cam waved her away from the door and he crept through it, squeezing past her.

She followed him down the hallway to the bar…and then wished she hadn't.

Tony was still here all right—slumped at a table, his head resting in a pool of blood.

Chapter Ten

The floorboards creaked behind him, and Cam whipped around from Tony's dead body, clutching his weapon.

Martha gaped back at him, her face white and her mouth wide.

"Get back. He's dead."

"What happened to him?"

Cam launched forward and ran down the hallway toward the back door, which they'd left propped open. He pulled it closed and locked it.

When he returned to the bar, Martha was leaning over Tony, both hands over her mouth. If she got sick all over the body, they'd have more explaining to do than he was prepared for.

"Martha, what are you doing?"

"He left us a message."

"Tony?" He joined her at the table and then jerked back. Someone had written on the table in Tony's blood: "Back off."

Martha stumbled back from the table, as if obeying the order written on it. "That's for us. He knew. He knew about this meeting, or suspected it and was watching Tony."

Cam backtracked to the mahogany bar and peered

over it at the register, gaping open. "He staged this as a burglary. Cleaned out the cash. He took care of the security cameras, too."

"And probably deleted the rest of the footage showing his meetings with Tony."

"We're done here." Cam leaned over the bar and grabbed a clean bar towel. "Did you touch anything at the table?"

"God, no." She shoved her hands in her pockets.

"Then we need to clean off our prints in the office—on the door and the computer keyboard—and at the back door. At least our images won't be on security footage, either."

As he made for the office, Martha grabbed his back pocket. "You mean we're going to just leave him here without calling the police?"

He glanced over his shoulder at her. "And how would that story go? We came here after hours to meet with Tony and get a look at security footage of his meeting with a man who knows you stole classified emails from your employer—the CIA?"

She sagged against the wall outside the office. "That's the problem with lying, isn't it? It never stops. You have to tell more and more lies to cover up the previous lies."

"I'd lie to hell and back to protect you, Martha. You don't need to get in trouble for something you did that felt right at the time."

"I guess that's what my father would've said. It felt right at the time. Your father, too."

He ran the towel across the computer's keyboard. "What we're doing doesn't compare to what our fathers did. Not even close. You sensed something was off about those emails—and you were right—but no-body believed you. You just took matters into your own hands."

"And made a mess of things."

Cam wiped down the front of the door and then, with the towel in his hand, closed it and finished off with the doorknob. "By keeping those emails, you forced Ben out into the open. He's running scared. If you hadn't stored those messages on a flash drive, Ben would've been home free."

"He might not have killed Wentworth, Casey and Tony though."

"Really?" Cam got to work on the back door, delet-ing their after-hours visit. "I think he would have. He didn't want to leave any witnesses."

"So we just leave Tony like this?"

"Nothing we can do for him now. He was playing with fire, and he knew it."

She tipped her head down the hallway. "What about the message on the table? Should we wipe that off?"

"Let the cops puzzle it out. If we wipe it up, the po-lice are going to be able to tell something was there. Why would a killer wipe up his victim's blood?"

Cam shoved the block of wood beneath the door with his foot to prop it open again, leaving everything as they'd found it when they arrived. "Now we just have to hope nobody saw us go in here."

"I was watching." Martha pulled her keys from her purse. "Nobody saw us."

They slipped into the alley, and Cam did a quick survey of the surrounding businesses. "I'm pretty sure Tony's killer took care of the other cameras in this alley that would have a shot at the Insider's back door."

"He's protecting us at the same time he's protecting himself." Martha sidled along the back wall of the building for good measure.

When they got to the street with the car, they ducked inside, just a couple of late-night bar-hoppers along with other stragglers on the sidewalk "This is going to be all over the news tomorrow. Do you think the police will make the connection between Casey and Tony?"

"They're going to look at him more closely because of that message, but I don't know why they'd connect him to Casey. As far as the cops are concerned, Casey's death is a suicide and they don't seem to be going through her contacts." Martha put the car in gear and eased away from the curb.

"They might be going through the contacts of her burner phone—if they had it."

She pulled around the corner, checking the rearview mirror. "And you're thinking if Ben had that phone, he wouldn't be running around murdering people and sending me warnings?"

"Oh, he still would've murdered Tony because he had access to that footage showing Ben meeting with him and Casey in the Insider."

"He obviously didn't think that footage was important enough to kill for—until we showed up. He must be following us. He knew we'd paid a visit to Tony."

"He could've been watching Tony. Where are you going?"

"To drop you off at your hotel."

"If you think I'm letting you go back to your mother's place alone tonight, you're crazy. I'm camping out on that ritzy sofa in the living room."

Cam could just make out the pink tint to Martha's cheek. She wanted him there. Maybe she even wanted *him*.

"Okay. Th-that actually makes me feel better, safer. If he thinks I have something he wants, who knows what lengths he's willing to go to get it?"

"And if it's that phone, it could blow his cover if Casey has texts with him on there."

"If his phone is a temp, too, how is Casey's phone going to incriminate him?"

"There could be ways to track those phones. Just the fact that Casey might have texts giving her instructions on what to do about Wentworth would be huge, especially if those instructions mention Denver and our assignments."

Her hand slid from the steering wheel and dropped to his thigh. "That might not be enough to clear his name. There's more evidence against him than what was uncovered as a result of those damned messages."

"I know that, but it's a start. If bogus, planted emails initiated the entire investigation, it'll cast suspicions over the rest of the so-called evidence."

"You'll never give it up, will you? Major Denver means that much to you?"

"Everything." Cam closed his eyes as a sharp pain pierced his gut.

The pressure of Martha's hand on his leg soothed his hurt and frustration.

"I understand." Her whispered words floated toward him. "When my father first came under investigation, I believed with all my heart that he was innocent. I was willing to do anything to prove it. I think that's why he finally admitted his guilt."

"Why?"

"He couldn't stand to see my vehemence in his defense when he knew it was all a lie."

Her voice broke, and he covered her hand with his—the soothed become the soother.

"He loved you though, despite his shortcomings." He traced the tips of her fingers, outlining her hand. "And you love him, despite your disappointment in him."

She sniffled. "I tried to hate him, but I didn't have it in me."

"He made a big, big mistake and he's paying for it. Don't charge him an even bigger price by withdrawing your love from him."

Her head jerked toward him and then back to the road. "You wouldn't be so forgiving of your father, would you?"

"Two different situations." He rubbed a circle in the condensation on the window with his fist. "Your father did what he did out of greed. Sure, he wasn't thinking of the consequences to his family, but he never stopped loving or caring for that family. My father didn't give a damn about my mother or me and my sister."

"I guess." She slid her hand from beneath his and wrapped her fingers around the steering wheel. "Totally different situation between my father and Major Denver, too. You're convinced he's innocent."

"Absolutely." He smacked a hand against his thigh. "He's being set up, and we're going to figure out by who and why."

"We?"

"The rest of our Delta Force team. Most of us don't believe the charges against him, and we've made a pact to clear his name."

"Then I'm glad to be part of that. If my father isn't deserving of my efforts, I believe you when you say Major Denver is."

They drove the rest of the way back to Martha's mother's house in silence, his thoughts on his good-for-nothing father and hers probably on her own father—two men who couldn't be more dissimilar, from two different sides of the tracks, but who'd both made bad choices that ultimately hurt their families.

If he ever got the opportunity to be a father, he'd do things differently, but he'd need a partner who could tame him. He slid a sidelong glance at Martha's profile, her pert nose and wide mouth, giving her a look of innocence. Maybe her sweet expression gave people the impression they could take advantage of her.

She pulled into her mother's driveway and cut the engine. "We should've stopped by your hotel so you could pick up some of your things. My mom has plenty of extra toothbrushes and toiletries, but I'm pretty sure you don't want to wear any of my dad's clothes now that orange is his new black."

"Probably not, but I'll take the toothbrush."

While she disarmed the alarm system and unlocked the door, Cam faced outward, his muscles tense. He'd made sure they weren't followed from the bar, but he'd bet Ben knew about Martha's mom's house out here on the bay.

Martha pushed open the door, and Cam followed her inside, close on her heels. She locked up from the inside and entered the alarm's code.

She tossed her purse and coat onto the nearest chair and covered her face with both hands.

"You okay?" Cam stroked her back, which arched slightly like a satisfied cat's.

"It's been a long, long day." Her hands moved from her face through the coffee-colored strands of her hair. "I can't believe we were so close to getting a look at Casey's contact and to have it all end in Tony's gruesome murder. I'd never seen a dead body before in my life, and I just chalked up three. How is that possible?"

"I know." He touched her arm. In fact, he couldn't seem to stop touching her. "I'm sorry you had to see any of it, but I'm glad you're still safe."

She turned wide eyes on him. "For how much longer? He's looking for something of Casey's, and he wants to find it before I do. If he doesn't, he may just be satisfied with making sure I never find it either, and the only way to do that is by making sure I meet the same fate as Wentworth, Casey and Tony."

"Do you think I'm gonna let that happen?" He gripped her shoulders.

"You do have a life, a job, outside of saving Major Denver." She dropped her gaze. "Saving me."

"Not yet. We have time. We're going to find what this guy's looking for, and we're going to implicate him. I'll be here for you, Martha."

Tipping her head to the side, she rubbed her cheek against the back of his hand. "Are you saving me because you can't save him, Cam? Or is saving me mixed up in your mind with saving him?"

"What does that mean?" He stepped back. "Do you think you're some sort of substitute for Denver?"

She raised her shoulders, rolling them at the same time, dislodging his hands. "If you could prove his innocence tomorrow in some other place, with someone else's help, wouldn't you?"

His brows shot up. "And leave you? Leave you in this situation without protection?"

Her chin began to dip, and he pinched it and tilted her head back.

"I want to help Denver. That's why I came out here in the first place, but you're my first priority now, Martha."

A tear danced on the ends of her long lashes. "I don't think I've ever been someone's first priority before."

His hand slid along her jaw, and he captured her earlobe between his fingers. "I may not be the brightest guy in the world, but I know a precious gem when I see it."

She blinked, dislodging the tear, which splashed on the back of his hand. "Some of the brightest guys in the world don't have kind hearts like yours."

The side of his mouth twitched into a half smile. "I've never heard that one before."

Crossing one hand over the other, she pressed them against his chest. "That's because you've never bothered to let anyone in before. Too busy being the big, macho lug."

His heart thundered under the pressure of her hands, and he expanded his chest. "You found me out."

She looked around, as if aware of her surroundings for the first time. "Why are we still standing here in the entryway? It's almost dawn."

"Good thing neither of us has a job to go to." A slow pulse beat in his throat as he looked down into Martha's face. He just needed some sign from her. Anything they did had to originate from her desire. He had to avoid even a hint of coercion or persuasion.

Her gaze meandered to his mouth, as her own lips parted and her fingertips curled into the material of his shirt.

He brushed a kiss across her forehead, and she sighed, dropping her shoulders. His next kiss landed on her cheekbone.

This time she shifted from one foot to the other, moving closer so that the tips of her breasts made contact with his chest.

He swallowed. "Do you want to sit down?"

She rested her forehead on his collarbone. "I want to go to bed—with you."

Her simple request lit a fire in his belly, and he pulled her against his body, wrapping his arms around her waist and resting his cheek against the top of her head.

"I want that, too." As he spoke, the stubble on his chin caught the wavy strands of her hair. This slow burn between them made him harder than if she'd ripped his clothes off.

"Shouldn't we make a move upstairs?" She pulled away from him, but they were still connected through her wisps of hair that clung to his chin.

That's how he felt with Martha—connected—as if she always had some hold on a part of him.

MARTHA'S STOMACH DROPPED. Cam didn't really want her. He was being polite…too damned polite. She turned away from him quickly and stumbled on the first step of the staircase, grabbing the bannister.

He caught her around the waist, more to steady her than make a move on her. "H-have you changed your mind?"

"No, but I think you have." She broke away from him and charged up the stairs.

His footsteps pounded behind her. She felt the air at her back as he made a swipe at her blouse, and she took the next set of steps two at a time.

"Martha, wait." This time he grabbed her swinging arm and pulled her down one step. "What did I do wrong?"

Her whiskey eyes flashed at him. "I just told you I wanted to go to bed with you. Maybe it was clumsy or whatever. Maybe I should've batted my lashes and swiveled my nonexistent hips, but I thought it was pretty direct."

A slow flush crawled up his neck. "And I thought my answer was direct. It's what I want, too."

"But then you—" she wrinkled her nose "—you hugged me, put your cheek on my hair. Comforted me."

"So." He spread his hands and hunched his shoulders. "What does that mean? We just came from a murder scene. I figured you needed some comfort."

She bit her bottom lip. What did it mean? It had felt…brotherly. She was done being everyone's favorite little sister.

"It's just not the reaction I expected after telling you I wanted to sleep with you."

"What did you expect?" Cam leaned against the bannister as if waiting for a long, drawn-out explanation.

"I expected you to j-jump my bones. Rip my clothes off." A hurt little bark escaped from her throat. "I guess I just don't inspire that kind of passion."

A slow smile crept across his mouth, and before she had time to ask him what it meant, he had her against the wall, pressing the full length of his body against hers.

He captured her wrists in one hand, dragged her arms above her head and pinned them to the wall. He growled, his lips one hot breath away from hers. "You talk too much."

The kiss he planted on her mouth heated her blood. Her knees wobbled. Her skin tingled. Her lashes fluttered closed and as his tongue invaded her mouth, she wrapped one leg around his in an attempt to stay upright.

When he finished draining her with that one kiss, he unbuttoned her pants. To allow him to pull them down easily, she arched her back. Instead, with her pants still around her hips, Cam plunged his hand inside her panties, and she gasped at the sweet invasion.

He toyed with the swollen folds of her flesh, and she closed around his fingers as she rocked against him.

She couldn't just let him do all the work, but his other hand still held her wrists captive. She rested her head on his shoulder and pressed her lips against his neck.

As she got closer to her release, she bared her teeth against his skin and nipped at it.

And then it happened. Her orgasm clawed through her body, and her head fell back against the wall, banging it.

Cam tucked his hand beneath her bottom, his fingers still toying with her, as she rocked against him.

He released her wrists, and she grabbed the front of his shirt. With shaking fingers she unbuttoned it, fanned it out and slipped it from his arms.

His broad chest looked chiseled from granite. With a fever burning in her veins, she trailed her fingers from his throat to the waistband of his jeans.

As she worked on the fly, Cam braced his hands

against the wall on either side of her and kept dipping his head to tease her with kisses.

"I thought you were supposed to be ripping my clothes off. You're kinda slow."

She yanked his fly open and skimmed her palm over the bulge in his briefs. "Oh, I want you."

He toed off his shoes and kicked them down the stairs. Then he shed his jeans and his underwear at the same time and kicked them off the side of the staircase.

He tugged at her clothing, not quite ripping it off, and dropped each piece over the bannister to the floor below to join his clothes.

For a brief moment she thought he'd taken her hand to lead her up the rest of the staircase to her bedroom. Instead, he urged her down to the step directly beneath her.

She sat with her legs extended down the stairs, as he crouched beside her. Looked like she'd have to wait to have him because he seemed intent on having her again.

He spread her legs, and the toes of her left foot curled around the wooden balusters that drilled into each step. He positioned himself between her thighs a few steps below her.

When his tongue touched her aching flesh, her bottom bounced from the step.

"You're not going anywhere." He flattened his palms against her inner thighs and dipped his head to renew his tender assault.

She didn't even last as long as the previous time, and the heat surged through her body and into her cheeks as her orgasm raced through every cell of her body.

He came up for air and rested his chin on her mound as she still writhed beneath him. "That didn't take long.

Either you haven't had sex in a while, or I'm the great-est lover known to womankind."

"It's been years."

Cam's eyes popped open, and Martha giggled as she ran one foot up the back of his leg and planted it against his muscled buttocks. "I'm just kidding."

"You're cruel." He reached up and cupped one of her breasts. "And who knew Martha Drake giggled?"

"Only when she's with the greatest lover known to womankind."

He rose above her, as if doing a push-up over her body, and skimmed the tip of his erection along her belly. "I haven't even gotten started yet."

He grabbed the bannister and pulled himself up, hooking one arm around her waist. He pressed his naked body against hers and kissed her hard and long.

"Where the hell is your bedroom in this dump?"

She traced his perfect form with her hands on either side of his body and trailed her fingertips across his smooth, tight skin. "I thought you'd never ask."

"I could take you right here on the staircase if you want." He tapped the hard wood of the bannister. "Lean you right over and claim you from behind."

"But my bed is so soft and warm."

"Just like you." He swept her up in his arms, cradling her five-foot-ten-inch frame against his chest like she was a teddy bear.

Her head fell into the hollow of his shoulder, fitting perfectly, and her mouth watered as she anticipated the other perfect fit between their bodies.

She directed him to her bedroom, and he kicked open the half-closed door, which gave her a thrill. As he dropped her on the bed, she reached for him with greedy hands.

Grabbing those hands, he kissed her fingertips. "You're so beautiful. I watched your face during your first orgasm, and it was like witnessing the birth of a butterfly."

A wash of red immediately claimed Cam's cheeks. "Was that the stupidest comparison ever?"

A tear leaked out of the corner of her eye. "That was the sweetest thing anyone has ever said to me. The best bit of poetry I've ever heard."

"You're just saying that." He stretched out beside her and caressed every inch of her body as he rained kisses all over her face.

She wanted to pleasure him, too, but he wouldn't allow it.

He whispered in her ear, "This is all about you tonight. I want you to feel pampered, desired…"

Loved. She wanted to feel loved, but what right did she have to expect that from Cam? She'd practically dragged him into bed. What was he going to do, turn her down? Cam Sutton was a hot-blooded, all-American male. Men like Cam didn't turn down invitations to sex—ever.

As he began moving against her, spreading her open, entering her, all her insecurities slipped away in breathless wanting. He filled her up, seemed to find every deficit in her soul and had an answer for it.

This time, she got to watch him as he experienced his release, and the sheer pleasure that spasmed across his face gave her a sense of power and tenderness at the same time. For several moments, she held his joy cupped within her.

As he shifted off her body, he nuzzled her neck. "I don't know if that just made the situation between us better or worse."

She froze, her fingers ceasing their combing his hair back from his forehead. "What does that mean? How can what we just experienced make anything worse? Unless I just misread everything that happened."

"You didn't misread a damned thing, Martha." He rolled to his side and propped up his head with his hand, his elbow digging into the pillow. "That was incredible and we both know it, but I still have to protect you. I don't know how I can do that job with a clear head now."

"It'll be better." She traced his bottom lip with her thumb. "Now that we've gotten the sex part out of the way, we'll be able to focus better on the issues in front of us."

His eyebrows shot up. "The sex part?"

"You know, all that tension between us, or at least on my side?" She tried to keep the insecure questioning out of her voice but failed miserably.

"I know exactly what you mean." He kissed the pad of her thumb.

She cupped his jaw briefly with her hand. "I'm going to pick up our clothes downstairs."

He grabbed her hand as she rolled from the bed. "I can do that if it's driving you crazy knowing they're in heaps on the floor."

"That's okay. I'm going to get some water, too."

Yawning, he settled back against the pillow. "Hurry back."

From the edge of the bed, she surveyed his heavy lids and slow, steady breathing. She rolled her eyes.

Even if she hurried, he'd probably be sleeping by the time she came back.

She tiptoed from the room and crept down the stairs, picking up items of clothing as she went. She gathered up the rest of their things where Cam had dropped them over the bannister, and her lips twitched. He'd really shown her a night of passion.

She bundled the clothes on a chair and flicked on the lights beneath the kitchen cabinets. She grabbed a glass from the cupboard and turned toward the fridge.

A quick movement caught her eye, and she glanced at the sliding glass doors to the back. She let out a scream and dropped the glass on the floor where it shattered.

But she still couldn't tear her gaze away from a pair of gleaming eyes that had caught her in their malevolent stare.

Chapter Eleven

A crash and a scream from Martha yanked Cam to full consciousness. He bolted upright and reached for his gun...which he'd left downstairs in his jacket.

"Martha!" Scrambling from the bed, he scanned the floor for his briefs and remembered he'd dropped them over the stairs. "Just great."

He stumbled for the door and charged down the stairs, calling Martha's name again. He followed the glow of the low light emanating from the kitchen.

He almost plowed into Martha's back as he launched into the kitchen.

She stumbled forward, and he caught her around the waist as she raised her arm, pointing toward the sliding door to the back of the house.

He peered at the darkness beyond the glass, beyond the reflection of the two of them naked and entwined in some other kind of dance from the one they'd left upstairs. Martha's body was stiff and unyielding, and she hadn't said one word to him since that scream had echoed throughout the house.

Giving her a little shake, he asked, "What's wrong? What happened, Martha? Did you see something outside?"

She cranked her head to the side and worked her

mouth for a few seconds before she finally found her voice. "A man. A man with a black ski mask covering his whole face was looking in at me."

Adrenaline ripped through Cam's body and he lunged for the door, but Martha grabbed his arm.

"Wait. There's glass on the floor and…and you don't have any clothes on."

"More importantly, I don't have my weapon." He spun around and strode to the chair where he'd left his jacket. He plunged his hand in the pocket and grabbed his gun. He swiped his jeans from the same chair and struggled into them on his way back to the kitchen.

This time he nearly tripped over Martha, on her hands and knees, sweeping a towel across the kitchen floor.

"You need shoes. I think I pushed most of the glass aside, but it's freezing out there. Your shoes are under the chair where I put our clothes."

With the intruder most likely putting more and more distance between himself and the house—and Cam's gun—Cam turned and stuffed his bare feet into his shoes. Finally, he charged outside.

Martha had turned on the outdoor lights, and Cam scanned the small patio and the lawn beyond it, which tumbled down to the boat dock and the bay. He took the corner of the house and ran in a crouched position to the front.

He peered around the corner to the driveway, but if the masked man had arrived in a car and driven up to the front of the house, he was gone now. It made sense that Ben would know about this place. He seemed to know everything else about Martha.

The cold night air seeped into his bare flesh as he

made his way to the circular driveway. He cocked his head, listening for—anything, a receding car, the squeal of a tire. He heard nothing but his own heart slamming against his chest.

He returned to the back patio where Martha hovered at the sliding door, his jacket clasped to her chest.

"Nothing out front?"

"No."

She thrust the jacket at him when he got close. "Put this on. It's freezing out here."

Poking his arms through the sleeves, he asked, "What was he doing at the door? What did you see?"

"Not much." She hugged herself. "I glanced up and saw his face at the door, except it wasn't really his face. His face was completely covered by a ski mask."

"Did he try to get in?"

"I-I'm not sure. He didn't run away until you got down here."

"Close the door. I want to check something."

Martha stepped onto the patio next to him and slid the door closed.

Cam ran his hand over the window closest to the door handle, skimming his palm over the chilly glass. Then he felt it. His fingertips traced over a rough edge in the glass.

"Did you find anything?"

"I did. Feel this." He took her hand and guided her fingers over the damaged window.

She snatched her hand back and wrinkled her nose. "It's cut."

"He used some glass-cutting tool. He was going to slice out a part of the window and reach in to unlock the door."

She jerked upright. "He knows about this house."

"Of course he does, Martha."

Flicking her fingers at the window, she jerked upright. "That's what he was doing when I discovered him. He stopped because you came onto the scene. I guess he wasn't expecting anyone else to be here."

"Too bad I wasn't prepared for him." He snapped his fingers. "The camera system. I noticed the house has cameras on all corners. Can you pull that up on the computer?"

"Yes." She sighed. "The sun's going to be coming up soon anyway. Who needs sleep?"

He caught a strand of her hair and wrapped it around his finger. "I'd rather do what we did instead of sleep any day of the week."

"Me, too."

He tugged her forward by her hair and kissed her sweet lips. "Video."

"Maybe you could put on the rest of your clothes, so I won't get distracted." She wiggled her fingers in the air over his bare chest, and his skin tingled as if she'd actually touched him.

"Yeah, distractions." He yanked open the sliding glass door and stalked to the chair where a lone shirt hung. Martha had already put on all her clothes from last night.

At the entrance to a door off the main hallway, Martha crooked her finger at him. "The office. My mom's desktop computer is in here, and we can look up the footage."

Martha stationed herself behind the big desk and clicked on a lamp. "Let me see if I can remember how to retrieve it."

"It's all pretty standard." He leaned over her shoulder as she clicked through the files on the computer's desktop.

The monitor displayed four squares, and Martha poked at each one as she identified it. "Driveway, front door and porch, back door, boat dock."

"Time?" He swirled his finger around the date and time stamp in the lower-right corner of each panel.

Martha enlarged the driveway display and moved the cursor to the menu. She adjusted the time to just about thirty minutes before she went downstairs.

Cam squinted at the video. "Is it motion-activated?"

"I honestly don't know that much about it, but I think so. It's just dark, isn't it?"

"Do you know for sure if it works?"

She slumped against the deep, leather chair. "No."

"Maybe he didn't come up the driveway. He wouldn't be that obvious, would he? I didn't see or hear any evidence that he had a car out front. Switch to another view. We know for sure he was at the back door."

Martha switched to the video panel showing the back door and made it bigger. She set the time back, and they both stared at the murky display again.

The image came to life and Cam let out a breath. "There he is."

A figure moved into the frame, a ski mask pulled low over his face, dark, baggy clothing loose around his body.

Martha bolted upright. "That's our guy."

"Unfortunately, that could be any guy. That could be me or even you. Just like using a disguise at the Insider, he's covering up."

The man came in from the side and crowded the door for several seconds, hunching over.

"He's probably working on the window."

The man stood still, placing gloved hands against the door, staring into the house.

"Ugh, that's probably when I noticed him."

The intruder sprang back from the door, stumbling over a potted plant. He dashed toward the lawn and out of the camera's view.

"He's heading toward the boat dock." Martha pulled up that panel, but the camera recorded nothing, no movement at all. "That one might be broken."

"We wouldn't have been able to identify him anyway, not with that ski mask."

Martha shoved back from the desk. "I wish I knew what he wanted. He must've come here to break in and do a search."

"If all he wanted to do was search your place for whatever he thinks Casey left you, he would've taken off when you appeared in the kitchen and caught him red-handed."

Slowly turning the chair to face him, Martha asked, "Do you think he wanted to harm me this time?"

"You said he didn't leave until I stumbled onto the scene. You'd already noticed him, and that didn't make him go away."

"So, he's reached the point where he doesn't want to take a chance that I'll discover his identity from something Casey might have left behind." Martha's fingers clawed into the arms of the chair.

Cam bent forward and smoothed his hands down her arms. "Maybe he just wanted to question you."

"Question?" She tilted her head back to meet his

eyes. "Is that a nice way of saying interrogate under a single bright light? The man's a killer, Cam. He's proven that three times now."

"He *is* desperate to protect his identity. He probably never figured you'd find Tony and never figured Tony would fess up to being Casey's pimp."

"But I did, and Tony did and now we have a chance to discover who this guy is and why he set me up with those emails about Major Denver."

"And who's giving him orders." Cam's jaw tightened. "I'd like to get *him* under a single bright light to find that out."

"He must know we don't have this super-secret thing he's searching for because he's still after it—and us. I don't understand why he doesn't just disappear." She cupped his jaw with her hand. "Even if we get a good look at him and we're able to convince the FBI or the CIA to investigate him for those emails, it's not going to change anything for Denver, is it? There's still the rest of the evidence against the major that these emails brought to light."

"It's a start. It's a connection. Right now, we don't know who set him up or why. If this Ben can give us some insight, maybe we can unravel the rest of it."

"Then it's a game of cat and mouse, isn't it? We try to find the evidence, and he tries to make sure we don't. When is he going to give it up?"

Cam shrugged and pulled her out of the chair. "When he's tired of playing cat and mouse."

"Or when I'm dead."

"Don't say that." He placed his hands on her shoulders and drove his thumbs into her skin.

"We both know the reason why he hasn't taken his shot at me yet."

"We do?" Cam ran his tongue over his dry lips.

"It's because you're here, Cam. He knows I have some kind of badass bodyguard dogging me, and when you leave—" her shoulders tensed beneath his hands "—I'm a goner."

"I'm not going anywhere."

"Yet." She tucked her head beneath his chin. "How many more days until you leave?"

"Shh." He dropped his hands to her waist and pulled her body against his. "We have time. I'm gonna catch this guy and when I do, he'll pay—for everything."

LATER THAT MORNING, Martha, still sleepy-eyed, greeted him in the kitchen, holding up a plate of eggs. "Scrambled. Is that okay with you?"

"You didn't have to make breakfast…but I'm glad you did." He straddled the stool at the island counter. "I'd like to have a look out back now that it's light and see if Ben left anything. Would also be interesting to figure out how he got here. Unless that camera out front is broken like the one at the boat dock, he didn't come up the driveway."

She dropped two slices of toast on his plate and put it on the place mat in front of him. "I wanted to show you the boat dock, anyway. It's not as big as the one we had when my dad was a free man, but it's similar."

"Must've been an idyllic childhood."

"It was lonely. I didn't make friends easily, and my mother insisted on sending me to a private school, miles away from our house. My parents' home wasn't exactly part of a neighborhood." She waved her fork around.

"Kind of like this place. I couldn't run down the block to play with friends. That's one of the reasons why I read a lot—and hung out with my dad."

"At least you had a dad you could hang out with... and at least you could read." Cam shook his head as soon as the words left his lips. "I sound like a self-pitying idiot."

She smiled, and his world got brighter by several shades.

"A little, but it's safe to do that with me. At least you had godlike good looks and athletic abilities. You must've been Mr. Popularity growing up."

"Yeah, but that can get kind of lonely too in its own way."

She sat on the stool next to him and bumped his shoulder with hers. "Two lonely kids and now here we are."

"No place I'd rather be." He dabbed a crumb from the corner of her mouth. "When I discovered the identity of the CIA translator who turned over the emails that upended Denver's life, I was ready to give you the third degree. I thought you might've even been involved in the setup—until I met you. Then I knew exactly why you'd been the conduit for those emails."

"Because of my rigid adherence to protocol."

"But you surprised me, and you sure as hell surprised Ben."

She twirled her fork on her plate. "Do you think the patriot and Ben are the same person? We've been assuming they are, but maybe we're dealing with two different people—the computer geek and the killer."

"Could be." He brushed the toast crumbs from his fingers into the napkin on his lap. "The patriot warned you the night before Wentworth's death. That's for sure. He knew that was coming."

"Just seems like we're dealing with someone who has two very different sets of skills."

"A computer nerd can't be a killer? Or an assassin can't also be well versed in computer programming?"

"Anything's possible, but I dated a tech whiz and I couldn't see him taking out Tony like that."

So, Martha did date. Cam stirred the eggs around his plate, intently studying the pattern they made. "What happened to that relationship?"

"Bad idea all around. We were too much alike, and I worked with him or at least near him."

"CIA analyst?"

"Not nearly that exciting. CIA tech guy."

"Who broke it off?"

"I sort of did. It wasn't that serious to even be called a breakup. We talked a lot. We were friends first, and then he got the bright idea to ask me out. He never even saw the inside of my bedroom."

Cam raised his eyebrows. Was that Martha's way of telling him she hadn't slept with the guy? "Still friends?"

"We chat when we see each other at work." She picked up her plate and held it out toward him. "Are you done?"

He stacked his plate on top of hers. "That hit the spot. Now let's bundle up and take a look around outside."

Martha left their plates in the sink, and they grabbed their jackets. When they slipped through the back door that had been compromised the previous night, Cam stepped back and looked at the scratches on the window.

He rubbed the rough patch of glass. "You should get

this fixed. It wouldn't take much to punch that out. He was probably minutes away from doing that."

"Add it to my list, which includes getting my Georgetown locks changed."

Cam crouched and searched the ground in front of the door. The mat seemed undisturbed, and the brick beneath didn't show any marks or footprints, not even theirs from last night.

He took two steps back, grazed the edge of the planter with his leg and squatted beside the container to study the plant for threads.

"You're retracing his steps?" Martha tilted her head.

"Yeah. It looked like he ran straight back to the boat dock and the bay."

Martha turned and faced the water. The brisk breeze blew her hair back from her face. "He must have, unless he circled back to the front, but we didn't see anything on the camera footage. Maybe he came up by water."

"You did want to show me the boat dock."

She stuck her hand out behind her. "Let's go."

In two strides he joined her and grabbed her hand. Their footsteps crunched on the gravel path leading toward the dock.

Cam stopped and dropped to one knee. "If he took this path, he would've left footprints."

Martha crouched beside him and poked at the gravel with her finger. "Looks like he may have even smoothed this over by shuffling his feet."

"Maybe, or the wind covered his tracks." Cam cupped her elbow and helped her rise. "I think we're on the right track here."

When they reached the dock, Cam stomped on it. "Sturdier than it looks."

"It has to hold up to the weather, especially this time of year." She pounded on the side of the shed that was designed to hold a small boat. "This, too, even though my mom doesn't have a boat."

Cam peered around the corner at the water stirring inside the empty boat shed. "Maybe he parked his own boat here when he came up."

Martha placed her hands on her hips and stared at the gray water lapping at the shore. "He could've come from the public dock, moored here and then attempted his break-in. When you showed up, he hightailed it back to his boat and took off, probably knowing you'd look for a car out front."

"I probably could've caught him if I'd come straight back here instead of wasting time putting clothes on and going to the front of the house." He fired a pebble into the water.

"You couldn't have come out here without your clothes." Martha moseyed to the edge of the dock and kicked at the mooring.

"Don't fall in." Cam leaned over to gather a few more stones for skipping, and a half-smoked cigarette on the shore. He pinched it between his thumb and forefinger and held it up. "Look at this. Does your mother smoke?"

"No."

He cupped it in his palm and bounced it in his hand. "This looks hand rolled. Would anyone else be down here? It's dry. Looks like someone meant to toss it in the water and missed—maybe because it was dark."

"My mom's handyman smokes. He's married to the housekeeper, and he comes down here sometimes when MayBeth is working, but I don't think he rolls his own."

"When was the last time he was here? If this had

been tossed here any earlier than last night, it would be wet by now or swept into the bay."

"I don't know for sure, but MayBeth usually comes on Fridays. Maybe Ben smokes."

"I'm hanging on to this." He slipped the cigarette into his pocket. "He knows you're staying at your mom's. He knows how to get here, and he tried to break in."

"And he knows you're here too—for now."

"You've been checking your texts? We know he has your number from Casey's phone."

She patted her jacket pocket. "All the time. He's gone quiet after weeks of harassing me."

"Then he was just trying to intimidate you into keeping quiet about your suspicions."

"Now he's afraid I'm going to find him out and report him. If he hadn't started murdering people, I wouldn't have had a clue to his identity."

"Those murders were always in his playbook—maybe not Tony's—but he wanted to cover his tracks and get rid of Wentworth and Casey. She could tie him to both Wentworth and the emails, and he wanted to erase that link. The only loose end left was you holding on to those emails for some reason he can't figure out."

"Believe me. I couldn't figure it out at first either, but now I know it was instinct that led me to hold on to them." She tucked her hand in his pocket. "And that instinct led you to me. It all happened for a reason."

He inserted his hand and folded it around hers. "I feel it, too. We're like puzzle pieces, and we both fill a part in this mosaic."

She pressed her arm against his as she hunched her shoulder. "I'm cold. Let's go inside, and I'll find someone to fix that window."

A phone buzzed and Cam dipped his hand into his other pocket. "That's yours."

Martha pulled out her phone and cupped a hand around the display to read the text. "It's my friend Farah. She's a translator who works with me."

"I'm assuming everyone at work knows what's going on with you."

"Yeah." She looked up from the phone. "Farah wants to meet for drinks tonight to tell me what's going on, what people are saying."

"Can she be trusted?"

"Farah? Absolutely."

"Then I think it's a good idea. Get the pulse of what's going on there."

"I think you're right." Martha cupped the phone with one hand and texted with her thumb.

She had two more exchanges with Farah and then pocketed the phone. "We're all set for eight o'clock tonight."

Cam took her hand. "Plenty of time to replace the glass in the window, get your locks changed and make a trip to and from my hotel."

"To and from?"

"To pick up my stuff and bring it here." He pressed a kiss against her temple. "After what happened here this morning, you don't think I'm going to allow you to stay on your own, do you?"

Cam pulled her close on their walk back to the house, inhaling the crisp scent of the bay that clung to her hair. He didn't know how he was ever going to leave Martha on her own as long as this killer had her in his sights.

SECURITY BUSINESS AND errands ate up the rest of the afternoon. Martha had a locksmith change the locks to her town house, got the glass replaced in the sliding glass door and Cam moved from his hotel to Mom's house.

Too tired to cook and too frazzled to go out, they picked up a pizza on the way back to Mom's. Martha patted her full tummy and curled one leg beneath her on the sofa. "I was relieved to see that our friend hadn't made a return visit to my town house."

"Not that we know of, anyway. You should've followed your mother's example and wired that place with a security system."

"He probably would've disabled that like he did the one at the bar." She nudged the pizza box with the toe of her shoe. "There are two pieces left. Do you want them, or should I wrap them up and put them in the fridge?"

"People actually wrap and refrigerate leftover pizza instead of just eating it in the morning?"

"Ugh." She wrinkled her nose as she eyed the gooey cheese congealing on top of the slices.

Reaching forward and ripping the pieces apart, Cam said, "I'd better do them justice now."

As a shot of the Insider flashed on the muted TV screen, Martha lunged for the remote and turned up the volume. "I wonder if they have any suspects yet."

"You and I both know the police will never find the real killer."

They listened to the story for a minute, and then Martha muted the sound again. "They're still putting out the burglary story. Maybe they don't want to reveal the message on the table to the general public."

"Well, he did clean out the cash drawer and the safe to make it look good."

"And destroyed the security system."

"Good thing he did that or we'd be on it, front and

center." Cam dragged a napkin across his mouth. "I haven't heard anything yet about Tony's extracurricular activities."

"Or his connection to Casey."

"Just another vicious murder in DC."

"Georgetown, and that's why it's getting so much air play."

"Is this bar we're going to tonight near the Insider?"

"Not far." Martha sniffed the air. "What is that smell? Tobacco? I've been smelling it on and off all day."

Cam reached across her and plucked his jacket from the arm of the sofa. "It's that cigarette I picked up by the boat dock. The tobacco is kind of sweet, isn't it?"

"And strong." She pushed up from the sofa. "I'll get you a plastic bag from the kitchen."

As she made a grab for the pizza box, Cam snatched up the last piece of pizza. "I'm saving this piece from the fate of being wrapped and stored."

She snorted. "A great sacrifice for you, I'm sure."

An hour later, they were on their way to another bar in Georgetown, and Martha hoped for a better outcome than last night.

She yawned as she pulled into a public parking lot on the crowded street. "I'm not sure I should have a drink tonight. I'm ready to fall asleep as it is."

"I wouldn't make any promises you can't keep." Cam tapped on the window to point out an empty parking space. "You may need a drink after listening to what your friend has to say."

They walked the two blocks to the waterfront bar hand in hand, and Martha could almost imagine they were on a regular date. She couldn't help noticing the admiring glances women threw at Cam, and she was just superficial enough that the attention to her date brought a smile to her face.

She tugged on Cam's hand as the bar came into view. "This is a date, right? You're not in Delta Force, you didn't track me down to interrogate me about the Denver emails, you never met Casey or saw Wentworth at my place."

"Just like we discussed." He opened the door for her and put his hand on her back as he whispered in her ear, "Do you see Farah?"

Martha swept the bar with her gaze and spotted Farah at a table with the guy she'd met on a dating website a few months ago—the married guy. "She's over there, and…"

Cam didn't give her a chance to finish her sentence. He crooked an arm around her neck and pulled her around for a kiss on the mouth.

For a few seconds Martha forgot she was standing in a crowded bar, forgot she had a three-time killer stalking her, forgot she was going to lose Cam in a week.

Her arm curled around his waist, and she sagged against him as a pool of heat ached between her legs.

He ended the long kiss, punctuated by another peck on the lips. "There. That should put any doubt about this being date night to rest."

Martha blinked and adjusted her glasses. She cleared her throat. "Right."

She yanked on his sleeve. "What I was going to say before you ambushed me is that Farah is here with her scumbag boyfriend."

"He's a scumbag?"

"He's married."

"Oh, that kind of scumbag." He rubbed her back.

"You weren't planning to get top secret with Farah anyway, were you?"

"No."

"Then let's see if she can tell you what they're saying about you in the office." He nudged her back, and she led him to Farah's table.

Farah rose from her chair, her wide, dark eyes darting from Martha to Cam. She gave Martha a one-armed hug and said, "You take a day off work and collect a boyfriend along the way?"

Martha kissed her friend's cheek. "Farah, this is Cam. Cam, this is Farah and Scott."

Everyone shook hands, and Martha and Cam crowded around the small table, as Cam craned his neck. "Waiters coming by?"

"Not often enough." Scott raised his almost empty bottle of beer. "I need to hit the men's room. I'll swing by the bar on the way and get us a round. Farah?"

She covered her wineglass with her hand. "I'm good."

Cam tapped Scott's bottle. "I'll have one of these."

Martha pointed to Farah's glass of wine. "And I'll make it easy and have a glass of white wine, thanks."

Scott kissed Farah on the top of the head. "Be right back."

"Thanks, babe." Wiggling her fingers over her shoulder, Farah flicked back her hair. "I'm glad you came out, Martha. I just wanted to give you a heads-up about work. First of all, are you okay? My God, to find Wentworth dead in your town house and then Casey the next day. I can't even imagine what you're going through."

And Farah didn't even know about Tony. Martha shot a look beneath her lashes at Cam. "It's been a pretty rough few days. What are they saying at the office? What's *Gage* saying?"

"Just, you know." Farah swirled her wine in the glass. "Lots of gossip about the congressman and your roommate."

Martha narrowed her eyes. "What's the real reason Proffit asked me to take a few days off?"

"I don't know." Farah hunched forward and twisted her head toward Cam. "Is he okay?"

"You can say anything in front of Cam."

Farah's tongue darted out of her mouth in a quick sweep of her lips. "Martha, they're looking at your computer."

Martha's jaw dropped, and a tickle of fear crept up her neck. "D-did they remove it from my cubicle."

Cam pressed his knee against hers and she welcomed the contact, although it did nothing to alleviate the panic galloping through her veins.

"No, but they've been in your cubicle a few times— all hush-hush. What else would they be doing in there?"

Cam asked, "Who's they? Who's been in Martha's cube?"

"Gage, Proffit and that tech guy." Farah tapped a fingernail against her glass. "Sebastian Forsythe, the one you dated a few times."

"That's not good." Martha grabbed Farah's glass and took a gulp of wine.

"You don't have anything to hide, do you, Martha? No, of course you don't, but if the Agency is looking at your work computer that may not matter."

"You're right. It may not matter. Thanks for clueing me in, Farah."

She nodded and then put a finger to her lips as she glanced to the side. "Zip it."

Martha looked up to see Scott with three drinks gathered in his hands.

"Success." He placed the drinks on the table in a huddle, and then slid them to their owners. "Wine, beer, beer. I can go for another round if you need me to."

Farah squeezed his hand. "Thanks, babe. Maybe later. Let's toast."

"To Mondays." Scott leaned in and clinked his bottle to Martha's glass, and she instinctively drew away.

She'd never liked Farah's taste in men. She'd met Scott just a few times, but any guy who claimed to have an arrangement with his wife raised a red flag with her. She gave Scott a weak smile and took a sip of her wine. Cam had been right. She might need the whole glass to get through this get-together.

"Oh my God, did you hear about that bartender who was murdered during a robbery? It happened not far from here." Farah twisted the gold chain around her neck with her fingers. "Terrible."

"I did see that on the news." Martha shook her head. "Why'd the guy have to kill the bartender?"

"Maybe he didn't expect the bartender to be there, and he didn't want the bartender to ID him." Scott ran a thumbnail through the damp label on his bottle.

"Well, it was probably all for nothing anyway. I know that area, and there are CCTVs in all the bars." Farah pointed to a corner of the ceiling. "Probably in here, too."

"The robber took care of the cameras." Martha

picked up her glass for another sip of wine, and someone kicked her under the table.

She choked on her wine and ended up taking a
deeper gulp. She avoided looking at Cam. Who else
would kick her?

"Took care of the cameras?" Farah tilted her head
to one side.

Scott asked, "You mean disabled them? We didn't
hear that."

Martha could've kicked herself—in the same spot
Cam had kicked her. She'd better stick to translating
because she clearly didn't have the makings of a spy.

"I think we heard something like that on the news
before we left." Cam dragged his napkin over a few
drops of wine on the table in front of Martha. "Do you
follow football, Scott?"

The men talked football while Farah filled Martha
in on other office gossip.

Several minutes later, Scott patted his front shirt
pocket. "I'm going to head out to the deck for a smoke.
Join me, Cam?"

"I don't smoke, but I do need to hit the men's room."
Cam scooted back from the table and winked. "We'll
leave you ladies to exchange secrets if you want."

Cam and Scott walked several feet together until
Scott peeled off for the deck on the side of the bar, and
Cam continued to the back and the restrooms.

Farah bent her head to Martha's and whispered, "Is
it those emails, Martha? I didn't want to say anything
in front of Cam, but do you think Proffit knows you
copied those emails onto a flash drive?"

"I don't know how he could...unless someone told him."

"Not me, I swear." Farah drew a cross over her heart with one long fingernail. "Did you tell someone else?"

"No, but…" She snapped her mouth shut as she saw Scott coming in from the patio. "That was fast."

"Oh, he's trying to quit, so he doesn't smoke his cig all the way down. Screwy method if you ask me." Farah rolled her eyes and touched her glass to Martha's.

Martha cupped her wineglass with one hand and swirled another sip of the oaky chardonnay in her mouth, her eyebrows knitting over her nose as she followed Scott's progress back to their table.

Even as Cam appeared several feet behind Scott with a bottle of beer in each hand, Martha pinned her gaze to Scott, tracking his every movement. He stuffed something, a pouch, in the pocket of his jacket.

Martha jerked her head once and allowed the wine to run down the back of her throat. That pouch could be anything. Maybe it wasn't even a pouch. It didn't have to be loose tobacco, and plenty of people didn't smoke their cigarettes all the way down to the butt. He probably wanted to get back to Farah.

Eyeing her half-empty wineglass, Martha pushed it away from her as Scott reached their table.

He leaned in to kiss Farah on the mouth, and she shooed him away with both hands. "You know I can't stand smoking. I grew up with just about every member of my family lighting up, and I can't stand it—especially that tobacco and especially those roll-your-own cancer sticks."

Martha froze. This time when Scott sat down and pulled his chair up to the table, instead of moving away from him, she moved closer and inhaled deeply.

Her heart slammed against her rib cage. The odor of the tobacco from his breath caused a cold dread to snake up her spine.

Chapter Twelve

Cam placed the beers on the table and nodded to Scott. He didn't want to stay much longer, but he owed Scott a round. Unless Farah had dropped a bombshell in the past ten minutes, she'd told Martha everything she knew about the office. Wasn't much Martha could do about it now.

Someone kicked his shin under the table, and he shifted his leg to the side. Then Martha scooted her chair toward him and dug her fingernails into his thigh—at least he hoped those were Martha's fingers so close to his crotch.

Picking up his beer, he met her gaze above the bottle and almost choked on the liquid running down his throat. Her pale face and her lips pressed together in a thin line made his stomach drop. Had Farah delivered more bad news?

Martha made a grab for her wineglass and knocked it over. She jerked back from the table. "Sorry."

Scott tossed his napkin on top of the spreading pool of wine. "Do you want another?"

"No!" Martha shoved her chair back from the table. "No, thank you. I think we'd better be going. I—I have to let my mom's dog out."

"Your mom has a dog?"

As Farah tilted her head, Cam drew his eyebrows together. What had lit a fire under Martha? Farah didn't seem to know.

Martha jumped up from the table. "Thanks so much for the heads-up, Farah. If anything else happens, let me know. Hopefully, I'll be back at work next week once the Agency realizes I wasn't at all involved in Casey and the Congressman's relationship."

"Sounds like a movie of the week, Casey and the Congressman." Farah stood up and gave Martha a one-armed hug and shook Cam's hand. "Nice to meet you."

Scott stood up, as well, and everyone said their goodbyes, which couldn't happen fast enough for Cam. Something had obviously happened to spook Martha when he'd been absent, but that something hadn't come from Farah.

Cam slid Martha's coat and purse from the back of her chair. "We'll have to do this again."

As he handed Martha's purse to her, she elbowed him in the ribs, and he sucked in a breath. He helped her into her coat and she grabbed his arm, practically dragging him out of the bar.

When they hit the sidewalk, Martha folded her arms and continued her quick pace.

He bumped her shoulder. "What's going on? Where are we going? Your mother doesn't even have a dog."

She didn't say one word until they got into the car and closed the doors. Then she turned to him and grabbed his sleeve.

"Farah's boyfriend? Scott?"

He nodded. "Yeah?"

"He's our guy."

"Our guy? The one who hacked you?"

"The one who killed three people."

"How do you know that?" His gaze darted to the side mirror.

"Did you smell him when he came back to the table?"

"I don't usually make a habit out of sniffing other dudes."

She slugged his shoulder. "I'm serious, Cam. He smelled sweetish, just like that cigarette you picked up on the boat dock."

"Same tobacco?"

She licked her lips. "It's more than that. He rolls his own cigarettes, and when he came back from his smoke after just a few minutes, Farah told me he's trying to quit and smokes only half his cigarette."

"The one on the dock was only half smoked." He rubbed his knuckles against his jaw. "Maybe you're onto something."

She closed her eyes and pressed her fingers against her temples. "I think I am. It's too coincidental."

"When did Farah start dating him?"

"About four months ago. Met him online, and he told her he was married right away. She's not looking for something permanent, so that didn't bother her."

"He told her he was married to explain why he didn't bring her to his place or introduce her to his friends."

Martha started the car but didn't make a move. "He started dating her to get close to me. Just like he ordered Casey to keep an eye on me. Everyone around me is proving to be false."

He grabbed her hand. "Not me. Do you think Farah's in on it? She could've been the one who identified you to be the conduit of those emails."

"No way. Farah wouldn't do that."

"That's what you thought about Casey, too." He entwined his fingers with hers. "It's like they're forming a snare around you, Martha. They wanted people on the inside, watching you—from work and from home."

"That doesn't make sense." The chattering of her teeth swallowed up her last word.

"Sure it does." He turned up the heat in the car. "On some level you know it. You recognized the smell of that cigarette when it had been in my pocket. It struck a chord with you because you'd smelled it before—on him."

"If it's all true, if Scott's the killer, we can't leave Farah to him. I'm not going to allow her to be alone with a killer."

He reached over and cut the engine, and then grabbed the door handle. "I wish you would've told me this sooner, right outside the bar. I could've confronted him then."

"What are you doing?"

He cranked his head over his shoulder. "I'm going back. He's right under our noses. I'm not going to let him slip through my grasp now after trying to ID him for days."

"Wait." She put her hand on his back. "Do we really want him to know we're onto him? What do you think he was planning in there? He *did* get us our drinks."

Cam ran his tongue around the inside of his mouth. "What would be the point in drugging us in a public place, in front of his supposed girlfriend?"

"Maybe he wanted to drug us for later. Knock us out at my mom's house and break in without disturbing us."

"That's some long-acting drug."

"I don't know." She flattened her palm against her chest. "You do know that he arranged this meeting to-night, don't you? Somehow, someway, he got Farah to invite me out."

"I agree. None of this is coincidence." He pushed open the door. "And I'm going to find out why. I'm going to find out who put him up to this, and why they want to bring down Major Denver."

"Cam!"

The urgency burned in his gut. On some logical level he knew Martha was right. Why show their hand now? But he might never get a crack at this guy again. He was two blocks away. He had to make a move.

Cam broke into a jog, even as he heard Martha call-ing behind him. He dodged a couple of cars to cross the street to the restaurant and burst through the doors.

The chairs where the four of them had sat were empty, the table still littered with their glasses and bot-tles. He threaded his way through the bar and loomed over the table.

"Forget something?"

He spun around and almost knocked into the wait-ress. "The other couple, they left?"

"Right after you did." She balanced her tray on her hip and repeated her question. "Forget something?"

"It's all right. I'll call them later." Cam backed up to the table and wrapped his fingers around the neck of Scott's beer bottle. He shuffled around the waitress, keeping the bottle behind him. "Thanks."

Outside the bar when he reached the street corner, Martha pounced on him. "What were you doing? How could confronting him in public possibly work?"

"Don't worry. They'd left." He presented the beer

bottle with a flourish and held it in front of Martha's face. "And I snagged this."

"His fingerprints."

"Exactly. I have a buddy with the PD in Virginia who can help out with the prints."

She slipped her fingers in the back pocket of his jeans as they walked to the car. "Scott's playing with fire. How did he know we wouldn't be able to ID him?"

"He probably felt secure since he was obviously wearing a disguise when he met with Casey and Tony, and he had a mask on this morning at your mom's house. When Tony described him with the beard and glasses, we already figured he'd donned a disguise."

"We can't prove anything based on a tobacco brand, Cam."

"Who knows? We could even be wrong about him, but I doubt it."

When they reached the car, Martha leaned against it, shoving her hands in her pockets. "Farah. We can't leave her alone with him."

"Would they go back to her place?"

"They never go to his place. He's conveniently married, remember?"

"We can't go charging into Farah's place. We need a plan." Cam rubbed his hands together against the chill of the night. "But let's do it in the car with the engine running and the heat blasting."

Once in the car, Cam turned to Martha. "Do you know where Farah lives?"

"A town house not far from here."

"We could drop by on some pretext—you left your phone at the bar, or something work related. If Scott's still there, you could get Farah alone. Maybe you could warn her against him."

She worried her bottom lip. "If he's at her place and you see him again, will you be able to control yourself? You charged back to the bar, ready to get some answers from him."

"If he is there, it might be the perfect opportunity to get some answers." Cam drummed his thumbs against the dashboard. "He'd be in a private place. I could let him know we have his prints and are going to the police with our suspicions."

"Like you said before, we have nothing to tie him to the three murders. Heck, the cops aren't even calling Congressman Wentworth's death a murder." She rolled her eyes. "I don't think a cigarette is going to do the trick, do you? We never even reported his attempted break-in to the police."

"We know that, but he doesn't. It might give us a little leverage with him. He's gonna realize he dropped a cigarette at your place, so that'll ring true." He slapped his hand against the dashboard. "It's worth a try. I'm not letting this guy slip away."

Martha threw the car into gear. "I agree, but I don't want anyone getting hurt."

"Nobody's going to get hurt." He ran a hand down her thigh. "Especially not you."

"Or Farah."

"Or Farah."

"Or you."

"Got it."

Ten minutes later, Martha parallel parked at the curb and pointed to a row of town houses. "Farah's is on the end."

Cam twisted around and peered out the back window. "Quiet street."

"Well, it is all residential and it's a weeknight." She turned off the engine and blew out a breath. "Ready?"

"We're ready." He patted his jacket pocket, feeling the hard outline of his weapon.

Martha's gaze followed the gesture. "Nobody's getting hurt, right?"

"Would you really care if Scott-Ben-Patriot got hurt? He murdered three people—that we know of—and he's after you and using Farah, putting her in danger."

"I know you're right, but you can't just run around shooting people based on a half-smoked cigarette—even if you are a hotshot D-Boy." She touched his face. "I'm more worried about you than him. I don't want you getting into any trouble."

He captured her fingers and kissed the tips. "And I don't want you getting into any trouble. Nobody's going to know you took those emails."

"My hand may be forced in the end if we want to put a stop to this guy." Closing her eyes, she sighed.

"You're not going to end up like your father." He squeezed her fingers before releasing them. "Let's go."

When Cam slammed the passenger door, a dog popped up at a window of a town house and barked. "At least someone's on guard around here."

"Let me do the talking." Martha pocketed her keys and took the lead to Farah's place on the corner.

This neighborhood lacked the understated elegance of Martha's with the fronts of the town houses closer to the edge of the sidewalk, but still nobody glanced out their windows at them as they passed by.

The area didn't scream high crime, but Cam shoved

his hand in his jacket pocket and caressed the handle of his gun anyway. The silence of the street had him coiling his muscles in expectation of…something.

Martha drew up to the steps of Farah's town house and pulled back her shoulders. "This is it."

Cam looked over Martha's head at the glow from the front window, the drapes tugged close, keeping the warmth and light from spilling onto the sidewalk. No light gleamed from the window to the left of this one, and the town house seemed draped in silence like the rest of the block.

Martha breezed up the steps and rang the doorbell. Shifting to the side, she said, "I want her to see me from the peephole."

Cam kept his eye in the square of light that was the front window, searching for movement or shadows.

He swallowed. "I don't think she's home, Martha."

"Not home?" Martha jabbed at the doorbell again. "Where would they be?"

Cam lifted a stiff shoulder. "Don't know."

Martha stepped back, tilting her head to scan the windows of the second story. "No lights on up there. Maybe they're in bed."

"Farah and Scott?"

Martha stuck her finger in her open mouth to mimic gagging. "I know. It makes me sick to think about it."

"Maybe you should call her." Cam's jaw ached with the insidious tension that had crawled through him ever since he stepped from the car. "Call her."

Martha shot him a sharp glance and then fumbled with her phone. She tapped the screen and listened for several seconds. "It's Martha. I'm on your front porch.

Something I need to ask you, so give me a call when you get this or let me in if you're home."

"This place has a side door and a back door?"

"Back door, I think." Martha folded her arms, clutching her purse to her side. "Why?"

"I want you to go back to the car, Martha. Just sit inside and wait for me. I'm going to do a quick check."

Her eyes got round behind her glasses. "Why?"

"Just want to make sure."

"Make sure about what, that Farah's not dead behind those doors? Like Casey? Like Tony?"

Her voice had risen to a squeal, and Cam put a finger to her soft lips. "We came here to check on Farah, didn't we? To make sure she was okay. I'm gonna do that now, and you're gonna go back to the car and wait for me."

He put his hands around her waist and twirled her toward the car as if they were on the dance floor. "It's just a precaution. I'm sure she's fine."

She cranked her head over her shoulder and covered her mouth. "What if we endangered Farah's life by taking off like that? Maybe Scott realized we'd made the connection. I said my mom had a dog. If Scott was the one prowling around this morning, he's going to know there's no dog at that house."

He stroked her back. "That's not a given. Could be a lapdog, one of those little fur balls. Don't think that way. I won't be long."

He watched as she stumbled toward the car, and then he slipped around the side of the town house. If something had happened to Farah, Martha didn't need to bear witness to it.

He crept up to the first window and touched the glass with his nose, squinting to see through the gap in the curtains. He saw a slice of neat, undisturbed kitchen, and the threshold of the living room beyond.

He tried raising the window, but it didn't budge. If he did break in and discovered Farah and Scott in bed, he'd have a lot of explaining to do—especially if Scott really was just some cheatin' dog and not a killer.

Hunching forward, he made his way to the back of the town house where a short gate blocked his path. As he reached over the top to feel for the latch, he froze.

The eerie silence of the neighborhood had been broken by something much worse—Martha's scream.

Chapter Thirteen

About five feet from the car, Martha aimed the remote to unlock the doors. A sick feeling had been gnawing at her gut ever since Cam's true purpose for searching Farah's place and sending her to the car had dawned on her.

If anything happened to Farah, she'd never forgive herself. How many people had to pay the price for her stupidity of snagging those emails for herself?

A pair of headlights flooded the street, and Martha caught her breath. Maybe Scott and Farah had come back and if so, she'd have to waylay them out here until Cam finished his search—and then somehow explain where Cam had gone and why.

The car slowed down, and Martha ran her tongue along her bottom lip as she recognized Farah's vehicle. She whispered, "C'mon, Cam."

The car double-parked next to her own, and just as Martha pasted a fake smile on her face, the driver's door sprang open.

"Hey, Farah, we—"

Martha broke off as the figure moved toward her, the black ski mask covering his face. She tripped backward, throwing her arms out to her sides to recover her balance.

The man circled behind her and took advantage of her unsteadiness. One strong arm curled around her chest, dragging her to the street and the idling car—Farah's car.

She used her last burst of air to scream. She dug her heels into the pavement. They scraped against it as her attacker pulled her to the street. When he reached Farah's car, he pulled open the passenger door and scrambled in backward, pulling her along with him even as she clawed at his arm and kicked at his legs.

"Hey, hey!"

Martha sobbed as Cam's shouts echoed in the night.

The man holding her grunted as he landed behind the wheel, and he threw the car into gear. As the car jerked into motion, he growled, "Stay out of this, or I'll be forced to kill you."

He'd released his hold on her, but the car was now in motion and her body was half in and half out, one foot inches off the ground.

She felt rather than saw Cam launch himself at the moving car. With one hand, he grasped onto the door as it swung wide, his other hand clutching his weapon pointed futilely at the ground. His legs scrambled beneath him, as they tried to keep pace with the moving vehicle.

Martha screamed again as the car veered toward a pole. The masked man would crush Cam if he could.

Through his panting, Cam said, "Get out, Martha. You have to get out. Fall on me."

The driver punched the gas pedal, and the car leaped forward. The car door swung back again.

Martha braced her foot against the seat as her attacker made a grab for her leg. She twisted and kicked him in the side.

Her new position gave her a view of the back seat, and she choked. "Cam, Cam."

"Out now!"

Cam yanked her by the arm, and she felt suspended in air for a second before landing on top of Cam's solid body. His arms wrapped around her, and they rolled together for several feet along a stretch of foliage.

They came to rest against a rise that broke their momentum, and Martha squeezed a painful breath from her lungs.

"Are you all right?" Cam's hands brushed across her face.

"I—I think so." She heaved a strangled sob.

"My God. He was trying to get you into the car." He smoothed the hair back from her face. "I should've never left you."

"Cam." She bunched fistfuls of his jacket in her hands. "He had Farah."

"What do you mean? That was her car?"

"He had her in the back seat. She was knocked out or..." She buried her face against his chest.

Cam struggled to sit up, brushing bits of leaves and twigs from his sleeves. "We have to call the police now. We'll stick as close to the truth as possible, but we need to report Farah's kidnapping and his attempted kidnapping of you."

"He warned me again. When it became clear he wasn't going to succeed in his abduction, he told me to back off. He said something weird."

Cam curled his arm beneath her back, and she winced as she sat up. When a car drove by, they both hunched toward the ground, but the driver rolled by without even noticing them.

"What was weird?"

"He told me to stay out of this or he'd be forced to kill me." Martha combed her fingers through her tangled hair. "Forced to kill me. He doesn't want to, but why? If he took me out now, he wouldn't have to worry about my finding anything else that Casey left behind for me."

"How would that look?" Cam rose to his knees, and cupped her elbow to help her up along with him. "A CIA translator is the conduit for a batch of emails implicating a Delta Force commander in colluding with the enemy. That translator's roommate kills herself after her congressman lover dies, and then the translator accidentally dies? Disappears? Is murdered? If Wentworth's death wasn't on the FBI's radar, your death and Casey's would definitely put it there."

"This is all blowing up for him and his plans to make the emails seem like some concerned patriot looking out for the good of the country."

"You're blowing it up for him. You and your out of left field decision to keep those emails." Cam touched her nose. "What happened to your glasses?"

"I don't know. I can't even remember if I had them when he pulled me into Farah's car." She bunched a fist against her midsection. "What are we going to do about Farah? He can't kill her, either. Even though she didn't receive the emails, she's a CIA translator."

"With no connection to Casey or Wentworth or as you just mentioned, the emails. He could make her death look like an accident."

"But we're friends." Martha clung to Cam as if she

were clinging to hope about Farah's safety. "That would look suspicious."

"If he doesn't kill her, she's going to report him."

"Maybe not." Martha took a wobbling step and grabbed Cam's arm for support. "If he drugged her wine and took her to the car where she passed out, she's not going to know any of this happened."

"Unless we call the police right now and tell them what we witnessed."

"Maybe that's not the way to go right now. We'd force his hand if he we do that."

"We have to go to the authorities at some point with what we know, Martha, or what would've been the whole point in all this? We have to let them know the emails were a plant to discredit Major Denver."

She slipped her hand in his pocket as they limped back to her car parked down the block from Farah's place. "What happened to your gun?"

"Dropped it." He pointed to the ground. "That's why I'm walking with my head down."

"What a pair we are." She leaned her head against his shoulder. "I guess Scott knew I realized his identity in the bar."

"Yeah, well, don't beat yourself up over that. If I'd put two and two together about those cigarettes, I probably would've assaulted him right then and there, and that wouldn't have been smart."

"It probably would've saved Farah."

Cam stopped suddenly and she bumped into him.

"Found it." He stooped to pick up his weapon, which had landed in the gutter of the street.

"You haven't seen a pair of glasses down there, have you?"

"I've been looking."

They reached the car, and Martha shivered when she saw the black skid marks in the street. If Cam hadn't come to her rescue, she'd be God knew where right now with a killer and a comatose Farah in the back seat of her car.

Cam swooped down and snatched up the keys she'd dropped during the attack. He dangled them from his fingers. "Are you okay to drive?"

She tapped her temple. "No glasses. You take the wheel." She looked up and down the empty street. "I can't believe all that commotion didn't prompt someone to call the police. Didn't anyone hear me scream?"

"I did." He opened the passenger door and helped her in. "That's all that matters."

As Cam walked around to the driver's side, two more cars drove by and Martha slid down in her seat.

He slammed the door and gripped the top of the steering wheel, stretching his arms in front of him. "We need to make a decision about Farah. She's incapacitated in the clutches of a killer."

"On the other hand…" She put one hand over her mouth. "Did I really say that after what you stated as the obvious?"

"This is me you're talking to, Martha." He thumped his chest with his fist. "I understand the gray areas. Let me finish your thought. On the other hand, if Farah's in the dark about being drugged, or kidnapped or Scott's wild ride with us clinging to an open car door, she's still safe and maybe we don't have to do anything at all right now to help her."

Martha nodded, happy that Cam had understood her coldhearted statement. "That's what I mean. Scott could take her to a hotel and tell her she passed out, got sick, whatever. He wouldn't have to harm her at that point because she never would even know she'd been in danger—except for us and if we call the police..."

Cam squeezed the bridge of his nose. "That's our dilemma."

"Cam." Martha spread her hands in front of her and inspected an abrasion on her knuckle. "I think it might be time for me to call an attorney. Gage at work was joking, but I *should* call my father's attorney. He's a family friend."

"Are you thinking of coming clean about the emails?" He traced a scratch on the back of her hand to her wrist.

"I think it's the only way now to protect Farah and tell the police and the FBI everything about Wentworth, Casey and Tony. I haven't heard any news about an autopsy for Wentworth, but they're still calling it a heart attack and Casey's still a suicide. The police haven't asked me anything else about her death or friends or state of mind."

"I don't want you to get in trouble, Martha."

"I did that all by myself." Her nose tingled, and she swiped the back of her hand across it.

"You tried to go through the right channels about your suspicions, but it didn't work. Nobody would listen to you."

"Coming clean would also help your cause. This guy, these people, have gone to great lengths, even murder, to set this all up and then deal with the loose ends. It will prompt an investigation of the emails and Major Denver."

"Like you said before. It still won't clear his name."

"But the doubt will be out there. What other evidence

was fabricated against him? The CIA will have to take a second look." She dragged her purse from the floor of the back seat and fished her phone from the side pocket. Scanning through her contacts, she said, "I'm not sure I have Sam Prescott's number on my phone, but it will be on my mom's computer."

"Whoa. You're going too fast." Cam splayed his hands across the steering wheel. "Don't you think you should talk to someone first? Get some advice?"

"That's why I'm going to call Sam." She pointed the corner of her phone at Cam.

"I suppose there's no point in waiting for Scott to bring Farah back home." Cam pulled away from the curb and made a U-turn in the middle of the street.

Martha's phone buzzed in her hand and she jerked it in front of her face. "I-it's Farah. It must be him."

"Answer it and put it on speaker."

"Farah?" Martha pressed a hand against her chest and her thundering heart.

"What's up? What's so urgent?" Hearing Farah's voice, clear if slow, sent a rush of relief flowing through Martha's body.

"You're okay?"

Cam put a hand on her arm and shook his head.

He was right. If Farah didn't know she was in danger, that just might save her. Her captor wouldn't have to kill her.

"Kinda woozy, but yeah. What's wrong? I got your voice mail from earlier. What was so urgent that you had to come out to my place?"

Martha cleared her throat. "Cam thought he left his cell phone at the bar and figured you and… Scott might've picked it up."

"I didn't notice any phone. We left pretty soon after you did. Are you going to tell me about Cam? He's a hot hunk of man, girl."

Martha snuck a peak at Cam, who rolled his eyes. He'd probably heard that line a million times.

"Where are you, Farah?" Cam poked her in her sore ribs. "A-Are you home now?"

"No. Scott treated me to a hotel suite. I was so out of it, he thought a nice spa day tomorrow would make me feel better. Isn't that sweet?"

Martha gritted her teeth. "He's still married, Farah. You need to get out of that relationship."

Farah giggled. "Shh. You're on speakerphone and Scott just heard that. That's just Martha, baby. You know this suits me just fine."

A chill snaked up Martha's back. She knew whose idea it was for Farah to broadcast this call.

Scott shouted from the background. "You're totally right, Martha. Maybe Farah and I should end this relationship—for good, but we'll enjoy ourselves for now. I'm not going to hurt Farah, and she's free to leave me whenever she wants—after I pamper her for a few days."

"Aww, see what you did, Martha? You let me worry about my own affairs...and you can concentrate on that handful of man you have. By the way, did Cam ever find his phone?"

"He did, thanks."

"Okay, then. I'll see you later."

"Be...have fun."

"We will." Farah ended the call on another giggle.

Martha cupped the dead phone in her hands. "That

call was a message to us. Farah is safe…for now, as long as she doesn't discover his true motives."

"He can't keep her at that hotel forever."

"Two days. I think she's taking a few days off this week for Thanksgiving, and as long as he has her there, we can't call the police." She tucked her hands between her bouncing knees. "He as good as threatened her."

"Do you still want to consult that attorney?"

"I have to." Her voice shook, and she shot a sideways glance at Cam to see if he noticed.

He reached over and pinched her chin. "I'm sorry you lost your glasses."

"I have contacts at my mom's."

By the time they reached her mother's house, it was past midnight. Martha's knees trembled as Cam opened the front door for her, and it wasn't due to the aches and pains racking her body from the tumble out of the car.

Would she and Cam share a bed again tonight? Would they make love? The clicking clock on their time together echoed in her head, marked her every breath.

Once she contacted Sam and came clean, she might lose her job, she might go to jail, but none of that mattered as much as the looming threat of losing Cam.

Could a member of Delta Force ever be involved with a spy, a federal criminal?

Cam tapped the alarm system. "Arm it, even though our guy will be spending the night somewhere else."

"Unless he drugs Farah again and sneaks out." She punched in the code for the alarm system and tossed her purse into a chair. "How long does he expect to buy my silence by holding a threat over Farah's head? Once I go to the authorities and tell all, Farah will know everything."

Cam walked to the kitchen with a hitch in his step and reached for a glass.

"I didn't even ask if you were okay." She followed him into the kitchen and wrapped her arms around his waist from behind. "You took the brunt of that tumble from the car."

He lifted his broad shoulders. "I took it like a football tackle. I know how to fall and roll."

"With a gangly woman attached to your body?"

He threw back the water and kissed her mouth with wet lips. "That was the best part. Should we undress each other slowly and inspect our bodies for injuries?"

"Is that a new line?"

"I don't know. Will it work?"

"You don't need any lines to get me into bed, Cam Sutton." She skimmed her hands across his face and flicked his earlobe, which sported a spot of dried blood. "But I do think we need a soak in the bathtub first to clean all our boo-boos."

"Is *that* a new line, 'cause I gotta tell you, discussing my…boo-boos is a total turnoff."

She rested her head against his chest. Her lips formed a smile, but a tear leaked from the corner of her eye and she sniffled.

Drawing away, he wedged a knuckle beneath her chin and tilted back her head. "I'm sorry. Boos-boos are a turn on. Gives me a chance to take care of you."

She sniffed, but he coaxed a bigger smile from her. "When I'm in federal prison sharing a cell block with my dad, will the army forbid you from fraternizing with an enemy of the state?"

He snorted. "I just might be in the next cell block over."

"What do you mean?" She wrinkled her nose. "You haven't done anything wrong?"

He lifted one eyebrow. "Really? I have knowledge about your theft of those emails and failed to disclose that intelligence. I helped you clean evidence off your computer. I stumbled upon a murder scene and didn't report it. I could go on, but I'm sure your attorney can fill you in."

Her chest tightened as she dug her fingernails into Cam's biceps. "I can't do it. I can't do that to you."

He scooped his hands through her hair. "You do what you have to do to stay safe, Martha."

"Not if it's going to put you in jeopardy."

He pulled her head down and kissed the top. "Let's talk to that lawyer first…but not before we take a bath and check out each other's bodies."

She took the glass from his hand and drank the rest of the water. "Deal."

Just in case Cam thought she was kidding about the bath, she threw open the door of the master bathroom and cranked on the faucets for the sunken, oval tub while he prowled around downstairs, securing every door and window in the place.

By the time he joined her upstairs, Martha had a tub full of steaming, scented bubbles and candles.

He hung on the doorjamb and whistled. "I should've brought up two glasses of wine."

"That would probably put me to sleep, and I'm still trying to get the taste of that other wine out of my mouth."

Two steps took him into the room, and he slid his hands beneath her robe and squeezed her shoulders. "Do you still think he put something in your wine?"

"He sure put something in Farah's."

"But you feel okay? No strange aftereffects?"

"I'll feel better once I crawl into that warm water." She dropped her phone on top of a basket full of rolled-up towels and dipped her toe past the bubbles and into the water. "It's perfect."

He slipped the robe from her shoulders and kissed the side of her neck. "You're perfect."

Cam shrugged off his clothes, they shared a long kiss before sliding into the tub together. Despite Cam's size, the cavernous bathtub allowed him to stretch out. He settled her between his legs and ran his hands gingerly across her back.

"You're going to have a few bruises back here."

"I'm glad that's all. I expected some broken bones." She scooped up a handful of bubbles and scattered them with a breath from her pursed lips. "Do you think Farah's okay?"

"He doesn't want to harm her. He doesn't want to harm you."

"Cam, why do you think he's still here? He planted the emails with me, or an associate did, he took care of his loose ends by killing Wentworth, Casey and Tony. What more does he want? He knows, or at least he thinks he knows, that I'm not going anywhere with the info I have. Where would I go? Implicating him implicates me."

"He's still looking for whatever Casey left behind." Cam's hands made waves in the water pooling over her belly. "He knows you don't have it, and he wants to find it before you do."

"We searched through her stuff. There's nothing

there that implicates him or anyone else. What could it be?"

"Maybe it was just his identity, and now that we have that—or at least who he's pretending to be—he has Farah. I guess he believes that will stop us from turning him in."

"Well, he's right, but how long can he keep her? Like you said before, he can't make her stay in that hotel forever. She'll have her spa day tomorrow, and another few days, but what then?"

His hands floated toward her breasts, and he cupped them. "You're safe. Farah's somewhat safe, and you're going to talk to your father's attorney tomorrow. There's nothing left for us to do tonight. Let me make you feel better."

She succumbed to the sweet kisses and gentle caresses that slowly stoked the embers of her passion, so different from the fiery explosions of last night.

By the time they returned to her bedroom, Cam had to pour her limp body onto the sheets. He whispered in her ear, "You're still going to need some ibuprofen tomorrow."

She burrowed under the covers. "Bring it on. I feel ready for anything right now."

The bed dipped as Cam snuggled in behind her. His arm draped heavily across her midsection, and his leg hitched over her hip. She felt engulfed by him, and she soaked up the feeling, trying to drown out the thought of his departure that echoed in her head like a hollow drumbeat.

The buzzing of her cell replaced the dirge, and her lids flew open. "It has to be him."

Cam bolted upright and made a grab for her phone. He squinted at the display. "It's not Farah. Unknown number."

"It's him." She snapped her fingers, and Cam held out the phone to her. She tapped in her password and swiped open the text.

"Is it Scott?"

Tilting her head to the side, Martha blew a wisp of hair from her eyes as she read the text. A cold fist squeezed her heart, and she dropped the phone with a gasp.

Cam snatched it up. "Is it him? Is it that bastard?"

"No. It's a text from a dead woman."

Chapter Fourteen

Martha's pale face stood out in the darkness of the room. Cam fumbled with the light switch on the wall to turn on the ceiling fans above the bed, and brought the phone close to his face.

"Casey? Is it from Casey?"

"H-how can that be?"

The letters on the display swam before Cam's eyes, the words they formed, nothing but gibberish to his brain. "What did she write? What does it say?"

"Read it." Martha had folded her hands together, her knuckles as white as the sheets beneath them, seemingly incapable or unwilling to take the phone from him.

He made another pass at the jumbled words on the screen, and then shoved the phone between her wrists. "I can't, damn it. I can't read it, Martha."

His words shocked her out of her stupor, and she picked up the cell and read aloud the words from Casey. "'Martha, it's me, Casey. If you get this message after I've disappeared, I locked myself out. I'm sorry.'"

"Locked herself out?" Cam tipped his head back against the headboard and stared at the ceiling. "If she locked herself out, she'd get the key from the zippered cover of the lawn chair, but we already looked there. She must be referring to the message she left you about Tony."

"Did she even send that message, Cam? How? How do we know it came from her?"

"She scheduled the text to be delivered at a later date. She obviously knew she'd taken a step too far, knew her life was in danger." He folded one arm behind his head. "Why wouldn't it be from her? You and she are the only ones who know about the hiding place for the key, right?"

"I never told anyone, and as flakey as she was, I don't think Casey did, either, well, except Tony."

"Another reason is that Scott would have no need to send you a message like that. Why would he want to further pique your curiosity or provide you with any more evidence to bring to the authorities that Casey was anything more than a suicide?"

Martha had been panting, sipping in short spurts of air. Filling her lungs, she closed her eyes. "I guess Casey really wanted me to talk to Tony."

"Do you think that's it?"

"What do you mean?" Martha asked.

"Maybe there's something more. Maybe this is what we've been waiting for, what Scott has been looking for."

"We looked in the cushion and found the key with the note. Are you saying there's something more?"

"It's a big, square cushion. You shoved your fingers into the zippered opening, found the key and the note. We didn't look for anything else. We didn't know there was anything else."

"The phone?"

"If we found that phone and it contained instructions

from Scott, aka Ben, regarding Congressman Wentworth and the emails, we'd have some real proof against
this guy. You wouldn't even have to admit to taking the
emails. Your roommate died, you got this message from
the grave and you found the phone. It all smelled like
yesterday's fish, and you did your duty as a citizen and
CIA employee and turned it over."

"You're making a lot of assumptions. Maybe she
did just want me to contact Tony. It could be nothing
more than that."

Cam flicked off the light and slid back beneath the
covers. "Or a whole lot more."

The following morning while they ate breakfast,
Martha called Farah. When she ended the call, she
picked up her fork and poked at the eggs on her plate.
"She sounds fine, happy."

"Was she suspicious that you were calling her?"

"A little. I don't know if you heard, but I told her I
wanted to check on her because she didn't sound well
last night."

"As long as you didn't spook her and didn't spook
Scott." Cam rinsed off his plate and stacked it in the
sink. "He's keeping your silence today by holding on
to Farah, but what about tomorrow and the days to follow?"

"Maybe he plans to leave the capital and isn't worried even if I do report him. Is Farah ever going to believe Scott drugged and kidnapped her? As far as she's
concerned, he's treating her to a spa day. What about
your friend on the police force?"

"I called him this morning, but I can't get the glass to
him until tomorrow. I could just hold on to it and turn
it over to the FBI once we report our suspicions about

Farah's boyfriend. And your father's attorney? Have you called him?"

"While you were in the shower. He wants a video conference with us later this afternoon." She held up her plate to him and he took it.

"Everything has to wait until we go back to your place and search that cushion for further evidence." He loaded the rest of their breakfast dishes from the sink into the dishwasher.

"You got a text." Martha held up his phone.

Cam dried his hands on a towel and hunched over the counter, holding out his hand for the phone. Martha dropped it in his palm and he opened the text.

"D-do you need any help reading it?"

He glanced up, a warm flush creeping up his neck to the roots of his hair. "Last night was just because of the stress of the situation. I'm okay."

"I'm sorry."

"Don't be. It's all right. I'm glad you asked." He held his phone under the light and read the text. "It's from one of my teammates, Joe. He's asking about my progress."

"Is he in the States?"

"Just arrived. He's taking leave for Christmas."

"What are you going to tell him?"

"The truth. That we're onto something and the emails were a setup, just as we suspected—not that we ever believed anything else."

"We'd better get going. If we find further evidence in that seat cushion linking Scott to the murders, we'll have something more to discuss with Sam."

On the drive to Martha's town house, Cam texted back and forth with Joe. He wanted to warn him, just as Martha kept pointing out to him, that even if they could prove some foreign entity planted the emails implicating Denver, there was still the rest of the evidence against him. They wouldn't be able to clear his name right away, but this had to be a start.

The reporters had cleared out from the front of Martha's town house. Another Washington scandal had already diverted their attention, and Martha hadn't been around for days.

She pulled her car up to the curb. "I might as well collect my mail while I'm here and water some plants."

"First things first." Cam looked up and down the street. A few pedestrians walked to and from their cars. One with a dog waved to Martha and she waved back. Nobody looked suspicious, but then Scott was guarding his pampered captive.

Martha unlocked the front door, and Cam nudged her aside to walk in first. "Anything out of place?"

"Not this time, but I'm going to check Casey's room again." She bounded up the stairs ahead of him, and his heart pounded as he followed on her heels.

"Wait." He stopped her before she opened Casey's door. Holding his breath, he pushed it open.

The neat row of bags and the suitcase they'd packed up the other day greeted him, and he blew out a gust of air. "At least nobody's been back."

"I'm sure changing the locks helped." Martha placed her hands on her hips and surveyed the room. "Incredible I haven't even heard from Casey's mom yet."

"Do you know if they've made arrangements for her body?"

"I couldn't tell you." Martha wandered to the window and pressed her nose against the glass. "The patio furniture's still where we left it."

"Let's go take it apart."

They went downstairs and out the back door. Martha crouched beside the same chair.

"It wouldn't be in the other one?"

"We always used the same cushion for the key." She pulled the zipper back. This time she shoved her whole hand into the cover, wrinkling her nose. When most of her arm disappeared into the cushion, she squeaked. "I got it. Cam, it's a phone."

His pulse jumped. "It must be the phone she used for contact with Ben."

Martha pulled out the type of phone typically sold as temp phones, and framed it in her hand. She pressed and held a button. "It's dead."

"Maybe she has a charger in her room. Did you see something?"

"I think just her regular smartphone charger." She pressed the phone to her chest. "This is huge, Cam. This is what Scott was looking for, what he was afraid I'd find."

"He must've thought Casey would have the phone on her when he lured her to that hotel room to kill her. When he couldn't find it, he took her keys instead and searched her room for it."

"It must have evidence pointing to him, or he wouldn't have wanted it so badly." A dog barked and Martha jumped.

Cam grabbed her arm. "Let's go inside and find the charger. I cleaned out her desk and dumped a bunch of items in a plastic bag. It could be in there."

Once inside, Cam took the stairs two at a time,

clutching the phone in his fist. If the FBI could use the evidence on this phone to tie Scott to the murders and implicate him in the faked emails, Martha could completely avoid scrutiny for stealing the messages.

He pounced on the plastic bag containing the items from Casey's desk and dumped the contents onto the floor.

Martha dropped beside him and pawed through the papers, pens and business cards. She grabbed a black cord, pulled it free from the mess and dangled it from her fingers. "This could be it."

He grabbed the swinging end and compared it to the outlet on Casey's phone. "I think it is."

He inserted the USB into the phone and it clicked into place. "That's it."

Martha sprang to her feet in one movement. "Let's charge it downstairs. I take back every bad thing I said about Casey. Would a flake think to hide her cell phone where she knew I'd find it?"

"Not so fast. She's still a spy who stole secrets from a US congressman and worse...put her roommate's life in danger."

They traipsed down the stairs, and Martha pointed him to an outlet in the kitchen.

"Let's get this going. I can't wait to see what's on this phone."

Cam plugged the power cord into the outlet. "I suppose we can sit here and stare at it until it juices up."

The doorbell echoed through the house, and Martha gripped the edge of the counter. "Scott wouldn't be ringing my bell, would he?"

Cam pulled his gun from his jacket pocket and jerked his thumb at the door. "Check it out."

Martha crept to the door, crouching below the fan-shaped window at the top so the visitor couldn't see her coming. Cam stayed to the side, his gun at the ready.

She ducked her head and peered through the peep-hole. She whispered. "It's Sebastian."

"That guy you dated from work?" Cam rolled his eyes. "What does he want, a date? You don't have to answer the door."

"Martha? It's just Sebastian. I know you're home because I saw your car on the street. No press out here if you're worried."

Martha shrugged and slipped back the dead bolt. She opened the door wide enough so that Sebastian could see Cam hovering behind her.

He'd pocketed his weapon.

"This is a surprise."

"Is it?" Sebastian's eyes behind his glasses darted from Martha's face to Cam's. "I've been worried about you. First the congressman, then Casey and now the suspension from work."

"Speaking of work, why aren't you there?"

"I'm taking the whole week off for Thanksgiving. Aren't you going to visit your mother?"

"With all this going on—" she swept her arm behind her to encompass Cam "—I completely forgot about Thanksgiving."

Sebastian smiled and seemed to dig his Oxfords into the mat on Martha's porch. If Martha thought she was getting rid of this guy, she wasn't reading his signals.

"D-do you want to come in for a few minutes? We were just on our way out. I'm not staying here."

"At your mom's?" Sebastian stepped across the threshold, and a muscle ticked in Cam's jaw. This guy seemed to know a lot about Martha's family, but she *did* date him. Probably had a genius IQ.

Martha nodded toward Cam. "Sebastian, this is Cam. Cam, Sebastian."

Cam gave him a handshake that could've brought him to his knees if he'd kept it up, but he released his grip just as a grimace started to twist the other man's lips.

Sebastian put his hand behind his back. "Nice to meet you. Friend of Martha's?"

"Uh-huh." Cam wandered back to the charging phone and perched on the stool next to it while Martha and Sebastian talked.

She offered him a soda and he accepted. She couldn't be rude and kick the guy out?

As she walked toward the kitchen, her back to Sebastian, she rolled her eyes at Cam and pointed at the phone.

He shook his head.

She returned to Sebastian with a can in each hand and joined him on the sofa, where he'd made himself comfortable.

Cam ground his back teeth. Why was Sebastian here, anyway? Martha had made it clear they were over.

Cam kept one eye on the phone, and one ear on the conversation between Martha and Sebastian. He couldn't help it. Since his reading skills had been so poor in school, he'd honed his listening comprehension skills to an art.

Sebastian knew a lot about Martha's family, her father's situation, her mother's house. Her likes and dislikes. Their conversation had turned to art, and Cam felt a little bit of panic. Did he know enough about art to converse with Martha about it?

Martha said, "I'm not sure I know that artist."

"His work is similar to the print you have in your room."

"The Gaspar?"

Cam snorted softly. What the hell was a Gaspar?

Then something clicked in his brain, and his head twisted slowly to the side. Her room? The print in Martha's bedroom? Unless she'd been lying, Martha had told him she'd never slept with Sebastian, that he'd been to her place just twice and had never made it past the entryway.

How could he know what was in her bedroom—unless he'd seen it from her laptop camera, which he'd hacked into as the patriot?

Chapter Fifteen

Martha swallowed. "The Gaspar? In my bedroom?"

Sebastian licked his lips, his tongue flicking out of his mouth like a snake's. "The one you told me about."

Martha's eye twitched. Two seconds later, Cam barreled across the room and grabbed Sebastian by the neck.

Martha shouted, "What are you doing?"

"He's the patriot, Martha. He's the one who hacked your computer. He's the one who IDed you as the CIA employee to set up. He sent Scott to your mother's house, and Scott probably sent him here to watch your place while he's with Farah."

Martha's mouth dropped open, but every word Cam said she knew to be true. Sebastian had set her up, and he'd probably set up Farah, too.

Sebastian gagged and choked as his face turned blue above Cam's powerful hand clutching his throat.

"Let him go, Cam. You're choking him."

He uncurled his fingers, and Sebastian slumped to the sofa, coughing.

Cam got in his face. "Start spilling."

Sebastian rubbed his throat. "You're crazy. I don't know what you're talking about."

"You can choose that route if you want." Cam pushed away from the sofa and held up the charging phone. "But we have Casey's burner phone. Is that what Scott sent you here to find?"

Sebastian dropped his head in his hands. "I—I didn't know it would go this far. It started with information. I was approached on an overseas trip. It was the money. They offered me so much money. You wouldn't know what it's like, Martha. You, with your privileged background. I had so much student loan debt, it was suffocating me."

"Oh, I thought you were doing it because you were such a *patriot*." Martha jumped up and took a turn around the room.

"How did this email plan start and why?" Cam slammed his fist in his palm. "Why Major Denver?"

Sebastian held up his hands as if deflecting physical blows. "I don't know anything about any of that. I was just asked to identify someone at Langley who would turn over a set of emails, no questions asked. I knew Martha would do it. I knew how she felt about her father's crimes."

"Oh my God. You used our conversations against me."

"It was nothing, Martha. You didn't have to be involved any more than turning over those emails—and then you broke bad."

"Ha!" She tossed her head. "That's quite a charge coming from someone involved in espionage against the government."

"It was more than just the emails. You helped Scott set up the liaison between Casey and Congressmen Wentworth, putting Martha in further danger."

"Martha was never supposed to be in danger."

"But she was." Cam smacked his hand against the wall, and Sebastian's eyes widened as his Adam's apple bobbed in his skinny neck.

How had she ever been remotely interested in him?

"I wanna know why Scott is still here. Why didn't he murder those people and get out of town?"

"I-I'm not sure."

Cam stalked toward him, and Sebastian shrank against the sofa cushion. "I swear. I don't know. Maybe it's the phone. He wants to make sure we secure Casey's phone first."

His fist clenched, Cam loomed over Sebastian. "Who's he with? Who is Scott working with?"

"I swear. I don't know any of that."

All three heads swiveled toward a buzzing noise from the phone.

"It's operational." Cam stepped away from Sebastian, flexing his fingers as if he'd gone through with the hit.

As Cam strode toward the counter, Sebastian half rose from the sofa, and Martha said, "Cam!"

He swung around and leveled a finger at Sebastian, who'd stopped in midrise. "Sit."

Cam grabbed the phone and tapped it awake. "No password."

"Check the texts." Martha cast a nervous glance at Sebastian, who looked ready to bolt at any minute.

Cam's eyebrows collided over his nose, and he thrust the phone out to Martha. "You look through it, while I watch our spy here."

She took the phone from him.

Martha saw just two sets of texts, and one was the single text to her phone. The other was to a number, no name attached to it. It had to be the man Casey knew as Ben and they knew as Scott, but Martha would bet her town house that both names were false.

"The most recent text is the one directing Casey to the hotel for a meeting. She must've received that text, scheduled her text to me and then hid the phone in the hiding place for our key." Martha held up the phone. "This is enough to cast suspicion on Ben, even if this is a temp phone for him."

"Ben? Who the hell is Ben?" Sebastian shoved his glasses up the bridge of his nose.

Cam growled. "Ben is your buddy Scott. You know, the guy you set up with your coworker Farah. The guy who murdered three people."

"Ben?" Sebastian emitted a high-pitched, hysterical laugh. "He got that from when I told him I felt like a regular Benedict Arnold, and I had to explain who he was."

"He didn't know Benedict Arnold?"

"I don't think so."

"You were right about those emails, Martha. They came from a foreign entity, a non-native speaker." Cam twirled his finger in the air. "What else? What other texts are between the two of them."

Martha backtracked through the conversation between Casey and Ben. "There's not a lot of substance here. It's mostly Ben setting up meetings. He must've been very careful about committing anything to text or probably even telephone conversations. I don't know why he was so worried about our finding this phone."

"Those texts are going to cast suspicion on Casey's death and Wentworth's. Maybe that's all we need."

Cam dragged a chair from the dining area, placed

it in front of Sebastian and straddled it. "Here's what you're gonna do. We're gonna contact the FBI, and you're gonna confess to your crimes. You're gonna tell them about those faked emails and give them everything you know about Ben or Scott or whatever he calls himself. I have his fingerprints on a glass, and maybe we can get his real identity from his prints—even if it has to come from Interpol."

"We have to wait the rest of the day, Cam. He still has Farah, and if he finds out Sebastian went to the FBI, he could harm her."

"I—I can't stay here the rest of the day." Sebastian looked wildly from Martha to Cam. "I have plans for Thanksgiving."

Martha tapped Casey's phone against her chin. "What are we going to do with him? If we let him leave, he might disappear. If we call the FBI now, we put Farah in danger."

"If we let him leave, he just might go back to the office and try to destroy the evidence that points to him as the one who got those emails to your computer."

"Wait. You can't keep me a prisoner." Sebastian shook his finger at Martha. "You're in a lot of trouble, Martha *Brockridge*."

"That makes two of us."

"We'll keep him here until Farah is safe. Maybe—" Cam drummed his fingers on the chair back "—we'll have him contact Ben and let him know he got Casey's phone."

"What? No!" Sebastian had turned even whiter. "He'd expect me to bring it to him right away."

"I still don't understand why tomorrow is some magic

date for Ben. He releases Farah tomorrow, and we go through with our plans to report him once she's safe."

"He obviously plans to leave tomorrow."

"But why not leave today?"

Sebastian's eyebrows jumped to his hairline. "Why are you two looking at me? I told you. I don't know any of his plans. I'm paid for my contacts within the Agency and my access to and knowledge of its computers. That's it. When Wentworth died and then Casey, I knew everything had exploded."

Martha smoothed her thumb along the curve of Casey's phone. "If he's willing to give up Farah tomorrow and take off, let him. I suppose he figures once he's out of the country, the FBI won't be able to track him down. But at least he'll be out of my life, and Sebastian can testify to the falsity of the emails."

"I won't know the why or who behind the setup of Major Denver though."

"Maybe once the FBI and CIA get a handle on Ben, it'll give them a good idea." She came up behind Cam and rubbed his shoulders. She couldn't help that Sebastian's bug eyes at the gesture gave her a thrill of satisfaction.

Casey's phone slipped from her hand and landed at Cam's foot. He bent forward to pick it up. "I'm not looking forward to spending the night with this guy, but… What's this?"

"What?" She leaned over his shoulder and looked at the phone cupped in his hand.

"Pictures. You didn't check the phone's photos, did you?"

"No." She knelt beside him, and even Sebastian hunched forward.

Cam's finger brushed across the display. "They're documents. Security plans and diagrams."

"For what?"

"I'm not sure yet. Casey must've gotten these from Wentworth. Tony told us she would get info from the congressman and pass it along to Ben. This must be part of that."

"Why would Ben want this type of information?"

"To gain knowledge of the security plans for a building or place…and bypass it."

Sebastian exhaled a noisy breath. "A terrorist attack. You'd want intel like that to plan a terrorist attack."

"He's right." Cam's lips formed a thin line. "And this is what Ben doesn't want us to see. He knows these pictures are on this phone."

When Cam swiped to the next picture, his body jolted. "It's the Mall, the monuments on the National Mall."

Martha crossed her arms over her chest. "And it's going down tomorrow."

Chapter Sixteen

"Answer it." Cam handed Sebastian his ringing phone, pressing the button on the side to activate the speaker.

They'd forced Sebastian to text Ben from Casey's phone to let him know he'd found it at Martha's town house. The response from Ben had been instantaneous.

Sebastian cleared his throat. "Scott."

"So you found it. How?"

"I—I remembered when I was dating Martha she told me Casey was always losing or forgetting her key, so they had a hiding place. I found the phone there."

"Did you look at anything on the phone?"

"Just the texts." Sebastian licked his lips. "Did you want me to look for something?"

"No, just bring it to me in two hours."

"Where are you?"

Cam dug his fingers into his biceps as they waited a beat for Ben's response.

"I took Farah to the St. Regis to get her out of the way while all this was happening. I didn't want her questioning Martha too closely about anything."

"Good idea."

"I don't need your approval, geek. Just bring me the phone."

Sebastian turned bright red. "Sure, sure. Am I supposed to see Farah while I'm there?"

"No need for that. We're ordering dinner up to our room tonight. I'll make an excuse to get ice or something, and you can meet me at the vending machines down the hall. Text me from the phone when you get here, so I know you still have it."

"Is this going to get me a bonus?" Sebastian wiped his upper lip with the back of his hand.

"Bonus?" Ben chuckled. "Sure, I'll give you a bonus."

When Sebastian ended the call, he gagged. "He's going to kill me."

Cam snatched the phone from his hand. "I'll try to save you…after I take care of Ben."

"And after I get Farah out of that room."

"Don't worry, Sebastian." Cam smacked him on the back. "This will all look better for you when you make your confession."

After a few informative hours at Martha's town house where Sebastian spilled his guts on video, Cam wiped Casey's phone clean and handed it to Sebastian.

"No tricks."

"Tricks? I don't have any tricks. I just want this to be over. I never imagined Ben would be planning a terrorist attack on our soil."

"So, it's okay on someone else's soil?" Martha yanked her coat from a hook by the door. "Your actions endangered so many lives."

"I didn't think."

"For a smart guy like you, that's quite an admission." Cam shoved his gun in his pocket. "Let's go."

With Sebastian in the back seat and Cam in the passenger seat beside her, Martha drove to the St. Regis near the Mall. "I guess he wanted to stay close to the site of his attack."

A valet took Martha's car, but they walked around to a side entrance. Their whole plan would blow up in their faces if Ben or Farah saw them in the lobby of the hotel.

They slipped through a side door and once inside, Cam prodded Sebastian in front of him until they reached an empty hallway leading to some restrooms. He slammed Casey's phone against Sebastian's chest. "Send the text."

He watched over Sebastian's shoulder as he texted the words, I'm here. Cam could read those words clear as day.

Less than a minute later, Ben called Sebastian on his own phone. Cam bent close to Sebastian's ear so he could hear the conversation.

"Where are you?"

"Lobby."

"I'm on the tenth floor. On one end of that floor, around the corner from the elevators, there's an alcove with vending and ice machines. Meet me there, hand over the phone and take your money. We're done."

"Will you be contacting me for further assignments?"

"We're done."

Ben ended the call.

Cam held out his hand. "I'll take that."

Sebastian dropped his phone into Cam's palm. "I just hope he doesn't call me again on my phone."

"Why would he?" He slipped Casey's phone into Sebastian's front pocket. "If you use that phone to double-cross me, I'll make sure I kill you both."

A bead of sweat ran down the side of Sebastian's face. "I'll follow the plan."

Cam turned to Martha. "As soon as I give you the signal from the stairwell, you text Farah and tell her to get out of that room as soon as she can. Once she's safe, call that number I gave you for the FBI. I'll surprise Ben in the vending room."

"Be careful." Martha grabbed his hand and pressed her lips against his cheekbone. "I may be losing you in a week, but I'm not going to lose you forever."

"I'm not gonna let that happen. Who's going to help me read my texts?" He kissed her mouth as Sebastian watched their exchange with round eyes.

"And you." He poked his finger in Sebastian's chest. "Give us a few minutes to climb ten flights of stairs before you even punch that elevator button."

"Got it."

They edged around the corner of the hallway and started to cross the lobby for the bank of elevators and the stairwell across from it. Their path took them past the crowded lobby bar.

"Martha?"

The voice sent a surge of adrenaline through Cam's veins, and he spun around. He made a grab for Martha's hand, but Farah had moved between them.

His gaze met Ben's above the women's heads, and his gut twisted.

Sebastian made a strange gulping sound beside him.

"Go, Martha!" His shout barely made it above the music and conversation spilling out of the bar. He'd reacted too late, anyway.

Ben had Martha's arm and was pulling her back toward him.

Farah's dark eyebrows formed a V over her nose. "What's going on? What are you doing here? Sebastian? What are *you* doing here?"

Cam saw the flash of the blade in Ben's hand as he pressed it against Martha's side.

"Now I have a bigger prize." Ben smiled through his words as if they were all part of the convivial bar scene behind them.

"I—I don't understand." Farah's head was snapping back and forth between Ben and Martha, and Cam and Sebastian.

Cam took Farah's hand and pulled her toward him. "You're safe now."

"Safe?" Farah sobbed and stretched her hand out. "Martha?"

Martha drew back her shoulders and straightened her spine, standing taller than the man who held her at knifepoint. "The man you know as Scott is planning a terrorist attack."

"No, I…"

"Shh." Ben put his finger to his lips. "Quiet, Farah, unless you want to see your friend hurt. I at least had some feelings for you. Her? I don't care about her at all."

Farah's shoulders slumped and she dropped her head.

Cam pulled Farah behind him. "What are you going to do with Martha?"

"Just like Farah, Martha stays with me until I can conduct my business tomorrow."

Cam ground his words through his teeth. "Your business is terror, mayhem, murder of innocents."

"So is yours, Sergeant Sutton."

A lash of heat whipped through Cam's body, and he

curled his fists. "You'll have to kill all of us to carry out your plan. We all know."

"I think I just need Martha. Do you want to see her die right here and now to save a bunch of strangers on the Mall tomorrow? And how do you know I don't have others to take my place?"

"Oh, we'll be prepared for you and others like you. Planning a truck or van attack, aren't you? Planning to mow down some civilians? Once I outline your plans to the FBI and DC Metro Police, they'll be ready for you."

That got him.

Ben's eyes, which had been focused on Cam the entire time, widened, and his arm slipped an inch from Martha's waist.

Cam would have to act here and now in the hotel lobby. He'd never allow this man to take Martha away from him—not now, not ever.

A muscle in his jaw twitched as he sensed movement behind him from Sebastian, who'd remained speechless and frozen up until this point.

Sebastian took a deep breath and shouted. "Help! Help!"

Ben's head jerked up, and Martha wrenched away from him, creating just enough space for Cam to make a move.

Cam lunged forward and grabbed the wrist of the hand that held the knife, and twisted. A woman in the bar screamed.

Ben made a thrusting motion to the side, and Cam slammed his body against Ben's, knocking him over, his hand still grappling for the knife.

They landed with a thud, and people began shouting

around them. Hands grabbed at the back of Cam's jacket as moisture began seeping into the front of his shirt.

Ben released the knife, and Cam found himself in sole possession of it. He pushed himself off Ben, and the wound beneath Ben's heart began gushing blood.

"Cam?" Martha dropped to the floor, her hand on the back of his neck.

"I'm fine. It's not me." Cam looked into the dying man's eyes and grabbed the front of his shirt. "Not yet, you bastard. Who sent you? Why'd you set up Denver?"

A trickle of blood seeped from Ben's mouth as his lips curled into a smile.

Epilogue

Martha stretched out on the huge bed in the penthouse suite of the St. Regis and curled her toes. "It's a shame we have this big bed and end up crowding together in one corner of it every night."

"A shame?" Cam grabbed her foot and kissed her arch. "We can just crowd together on another corner of the bed if you want to make good use of it."

She sat up and wrapped her arms around Cam, burying her head against his chest. "Promise me you'll come back to me safe and sound after this deployment."

"That's the easy part." He ran his knuckles down her spine. "Promise me you won't engage in any more illegal activities."

"I'm done breaking bad, as Sebastian put it, although he's the one who's going to be spending time in federal prison."

"His actions after we confronted him went a long way toward reducing his sentence."

"And his sheer cowardice when he screamed and started scrambling for his own safety allowed you to take down Ben." Martha suppressed a shiver. "I can't believe we wound up uncovering a terrorist attack. He had the van already rented and everything. There would've been plenty of people on the Mall the day before Thanksgiving."

Cam's muscles tensed beneath her touch. "He died before I could get any answers out of him, although we know he killed Tony and Casey and made sure Casey got together with Wentworth to get info from him about Denver."

"He must've killed Wentworth too after Casey got the info about Denver out of him, even though the authorities are still calling Wentworth's death a heart attack. Maybe they'll take a second look at that now that Interpol identified him as Alain Dumont, a Frenchman of Algerian descent, a man involved in petty crimes but with no known terrorist ties…but we know he's not working alone."

She rubbed his back. "His involvement with the emails is forcing the CIA to take a closer look at the evidence against Major Denver."

"A closer look is not clearing him."

"I know. I'm sorry." She flattened her hands against his chest and pushed away from him. "If you say he's innocent, I believe you and others will, too."

"Even Asher, one of our own teammates…" He shook his head. "I don't want to get into all that when we have just a few days left together. How's Farah holding up?"

"She's fine. Feels humiliated, but maybe this whole thing cured her of her propensity for unavailable men."

"No way she's going to top that guy for unavailability." Cam ran his hand up her thigh. "And you? Looks like you wound up with someone unavailable yourself."

"I'm willing to wait."

"Good, because I fell in love with the smartest girl

in class, and I'm not about to let her slip through my hands." He scooped her into his lap and tore off her robe.

"Oh, I like where this is going, D-Boy." She reached for her glasses, and he grabbed her hand.

"Nope, I wanna make love to you wearing nothing but your glasses."

And then he did and the sparks flew.

* * * * *

COMING SOON!

We really hope you enjoyed reading this book. If you're looking for more romance, be sure to head to the shops when new books are available on

Thursday 15th November

To see which titles are coming soon, please visit
millsandboon.co.uk

LET'S TALK
Romance

For exclusive extracts, competitions
and special offers, find us online:

- **f** facebook.com/millsandboon
- 🐦 @MillsandBoon
- 📷 @MillsandBoonUK

Get in touch on 01413 063232

For all the latest titles coming soon, visit
millsandboon.co.uk/nextmonth